SOUTH COUNTRY

JOHN STONEHOUSE

Copyright © 2023 by John Stonehouse

All rights reserved.

No part of this book may be reproduced in any form or by any electronic or mechanical means, including information storage and retrieval systems, without written permission from the author, except for the use of brief quotations in a book review.

This book is a work of fiction. Names, characters, places and incidents are either a product of the author's imagination or are used fictitiously. Any resemblance to actual people, living or dead, events or locales, is entirely coincidental.

ISBN 13: 9798399202600

Cover Design by Books Covered

CHAPTER ONE

Presidio County, Tx

Desert road stretches out through the windshield of the Silverado, the fence lines of ranch land caught in the edge of the truck's hi-beams.

Deputy US Marshal John Whicher eyes the empty two-lane highway, lightning flickering, pulsing in the night sky overhead.

The sparse lights of the town of Presidio are ahead of him.

Across the border, the faint glow of Ojinaga.

Whicher checks the clock on the dash of the truck—coming up on 9.30.

Nothing moving on sixty-seven, barely a sign of life ahead.

A handful of trailer homes and one-floor houses sit back from the highway, block shapes among the ocotillo and desert scrub.

He sees the turn for the dirt-colored farm-to-market —takes it.

Half a mile up the road, the lights of the Border Patrol station shine from the dark.

The marshal sits up behind the wheel, bunches his shoulders beneath the jacket of his suit. Feels the weight of the large-frame Ruger revolver in the shoulder holster.

Approaching the Border Patrol station pole lamps light up a compound of metal-sided buildings, white-and-green painted vehicles, a single black pickup parked to one side, the word *Police* picked out on its door.

Whicher stops at the gate, cuts the motor on the Chevy.

He climbs out. Sets his tan, felt Resistol hat.

The door of the police truck opens, a man in a blue uniform shirt steps out. Dressed in jeans, a white hat. Thick-set. His face flat, like a boxer.

Whicher sees sergeant's stripes on the man's shirt. He takes out an arrest warrant from his jacket. Calls over; "US Marshals Service."

The sergeant walks to a gate in the fence, opens it. Nods. "Arturo Diaz." He indicates a metal-sided building with a single steel door. "In there."

The marshal eyes him.

"Cuffed and chained," the sergeant says. "Didn't figure on sitting with him, mano."

"You make the arrest?"

Diaz shakes his head. "Border Patrol. Running vehicle checks on the highway."

Whicher reads from the arrest warrant. "Marco Zambrano. Colombian national."

"Patrol said he gave a false name," Diaz says.

"We know it's him?"

The sergeant's eyes are hooded. "Federal arrest warrant, we call you guys, mano..."

The marshal reads on; "Wanted on charges of homicide,

He'd have to book Zambrano into the Reeves County Jail.

Then drive home across town. Get back maybe one in the morning. The house empty, Leanne and Lori gone, his wife and daughter visiting with Leanne's folks for Spring Break.

Ruined buildings form out of the darkness in the canyon; old stone, crumbling adobe.

By the guard rail at the edge of the road, the name *Shafter* is picked out on a highway panel, white on green.

The bell tower and stucco walls of a church light up in the sweep of the truck's hi-beams.

Whicher listens to the thrum of the truck tires. In his rear-view, sees Zambrano turning his face side to side. Restless. Twitching. Hair matted to his head.

He tries to tune out the presence of the man in the back of the cab. Used to transporting prisoners, men worse than Zambrano. Plenty worse.

Lightning ripples overhead in the distance, dry lightning.

He passes the strip airfield at Cibolo Creek.

The radio crackles in the Silverado.

The inter-op channel flashes up. "All units that can clear to assist...I have an emergency report of gunshots at the Mackenzie Ranch..."

The marshal turns up the volume.

"That's south sector, Presidio County. Gunshots plus a possible incursion."

Whicher stares through the windshield at the onrush of night.

Listens for anyone coming back on the radio.

Barely a handful of sheriff's deputies cover the whole of the county.

"Location is around fifteen miles east of Ruidosa," the dispatcher says. "On the border. Around nine miles northwest of Shafter—on sixty-seven."

The marshal reaches for the radio on the dash hook—

CHAPTER ONE

Presidio County, Tx

Desert road stretches out through the windshield of the Silverado, the fence lines of ranch land caught in the edge of the truck's hi-beams.

Deputy US Marshal John Whicher eyes the empty two-lane highway, lightning flickering, pulsing in the night sky overhead.

The sparse lights of the town of Presidio are ahead of him.

Across the border, the faint glow of Ojinaga.

Whicher checks the clock on the dash of the truck—coming up on 9.30.

Nothing moving on sixty-seven, barely a sign of life ahead.

A handful of trailer homes and one-floor houses sit back from the highway, block shapes among the ocotillo and desert scrub.

He sees the turn for the dirt-colored farm-to-market—takes it.

He'd have to book Zambrano into the Reeves County Jail.

Then drive home across town. Get back maybe one in the morning. The house empty, Leanne and Lori gone, his wife and daughter visiting with Leanne's folks for Spring Break.

Ruined buildings form out of the darkness in the canyon; old stone, crumbling adobe.

By the guard rail at the edge of the road, the name *Shafter* is picked out on a highway panel, white on green.

The bell tower and stucco walls of a church light up in the sweep of the truck's hi-beams.

Whicher listens to the thrum of the truck tires. In his rear-view, sees Zambrano turning his face side to side. Restless. Twitching. Hair matted to his head.

He tries to tune out the presence of the man in the back of the cab. Used to transporting prisoners, men worse than Zambrano. Plenty worse.

Lightning ripples overhead in the distance, dry lightning.

He passes the strip airfield at Cibolo Creek.

The radio crackles in the Silverado.

The inter-op channel flashes up. "All units that can clear to assist...I have an emergency report of gunshots at the Mackenzie Ranch..."

The marshal turns up the volume.

"That's south sector, Presidio County. Gunshots plus a possible incursion."

Whicher stares through the windshield at the onrush of night.

Listens for anyone coming back on the radio.

Barely a handful of sheriff's deputies cover the whole of the county.

"Location is around fifteen miles east of Ruidosa," the dispatcher says. "On the border. Around nine miles northwest of Shafter—on sixty-seven."

The marshal reaches for the radio on the dash hook—

narcotics and arms trafficking. Alright, well, I'll take him off your hands."

"Just you?" The sergeant looks over at the metal-sided building. "That's a bad hombre in there. Acting up. We get a bunch of 'em…"

"I'll get him upcountry," Whicher says. "We'll find out who he is. Any idea what he was doing here?"

"This close to the border, most likely looking to cross. But something's wrong with him." The sergeant's eyes come up on Whicher's. "I think he's on something…"

The marshal studies Diaz a moment, reads tension.

Diaz grunts. Turns. Stalks toward the scuffed, steel door in the metal-clad building. "All I'm saying, mano, just be careful…"

* * *

Scrub desert gives way to the shapes of hills looming from the darkness on 67. In the wash of the headlamp beams, chino grass and rock line the sides of the empty highway.

Whicher eyes the man now chained to a D-ring in the floor in the back of the cab.

Marco Zambrano.

According to the Warrant Information System, a career criminal wanted in Bogota. Known to be hiding in the US. An open file on him at FBI—Marshals Service tasked with bringing him in, securing him for extradition.

Zambrano stares out of the blackened windows. Short, slight, dark-complexioned. His eyes jittery. Sheen on his skin.

Whicher catches his own reflection in the rear-view mirror—wide-set eyes, hazel to green above a broken nose.

He shifts grip on the wheel as the road starts to twist and turn through a canyon.

Two and a half hours back to Pecos.

Half a mile up the road, the lights of the Border Patrol station shine from the dark.

The marshal sits up behind the wheel, bunches his shoulders beneath the jacket of his suit. Feels the weight of the large-frame Ruger revolver in the shoulder holster.

Approaching the Border Patrol station pole lamps light up a compound of metal-sided buildings, white-and-green painted vehicles, a single black pickup parked to one side, the word *Police* picked out on its door.

Whicher stops at the gate, cuts the motor on the Chevy.

He climbs out. Sets his tan, felt Resistol hat.

The door of the police truck opens, a man in a blue uniform shirt steps out. Dressed in jeans, a white hat. Thick-set. His face flat, like a boxer.

Whicher sees sergeant's stripes on the man's shirt. He takes out an arrest warrant from his jacket. Calls over; "US Marshals Service."

The sergeant walks to a gate in the fence, opens it. Nods. "Arturo Diaz." He indicates a metal-sided building with a single steel door. "In there."

The marshal eyes him.

"Cuffed and chained," the sergeant says. "Didn't figure on sitting with him, mano."

"You make the arrest?"

Diaz shakes his head. "Border Patrol. Running vehicle checks on the highway."

Whicher reads from the arrest warrant. "Marco Zambrano. Colombian national."

"Patrol said he gave a false name," Diaz says.

"We know it's him?"

The sergeant's eyes are hooded. "Federal arrest warrant, we call you guys, mano..."

The marshal reads on; "Wanted on charges of homicide, narcotics and arms trafficking. Alright, well, I'll take him off your hands."

"Just you?" The sergeant looks over at the metal building. "That's a bad hombre in there. Acting up. Whole bunch of 'em..."

"I'll get him upcountry," Whicher says. "We'll find out who he is. Any idea what he was doing here?"

"This close to the border, most likely looking to cross something's wrong with him." The sergeant's eyes come to Whicher's. "I think he's on something..."

The marshal studies Diaz a moment, reads tension.

Diaz grunts. Turns. Stalks toward the scuffed, steel in the metal-clad building. "All I'm saying, mano, just careful..."

* * *

Scrub desert gives way to the shapes of hills looming from darkness on 67. In the wash of the headlamp beams, grass and rock line the sides of the empty highway.

Whicher eyes the man now chained to a D-ring in floor in the back of the cab.

Marco Zambrano.

According to the Warrant Information System, a criminal wanted in Bogota. Known to be hiding in the US open file on him at FBI—Marshals Service tasked bringing him in, securing him for extradition.

Zambrano stares out of the blackened windows. Sh slight, dark-complexioned. His eyes jittery. Sheen on his sk

Whicher catches his own reflection in the rear-v mirror—wide-set eyes, hazel to green above a broken nose.

He shifts grip on the wheel as the road starts to twist turn through a canyon.

Two and a half hours back to Pecos.

presses to send. "Yeah, this is Deputy Marshal Whicher, USMS—I just drove through Shafter."

He glances at Zambrano in the rear-view, sees the man's eyes unnaturally bright.

"Can you assist?" The dispatcher's voice drops out. Comes back on air. "You're north of Shafter? You'd be closest unit."

"I'd need directions..."

A burst of static hisses.

"Copy that. Did you pass a road yet?" the dispatcher says. "Coming in on your left?"

The marshal thinks about it. "No, ma'am."

"Alright, well I can get you out there."

Whicher shifts his grip on the wheel. Feels his pulse tick up. "Alright," he answers. "Alright, go ahead."

"Watch for a road on your left, a ranch road," the dispatcher says. "I'll take you over toward Pinto Canyon—I can get you right there."

* * *

Thirty minutes later the ranch is visible from an overlook—remote, isolated—dim points of light in a desert moonscape.

Whicher stops the truck on a dirt road, kills the headlights. Steps out to listen, staring down at the ranch through the dark. Hearing only the wind.

Vehicles are parked around a main house and a scattering of outbuildings.

He sees no one, senses no movement.

Stepping to the truck, he pulls open the rear door. Eyes Zambrano.

Sweat is running down the side of the man's face.

The marshal checks the prisoner's cuffs, checks the chain fixed to the floor.

He reaches beneath the back seat—unlocks a custom-fit

gun safe. Pulls out an 870 Remington. Checks the shotgun over.

Glancing down at the ranch he takes off the suit jacket, throws it up front in the cab. Border Patrol and the county sheriff are rolling units—estimated time of arrival unknown.

From the gun safe, he drags out a Kevlar vest.

Zambrano shifts in his seat, pulls his arms against the chain.

"Quit that." Whicher takes off the Ruger, puts on the vest.

From the safe he grabs a nylon belt and speed clips, each clip loaded with four shotgun shells.

He loops the belt around his waist, clear of the service-issue Glock. Puts the shoulder holster into the safe, locks it. Shuts the rear door of the cab.

He swings in behind the wheel, puts the shotgun into the footwell.

Drives down the track, heart rate rising—scanning the ground out before him.

At a set of locked gates, he stops, pulls the keys from the ignition. Switches on a set of blue, flashing lights mounted in the truck's front grille.

Zambrano yanks his cuffed wrists, the chain snaps tight.

Whicher turns, stares at him.

The man sways side to side, mouth working.

"Shut up. Sit there, stay quiet..."

Stepping from the truck, Whicher tracks to the side of the gate.

He swings over a post-and-rail fence, gets low. Checks for cover ahead—the army scout he once was taking over.

He fixes on a low, stone wall, some kind of animal enclosure. Runs forward at a crouch.

At the main ranch building, a shape appears beneath a porch lamp—a man holding a rifle.

Whicher raises the shotgun. "*US Marshals Service,*" he calls out, "*put your weapon down.*"

The man stands stock-still.

"*Put down the gun...*"

The man raises both arms, one hand gripping the forestock of the rifle. "I work here," he calls out.

"Put it down."

The man lowers the rifle. Places it onto the ground. He's dressed in jeans and boots, a fleece jacket. Light from the porch shines on his white straw hat.

Whicher moves from the animal enclosure, leads with the shotgun.

A second man appears at the side of the house.

"US Marshal—stay where you are..."

The second man is older, bareheaded. Wearing a Carhartt coat. "This here's my family ranch—name's Mackenzie, Larry Mackenzie..."

"You made the emergency call?"

"Yes, sir."

Whicher lowers the barrel of the twelve-gauge. "Anybody hurt here?"

Mackenzie steps forward. "No. But something's going on." He points toward the dark land at the south. "Out there. Somebody's firing shots...we saw a flare, too. Up in the sky."

"What kind of flare?"

"Big flare," Mackenzie answers. "Just hanging..."

The marshal squints at the man in the white hat.

"This here is Glen Carr," Mackenzie says, "he works here."

"How many shots?"

"A dozen," Mackenzie answers. "We saw muzzle flashes."

"Where?"

Carr points south, tracks his arm in a line.

"How long since the last shots?"

"Five minutes?" Mackenzie says.

Carr nods.

"They were shooting at you?"

"Hard to tell," Mackenzie says. "But it sounded like bullets whining in the air. Plus some things getting hit."

"You think you had rounds come in here?" Whicher says.

Mackenzie stares at him. "I think so, yes."

"How many people here at the ranch?"

"Six, including us."

"Where are they?"

"Inside."

"Keep 'em there," Whicher says. "Border Patrol are headed up, they should be here soon—I'll go out, take a look."

Carr steps from the porch. "You need help?"

The marshal shakes his head.

"I know the land pretty good."

"Glen's my main hand," Mackenzie says, "he's worked out here a long time. He knows the terrain."

Whicher eyes the younger man, in his thirties. "I need you to stay here, y'all stay inside."

"We have rifles," Carr says.

"I need to know where you are," Whicher tells him. "I don't want anybody caught up in something."

"Well, if you're fixing to head out," the hand says, "head west, there's higher ground—you might get a view to the south."

The marshal looks into the desert night, flashes of blue from the truck light strobing across the scrub. "Open up the ranch gates," he says to Mackenzie. "Border Patrol will be coming in. But keep away from my vehicle. Just open up the gates—then get inside."

* * *

Descending from the perimeter wall of the ranch compound, the marshal reaches a dry watercourse at the foot of an adjacent hill.

He climbs, moving silent, pushing fast onto higher ground. Shotgun at the waist, heart pumping, senses awake—senses honed on overseas ops, and years since in law enforcement, alive to unseen danger—switched on, alert.

At the rounded top of the hill he crouches in the short grass, snugs the 870 to his shoulder. Sweeps the indistinct, dark plain before him—knife peaks of hills in the distance, outlined against the sky.

Shapes form and disappear. Reform in the heat lightning beneath moving cloud.

A quarter mile off, the Mackenzie Ranch is a solitary glow.

The blue flashers on the truck turn in a sea of darkness.

He thinks of Zambrano.

Nothing cuts the landscape of mountains to the west, the desert extending south and east into black.

The border is maybe fifteen miles over the mountains.

People could be running drugs, coming through with illegals.

He moves across the hilltop. Settles low. Scans the darkened land below.

Sees no lights, hears no shots. No sounds or voices in the air.

Holding still, he tries to pick up on anything. Only listen. Watch. Breathe. Give rein to the sixth sense, awakened years back in a war zone; animal instinct.

Seeing nothing.

Hearing nothing.

Something registers in him all the same.

Something is out there.

CHAPTER TWO

Two Border Patrol Chevy Tahoes and a Ford Super Duty pull up in front of the ranch, their lights flashing.

Whicher moves at a run from the dark.

He stops at his own truck, yanks the rear door open.

Marco Zambrano stares out, tension rippling his body, the chain to the floor pulled taut.

"The hell's wrong with you?"

Zambrano mouths words in Spanish, too fast for Whicher to catch. His eyes are wild, the veins and tendons bulge in his neck.

"You sit there, you calm down—understand?"

Another set of headlamps appears on the dirt road.

Whicher eyes the cuffs at Zambrano's wrists—he swings the door shut.

A female Border Patrol agent steps from the Ford truck, two men exit the Tahoes. All three dressed in olive fatigues, caps and boots, the two men carrying M4 carbines.

The marshal glances back up the dirt road at the headlamps of the oncoming vehicle—a light bar flashes above its roof.

It slows.

Whicher sees the sheriff's department sign on its door.

The driver rolls the window, takes in the USMS vest, the shotgun. "Deputy Garcia," he says. "Responding to reports of shots?"

Whicher gestures to the ranch. "I need to talk with the Patrol, they just got here..."

The deputy nods, drives the black Toyota through the ranch gates.

Whicher jogs into the compound.

Mackenzie and Carr are out on the porch.

The female Border Patrol agent speaks with them.

The two male agents watch the black pickup enter the yard—then turn to look in Whicher's direction.

"With the Marshals Service," Whicher says, "I got here five minutes back."

The woman steps from the porch. "Agent Lozada. Senior agent, Presidio Station."

"John Whicher."

Deputy Garcia gets out of his truck. "Adriana," he says to the woman.

She nods. Indicates the two men with her, one Hispanic, short, the other Anglo, heavy, with a goatee beard. "Agents Matos and Webber."

Whicher steps in close.

Lozada is mid-thirties, dark-eyed. "Owner's reporting shots fired to the south," she says.

"I took a look," Whicher says.

"You see anything?"

The marshal shakes his head.

"Nobody's hurt?" Lozada says.

Mackenzie comes down off the porch. "We don't know what the hell happened. But shots were coming out of the dark, a whole bunch of 'em. I have people here, I have their safety to think of."

"Been nothing since I arrived," Whicher says. "There's high ground a shooter could use. Low ground you could get a line of sight up here, too."

Deputy Garcia steps forward—tall, rangy, dressed in uniform shirt and blue jeans. He turns to Lozada. "You have night vision with you?"

"Some. We were going off watch. We've got infrared binoculars, everybody else is on line watch, we heard the call, we came out with what we had."

Deputy Garcia turns to Mackenzie, "Larry? You're sure they were shooting at you here?"

"Somebody was." Mackenzie turns to Carr. "We all saw it, and heard it..."

Agent Webber angles his M4 carbine to the ground. "We can go out, take a look around."

"They'll be long gone, man," Agent Matos says. "South, or west. Maybe back into Mexico they get a look at all this..." He gestures at the lights flashing on the SUVs and trucks.

"They shot a flare in the sky," Mackenzie says.

"Signal flare?" Lozada turns to Deputy Garcia. "Carlos. You want to post up here, secure the ranch? We can take a look around, see what we can find?"

The deputy nods.

"Marshal?" she says.

On the ranch porch, two more men appear—in their fifties, dressed in camo gear.

Whicher turns to Mackenzie. "I want to speak with everybody you got staying here."

Lozada cuts the marshal a look. "We'll go take a look, see if anybody's still out there..."

* * *

Inside the house, in a lounge room built from rough stone and heavy timbers, Whicher props the 870 Remington in a corner. He turns to survey the assembled group.

The two men dressed in camo gear sit on a hide-covered couch. Patrician-looking—one lean, taller, dark—the other heavy-set, with sandy hair.

Larry Mackenzie and Glen Carr sit with two women at a Spanish dining table. One of the women dressed in running gear, a track top and body warmer, her hair a mass of tight brown curls. The other is younger, dressed in a T-shirt and jeans, her long black hair worn loose.

"This is my wife, Patricia." Mackenzie indicates the woman in the running gear. "And this is Amber, Amber Lester, she works for us here, keeping house."

The marshal nods.

"These gentlemen are our guests. They're on a hunting trip," Mackenzie says, "they've been with us a couple days, they're here for the week."

The shorter man speaks; "Eliot, Donald Eliot."

"And Vaughn Richardson," the taller man says.

The second man's name is remotely familiar.

"I need to ask what anybody saw of the shooting incident out there?" Whicher says.

Donald Eliot speaks. "We saw it from the guest lodge. Vaughn heard something when he was outside getting some air."

"You went out?" Whicher says.

"I went out to smoke a cigar, look at the stars," Richardson answers. "After a while I heard something. Then I saw something. Bright flashes. I came into the house, spoke to Larry, Mister Mackenzie. And Glen. They said they'd take a look, told us to go in and stay inside."

"Safety's the priority," Mackenzie says.

Richardson continues; "We turned out the lights—so we could see better from the windows. Don and I watched it."

"We saw a flare go up," Eliot says.

The marshal looks to the two women. "Either of you see any of this?"

Patricia Mackenzie speaks; "Larry didn't want us outside. We watched it from inside the house."

"I've never seen anything like that before," the younger woman says. "Not out here, this close to the ranch."

Mackenzie cuts in, "We never get trouble like that here."

"There was that break-in over at the Gusterson Ranch," Patricia says, "three weeks gone."

"That's miles away."

"You got everybody inside," Whicher says, "you called 911?"

"We're a long ways from anyone out here," Mackenzie says. "Glen and I were watching it, listening to it. We thought maybe it could've been a fight. Nighttime it's not real difficult to imagine something spilling over, coming this way. We're the only property for miles around, the only lights you'll see. Then all of a sudden, it felt like we were getting shot at..."

"You still think that?"

Mackenzie nods.

"How about the rest of you?"

"I don't think we were actually aware of anything like that," Vaughn Richardson says.

Donald Eliot shrugs. Turns his hands outwards.

The housekeeper, Amber, looks at Patricia, uncertain.

"Border Patrol are outside," Whicher says, "along with the sheriff's office. I need y'all to stay in here, stay together, till we figure out what's going on."

* * *

Back at the Silverado, Whicher checks on Zambrano, still agitated, twisting, turning in the rear of the cab.

He studies the man in the strobing blue and red lights of the assembled vehicles—working his wrists, chain pulled tight to the floor. "What the hell's the matter with you?"

Zambrano doesn't answer. He only stares at the marshal, searches his face, his breath coming short.

Whicher steps away from the truck.

The beam of a flashlight is moving, tracing timbers and the wall of an outbuilding. Garcia—Deputy Garcia, searching.

From the thin scrub at the south of the property, the female Border Patrol agent, Lozada, walks toward the perimeter wall of the ranch.

"Anything?" the marshal calls out.

"Nothing so far," Lozada answers. "We pushed down a half mile, there's a deep gully running east, a dry creek you could hide out in. Head west, you're in the hills. It's too dark to search without better equipment. But there's no sign anybody's out there."

Deputy Garcia crosses the yard, turns off the flashlight. "I don't see any evidence of incoming rounds—but we'd need working lights—or daylight."

"The folk in the house all say the same thing," Whicher says. "Gunfire. And a flare, some kind of flare."

Lozada purses her lips.

Garcia pushes back his hat. "You think anyone would still be out there?"

"If they're narcos, no," Lozada says. "First sign of law enforcement, they'll get out, fast."

"Non-docs, they're not going to be shooting things up," Garcia says.

Lozada looks at him. "Fights happen. Between people in a group. Or with the coyote."

"Why the flare?" Whicher says.

The deputy shrugs. "Maybe somebody got lost?"

The marshal thinks it over. Thinks of his own feeling—the sense of something wrong.

Garcia addresses Lozada. "What do you want to do, Adriana?"

"My guys are off watch—they're back on again tomorrow. Right now, I don't know what else we can do..."

"I could stay," Garcia says.

"How about you, marshal?" Lozada says.

"I have an arrestee on a federal warrant in my truck." Whicher gestures over his shoulder. "I have to get him upcountry."

"We got this, mano," Garcia says. "If you need to go."

Lozada eyes him. "I don't think there'll be any more trouble here tonight."

"Let me talk with Larry," Garcia says, "see if he wants a presence, I could stick around."

"Who's the arrestee?" Lozada says.

"Foreign fugitive. Picked up this evening."

"You're taking him where?"

"Reeves County."

Garcia glances at the Silverado. "Long drive."

Whicher rubs at his jaw. "He might've taken something. Drugs maybe. I need to be sure he makes it in, I don't need a medical emergency."

"We'll talk with the owner," Lozada says, "see what he wants to do. We can get people out here. But I don't think there's any need."

The marshal eyes the dark land.

With still the same sense of unease.

* * *

Lying flat in the dirt at the high ground north of the house, Aquino stares at the truck now leaving up the dirt road—the first vehicle to arrive. The man driving it, the tall man in the hat—the searcher. The man that moved up silent on the hill.

Aquino watches the truck's twin headlamp beams pass below—bumping, arcing through the night.

At the ranch, in the light of the SUVs of La Migra, two men watch the land to the south and west, carbines held at their waists.

The woman officer is gone into the house with the thin man in the uniform shirt.

Settling against the dirt, Aquino lowers his eye to the night vision scope of a Heckler & Koch 416 rifle.

He trains it onto the squat agent from La Migra at the near end of the ranch compound.

The man turns.

Presents his back, full to the scope.

Aquino rests the center of the aiming reticle between his shoulders.

Inches up.

To hold on his head.

CHAPTER THREE

Alone in the house in Pecos, Whicher sets the drip-brew coffee maker in the kitchen for the first cup of the morning. He pads into the bathroom, strips his T-shirt to shave in the sink.

He eyes himself in the mirror—in shape at fifty-two. The muscles of his upper body taut. Face fatigued from a lack of sleep.

He runs water from the faucet, smooths his short, brown hair.

Foams his face, shaves, rinses off.

Thinks of Marco Zambrano—arriving with him in the early hours of the morning, booking him into the Reeves jail. Still pumped, amped, still intense.

Returning to the kitchen, the marshal checks his phone—aware of checking it. Unsettled. Preoccupied from the night before. He stares out through the glass sliders at the yard outside.

No word.

Nothing from anyone.

He pours coffee. Thinks of Leanne. Of Lori. Back in Austin with Leanne's folks. The house unnaturally quiet without them.

Walking to the bedroom, he searches out a crisp white shirt from the armoire.

Puts it on. Checks his watch.

Two hours till he has to be there.

An hour and a half by road.

He dresses quickly, puts on a dark gray suit, selects a tie.

Re-enters the kitchen, takes a sip on the cup of coffee.

Despite himself, glances at his phone.

Fifteen miles west of Marfa on US 90, a flat sweep of West Texas is backlit beyond the dust-streaked windshield.

Whicher slows the truck, looking for the turn from the highway.

To the north, gray-blue foothills of the Davis Mountains edge the skyline.

A low wall and gate mark the entranceway onto land running south.

The marshal checks his rear view. Sees the name on the iron sign by the gate.

Zimmerman.

He makes the turn through the gateway onto a gravel road —toward a cantaloupe farm.

The phone lights up in the holder on the dash.

Whicher sees the name on screen, presses to answer. "Leanne?"

"Morning."

"Everything alright?"

"Sure," his wife says.

"Lori alright?"

"Everybody's fine."

The marshal feels tension ease across his shoulders.

"I tried to call last night," Leanne says. "Where were you?"

"Picking up an arrestee." Whicher scans the gravel track, the rising hills in the distance.

"The calls went straight to voicemail."

"I was down on the border. No coverage out there. I picked up this guy, then there was something up at a ranch—in the mountains. I didn't make it back till four."

"Oh?" Leanne says. "What happened?"

"Some kind of a shooting incident. Up in the Chinati Mountains. I was closest unit. Border Patrol came out. Plus the county sheriff."

Leanne is silent on the line.

"Kind of a long night," the marshal says. "Anyhow, I'm fine. How's Lori? How're your folks?"

"They're good. Lori's a little…whiny."

Whicher steers around a turn in the track. "How come?"

"Because she's twelve? I thought we'd go downtown today, into Austin," Leanne says. "Get lunch. Maybe look at clothes."

"Mm-hmm."

"I know you'll be sorry to miss that…"

Whicher grins.

Ahead are farm buildings—along with a two-story, white stuccoed house. A shaded gallery runs along its front beneath red clay tiles. In the farmyard are vehicles, a law enforcement SUV.

"So, you're alright?" Leanne says. "Did you eat?"

"Uh-uh…"

"Eat something…"

"Listen, I'm meeting with the sheriff outside of Marfa..."

"What's going on?"

"Somebody missing," Whicher says. "Farm worker. Sheriff's office is pretty stretched, they bumped it up the line, asked for federal assistance."

Approaching the buildings closer he sees a man step from the SUV, talking into a radio transceiver—dressed in tan uniform shirt, a Western hat.

"It's probably nothing," the marshal says.

Sheriff Torres raises a hand.

"Listen, I got to go."

Leanne's voice is low, warm. "Alright, well take care of yourself."

"I will."

Whicher clicks off the call.

Pulling in alongside the sheriff, he shuts down the motor.

A young, Hispanic woman climbs from a battered, green, Isuzu Trooper.

The marshal steps out, fits the Resistol. Buttons his suit jacket over the Ruger in the shoulder holster and the Glock at his waist.

The young woman leans against her vehicle, folds her arms over a faded T-shirt.

Sheriff Torres is in his mid-fifties, with hard-looking eyes. His brow furrowed beneath his hat, face weathered. "Heard you were out here, last night? Down in the south country?"

The marshal nods.

"My deputy, Garcia, is going down there again this morning—to run a search in daylight."

The woman stares across at the sheriff, eyes flat.

From the house, a man emerges, dressed in a checkered shirt, the sleeves rolled.

The sheriff glances in his direction. "Emmett Zimmerman," he says. "Owner of the property." Torres turns toward the young woman at the Isuzu. "And this is Josefina Olvera. Josefina made the missing person report."

Whicher raises the Resistol. "Ma'am. Good morning."

She only stares back, mute.

Zimmerman approaches, balding, heavy-set, tanned from the sun. "Saw y'all from the window," he says. "Sheriff. Josefina." He looks to Whicher.

"United States Marshals Service. I'm a criminal investigator, out of Pecos."

The farm owner looks unsure. "Pleased to know you, sir."

"We just need to talk with Ms Olvera, right now," the sheriff says. "If you don't mind."

"Of course," Zimmerman says. "I thought—if I could be of any help..."

"We'll need to talk with you. And talk with Santiago," Torres says. "We need to speak with Ms Olvera first."

Zimmerman nods. "I'll be right in the house."

Torres turns to Whicher—he gestures toward an automobile parked in the shade of a barn at the side of the yard.

The young woman pushes up from the side of her car.

"This here vehicle belongs to Matias Cardenas," Sheriff Torres says.

Whicher and the woman follow across the yard to a twenty-year-old Buick Regal Sedan sitting low on its shocks.

"Matias is twenty-eight. He works here at the farm, lives outside of Marfa."

"He's been missing five days," the woman says.

The sheriff stands by the dilapidated sedan. Tips back his hat. "Ms Olvera reported him missing—so far, nobody's seen him in that time, from what we can tell."

"Five days?" Whicher says.

Josefina Olvera levels her eyes on him.

"What relationship do you have with Mister Cardenas, ma'am?"

"We're together."

The marshal takes out a lined notepad and a pen from his jacket. "And you've had no form of contact with him since then?"

"Nobody's seen him," the sheriff says. "Nobody heard a thing."

The marshal looks at the Buick. "His car's been out here the whole time?"

The woman nods, chews on a nail.

"It's unlocked," Torres says.

"He left for work last Thursday," Olvera says. "He came here."

"He was here all day?"

The sheriff looks to the farmhouse. "Mister Zimmerman says he was, so far as he knows. But he was up in Marfa, on business. By the time he got back, he noticed Matias's car, he thought maybe he got a ride home with Santiago."

Whicher makes a question with his face.

"Santiago Guevara," Torres says, "he works here."

The marshal looks to Josefina Olvera. "Anything like this ever happen before?"

Her eyes narrow. "Never. Anybody who knows him will tell you that."

"He acting any way different? Before this all happened?"

The young woman's gaze shifts beyond the barn to the mountains rising in the south. "No," she says. "I don't know. All I've been doing is thinking about it..."

The sheriff cuts in; "Santiago Guevara says he saw Matias get into a car with two men. Couple days before this all happened."

Whicher taps the pen against the notepad.

"He said he thought he looked maybe—like he was under duress."

"He use those words?" Whicher says.

"Santiago told me he looked scared," Olvera says. "Like these people came here, they wanted him to get in their car, he didn't want to—then they made him."

"I talk with the guy?" Whicher says.

The sheriff nods.

"Ma'am, you have any idea what might've happened?"

The young woman only stares back.

"He have any problems that you know of? Money problems? Problems with other people?"

"No." Olvera's voice rises, "And so far, nobody's doing nothing..."

"Josefina," the sheriff says. "Matias is a grown man, we can't open up an investigation without evidence..."

"So where is he?"

"People go missing, they have all kinds of reasons," Torres says. "Mostly, if you can't find them, it's because they don't want to be found."

Heat is in Olvera's face now. "I told you, he's not like that."

"That's why I brought in the marshal here," Torres says, "to take a look at this. Marshals Service find people, that's what they do."

Whicher puts the notepad into his pocket. Lets his gaze run past the beaten-up Buick to the land running south. "Let me talk with this guy, Guevara."

***

In the shade of a packing shed to the west of the main house, a Hispanic man sits on a stack of unformed cardboard boxes piled flat by a harvesting rig.

Whicher regards him.

Santiago Guevara stares back—wary at the unfamiliar figure in the suit and hat; six-one, hard-eyed, tough-looking.

The farm owner, Emmett Zimmerman, addresses him. "Santiago. This here's the marshal. Down from Pecos."

Guevara's eyes are deep-set, mistrustful, in a fleshy face. He looks to Torres and Josefina Olvera. "I already talked with the sheriff."

"We're just trying to make sure Matias is okay," Torres says.

"You saw him get into a car with two men?" Whicher says. "That right?"

Guevara picks at the edge of a cardboard packing box. He gives a bare nod.

"Two days before Matias went missing?" Whicher says. "A week back. You ever see these guys before?"

"No, señor."

"Have you seen 'em since?"

Guevara shakes his head.

"What'd they look like?"

"One was short. Small. A thin guy. The other was taller."

"Anglos?"

"Latino."

"Any body art?" the marshal says. "Tattoos?" He points to his neck, his face.

Guevara lowers his gaze. "I didn't see nothing like that."

The sheriff cuts in; "We don't get so many gangbangers down here..."

The marshal nods. "How were they dressed?"

"Shirts. Jeans."

"How about their hair?"

Guevara bugs his eyes. "Short."

"What kind of vehicle they show up in?"

"SUV," Guevara says. "A big Dodge."

"What color?"

"Black. A Durango."

"You get a look at the plate?"

"No, señor."

"What time of day this all happen?"

"Noon. A little after."

"There anything else happen that day? Anything unusual?"

"No, señor."

"So, two men in a black, Dodge Durango. This a new car?"

"Not new. Not real old."

Whicher writes down the few details in the notebook. "You told Ms Olvera Matias looked scared? Around them. Like he didn't want to get in this vehicle with 'em?"

Guevara swallows. Doesn't answer.

"What made you think that? They force him into it? They talk with him first?"

"They talked a little. Next thing, he got in the car with them, they drove off."

"How long were they gone?"

"Like, thirty minutes."

"You talk with him about it? After he came back?"

"I asked him what was going on," Guevara says. "He wouldn't say nothing."

Whicher turns to Josefina Olvera. "He mention any of this to you?"

She shakes her head. "Santiago told me. After Matias didn't show up no more."

Whicher studies on the farm worker.

Guevara shifts his weight on the stack of boxes.

"You know anything that might help the sheriff? Or Ms Olvera here?"

Emmett Zimmerman leans forward, trying to put himself in the man's line of vision; urging him to speak.

Josefina Olvera stands rigid.

Guevara's eyes only cut away.

* * *

Back in the farmyard across from the main house, Whicher stands by the Silverado, taking in the drilled rows of seedlings growing in a field to the east of the barn. "Anybody else see these folk show up?"

"I didn't see 'em out here," Zimmerman says, "but I was up to Fort Davis part of that day…"

"I thought you said Marfa?"

"This was two days before that," the sheriff says, "two days before Matias went missing."

Zimmerman nods. "I agree with Santiago; when I got back, I talked with Matias that afternoon, something seemed wrong with him he was real subdued. Kind of edgy."

"You know him well?"

"Not real well, no. But he's worked here near on three years."

"He a good employee?"

Josefina Olvera glares at the farm owner.

"He shows up, he works hard," Zimmerman says. "He's reliable."

"Exactly," Olvera says. "He's *reliable*…"

Sheriff Torres cuts a look at her.

"So, it's obvious something's wrong."

"How many people you have working here?" Whicher says.

"Right now, there's just Santiago and Matias," Zimmerman answers. "I do a lot of the work myself, along with my wife. We grow melons, onions, some peppers, pumpkins. Springtime it's pretty much just us. Department of Ag allows us some migrant labor for the harvest."

"You have any ideas?" Whicher says. "Anything that might help?"

The farm owner's face is pinched-looking. "I've thought about it a whole lot, I daresay we all have. That's what's worrying, there's really nothing. This whole thing is just right out of the blue."

* * *

The sun is climbing high as Whicher stands with Josefina Olvera and Sheriff Torres in the dirt yard—Emmett Zimmerman gone back inside of the house.

"We've checked the hospitals, clinics," Torres says, "whatever medical facilities we have. There's no report of any accident involving anybody that could be him. His vehicle is here."

Whicher stares at the car by the barn.

"Calls to his cell phone go straight to voicemail..." Sheriff Torres takes a plastic document wallet from inside of his SUV. "This is everything we've done so far. Personal details for Matias. Everything we have."

"So, what are you going to do?" the young woman says.

Whicher inclines his head. "I have to speak with my boss."

Olvera juts her chin.

"I can make some calls. Talk to people. Check out background." The marshal pins her with a look. "What do you think could've happened?"

Her voice rises, "I have no idea..."

"You been together a long time?"

"Two years." Her face drains. "We have a place outside of Marfa."

"And you can't think of anything that might've happened to him?"

She shakes her head. Looks at Torres. "I told you to call the FBI..."

"FBI won't investigate," the sheriff says, "Matias isn't any kind of vulnerable adult. He's free to do what he wants. There's no evidence of any crime. We don't know he crossed any state line..."

"But none of this makes sense."

"I have six deputies to cover the whole of the county..."

"Ma'am," Whicher softens his voice. "The Marshals Service has a lot of reach."

"Someone has to find him," Olvera says, "wherever he is..."

The sheriff nods. Doesn't answer.

Whicher meets the woman's eye. Holds it.

* * *

Only the Silverado and the sheriff's SUV remain outside the house at the Zimmerman farm—the marshal watches Josefina Olvera's green Isuzu disappearing up the dirt track—a dot of color on the tan land raising dust across the flats leading back to the highway.

He turns to the sheriff. "So, what do you think?"

Torres shrugs. "We don't have evidence for anything."

"But?"

"He could have gotten mixed up in something..."

The marshal nods. "Narcotics? People smuggling?"

The sheriff spreads his hands.

"He have family here?" Whicher says. "In Marfa?"

"Fort Stockton."

"You spoken with any of 'em?"

"I had the sheriff of Pecos County go talk with the parents," Torres says. "Seems like they don't know nothing either. I'd like to run a search. Big-scale search. There's mountains and canyons we have a hard time getting to—lot of remote terrain. I'd like to search by air, get a helicopter."

The marshal looks at him. "Why's that?"

Torres blows out his cheeks. Sweeps an arm in the direction of the land south and west. "I don't want to think he went out there somewhere—and we just didn't find him. Not here. Not in my own back yard."

CHAPTER FOUR

Marfa, Tx

At the bar and grill off Highland Street Whicher sits at a corner table. Ceiling fans turn the air in the cool, dark room. He finishes up a plate of rib-eye steak with fried okra and corn.

On the table is the folder from Sheriff Torres—details of Matias Cardenas, a photograph. Barely anything in it he hasn't already heard. Cardenas an unremarkable farm worker, with few known interests or friends.

Whicher takes out his phone. Keys a call to Chief Marshal Fairbanks in the Pecos office.

His boss answers on the second ring. "Marco Zambrano?"

"Ma'am?"

"You picked him up last night?"

Whicher pictures the chief marshal—in her mid-fifties with steel-gray hair. Tough. Little given to preamble. "Yes, ma'am," he says. "Yes, I did."

"I've got the fugitive task force in Houston demanding we get him out of here as soon as we can—DOJ and the Office of International Affairs want to start the extradition process. I need him gone today. But you asked for a medical assessment?"

"The on-call nurse."

"Why was that?" Fairbanks says.

"Guy was acting like he was jacked full of something," Whicher says. "I thought he could have a heart attack, maybe a seizure."

"Well, the nurse didn't see him, it wasn't classed urgent," Fairbanks says. "They said it was four o'clock in the morning, they weren't about to drag her on in. So now he'll need to see the doc. We've got to clear him for travel."

Whicher drains the last of a glass of mineral water.

"How come it got so late?" Fairbanks says.

"I picked up a 911 call. A report of shooting at a ranch. I was closest unit." Whicher sits forward at the restaurant table. "It was up in the hills. I went out. Border Patrol went out. We couldn't find anything. The sheriff's office is still looking at it."

"Oh?"

"I didn't make it back to Reeves till gone three."

"Did you meet with Sheriff Torres this morning?"

"I just came from there."

"On the missing person report?"

"Right."

"What did you think?"

The marshal raises a hand, catches the eye of a waitress to call for the check. "I'd say the sheriff's office could use some help. The guy's mid-twenties, a farm worker—missing persons, it's mostly people younger, or older."

"If anybody could find him, it's probably you..."

"It could be nothing." The waitress approaches Whicher's table. "There's a girlfriend, she says something's definitely wrong..."

"Look into it," Fairbanks says.

"Alright, I'll see where it goes."

* * *

Outside the restaurant, high cloud scuds across an azure blue sky. Cars and trucks roll by brick and stuccoed buildings from the twenties and thirties, Whicher eyes the cupola of the courthouse rising behind cottonwoods in the square.

He can head back.

An hour-forty up to Pecos.

He can call the doc. See if he could meet him at the jail, check on Zambrano, get him cleared to go.

Turning onto West Texas Street, he thinks of the woman at the cantaloupe farm—Josefina Olvera. Two Hispanics forcing her boyfriend into a car.

He reaches his truck on the tar-ribboned asphalt pavement. Climbs in behind the wheel, fires it up, drives by the First Baptist Church.

He makes a right, another, skirts the courthouse square.

The highway north will take him back up through Fort Davis. He can stop, see if he could find the family; Cardenas's family.

He passes the sheriff's office, the back of the county jail. Makes the turn onto 17.

The phone on the dash lights up—he doesn't recognize the caller.

He clicks to speaker. "Yeah, this is Whicher."

"Marshal." A man's voice, accented. "This is Carlos Garcia. Deputy Garcia? We met last night?"

"Deputy."

"My boss said to give you a call."

Whicher steers along North Dean, past the old silver water tower.

"Border Patrol found a body," Garcia says, "out at the river. Late this morning. No ID. Sheriff Torres said to call you, he said you're looking into our missing person case?"

The marshal sits up. "You think it could be Cardenas?"

"All I know is, they found a male Hispanic. Young."

Whicher signals, pulls in at the side of the road. "You have a location?"

"It's west of the ranch—about ten or twelve miles."

"The Mackenzie Ranch?"

"Out at the river. By Ruidosa. I don't know what's going on, mano," Garcia says. "I'm headed over to take a look."

Whicher checks the rear-view, turns the truck around. "I'll be there as fast as I can."

* * *

Heat radiates in the air above the scattering of tin-roofed adobe buildings and the ruin of a church up ahead.

Whicher slows on the two-lane farm-to-market. A black and white Chevy truck stands guard at the side of the road.

A collection of vehicles sits in a dirt lot on the riverside beyond the church.

Among the vehicles is a white and green Ford Super Duty, a white panel van, a Nissan pickup. Plus a Tacoma—the Presidio County Sheriff's badge on its door—Garcia's truck.

The marshal signals, pulls in.

A blue-shirted police officer approaches, heavy-set, Hispanic, in his thirties.

Whicher holds his badge and ID out of the open window. "Marshals Service, out of Pecos. Here to see Deputy Garcia."

"Down at the river," the officer says.

"They move the body yet?"

"Not yet, marshal."

Whicher shuts off the motor. "Am I clear to go down?"

The officer nods.

Whicher steps out, fits his hat. Feels the uptick of heat.

The riverbank is thick with dark green vegetation—granjeno and salt cedar, carrizo cane.

At the foot of a dirt path he recognizes the Border Patrol agent from the night before—Adriana Lozada.

Deputy Carlos Garcia stands with her and two other men at the water's edge.

A body is on the ground beside them—among horseweed and cane moving in a light wind.

A tall man in a cotton jacket and black-framed glasses speaks to a young sheriff's deputy with short-cropped hair.

Whicher recognizes the tall man; Preston Crawford, a county justice of the peace.

Garcia spots the marshal, starts to move up on the bank.

Border Patrol Agent Lozada looks across in his direction—the marshal tips a finger to the brim of his hat.

The body at the river is dressed in jeans, sneakers, a red t-shirt. The t-shirt adorned with letters, yellow and white, over some kind of graphic.

Garcia approaches, squinting in the sun.

The marshal tries to read his face. "Not Cardenas?"

"I don't know."

"Could it be?"

"He's been in the water a while."

Whicher looks at the corpse lying just out of the river.

"There's some post-mortem swelling, facial injuries," the deputy says. "He's been dragged, against the ground, most likely by the current. There's gravel and rock in the bed, sharp enough to cut the skin. It messed his face up pretty good."

"How long's he been here?"

"We don't know. The body's been under a while. Then washed up, exposed to heat, exposed to the air," Garcia says. "He'd be about the right age, right build. I don't think it's him, but I couldn't rule it out. We don't know where he went in—upstream somewhere, we don't know how far."

"I take a look?"

The marshal descends the riverbank.

The JP steps away from the corpse. "Marshal."

"Mister Crawford."

The young deputy regards him, hat held between his hands.

"This is Deputy Padilla," Garcia says.

The marshal takes a pace toward the river's edge.

The dead man's face is swollen, grazed, discolored.

Whicher pictures the photograph of Cardenas in the file. "He drown? Was he alive when he went in the water?"

"They'll have to autopsy," Garcia says. "I'd say it looks like he drowned."

"We don't know what kind of shape he was in when he went in the water," Preston Crawford says. "He may not have been well."

"Who found him?"

"Border Patrol," Garcia says, "on a regular sweep. They'll walk sections where the river comes near any road—people hide out, wait for nightfall to move..."

The marshal looks to Lozada.

"Undocumented non-citizen..." She shades her eyes.

"You think?"

"Right age. Dressed down, to avoid attention. People in the river, you need to ask why they're in there." Lozada folds her arms over her olive-green shirt.

"Are you going to move him?"

"We had to wait on the van from the sheriff's department," the JP says. "Deputy Padilla will take the body to a funeral parlor in Fort Davis, till I can find an ME to take it. We're currently sending them up to Lubbock." He spreads his palms. "I wish we had a better way of doing it."

The marshal nods.

Garcia takes a pace from the mud-brown water. "I was up at the Mackenzie Ranch. Running a daylight search. Sheriff wanted me to come down. I told him we'd wait for you."

"Y'all find anything up there?"

"They had a truck stolen."

Whicher looks at him.

"They didn't know it was stolen last night," the deputy says. "It was out at some old barn on the property. They just found out this morning."

Whicher turns back to the body. "T-shirt the guy's wearing? Cardenas has a partner, she might know if he had one like it."

"We could find out," Garcia says.

Lozada gazes out over the river.

Whicher takes in the body of the young man—somewhere in his twenties, he guesses. A whole life ahead of him.

"If he was sick," the young deputy, Padilla says, "if he's a non-doc, they would have left him behind."

"I'll contact the regular consulates," Preston Crawford says. "Mexico, Guatemala, El Salvador. Somebody might've been in touch."

"Some of them carry pieces of paper," Lozada says, "phone numbers of loved ones. The water probably did for anything like that."

"He could be local," Crawford says.

The Border Patrol agent's eyes grow dark. "He'll be from somewhere south of here. A long way south."

* * *

Up at the roadside Garcia, Padilla and the JP place the body bag containing the corpse into the back of the van. At the Silverado, Whicher keys a call, watches Agent Lozada speaking with the blue-shirted police officer at the side of the road.

The call picks up.

"Bob Hollis..."

"Doc? Doctor Hollis? John Whicher, USMS. You may have had a call from the Reeves Jail this morning? On account of me."

"Marshal, yes."

"About an inmate I was hoping you could see? I was wondering, could you make it over this afternoon?"

"The jail called," the doctor says. "Your inmate doesn't appear to be unwell right now. There's no emergency, it's not urgent. In which case, it'd have to wait till the end of the week."

"The guy's a fugitive on a foreign arrest warrant," Whicher says. "We're looking to get him shipped back to Houston."

"Is he fit to travel?"

"I'd think," Whicher says. "But we're on record asking for a medical assessment..."

"I'll see what I can do. But it won't be today."

Agent Lozada steps away from the officer standing guard at the road. She crosses the lot with Deputy Garcia.

"I'll let you know," the doctor says.

"Appreciate it."

Whicher finishes the call.

"We're done here," Garcia says, "I have to head back up to the Mackenzie Ranch. Adriana's headed back to Border Patrol."

"Sheriff's office will investigate," Lozada says. "I'm only down here to keep us in the loop. But people call sometimes, call us rather than law enforcement; non-docs, already living here. Expecting a family member—that never arrives."

"Could this have something to do with last night?" Whicher says. "At the ranch?"

A thought passes behind Lozada's eyes, she doesn't answer.

Garcia's face is clouded. "It bothers me somebody stole a vehicle out of there."

Lozada nods. "That's unusual."

"It bothers me they have a judge among the party..."

Whicher looks at the deputy. "How's that?"

"A judge," Garcia says. "Richardson. That tall hombre? He told me this morning. If we have an active situation here...it's pretty close to that ranch."

Whicher frowns. "I'm going to need to check on that. What's the level of risk right now? On the border?"

"Ordinarily," Lozada says, "this sector, not that high. Most of the mule routes pass east and west of here. Same goes for people smuggling. Only lately, we're seeing a few things change."

Garcia nods toward the van. "More folk are coming through. The guy there, he's evidence of that."

The marshal scans the deserted road, the few adobe buildings, the church. "I'll need to speak to Richardson."

"You coming up?"

"I could use a handle on what's going on here." Whicher studies the ground away from the river; scrub giving out to rising hills in the middle distance, the foothills of the Sierra Vieja running north. "If it's bad, I need this guy to know that..."

The Border Patrol agent catches his eye. "You have a change of clothes?"

"In the truck," Whicher says.

She gestures at the suit. "If you want to head into country, you can't wear that."

"You offering to take me?"

"If you want," she says, "I could show you."

CHAPTER FIVE

For ten miles, the Pinto Canyon Road climbs steadily away from the river through the desert lowland—a graded dirt and gravel track twisting through mesquite and creosote bush and ocotillo between denuded hills.

Above, the land is a crazed jumble—peaks and plateaus of lava rock, banks of crumbling shale, sheer limestone cliffs.

Dressed in a T-shirt, jeans and army boots, Whicher scans the empty landscape from behind the wheel of the Silverado —to the north, the Candelaria Rim Rock, a towering ridge of ochers, tans and grays.

South of the road the Chinati mountains unfold, their northern slopes cloaked in shade.

Ahead, Adriana Lozada steers her truck across the bed of a dry creek into a high canyon.

She slows, pulls onto parched earth and loose stone and wisps of grass the color of straw.

Whicher pulls in behind her.

Lozada climbs from her truck.

The marshal shuts down the motor, steps out.

Light wind blows between the rise of hills in the tangible silence.

The Border Patrol agent reaches inside her truck—takes out a folded map and a spotting scope.

Whicher eyes the rock peaks encircling the canyon—the vast land of the valley below.

Lozada starts toward a hill sparsely covered in dry, stunted scrub vegetation. She calls over her shoulder; "Up here..."

The marshal follows on behind her.

Climbing to a natural look-out point Lozada opens out a section of the map.

She holds out her arm, points at a near hill to the north-west. "Cerro de la Cruz," she says. "A waypoint. Gateway to the canyon." She gestures at the ridge of mountains twenty miles distant in the west. "The Sierra Quemada."

"In Mexico," the marshal says.

Lozada nods. "You can see the Rio Grande. In places. Make out the line of the river, in green."

Whicher gazes out over the low desert to the border.

"You cross that river," Lozada says, "next thing is; which way you'll try to come."

The marshal thinks of the distance from the Rio Grande, the unforgiving terrain, the long, hard climb.

"People look to come through here," Lozada says, indicating the rough track below. "Not by road, it's pretty likely somebody would spot you. But all of these hills have canyons and creeks between them. If you know what you're doing you can find a way. Nighttime there's no one out here..."

"There's no one out here now," the marshal says.

Lozada points at the side of a scrub covered hill descending toward the trail. "There's a spring, there. Ojo Acebuche. See where the vegetation shows green?"

Whicher picks it out.

"What people need the most, that they can't carry enough

of, is water," Lozada says. "There's springs all over, watercourses that come up from beneath the ground. They'll run along the surface for maybe fifty yards, then disappear back in the sand."

"Migrants can find them?"

"Coyotes can, good coyotes. Drug runners, too. The choice coming through here is basically speed or stealth. You want speed, you'll have to use a road, have somebody come pick you up. You're either gone fast, or you're stopped by the Patrol or law enforcement. Mostly, stealth is your better option. But the more remote you go, the more chance there is of dying. With migrants, a lot of them, they're already sick. They've been traveling a long time already. They get in here, dehydration will get them. Hypothermia. Falls. The temperature can drop overnight so fast you'll freeze. Drug mules packing sixty pounds of marijuana get exhausted, they get lost..."

"That's what you're seeing coming through?" Whicher says.

Lozada nods. "Marijuana. Plus cocaine. And some meth."

"Is there competition for routes?"

"Always." Lozada shows him the map, runs a finger north, starting from their position on the hill. She draws a line up the US side of the Rio Grande. "Sierra Vieja," she says. "The Rim Rock. Twenty-some miles of mountain wall blocking you in if you make it over the river."

She holds the spotting scope to her eye, looks out over the land.

Whicher surveys the colors of the mesa-like ridge—just visible from the valley—a hard divide between the high plain at Marfa and the desert floor at the river three thousand feet below.

"Sometimes you'll see a group traveling...."

"By day?" Whicher says.

"Drug mules. Younger guys. Fitter, stronger." She offers him the scope. "They'll move by day, try to make ground. They're running big-time risk compared to any migrant."

The marshal holds the scope to his eye, studies the vista of rocks and hills.

"This sector," Lozada says, "a lot of people cross further upriver—close to Candelaria. They'll hide by day, there's corridors they'll use. Capote Creek, they'll look to climb up the rim near the waterfall."

Whicher takes away the scope.

"We stop them all the time," Lozada says. "More always come."

"So is it drugs, mainly?" the marshal says. "Right now, here? Or illegal aliens?"

"Both," Lozada says. "But drugs are on the rise—detection rates are growing at the ports of entry."

"So they take to the hills..."

The Border Patrol agent nods. "This canyon and the tracks around here are another known way through."

"How far are we from the Mackenzie Ranch?"

"From here? Seven, eight miles."

The marshal considers it. "Walking distance."

"Sure," Lozada says.

"So, you know where these people are coming from, you know where they'll try to go..."

"We do. But it's always changing."

Whicher hands her back the scope. "It's changing now?"

"Looks like," Lozada says. She holds his eye. "Last night made me think it more. That's what I want to show you..."

* * *

Six miles south of Pinto Canyon, the climb up the dry bed of the watercourse is steep in the afternoon heat—a grueling half mile to the mountain top through deep gullies of rock and loose gravel and sun-bleached stone.

Greasewood and mariola and tasajillo line the banks of the dry stream. Heat radiates from the parched earth, trapped in folds of the land.

Lozada keeps a steady pace.

Baked air moves in waves off the scrub.

At the top of the gully, the ascent becomes a scramble—the sides deepening between high shoulders of sharp-edged rock.

The marshal climbs, breathing hard now, footing uneven, crumbling, giving out.

Gusts of wind dry the T-shirt against his back, lift the sweat from his skin.

Pressing on beneath a whitening sky, the Border Patrol agent reaches a slope of loose stone, she crouches low to climb.

Whicher follows—handing off from the ground, watchful of cacti, of spines and thorns on every plant.

Where the mountain flattens to a ragged plateau at its top, Lozada finally stops.

Hands on hips she turns, looks down, surveys the drop to the valley below.

She glances at Whicher. "You okay?"

"I'm good."

She grins.

"Little warm," he says.

"No kidding."

The marshal takes in the empty mountain valley below—the Silverado at the head of a bare dirt trail, Lozada's truck parked beside it.

"Cañón Cinco de Mayo." Lozada gestures with her arm. "We know people come through it." She points to the north. "They'll come up the Cañón de Caballo—the next one over."

"Headed where?"

"Cross country," Lozada says. "Eventually, they need to get to a road. Coyotes arrange transport, drug mules meet with someone."

"How far is the highway?"

"About a dozen miles. But most of them head for farm roads, ranch roads. Remote even for here. 2810 is around ten miles north. It's safer. You're less likely to be seen. Otherwise, you cross the Marfa Plain. Get on US 90 between Valentine and Marfa. That's lonely country, not much out there."

The marshal thinks of the cantaloupe farm, the Zimmerman place, he nods. "I was out there this morning."

"There's plenty of ways to transit through here," Lozada says. "We know a lot about the routes. We have cameras at the river, ground sensors, surveillance drones. The aerostat up at Marfa..."

"Downward-looking radar," Whicher says.

"Doesn't mean we can stop them. Not all of them, this is big country, we can't cover everything, not all of the time."

Whicher edges into the shade of a rock overhang, hot wind lifting dust in the gully. "Things change, you told me?"

"That's why I brought you up here. You get your breath back?"

"Try me."

Lozada nods east—across the broad plateau of the mountain.

* * *

A quarter mile across scorched rock and burnt-dry vegetation, the eastern downslope falls steep—a descent running in a twisting channel, a scrub-choked dry watercourse, the ground treacherous underfoot.

Whicher follows Lozada down the barren tract of the hillside, as if descending the mountains of the moon—into a world of desiccation and silence, oppressive; a land voided. In the air above, a red-tailed hawk turns on the wind—its shadow passing fleet and black.

At a pinch point on the drop Lozada slows.

The marshal sees a bright glare—sunlight on a body of water. The wall of an old dam curves above its surface—weathered concrete, stained, darkened with the passage of time.

Lozada approaches it.

The marshal follows.

"*Presa Llorona*," she says.

Whicher kneels at the reservoir—a dam forty feet across—fed by the slopes of the mountainsides. Dark water within it, low against its wall.

"You know, La Llorona?" the Border Patrol agent says.

Whicher thinks of the old Mexican legend. "The weeping woman?"

"The wailer," Lozada says. "The vengeful ghost."

"She haunts the water?"

"Drowned her own children," Lozada says. "So she lives forever in purgatory—roaming the earth, looking for them. Pulling other children to their deaths."

The marshal stares at the reservoir in the heat.

"Parents use it to scare their kids," Lozada says.

The hawk crosses the sky like the downward slash of a blade—dropping remorseless to an unseen prey.

"A fourteen-year-old girl was found here," Lozada says, "three days back."

The marshal looks at her.

"Deceased. From exposure, from dehydration. She must have been left behind. There was nothing to her, she would have been so weak..." The Border Patrol agent's voice trails off. "We don't know who she is yet. Perhaps we never will."

Taking off her olive-green ball cap, Lozada brushes back a strand of black hair. "Somewhere, someone will be waiting for her. I have a daughter of my own, not much younger than her."

The marshal nods. Thinks of Lori. Feels the weight; desolation in the surroundings.

Recoils from the thought of a child there alone.

Afraid. Alone and dying.

* * *

Fifty yards farther down beneath the wall of the dam Lozada points beyond the scrub-filled gulch—out beyond the long descent of the mountainside.

On a small plain, structures are visible—warped in the haze of heat, maybe three miles distant.

Whicher stares out at them.

Lozada hands him the compact spotting scope.

The marshal puts his eye to it. Recognizes the group of buildings, the land around them. "The Mackenzie Ranch..."

"Right," Lozada says. "There's evidence of people moving this way, recent evidence—there never used to be. We're finding water bottles, sleeping bags. Clothing, wrappers from food."

The marshal takes away the scope. The feeling of uneasiness deepening. "This is drugs smugglers?" He gestures with his head in the direction of the dam. "Or people like the girl back there?"

Lozada blows out her cheeks. "Right now, I think it's mainly coyotes. Foot guides bringing groups looking to get upcountry."

"You think mules could be starting to come this way?"

"Could be. People fight over new routes."

Whicher frowns. "I don't like a judge being at the ranch down there. And why fire on it?"

The Border Patrol agent doesn't answer.

"Garcia reckoned a vehicle was stolen out of there last night…"

"Anyone passing through illegally," Lozada says, "last thing they'll want is to draw attention."

"Yeah," the marshal says. "Well, they have mine now."

CHAPTER SIX

Descending the trail to the compound at the Mackenzie Ranch, Whicher sees Deputy Garcia's Tacoma pickup among a handful of vehicles parked close to the house.

He drives through the gates, parks near to Garcia's truck.

At the house, watching his arrival in the shade of the porch is the ranch owner, Larry Mackenzie. Behind him, the short, squat figure of Donald Eliot, the tall outline of the judge, Vaughn Richardson.

Whicher eyes the other vehicles in daylight; a ten-year-old F150, a new model Lincoln Navigator, a Ram pickup, a battered-looking Rav 4.

Deputy Garcia inspects a spot by a low-roofed, open-sided barn across the compound.

The marshal steps from the truck, raises a hand to the men on the porch.

Garcia takes a zip-lock bag from the pocket of his shirt. He holds it out.

"You find something?"

"Three rounds," the deputy says. "One out of a post in the

shelter here. And two in the cement plaster outside..." He points to the rendered wall at the far side of the compound.

Whicher crosses the dirt yard toward him. "From last night?"

Garcia pushes back his hat. "According to the owner."

"You getting any kind of a read?"

"The bullets in the wall were somebody firing from the plain out there," Garcia says.

Whicher glances at the red-tinged, flat land south of the ranch.

Garcia leads him across the animal enclosure to a timber post holding up part of the roof. He indicates a spot at head height. "But not this one..."

Whicher studies the graze on the wood in front of a sunken hole made by the round, compression indicating its angle of entry.

He turns to look to the northeast—at the mound of a small hill less than half a mile off. Impossible to pick it out the night before. "How about from up there?"

Garcia nods. "The round from the post we could maybe identify. The other two, I don't think."

"Rounds hitting from different directions?"

"So far it's all we have."

"I see 'em?"

Garcia hands him the evidence bag.

The marshal studies the bullets through the clear plastic. The round from the wooden post recognizable in form, the second two from the wall distorted, flattened out "High velocity. Five-five-six. Could be the same gun, could be different."

"I'll keep looking," Garcia says, "see if there's more."

Whicher takes in the men on the ranch porch. "What do folk here think?"

"They have the same story as last night," Garcia says. "Seeing shots out there, seeing things, hearing things."

"How about the stolen vehicle?"

"Dodge Dakota. Nineties model, blue in color. I gave DPS the license plate."

"They didn't know about it till this morning?"

"It's kept in a barn with a bunch of fencing gear," Garcia says. "There's no livestock, now, they hardly use it. Larry says they leave the keys in, nobody's stolen it in thirty years."

"Till now."

"So, you going to speak with them?" Garcia looks across at the house.

The marshal shakes his head. "I want to take a look at something first."

* * *

Standing in a gravel wash at the southern edge of the small plain, the marshal stares back at the ranch in the late afternoon heat.

Beyond the buildings are barren hills of scrub—to the east, mountain and desert as far as the eye can see.

On two sides of the plain are dry creeks— worn into deep depressions in the terrain. Filled with loose stone and boulders, lined with candelilla and coyote willow.

In the dark, a party could pass close to the property. Use either creek in a concealed approach.

Pass close. Unseen.

Beyond the ranch and the hills, only mountain desert and emptiness stretch out. Thirty miles to the main highway. Nine or ten to the ranch road out of Pinto Canyon.

He lets his gaze follow the dry watercourse beyond the gravel wash—all the way back up the valley into the Chinatis

—toward the folds of hills, the dam on the mountain side—the Presa Llorona.

Two miles? Two and a half?

Walking distance. From there, another mile to get up past the ranch.

Climbing the dirt slope back up to the plain, the marshal feels heat pulsing from the burro grass. He studies the buildings around the compound, thinks of shots striking the outside wall.

Fifteen hundred yards?

From the edge of the plain.

Too far.

The shooter would be much closer, unless he were firing into the air; firing wild.

Night conditions, five to six hundred would be considered good accuracy. More likely, the shots would have come from much closer than that.

He stares at the ranch in the dense, still heat.

Unable to shift the gut feel.

Too near.

Too close.

* * *

In an office room off the main hall inside the house, Whicher lowers himself into a chair opposite Larry Mackenzie at a heavy oak desk.

A ceiling fan turns the air, smoke from Mackenzie's cigar trails out of an open window.

The housekeeper, Amber Lester, brings a tray with coffee, bottled water, tall glasses.

She sets the tray down on the desk.

Whicher sees the strain in her face.

She looks to Mackenzie.

The ranch owner nods.

She withdraws from the room.

"She alright?" the marshal says.

"I guess a little rattled."

"How about your hunting party? You expecting them to stay?"

Mackenzie considers it. "They say they want to. We had to cancel today's hunt—with the sheriff's office being here. We've only managed to get them out hunting a couple times, they've paid for a full week."

"Did you know that one of those men is a judge?"

"Yessir," Mackenzie says. "I did."

"Last night you were concerned for your guests' safety. You're not concerned now?"

"Should I be? I don't really know what to think."

"How long have you had the ranch?"

"Forty years, I guess. It's been in the family a while, my dad had it before me."

"You ever have any other incidents like last night?"

"Nossir."

The marshal picks up a mug of coffee from the tray, takes a sip. "Tell me about the truck that was stolen?"

Mackenzie sits forward, bunches his shoulders. Takes a puff on his cigar. "We didn't notice it was gone till this morning. Glen went out, headed down to Presidio…"

"Glen; your ranch hand?"

"Glen Carr, right. He was driving by, he saw the door of the barn was wide open from the road out. He went to check, he saw the truck was gone."

"Where is this?"

"About a mile from here. You would've passed it coming in."

"How come you leave it out there?"

Mackenzie shrugs. "The bed's full of tools and fence gear. We just swing by and pick it up, saves loading and unloading."

"You leave the keys?"

"We never had a problem, till now," Mackenzie says. "Nobody's out here. The truck's old, my dad bought it years gone, we don't use it much. We moved some of the horses last week, we used it then to check we had 'em fenced in."

"Nobody heard anything last night?" Whicher says. "Or saw anything?"

"We wouldn't see, the way the land is—there's a hillside between there and here. Nobody heard anything, that's for sure."

"So, no idea what time this was?"

Mackenzie shakes his head.

"Y'all have livestock as well as horses?"

"Not any more. A wet year, you'll get some good grazing. Dry years, you can run sheep or goats but not cattle, not at scale."

"So you take hunting parties?"

"Or anybody else that wants to come," Mackenzie says. "We're not a dude ranch but we'll have parties come up to ride, camp out, whatever. Experience some wild country. Look at the stars. We do whatever we can to pay for the upkeep."

"Y'all make your money elsewhere?"

"Patricia and I have various business interests outside of here," Mackenzie says. "But this place is sort of in the blood, it gets in you. We'll hang on to it as long as we can."

"There a lot of land?"

"Ten thousand acres."

"And nobody on it?"

"Nobody except for us."

Whicher takes another sip of coffee. "This barn? It's on the way back up to the road to Pinto Canyon?"

"Yessir. Carlos has the details," Mackenzie says, "Deputy Garcia. You think you'll be able to find it?"

"State Patrol are looking."

The ranch owner regards him. "What do you think might've happened last night?"

The marshal drinks the coffee, doesn't reply.

* * *

Outside, in the shade of a horse barn at the far side of the ranch complex, Deputy Garcia searches the weathered timbers forming one side of a small stable.

At the western side of the house, Vaughn Richardson and Donald Eliot sit beneath a sunshade on a raised deck to one side of a guest lodge.

"Any more rounds?" Whicher says.

"Unless I missed them, no," Garcia answers. "We could search for shell casings." He points toward the plain at the south. "But we'd need more people, a search team. I can talk to Sheriff Torres, I don't think there's enough here to justify it..."

"You're going to write it up as vehicle theft?" Whicher says.

"Some kind of incursion," the deputy answers. "Armed incursion, plus the theft. This close to the border, there's no telling who it might've been."

From the corner of his eye, Whicher sees the two men at the guest lodge rise from their seats.

They step from the deck, start to walk across the yard.

"How about you, marshal?" Garcia says. "What do you want to do here?"

"People came pretty close last night," Whicher says. "According to Border Patrol, there may be new routes opening up."

Garcia looks at him. "Adriana was shaken up—by that girl they found, up in the mountains."

"Not real far from here..."

Vaughn Richardson steps into Whicher's eyeline. "Good afternoon." He gestures with his head toward the guest lodge. "May I speak with you a moment? I'd like to know what developments there have been?"

The marshal nods, crosses the yard with the two men.

"We heard the sheriff's office found bullet fragments," Eliot says.

"Three rounds," Whicher says. "And I guess you know about the vehicle getting stolen?"

"We heard."

"So, we weren't seeing things."

"No, sir. A person or persons unknown came through here last night."

Richardson steps up onto the raised deck. "And now they're gone. Or do you believe people might still be out there?"

"There's a concern people could be coming back," the marshal says.

"Is Mister Mackenzie worried about that? Do the sheriff's office share your concern?"

Eliot climbs the steps to the deck. "Why would anybody be coming back?"

"Well, sir." Whicher cuts a look at him. "There's evidence people might be starting to come through here. Pass through close."

"What people?" Richardson says.

"This near to the border, walking distance, most likely illegal migrants. Or narco traffickers."

"Neither of which group is likely to want to trouble us," Richardson says.

Whicher studies the man's face.

"Marshal, I'm a judge, before that I was an attorney with the Department of Homeland Security. I know the situation on our border. I don't think this was anything more than a... freak incident."

Whicher points to the ground south of the ranch. "There's pack trails through the mountains. Those trails come down just a couple miles from here."

Richardson shoves his hands into the pockets of a pair of desert camo pants. "Somebody was out there and they started shooting, that much is clear. Almost certainly drugs mules. I think the most likely explanation is some kind of fight. Who can say what might have gone on? They may have been half-crazed on their own product, for all we know, shooting at lights here at the ranch."

Whicher rubs a hand across his jaw. "Somebody put a flare up."

"A signal?" Richardson says. "For a drop by air? That kind of thing is becoming common in south Texas..."

"Not here in the mountains."

Richardson takes his hands from his pockets, folds his arms over his chest. "I'd appreciate if you could assure Mister Mackenzie it will be safe to allow us to stay on and finish our trip."

"Larry seemed pretty anxious last night," Eliot puts in. "Today he seems unsure what to do..."

"Mackenzie's the property owner," Whicher says. "It's his decision."

"We have three more days booked here, we really want to continue."

"And we appreciate the sheriff's office has to investigate," Richardson says. "We're grateful, too—that you responded last night."

Whicher scans the bleak country surrounding the ranch complex. "Sir, in all honesty, I'd think the pair of y'all would be better cutting short the trip. Speaking as a US Marshal." He looks at Richardson. "Marshals Service have responsibility for the safety of all officers of the courts. Including judges, as I'm sure you know…"

The tall man bridles. "Which is exactly why I don't want anybody overreacting."

Whicher stares at the line of hills in the distance.

"We don't get the chance to do something like this all that often," Eliot says. "We want to stay on, complete the trip. Vaughn and I have talked it over."

"We intend to stay," Richardson says, his voice flat. "If anything, we're forewarned, now. The hunt ends when we take a trophy ram; that's the way this works. We take one, it's done, we go home. But not before."

Whicher meets the judge's eye a moment.

"There's plenty of us," the man says. "We're well armed."

CHAPTER SEVEN

The road across the high plain into Marfa stretches out across the desert grassland. Through waves of heat off the smooth-worn asphalt, Whicher sees vehicles and the shapes of people up ahead—a checkpoint—Border Patrol working the road.

He slows the truck as vehicles ahead in the distance begin to slow.

Keying a stored number on his phone, he pushes back in the driver's seat against the wheel.

Chief Marshal Fairbanks picks up the call. "Marshal. Did you hear from Doc Hollis?"

"Yes, ma'am. Says he can't make it to the jail today. Said he'd call, let me know."

"You tell him we need to ship Zambrano out of here?"

"I told him. But the jail told him the guy's okay today—any medical visit gets bumped…"

"We need to move him to Houston."

"I'll go see Zambrano when I get back."

"Where are you now?"

Whicher lets the Chevy slow against the road. Watches a

group of Border Patrol agents surround a car, two agents standing back with lowered carbines. "Still in Presidio County. I got dragged into something—on that missing person case. Sheriff's office were called to a body found washed up at the river. With no ID."

"Was it him?"

"It's a male, right age, unidentified, as yet. The river messed him up some. I'll try to have his clothing checked out. But there was something else—I found out one of the guests at that ranch incident last night is a judge..."

"Say again?"

"Vaughn Richardson. You know him?"

"Out of Houston? He's a trial judge with the criminal court."

"One of the deputies at the river told me about it," Whicher says.

"Richardson's a big hitter—he's going up to the Court of Criminal Appeals."

The marshal thinks it over. "In Austin?"

"He was just appointed a couple of months back," Fairbanks says. "The guy's a pretty big deal."

Whicher slows to a stop at the end of a line of waiting vehicles. "I had a BP agent show me around," he says, "to get me up to speed with the situation on the ground. Plus I went on back to the ranch—I'm not real sure it's safe for a judge. Sheriff's department found three rounds fired into there."

The chief marshal falls silent on the line.

Along the row of vehicles directly ahead on the road, a Border Patrol agent in fatigues walks slow, looking in at every window.

Whicher takes out the USMS badge and ID. "They had a vehicle stolen from the property last night, also..."

"Really? You think it warrants a threat assessment?"

"That's why I was calling. I get back, I want to see what

the FBI has on him. I advised him there could be an ongoing risk."

"Agreed," Fairbanks says. "Well, listen, find out what you can."

Whicher holds his badge out of the truck's open window.

The BP agent moves in close to check it.

"Things happen on the border," the chief marshal says, "we all know that."

"I'll see if there's anything live," Whicher says, "any active threat."

"Stick with it. Keep me in the loop."

* * *

At the Reeves Jail downtown on Oak Street, the interview room is small, bright-lit, AC running from a unit on the wall. Marco Zambrano sits on a metal-frame chair, handcuffs attached to a Martin chain around his waist.

Whicher takes in the seated man.

His hair matted, clumps standing out from his head.

His face is slack now, a residual wildness shows about his eyes.

"You know why you're in here? You understand why you're under arrest?"

The man regards him, mute.

"There's a warrant for your arrest and detention. I'm a US Marshal. I deliver you to court. The court will hear your case, decide what happens next."

No response.

"Last night I thought you were sick. You take something?" The marshal studies on Zambrano. "You were agitated. Worked up. Were you high? Alto en Drogas?"

Zambrano bunches his shoulders, shakes his head.

"You were stopped close to the border. By La Migra. What were you doing there?"

"Nada. Nothing."

"You trying to cross into Mexico?"

Zambrano shifts in his prison whites, rubs a tattooed arm.

"Trying to flee the country?"

The man gives no answer, only eyes the paint-scuffed walls.

"Are you sick now?" Whicher says.

Zambrano shrugs.

"A doctor will see you."

"I want a lawyer." Zambrano finally looks at him.

"You're not under questioning," Whicher says. "You're not answering any charge."

The man's gaze is fully focused, now. He sits forward in his chair.

"You're going out to Houston—tomorrow, the next day, maybe. I just came to tell you that. So get used to it."

Zambrano looks at him directly. "I need to speak to someone. Understand? Abogado. Let me speak to a lawyer."

* * *

Across the street in the USMS office above the courthouse building, Whicher sits at his desk looking over the slim folder of details from Sheriff Torres on the missing farm worker—Matias Cardenas.

He checks his watch—coming up on five.

A single civilian support worker, Ramona Fonseca, sits at the far side of the room.

Whicher grabs the phone from his desk, keys a number.

It picks up. "Preston Crawford..."

"John Whicher. Calling about the body recovered at the Rio Grande today."

The justice of the peace clears his throat. "Marshal, yes."

"I was wondering where the body will be now? I think you said Fort Davis?"

"Funeral home there, yes."

"I need to speak with them."

"Oh? I can give you their number?"

"I'm guessing the body will still be there?"

"It could be there a while—until the county can make arrangements," Crawford says. "Gonzales is the person you need to speak to, Julio Gonzales." The JP reads out a number.

Whicher writes it into a notepad on the desk.

"I don't anticipate we'll get a forensic pathology lab to receive the body imminently," Crawford says.

"No identification was made so far," Whicher says, "I don't suppose there's been any change to that?"

"No, marshal."

"I just had a couple questions. I'll see if I can catch them. Thanks."

He clicks off the call, keys the number from the notepad. Eyes the thin folder.

A voice comes on the line. "Gonzales Funeral Home..."

"Mister Gonzales, Deputy Marshal Whicher—calling from Reeves County. About an unidentified, male Hispanic—recovered at the Rio Grande today."

"Yes?"

"You have the body?"

"It was delivered here earlier today, marshal. How may I help?"

"My office is currently looking into a missing person case for Presidio County—the deceased at the river would be about the right age for the person I'm looking for. I was hoping to use the deceased's clothing—see if we could rule him in or out. You think you could send over a photograph of what he was wearing? The T-shirt, the sneakers? Somebody might recognize it."

"I could do that," Gonzales says.

"Could you send images here to the USMS office, in Pecos?"

"I have to head out—but I could have something with you by the morning."

"I'd appreciate it." Whicher gives contact details to the man. "One more thing—Border Patrol told me migrants sometimes carry phone numbers to call? Pieces of paper in their pockets—in case they're found."

"There was nothing like that," Gonzales says.

"If you could double-check?"

"Alright. I can't promise anything before the morning."

"Tomorrow morning will be just fine. And thank you for your help."

The marshal finishes the call. Writes a note on the pad to check for the photos.

The chief deputy's door opens—Fairbanks steps from it, dressed in a black business suit and skirt, metal-frame glasses pushed up into her steel-gray hair.

In one hand she holds a leather briefcase. She nods to Ramona Fonseca, looks across to Whicher. "Did you make it over to the jail?"

"I just came from there..."

"You check on Zambrano?"

"He seems okay. But he's asking to talk with a lawyer."

Fairbanks frowns. Drops her shoulders a fraction. "He'll get a lawyer when he needs one. Did you speak with anyone about Judge Richardson?"

"Not yet. I'm trying for an ID on the body at the border this morning."

She glances at her watch. "Let me buy you a drink?"

Whicher looks at her.

"If you've got the time there's somebody you ought to see."

*   *   *

Mo Fairbanks steers the big Chrysler 300 along Oak Street, makes the turn onto West 8th across town.

"I called a friend this afternoon in Houston," she says, "at the FBI field office."

"Oh?"

"They gave me some background on Richardson. They also advised we call Alec Strickland at the resident agency, over in Alpine. I spoke with him, he was up at Midland today, he's swinging by on his way back. There's a draft beer place along here, you know it?"

"Booker Tillman drink there?" Whicher says.

"That's the one." Fairbanks slows at an intersection. "So, anyhow—Vaughn Richardson—before he made judge on the criminal court circuit, he was a prosecutor at the Department of Homeland Security. Also, assistant DA at Tarrant County. Houston says he worked some big-scale narcotics cases, some involving South American nationals, some pretty big wheels."

"He did?"

"There's always a concern about retaliatory action—South America, it's common practice to target the judiciary, the prosecuting teams."

"There anything specific?" Whicher says.

"Nothing under active investigation." The chief marshal cuts her eyes at Whicher.

"So, no live file?" the marshal says.

At the side of the road is the bar—by a barber shop and a pizza joint.

His boss signals, pulls over, parks up in the lot.

* * *

Inside, the bar is cool, spacious, a half dozen customers at the counter, an NBA game showing on a bright-lit screen.

Whicher sits opposite Alec Strickland at a table by the window—the FBI agent slim, dark, in a dress shirt and chinos, his eyes lively.

Fairbanks takes a sip from a glass of Tecate Light. "So, you talk about any of this at the field office up in Midland?"

"I did some asking around," Strickland says.

"We've got a senior judge currently staying at a ranch in the Chinati Mountains."

"Close to the border?"

"Close enough. Following events last night, Marshal Whicher and I think there could be some danger—given the remoteness and the isolation of the locale."

"There was a shooting incident?"

"And a vehicle theft from the property," Whicher says.

"The governor appointed this guy to the Court of Criminal Appeals," Fairbanks says, "he's high grade, a sensitive asset."

Strickland considers it. "El Paso and Midland feel like the background prosecuting narcotics cases could be our main issue."

Whicher nods. "But no live files are active on him?"

"True..."

The marshal sips at a draft Shiner. "What's the general level of criminal activity in the area?"

"Narcotics smuggling, we're seeing about the same levels in terms of transshipment," the FBI agent answers. "A lot of cocaine and marijuana coming through, going east, going back to Atlanta. Plus we have heroin and meth. Also diverted pharmaceuticals, precursor chemicals."

"Any new DTOs?" Fairbanks says.

"Pretty much the same six drugs trafficking organizations this sector for the last year or so. DEA say the Mexican warehouses and stash houses near the border are pretty full."

"Any sign they're using more people to move it over?" Whicher says. "Looking for more routes?"

Strickland pulls at a Crawford Bock. "I mean the thing is, it's mostly coming through the ports of entry, El Paso, mainly. In terms of tonnage. Most of the road and rail freight is still uninspected."

"But there's always the foot traffic," Fairbanks says.

"Are levels of violence rising?"

Strickland thinks it over. "Most of the violence is between competing DTOs."

"Is it on the up?" Whicher says.

"There's competition for turf. It's been a while since we had encounters between armed traffickers and US law enforcement, this side. But it happens, you all know that. Sometimes they'll come with manpower and weapons, we can't do much about it—unless we know in advance."

Whicher thinks again of the possibility of a fight.

Fairbanks leans back from the table. "How about specific threats to Judge Richardson in the past?"

"A Honduran cartel wanted to take out an entire prosecuting team he was part of," Strickland says. "That was five years back. Nothing ever materialized."

"Anything else?"

"Colombian DTO tried to bribe and coerce officials this side of the border. A couple of years back. But nothing got off the ground."

"You don't think there's a reason to put a guard on him?" the chief marshal says.

Whicher angles his head. "Or advise him to leave?"

"You can go ahead and advise him," Strickland answers.

"Live rounds were fired into that ranch complex," the

marshal says. "We don't know who did it, we don't know why."

"What's Judge Richardson have to say about it?"

Whicher looks from his boss to Strickland. "He thinks it was likely just some local outbreak, maybe a drugs fight, something over and done. He reckoned they're well armed at the ranch—they're hunting out there. He wasn't rattled."

"Think you could rattle him?"

"Problem is, the man wants to stay."

* * *

Back home across town in the kitchen of the three-bed ranch, Whicher sits at the table, reading through the file on Matias Cardenas, a beer open, dishes waiting in the sink.

Matias Cardenas—twenty-eight. A farm worker of three years standing.

Two years into a relationship with Josefina Olvera. Living together in a trailer home outside of Marfa.

Five days missing.

No contacts, no sightings.

The guy's Buick Regal sedan sitting unlocked by a barn at the Zimmerman farm, his place of employment.

Whicher feels the tick of unease again—thinks of two men arriving the previous week—forcing Cardenas into a vehicle, according to the co-worker. He checks in his notes for the witness to it—Santiago Guevara. He'd told Josefina Olvera what he'd seen. Closed down when it came to talking with law enforcement.

The marshal thinks of the most common reasons for a disappearance—mental health issues, family trauma. Misadventure, accident. Some people ended up in jails, under assumed names, no ID, no way for law enforcement to know who they were.

The family back in Fort Stockton would be worth a visit.

Any criminality, it would probably involve money—likely some form of unpaid debt. Cardenas wouldn't make much working on a Presidio County farm. He didn't drive a fancy car, he lived in a trailer home—no suggestion of a lavish lifestyle.

Narcotics could come into it.

He'd need to find out if he'd been using drugs. Dealing, maybe, alongside using. He could've stepped in someone's patch, started selling in the wrong place.

If not drugs, there was the traffic angle—human trafficking.

The girlfriend, Olvera, seemed pretty straight.

He'd need to go down to Marfa, talk with her again, dig deeper.

He gazes out of the kitchen window—at the evening light descending over the land.

Somewhere there'd be something.

The silence in the room is broken—by Whicher's ringing phone.

The marshal sees the caller name. Picks up.

"Leanne?"

"It's Lori."

An image of his daughter flashes in his mind's eye.

"The battery's almost out on my phone," she says.

"You alright?"

"Mmhm."

"What's going on?"

"Nothing. Mom just said to call."

"Well, good. It's good to talk to you."

"Mmhmm."

"Did you go into Austin today?"

"Yeah."

The marshal sits forward at the kitchen table. "You look for something to wear?"

"Uh-huh."

He lets a beat pass. "So, you get something?"

"I got a new pair of jeans and some new Converse."

"Oh."

"And new tops."

"Okay."

"Mom says did you eat?"

"Tell her yes."

A pause. "She wants to know what."

"Tell her steak. There was steak in the fridge."

His daughter yells off of the phone. "He had *steak*..."

"So, you get lunch in town?" Whicher says.

"We went to this place, Flower Child, it was neat, it was really, really good. They have everything, it's like this amazing vegan menu, and everything looks really cool..."

"Huh. Sounds good."

"It is..."

"How's grandpa and grandma?"

"Yeah, they're good."

"Say hi from me."

"Mom says you didn't go to bed last night, she says you better go tonight."

"I will." He grins. "Don't worry."

"What were you doing?" Lori's voice is quiet now, a note in it.

"I was out at the border. I had to go check something."

"Well, what?"

"Some folks at a ranch called the cops. I was kind of close, I went over."

"In the middle of the night?"

"I was on my way back here, it just came up." The marshal

thinks of shifting the talk to something else. "It's just something that can happen sometimes."

"What're you doing tonight?"

"I'm going to bed. I'm tired." The marshal smiles, picturing his daughter. "And don't worry about me, I'm fine. Does mom need to talk?"

"Wait a minute..."

The line goes quiet.

Lori comes back. "She says she's okay."

"Alright. So, what're you going to do tomorrow?"

"I don't know yet. We might go check out an art museum or something, for my project."

"Yeah? Good idea."

His daughter laughs, suddenly, into the phone.

A warm wave passes along the length of his spine.

"I'm not telling him *that*..." she says, still laughing. "Mom says to go to bed early..."

"Tell her I will." He shifts at the kitchen table. "I miss you. Say hi to everybody."

"Okay."

"Alright, well, good night sweetheart."

"Night dad."

He finishes the call.

Stares out of the window at the darkening sky.

Till the image of his daughter fades.

Replaced with thoughts of Josefina Olvera.

Of the Presidio County Sheriff, Armando Torres. Torres looking to run a bigger search, bring in air support from DPS. Make sure Cardenas wasn't out there—somewhere, in some deserted canyon.

He pictures the mountains, the old water tank up in the hills.

Presa Llorona.

The weeping woman. The dead girl on the hillside.

He stares at his few notes on the table. Gaze falling on the one thing he can't get past.

Two men visiting Cardenas. A week back. Forcing him into a car.

Five days, nobody seeing him.

Only the vast night out there.

Vanishing belief he could be coming back.

CHAPTER EIGHT

The drive down from Pecos to Fort Stockton is fifty miles through grazed-out land dotted with greasewood and mesquite. US 285 empty, morning sun still low in the east.

Whicher thinks of the single phone call—to Matias Cardenas's father, Pablo. A construction worker, according to the county sheriff report. Married to Matias's mother, Guadalupe, a part-time worker at a local grocery store.

Approaching Fort Stockton, the highway widens into four lanes nearing the sprawl of Interstate Ten. Whicher drives past the fire department and the sheriff's office. Signals to pull into a gas station and Stripes store.

The father had been wary—caught between reluctance to talk with law enforcement and the need to find out about his son.

The marshal's phone rings. Whicher sees the caller name on screen.

He steers away from the gas pumps, parks in a bay to the side. Picks up. "Sheriff Torres. I do something for you?"

"I got news this morning," Torres says. "That truck that was stolen out of the Mackenzie Ranch?"

"What about it?"

"Turned up over in Valentine..."

Whicher shuts down the motor, pushes back in his seat.

"Blue Dodge Dakota. It's on a dirt lane just off of the highway among a bunch of houses," Torres says. "Somebody called the Jeff Davis Sheriff's Office—a homeowner, he thought maybe it'd been dumped."

"There anything with it?" Whicher says. "Anything we could use?"

"I told the sheriff to get a crime scene officer out there. Dust it down, check it for prints, whatever else."

"Tell 'em to pull everything they can get from it, bill the Marshals Service."

"That's what you want?"

"Whatever's in there I want to know about it," Whicher says. "Have you seen it?"

"I just heard."

"There be any reason to dump it in that locale?"

"It's residential, according to the sheriff there. A bunch of older houses, not much more."

"Listen, I saw Deputy Garcia at the Mackenzie Ranch yesterday," Whicher says. "He found some rounds or bullet frags out at the ranch?"

"Right."

"Where are they?"

"He brought them back here," Torres says, "they'll be in storage, in the evidence room."

"I might get a ballistics report."

"You want them, you can have them."

"Alright. Maybe hold them for now."

"Will you head over to see the truck?" the sheriff says.

"I'm about to go talk with the Cardenas family. The father agreed to see me. I'm right outside of Fort Stockton."

Torres grunts. "I talked with him. I can't say it did any good."

"His son's been gone six days, nobody's seen him. I want to know what he has to say."

* * *

The house on Chaparral Lane is single story, paint flaking from its walls, tin roof bleached by the sun. Beneath a carport of rough timber is a rusted E-Series van. A tube steel fence marks out the edge of the property, enclosing a bare dirt yard.

Pablo Cardenas stands in the shade from the house, looking out at the marshal's truck. Short, heavy. Wearing jeans, a stretched t-shirt. Eyes narrow in a lined face.

Whicher steps from the Silverado. Takes the USMS badge from his suit.

He holds it out, approaches the broken gate in the fence. "Mister Cardenas?"

The man nods.

"We spoke this morning, Deputy Marshal Whicher?"

Cardenas runs a hand through his dark, wiry hair.

The marshal puts away his ID, steps through the gate into the yard.

Cardenas leads him inside, into the house, down a narrow hall, to a living room. A ball game playing on a TV in the corner, a rerun of a night game, the sound on mute.

Cardenas sits on a sagging couch, picks up an open can of soda.

Whicher pulls out a chair from a table by the window. "I take a seat?"

Chilled air blows across the room from a noisy A/C unit.

"I just need some background on your son," the marshal says. "Anything that might help locate him. His partner, Ms Olvera, Josefina? You know she's pretty concerned?"

Cardenas takes a sip from the can of soda.

"How long has your son lived down in Marfa?"

"Coming on three years."

"Before that?"

"He was here. He lived here."

"Doing what?" the marshal says.

"He worked in oil. On the drill sites. Then servicing. Driving, delivering parts. He did that a while. A bunch of years. Then he quit. He worked a couple of the big ranches. He liked it better."

"He liked the ranches better than oil?"

"He likes to work the land. Work with livestock." Cardenas turns the can of soda. "Ranchers pay less..."

"So, he moved down to Marfa. Got a job on a farm. He come back? Visit?"

"He's got his own life," Cardenas says. "His woman."

"It's what, an hour and a half? He doesn't get back much?"

The man shakes his head.

"When was the last time?"

"Couple of weeks."

"You talk to him? On the phone?"

"His mother calls him."

"Last time you saw him, he okay?"

Cardenas puts down the can on the floor. A blank look on his face.

"Has Matias ever had any problems?"

No answer.

"Money problems? Disputes with anyone?"

"No."

"Do you know if your son uses drugs?"

Cardenas looks at him.

"Recreationally. I'm not interested in bringing charges," the marshal says, "I just need to know is all, it could have a bearing."

"He smokes a little weed sometimes. With a beer."

"Oil business," Whicher says, "plenty of drugs go around."

"Yeah, well. He quit all that."

"So, what's he like to do? Him and Josefina. When he's not working?"

"They hang out."

The marshal looks at him, waits for more.

Cardenas offers nothing.

"Could he have gotten into something he needed to get out of?" Whicher says.

"What do you mean?"

The marshal leans forward in the seat, spreads his palms. "With another woman. Or with money he might've owed. Somebody he might've gotten the wrong side of?"

"I don't know nothing like that."

"You don't think it's strange?"

Cardenas blows out his cheeks.

"Nobody seeing him? Hearing from him in six days. Most times, somebody disappears," the marshal says, "it's because they don't want to be found. If something went wrong in their lives, something they can't figure out how to fix. You understand?"

The man nods.

"Or else they got in an accident. I don't think your son got in anything like that. We would've seen something, some report. From the hospitals. Or from the highway patrol."

Cardenas looks at a spot six inches in front of his face.

"So, either he's gone from the area. Someplace far away. Or else something happened to him..."

"Maybe he'll come back," Cardenas says.

Whicher eyes him. Lets silence fill up the room.

Through the window he sees a car pull onto a double-wide strip of concrete at the side of the yard—an older model, compact Ford.

He watches the woman behind the wheel as she stares at the unfamiliar truck parked outside her house. Alarm in her face.

She steps from the car—dressed in a white cotton blouse, a blue skirt, her hair pulled back, her shoulders rounded.

She walks quickly to the door.

At the sound of it opening, Cardenas calls out; "In here..."

The woman appears in the doorframe, a look of panic in her face.

Whicher stands.

She looks at her husband. "Has something happened?"

"No, ma'am," Whicher says. "I'm from the Marshals Office. I'm here about your son. Sheriff Torres called me. I'm here to try to help find him."

She puts a hand to her chest. Breathes. Her quick, dark eyes search his face.

"You want to sit down, Guadalupe?" Cardenas says.

The woman pulls out a chair opposite Whicher at the table. She sits.

The marshal sits. "Your husband was telling me about Matias. About the places he worked, what kinds of things he did before he moved out to Marfa."

"He's like his grandfather," the woman says, "campesino, granjero, a farmer, in Mexico."

"He's happy working on the Zimmerman farm?"

She nods. "Yes. Happy."

"How about Josefina? Ms Olvera? Do you know her well? Are things between them...okay?"

"Josefina reported him missing," the woman says, her eyes downcast. "It took a while..."

The marshal looks at her. "You think she could've done it sooner?"

Cardenas cuts in; "Matias is a grown man."

The marshal takes a folded piece of paper from the inside

pocket of his suit. A printed copy of a digital image from the funeral home in Fort Davis.

He clears his throat. Softens his voice. "I have a photograph of an item of clothing. I'd like you both to take a look at it."

The color drains from Guadalupe's face.

"It may be nothing," Whicher says. Unfolding the sheet of paper, he holds up the photograph of the T-shirt worn by the drowning victim at the Rio Grande.

The man and the woman both stare at it.

"Do either of you recognize it? Did Matias have a shirt like that?"

The woman blinks once. "No. I don't know. I've never seen it."

Cardenas shakes his head.

The marshal puts the photograph away.

"Why show us that?" Guadalupe says.

"It was found, yesterday," Whicher says. "At this point, I can't tell you much more than that." He looks at her. "Has anything like this ever happened before?"

"When he worked the oilfields," she says, "he'd be gone, he would go away."

"That was with a crew," Cardenas says.

"He stay friendly with any of those folk?" Whicher says.

The man shrugs. "Oil workers? A few, I guess."

Guadalupe Cardenas stares at him. "You think he could be with one of them?"

"Would anybody know about it?" the marshal says. "If he was?"

Cardenas turns down the edges of his mouth. "If he was on a drill site, he'd be gone for days. Or weeks."

The marshal takes out a notepad from his jacket. "You think of anybody from that time I could speak with?"

Guadalupe looks at her husband. "There's Rodrigo. Or Juan, or Marco…"

"You have numbers for any of them?" the marshal says.

"I know their mothers. I can find out."

"If you can find someone, I'd like to talk to them."

She nods her head, "I will, I will."

Pablo Cardenas stares at the foot of the wall.

Guadalupe grips her hands with her fingers. "Why would he be on a drill site?"

"Maybe if he thought he'd be safe," Whicher says. "With people he might think could help him. Would Josefina know any of the people from that world?"

"I don't know—they're from this area…"

Whicher looks at her. "How well do you know Josefina?"

"Not so well." Guadalupe shifts at the table. "They seem happy. I think it's serious, I think she wants a family someday. They have a home. Her uncle lent her money."

"I met her at the Zimmerman farm with Sheriff Torres," Whicher says.

Pablo Cardenas sits forward on the couch. "What's the sheriff planning on doing about all this?"

"He'd like to run a wider search," Whicher says. "Make sure your son's not out somewhere in the surrounding land. At the Rim Rock, or around one of the valleys. Y'all know his car is out at the Zimmerman farm, still, Matias's car?"

"Sí," Cardenas says.

"He have some other way of getting around, another vehicle?"

Guadalupe presses her lips together.

"No?"

"No."

"Somebody drove out to see him there—did you know that? A couple days before Matias was last seen."

"Josefina told me," Guadalupe says, "she called me. She said it made her afraid."

"A witness at the farm saw it. Y'all know anybody who drives a Dodge Durango? Late model, black, Dodge Durango?"

The woman swallows. Her eyes search the room.

Cardenas's face is stone.

"The guys seen out at the farm were driving one. Small guy—plus a taller man. Any of that mean anything to you?"

Gaudalupe looks at Whicher. "The man who saw it told Josefina they made Matias get in their car—Matias looked like he'd seen a ghost. Like he was scared, like he was about to throw up. He said the tall man looked like..." Her voice wavers.

Pablo Cardenas shakes his head, his brow furrows.

"*El diablo*," she says. "With dead eyes. He said he looked like the devil..."

* * *

Back outside on the lane, Whicher stares along the dust-blown road.

From the passenger seat of the truck, he takes up the notes from Sheriff Torres's office. He finds a number, keys a call. The phone rings over and over.

It clicks to voicemail—a young woman's recorded voice; "Hola, you've reached Josefina. I can't take your call right now, but leave a message, I'll get back."

Whicher stares at the Cardenas house, at the featureless terrain beyond it. Mesquite and prickly pear and burnt-dry grass. The deserted strip of road and the house lifeless. As if palled by some absence, as if something were gone.

"This is Deputy Marshal Whicher, we met yesterday—at the Zimmerman farm. Call me when you get this." He speaks out loud his number. "I need to see you. You and I need to talk."

* * *

Ojinaga, Mexico

At the southern edge of the town of Ojinaga, the concrete-block house sits behind a paint factory—the house derelict, its windows boarded up.

Aquino enters the building with the caporal—inside, in the dim light, six men lounge on filthy mattresses lining the floor.

Backpacks and clothing are everywhere, food debris, water bottles, cigarette stubs, flattened cans of beer.

The men in the room fall silent at the new arrivals. Every face staring at the caporal and Aquino. Each man sitting up from his place, pushing upright against the foot of the wall.

The caporal gestures to a bearded Latino in his twenties.

The young man gets up.

The others lower their eyes.

Aquino leads the young man out of a back door to a dirt yard.

Squinting in the glare of light, the youngster stands uncertain among broken-up lengths of timber, burnt-out oil drums.

"This is him?" Aquino says

The caporal nods.

From his jacket, Aquino takes out a cell phone sealed inside a dry-bag of clear plastic.

He gives it to the caporal.

The caporal holds it out. "When you get across the river you will climb into mountains..."

The young man nods.

"After the mountains, there is a ranch," the caporal says, "in the hills. We will tell you where."

Aquino's eyes drill the youngster.

The caporal gestures at the phone. "A number is stored on this. A single number." He gives the young man the handset.

"When you are close to the ranch," Aquino says, "you call the number."

The young man glances at him, quickly.

"You understand?" the caporal says.

A question is in his eyes.

"Call it," Aquino says, voice flat.

No more questions.

The young man nods, looks away.

CHAPTER NINE

Back at the house in Pecos, Whicher hangs his jacket on a kitchen chair. He checks in the refrigerator, finds a leftover dish of nachos and chili and refried beans for lunch. He takes out the dish, places it on the countertop. Grabs his phone from the table, keys the number for the duty doctor covering the Reeves Jail.

He sets the oven to heat.

The call picks up. "Doctor Hollis."

"Doc? John Whicher from the Marshals Office—calling about that prisoner transfer, Marco Zambrano?"

"Marshal, yes. If I get the chance, I'll try to see him today."

"I need the guy in H-Town. I saw him yesterday, he seemed well enough."

"If you think he's okay," Hollis says, "and the jail agrees, you can move him without my say-so."

"Yeah. My boss wants paperwork."

"Well, what did you think was wrong with him?"

"He was probably high on something," Whicher says. "I

wanted to make sure he wasn't about to have some kind of seizure."

"Listen, if I can do it today, I'll let you know."

"I appreciate it." The marshal finishes the call.

He searches in a cupboard for a plate. Takes out flatware from a drawer.

The phone buzzes on the countertop.

Sheriff Torres—from Presidio County.

Whicher picks up. "Sheriff? What's going on?"

"Did you see Cardenas?"

"I just got back from there. I saw him, I saw his wife."

"You get anything?"

"Maybe. Couple things. I have a line I'm thinking to try. Matias used to work the oilfields—a guy could lay up awhile in a drill camp, nobody'd know about it."

"Yeah? Could be something."

"I showed the parents a photograph of the t-shirt from the drowning victim at the river."

"They recognize it?"

"No."

"You think it rules Matias out?"

"Nope. At least it doesn't rule him in."

"Alright, well, listen," the sheriff says, "I'm calling about the Dakota—the stolen truck."

"Oh?" The marshal steps from the kitchen counter, searches his jacket for the notepad and pen.

"Jeff Davis county sheriff had somebody come out from El Paso," Torres says. "They contract with the PD for crime scene investigation. There's a bunch of latent prints on the truck, most of them likely belonging to people at the Mackenzie Ranch—but the CSI found trace evidence of explosives, too."

"Say again?"

"Some kind of nitrogen compound. Maybe you want to talk to the guy."

"I will," Whicher says. "What's happening now, they tow the truck?"

"Still in Valentine, far as I know."

"You have a name for the CSI?"

"Donovan," the sheriff says, "Reece Donovan."

"You have a number?"

The sheriff reads it out.

Whicher writes it onto the notepad. "I'll call him—I'll let you know what he has to say."

Opening up the oven door, the marshal slides in the dish of nachos and refried beans.

He sits at the kitchen table, dials the number from the pad.

"CSI Department, Officer Donovan speaking..."

"John Whicher—from the Marshals Service, over in Pecos —you processed a stolen Dodge Dakota this morning? I heard you found trace evidence of explosive material?"

"I just sent my initial report to the Jeff Davis County Sheriff's Office."

"Vince Pruitt?"

"Sheriff Pruitt, yes."

"Can you send a copy to the Marshals Office?"

"We're only talking about initial findings," Donovan says.

"What kind of explosives you think were in there?"

"Trace evidence of nitrogenous compounds," the CSI says. "Most explosives contain some nitrogen—there's no actual material in the vehicle to test, so far as I can tell. But the trace detector picked up readings."

"The truck's out of a ranch property," Whicher says. "Could it be agricultural?"

"Could be, yeah."

"I'll talk to the owner, find out."

"If that's not the source," Donovan says, "we'll need to look harder."

Whicher writes down a note.

"Are you working the case?" the CSI says.

"Looking that way," Whicher answers. "How about fingerprint evidence?"

"I lifted some good prints, we can get them developed here, get them into IAFIS."

"Anything else on the vehicle?"

"There'll be multiple samples of hair, fiber, DNA," Donovan says. "It depends how deep we want to look? We can go after the mud on the tires, gunshot residue in the cab, presence of blood, whatever you want…"

"If you can get the prints into the system, I'd appreciate it."

"You guys in a hurry on this?"

"Little complicated," the marshal says, "but there could be a situation—with an individual that needs protection. Listen, if you get jammed up on the prints, let me know, I'll get them over to USMS in Arlington."

"You really want them quick?"

The marshal steps to the window, looks out into the yard. "I want to be clear, is all. I want to know what we've got."

* * *

Moving fast down Interstate Twenty in the Silverado, Whicher spots the overhead panel at the split for El Paso and San Antonio.

He moves into lane for I-10 west, accelerating into a long sweep of sun-baked curve.

Above the desert scrub, peaks of jagged mountain rise in the heat-hazed distance.

He checks the clock on the dash.

Sheriff Pruitt from Jeff Davis County will be there by the time he can make it down to Valentine—another hour or so, seventy miles.

He thinks of the place—a onetime rail and ranch community, now a highway town. Few people living there, maybe a hundred strong.

Reaching for the phone on the dash mount, he scrolls a list of numbers, keys for Josefina Olvera—a third time now—with no response.

He listens to the ring tone on speaker in the cab.

Waits for voicemail.

A young woman answers.

"Ms Olvera?"

"Yes."

"Deputy Marshal Whicher—I've been trying to reach you…"

"I been working," she says, "I was going to call you. You wanted to see me?"

"Right now, I'm headed someplace. But listen, I talked with Matias's parents this morning, back in Fort Stockton. A couple things came up—I need to ask about them."

"Like, what?"

Whicher drops his speed, settles at the wheel. "Is Matias friends with anyone who works in oil? So far as you know?"

Josefina makes no response.

"Anyone on the rig sites?"

"I don't know."

"He ever talk about anybody from that world?"

"Not that I remember."

"How about folk from Fort Stockton? He keep in touch with friends he had growing up?"

"I guess. A few."

"You think you could find names for me? Numbers?"

"I could try."

The marshal stares through the windshield, thinking—makes a quick decision. Catches his reflection in the rearview, scowls. "Listen, there was something else—I don't really like to do this—but an item of clothing was recovered yesterday..."

"What?"

"Some clothing. From a particular site..."

Olvera's voice is small in her throat. "What is it?"

Whicher spots an exit for a rest stop, he slows the truck. "A shirt—a t-shirt. If it's one Matias owned, we might need to look into it further. If not, it would be good to know." He steers down the turn into the rest area, brakes to a stop. "I showed it to Matias's parents, they didn't recognize it. Could I send you a picture?"

"Oh..."

Doubtful sounding.

The marshal finds the image. "Could I send it on this number?"

"I guess..." Her voice barely a whisper.

Attaching the picture, he sends it as a message.

Feels his pulse quicken.

Long seconds tick by.

Staring at an empty picnic table by a trash barrel, he feels his heart sink.

The truck motor rumbles beneath the hood. He digs a thumbnail into his palm. Tries to think of some consoling words to say.

"No," she says, finally.

"No?"

"It's not his."

"Are you sure?"

"I'm sure."

"You've never seen it before?"

Her voice is firm when she answers; "I've never seen that. It's not his."

* * *

An hour later, driving into Valentine the marshal scans the few roadside homes—some vacant, fallen into disrepair. Bars and businesses are boarded up—old school buses and wreckers lie in disused lots.

He slows. Spots the entrance for Nevada Avenue—a dirt lane between the backs of houses.

He makes the turn.

A block from US 90, a black truck is parked—a sheriff's department Ford Ranger.

Alongside it, a blue Dodge Dakota; the stolen pickup.

Whicher pulls over.

Sheriff Vince Pruitt climbs from his truck. Trim at fifty, the brass badge is prominent on his dark brown uniform shirt. He runs a hand over a goatee beard, his hat tipped forward.

Whicher cuts the motor on the Chevy, steps out. "Appreciate your coming out. You get a look at it?" The marshal cants his head at the Dakota.

"Left it to the CSI," the sheriff says. "I took a squint when I got here. What's the Marshals Service interested in, anyhow?"

Whicher takes a pair of nitrile gloves from a pocket of his suit. "I need to take a look inside, that okay with you?"

"You do what you want to do, marshal. You talk to Reece Donovan?"

"I talked to him." Whicher tries the driver's door, it opens. He pulls it wide, peers inside. Scanning the dirt lane, he takes in the houses at either side. "You dealing with any kind of crime around here?"

"We'll get the odd dispute," Pruitt says. "Or theft. Or fight. It's working people mainly, families. A few older folk."

Leaning in through the driver's door Whicher checks the floor, the seats, the general condition of the cab. Dusty. Dirty. Grimed from work. No obvious sign of ground transfer, or fluids, or recent damage, cuts or rips.

The keys are in the ignition.

With a gloved hand Whicher turns them.

The dash lights up, he checks the fuel gauge.

Switches off.

Stepping away, he eyes the front end of the truck, the grille, the lights, the bodywork. The tires, the sidewalls—the fence gear and wire and tools in the open bed.

"What's on your mind?" the sheriff says.

"Why dump it here?"

Pruitt looks at him.

"There's gas in the tank," Whicher says. "Why stop?"

"What're you thinking?"

"Maybe meeting somebody? Why leave it here? Why not carry on?"

The sheriff shrugs.

"Who reported it?"

Pruitt points at one of the houses backing onto the lane. "Guy name of Rodriguez. Called my office, one of my deputies came by."

"Know if he's home?" Whicher crosses the lane, eyes the house—part stone, part render beneath a rusted roof. Texas live oak and Chusan palms frame a concrete path. A man's face is at the window.

Whicher stands at the fence line, takes out his badge and ID.

The back door opens.

The man steps out—in shorts, a vest, his face haggard, mouth open.

"Mister Rodriguez? US Marshals Service."

Rodriguez slouches down the path in slide sandals, looks at Pruitt.

"You reported the vehicle here?" Whicher says.

"It's been there two days," Rodriguez answers. "Some of us are trying to live around here, we don't need nobody dumping stuff."

"When's the first time you noticed it?"

"Tuesday."

"What time of day?"

"Morning."

"Early morning?"

"Early," Rodriguez says.

Whicher tallies it; Monday night the Dakota was taken from the Mackenzie Ranch—so, dumped the same night.

"You didn't report it till today?" Sheriff Pruitt says.

"It was there yesterday, there all night. I went out to it this morning, I could see keys in it. So, I called your office. According to the deputy that came out, it's stolen."

"You see anything overnight, Monday?" Whicher says.

The man shakes his head. "I turned in around midnight. The truck was there when I got up."

"You think anybody else might've seen anything?" the sheriff says.

"I asked around. Nobody saw nothing." The man's face hardens. "We don't want folks dumping no stolen cars."

"We'll get it taken away."

Rodriguez sniffs. Looks from the sheriff to Whicher.

"Notice any new people coming through here?" the marshal says.

"Like who?"

"Anybody different. Folks you won't normally see."

"Like narcos?" the man says. "Border jumpers?"

"Anybody."

"I don't know nothing about any of that." Rodriguez turns, slopes back up the concrete path to the house.

"Thank you for your time," the sheriff says.

Whicher steps back to the Dakota.

Pruitt looks at him. "So, what do you want to do? We need to move it, get it out of here. You want to let the owners have it back?"

The marshal shakes his head. "You have someplace you could keep it? My office will pick up the tab."

Sheriff Pruitt takes off his hat, smooths his short dark hair. "If that's what you want."

"Keep it clean. Keep folk out of it. Sheet it up if it rains."

CHAPTER TEN

A low sun hangs in the sky above the Mackenzie Ranch—reflecting in the windshields of vehicles parked around the yard as Whicher pulls in in the Silverado.

By the guest lodge, Judge Vaughn Richardson sits with Donald Eliot, the two men cleaning rifles by a meat smoker.

At the far side of the house, Larry Mackenzie watches as Whicher kills the motor, keys a number for Reece Donovan at El Paso PD.

The CSI picks up. "Marshal?"

"I been thinking about the prints..."

"I've got the lab working on them," Donovan says, "developing, editing. They've isolated five distinct sets. We could use exclusion samples; that's a working vehicle, we need to rule out legitimate users."

"I just got down to the ranch, I'll talk to them about that," Whicher says. "But there's something I wanted you to take a look at. Can you run the prints through the Interpol AFIS database?"

"You're thinking overseas?" Donovan says. "International?"

"I think it could be, yeah. The ranch is down real close to the border—people are coming through here."

Donovan pauses a moment. "That's probably a good call…"

"Interpol database can be spotty," Whicher says, "especially the South American section. But run everything through, if none of the latents match, we'll put everything through IAFIS at FBI, plus the state police records."

"You got it."

"They have limited slots available but put in the request—international results can come back fast. I need to get this moving…"

"I'll get on it."

Whicher finishes the call.

Larry Mackenzie starts across the yard toward him.

Whicher steps down from the truck.

"Marshal," the ranch owner says. "Sheriff Torres called me. He says law enforcement found my truck?"

"Yes, sir."

"Have you seen it?"

"Yes, sir, I've seen it."

Mackenzie searches his face. "Is it alright?"

"There's no damage," Whicher says, "far as I can tell."

"So, can I get it back?"

"Jeff Davis Sheriff is holding it right now. We're running some tests."

At the house, Glen Carr appears beneath the shaded porch.

"What kind of tests?" Mackenzie says. "How long you think it will be?"

"I can't answer that," the marshal says. "But you'll get it back just as soon as everything's done."

Mackenzie nods. "So, what brings you out here, marshal?"

"Need to talk to you."

Glen Carr crosses the yard to stand by Mackenzie.

"A bunch of fingerprint marks have been lifted from the truck," Whicher says, "we need to exclude any that are legitimate."

"You need to take our fingerprints?" Mackenzie says.

"Anyone with access to the truck. We can get them scanned up in Marfa at the sheriff's office."

"Really?"

"It shouldn't take too long. It's just a ride up and back."

Mackenzie scratches at the back of his neck.

Carr regards him, saying nothing.

"A few of us use it," Mackenzie says. "There's me, Glen, Amber, my housekeeper."

"How about your wife?"

"Patricia, she'd be another."

"Deputy Garcia left out of here yesterday," Glen Carr says, "he didn't find but three slugs. He was searching the better part of a day..."

Whicher eyes him. "That's still three rounds."

"Somebody got in a fight," the ranch hand shrugs. "A couple loose shots hit in here..."

"I came out that night," Whicher says, "you people thought somebody was firing at you."

"Nobody came back since," Carr says. "Somebody found the truck, they got lucky, they took it. It sounds like they just dumped it. I don't see how it's that big of a deal."

Over at the guest house, Vaughn Richardson sets down his rifle by the meat smoker.

He stands, hitches up a set of desert camo fatigues. Calls over; "Marshal. What brings you out here?"

"Follow-up enquiries, sir. The truck that was taken out of here showed up."

Richardson approaches.

"I just have some questions for Mister Mackenzie. For his

staff." The marshal looks across at Donald Eliot by the smoker. "Y'all have good hunting this morning?"

"As a matter of fact, we did," the judge says. "I shot an aoudad. A pretty big one." He looks at Glen Carr. "Long-ish range?"

The ranch hand nods. "Good shot, clean shot."

The judge gives a self-deprecating smile.

"Sir, you plan to stay on?" Whicher says.

"Yes, we do." Richardson looks across at Eliot. "We're going out again tomorrow morning, early. With Glen. To see what else we can find. Are you going to get Larry his truck back? Why's the sheriff's department need it? They're never going to find the person who took it. They might as well just give it back."

"I need it," the marshal says.

"You need it? What for?"

"We just have some tests we need to run before we're done."

"Everything was quiet here last night," Richardson says, "completely fine. Completely normal." He looks to Mackenzie.

The ranch owner nods. "I don't think we have any ongoing problem."

Richardson regards the black, iron barrel with a stovepipe attached to its side. "We're smoking up brisket and hot links, what do you think of that?"

"Smells good."

"You bet it does." The judge grins. "The sun won't be long in going down, we can break out some cold margaritas."

"You got it," Mackenzie says.

"Have a word with the sheriff," Richardson says to Whicher. "See if you can get him to bring Larry back his truck, can you?"

The marshal doesn't respond.

The judge smiles a brittle smile, walks back across the yard to the smoker.

Whicher gestures to the low wall at the south of the compound. "I need to ask you about something?"

"Oh?" Mackenzie says.

The marshal starts to walk across the yard.

"Just me?" the ranch owner says.

"Both of you. Y'all wouldn't mind."

* * *

The view over the land from the compound wall is dominated west and south by mountains beyond the small, barren plain—Highway 67 somewhere east beyond the rise and fall of scrub-covered hills and hidden creeks. Whicher turns to Mackenzie. "I need to ask about explosives here on the ranch?"

Mackenzie frowns. "Excuse me?"

"Commercial explosives. Y'all use them?"

"Well, why do you ask?"

"We found trace evidence in your truck, sir. We need to know where it came from." Whicher looks from Mackenzie to Carr.

The ranch hand's face is blank. "I don't know about any explosives."

"Pop used to keep some ANFO, years back," Mackenzie says. "For blasting. They'd get a fall of rock on one of the trails. They'd break it up with that."

"You still have any?"

"I wouldn't imagine." The ranch owner thinks it over. "Matter of fact, he used to keep it out at the barn, there, you know? Away from the house."

"Where you keep the Dakota?"

Mackenzie nods. "There's nothing out there now, I don't think." He turns to Carr.

"I never seen any," the hand says.

"You want to go take a look, marshal?"

Whicher already has the keys to his truck.

***

A mile north of the ranch compound, a stone and timber barn sits off the trail in the lee of a rounded hill—the barn door open, cinched with a length of fraying rope.

Heat radiates from a sheet-metal roof as Whicher follows Mackenzie inside.

Lying about are old tires, gasoline and oil cans, reels of zinc wire, wooden posts.

"This is where we keep the Dakota…it's kind of a mess," Mackenzie says, "it gets to be a dumping ground."

At the back of the barn, rough shelves are set on iron brackets. The shelves piled with old tools, assorted storage boxes, a couple of ancient-looking saddles.

"Pop used to have an old John Deere out here," Mackenzie says. "We got to keeping the truck the same way. You know? One less vehicle up at the house."

"How about explosives?" Whicher says.

"I mean, it made sense…to keep all of that out of the way." Mackenzie searches among the shelves. He slides out a piece of white plastic sacking—red letters just visible on its side.

"That it?" the marshal says.

Mackenzie peers at it. "Yeah. That's ANFO."

"Ammonium nitrate," Whicher says, "and fuel oil?"

"Right. Pop had a buddy worked in mining, they used to make their own—take regular fertilizer, mix it up with diesel oil, I think. I mean, this all is a long time back."

"You still have any actual explosive?"

Mackenzie sifts through junk on the shelves, among lengths of chain and nylon rope and offcuts of lumber. "Nobody's bought any in years, I've never bought any. There might still be some ends of sacks or something..." He pulls out another piece of white plastic.

Whicher thinks it over. Easy enough for traces of nitrogen to transfer—anything in contact with the sacking, anything on the shelves.

He takes out the phone from his jacket, steps into the open doorway of the barn to call Reece Donovan.

"You won't get any kind of a signal out here," Mackenzie tells him.

On the phone screen, nothing shows for any network.

"You need to make a call," the ranch owner says, "we'll have to head on back to the house."

* * *

At the guest lodge across the yard, Vaughn Richardson and Donald Eliot drink from salt-frosted glasses beneath a sunshade on the wooden deck. The marshal feels the judge's eyes upon him. Checks the network signal—present, but weak.

He stands at the side of an empty horse barn, keys the number for the El Paso CSI.

It picks up.

Donovan speaks; "I've been trying to get hold of you, marshal—I called your office..."

"What's going on?"

"I spoke with the chief marshal there..."

"Marshal Fairbanks?"

"One of the prints came back a match—from the Interpol record—my tech ran it, it came back in less than an hour, we had a high-quality sample..."

"Really?"

"Guy by the name of Esequiel Aquino. Nasty dude. Real nasty..."

"Aquino?"

"A Honduran national."

"What's his rap sheet?"

"About anything you can think of," Donovan says. "Including assault, murder, extortion, intimidation, just about every kind of trafficking..."

"This a confirmed match?"

"It's confirmed," the CSI says. "And you know what, good call, nobody would've looked. I've been trying to get a hold of you..."

"I'm still down on the border."

"What do you want to do?"

"I have to call my boss." The marshal blows the air from his cheeks. "Listen, that explosive residue?"

"From the truck?"

"The vehicle's kept in a barn they used to store blasting explosives in the past. There's some old ANFO sacking in there."

"That'd give you cross-contamination," Donovan says.

"Do we need to check?"

"You could bring a piece of a sack if you want me to analyze it further. But most likely, that's what we have."

"Alright," Whicher says. "I've asked for exclusion samples, the folk at the ranch can get a fingerprint scan at the sheriff's office. Four people regularly drive the truck."

"Let me know when you have that?" the CSI says. "Do you want to bring up a sample of the ANFO material? It's up to you."

"I'll make some calls, I'll let you know," Whicher answers. "Right now, I need to look at this guy Aquino."

* * *

A ceiling fan turns in the lounge room of the ranch as Whicher follows Larry Mackenzie in through a double set of glazed doors.

Gesturing to the assorted chairs and hide-covered couches, Mackenzie sits, clasps his hands between his knees.

The marshal sits. "I need to ask you about the hunting trip y'all have planned for the morning?"

Mackenzie looks at him.

"Who's on it?"

"Glen. Judge Richardson. And Mister Eliot."

"That's all?"

"I may go with them," Mackenzie says.

"It's headed where?"

"I'd have to ask Glen. But they'll be going up into the Chinatis. To set up on a hillside a while—there's some good feeding areas to observe."

"They're going out when?"

"Before first light."

"How long would they usually expect to be gone?"

"Well, it depends. They're hunting Barbary sheep, aoudad, looking for a trophy-size ram. They take one, they'll stop, the hunt's over. If not, we'll generally bring folk back about midday," Mackenzie says. "It'll get warm, folk get hungry, they'll be tired."

"You run a lot of hunting excursions?"

"We sure do. It's a year round activity for non-native species—aoudad, feral hogs, fallow and axis deer."

"You ever run into folk out there?" Whicher says.

"Up in the hills? Not very often. Sometimes."

"Clandestine people?"

"Yes, sir."

"Then what?"

The ranch owner considers it. "Anybody coming through from across the border will usually do all they can to keep out of your way."

"That's not what happened Monday night."

Mackenzie lets his eyes meet the marshal's. "And that's the first time anything like that has ever happened."

"An agent from the BP station at Presidio showed me a trail up in the mountains—a trail she thinks people might be starting to use. Not real far from here."

"I can't speak to that."

"You know a young girl was found up there?"

"I heard about it." Mackenzie frowns. "And anything like that is a matter of tremendous regret. But look, people lose their lives coming through the land here the wrong way. Coming in illegally. Sometimes it can happen. Rarely here, but it happens."

"You have a young girl dying, signs of people coming through. Shots fired into your property—you're saying nothing much happens?"

"I've been here years," Mackenzie says, "my father before me—I'm talking long term, from long experience."

"I'm talking of recent things," Whicher says, "things changing."

Mackenzie looks off across the room. Looks back again. "Do we still need our fingerprints taken?"

"Yes, sir. I have a crime scene officer checking everything—it could speed things up, get your truck back faster."

Mackenzie stands. "I'll try to round up everybody, see if we can get it done tomorrow afternoon."

Whicher rises. Steps to the window, stares out at Richardson and Eliot drinking margaritas on the deck.

Glen Carr is at the meat smoker, feeding wood into a firebox welded at its side.

"Will that be all, marshal? I ought to see to my guests."

"Are they competent handling a rifle?" Whicher says, over his shoulder.

The ranch owner hesitates before answering. "To be honest, about average."

The marshal nods. "Average shooter's pretty poor."

"At a moving target, at distance," Mackenzie says, "I'd have to agree."

"Short range, too," the marshal says.

"Why do you ask?"

Mackenzie steps level with him at the window.

Whicher doesn't reply.

* * *

Behind the wheel of the Silverado inside the compound gates, Whicher keys a number for the Pecos office, eyes the parked vehicles spread out—Judge Richardson's new Lincoln Navigator, the housekeeper's battered Rav 4, the dust-covered F150, the Ram.

He holds the phone to his ear as Chief Marshal Fairbanks picks up.

"I just spoke with Reece Donovan," Whicher says.

"You know about the Interpol match? I tried to call."

"I'm still up in the mountains, coverage is pretty bad—but I spoke with him. We need to talk with Alpine FBI."

"Already done," Fairbanks says. "I talked with Alec Strickland. This Esequiel Aquino has extensive involvement in narcotics smuggling—from South America, through Mexico, on into the US. He's mid-to-low-level—but I made a couple of calls to FBI in Houston, to check for any link between Aquino and cases Richardson could have prosecuted."

"And what's the word?"

"Tenuous links only," Fairbanks says, "nothing direct."

"So, what was he doing here?"

"Nobody knows. But there's no evidence Richardson ever went after Aquino, or anybody he worked with."

"Doesn't mean there couldn't be a link..."

"I spoke with Strickland," Fairbanks says, "brought him up to speed. He called the other resident agency up at Midland, plus the main office in El Paso. Aquino's on a list of people they think come in and out of the country on a regular basis. So, maybe he came through by chance—and something happened. We know some kind of altercation took place—the folk at the ranch saw gunfire."

"Right," Whicher says.

"But if he intended to get to Richardson, why didn't he do it, while he was there? He stole a truck, he ended up, what, a hundred miles away?"

"Something like that."

"FBI presumption is he must have met with someone—then continued his journey out of there."

"Why come through somewhere this remote?" Whicher says.

"He'd have no choice. Law enforcement would arrest him on sight at any of the ports of entry."

The marshal scans the deserted land, vast in the twilight. An uneasy feeling nagging inside.

"FBI are interested in Aquino being back in the country," Fairbanks says. "He's a violent criminal, if only a mid-level target—but they're interested in what he does, where he goes, who he meets. They're interested to know where he's coming in. But the threat assessment against Judge Richardson remains unchanged."

"Something's not right out here."

"He's gone," the chief marshal says. "The evidence supports that."

"I've thought it since the first time I came here. The first night," Whicher says.

Fairbanks is silent on the line.

The marshal watches the hills, the light fading.

"You're a good investigator, John," Fairbanks finally says. "If you think something's wrong, I'd take that. But USMS aren't being asked to provide protection. And from what you've said, Richardson doesn't want it, either. Is the ranch owner asking for anything from the sheriff's office?"

"Nobody's asking for anything."

"Officially, there isn't any problem."

"They're a long way from anywhere," Whicher says, "if there is..."

* * *

Rummaging through the back of the cab in the truck's interior lights, the marshal slides the 870 Remington from the gun safe. He grabs the canvas carryall from behind the passenger seat, yanks it out, rifles through it. Inside are tan cargo pants, two t-shirts, socks and shorts. A sweat top, a navy, US Marshals jacket. In the rear footwell, the pair of army boots.

He steps away from the truck, swings the door shut.

Crosses the dirt yard in the dwindling light.

Larry Mackenzie and Glen Carr are at the smoker now, with Richardson and Eliot. Patricia Mackenzie exiting the house carrying a tray.

She sets it on a camp table on the raised deck of the guest lodge.

Glen Carr watches the marshal approach.

"Everything alright?" Mackenzie says.

Donald Eliot stands with a glass in hand—face flushed, a slack smile at his mouth.

Vaughn Richardson's eyes are sharp. "Larry says traces of explosives were found in the truck—but you've been able to account for that? Some old fertilizer sacks?" He looks from Mackenzie back to Whicher. "What're you worrying about now?"

"We have intel on activity in the area that's some concern—involving foreign nationals."

"Really?" Mackenzie shifts his weight.

"I'm going to need to stay," the marshal says. "Just while it gets checked out."

Richardson shakes his head. Takes a glass from the table, takes a swig.

Patricia Mackenzie sets down the tray. "You're welcome to stay."

The ranch owner nods; "Of course..."

The marshal looks at Glen Carr. "And I'll need to accompany you on your trip in the morning. Out in country."

Carr shrugs. "Alright with me."

"You have a change of clothes?" Mackenzie says.

"In the truck," Whicher answers. "Boots, some rough gear. I could use a jacket."

"Not a problem," the ranch owner says.

Carr regards him. "You need a rifle?"

"I really don't see the need for any of this," Richardson says.

Eliot looks at the judge. "It can't hurt, can it?"

"We're glad to have you," Patricia says. "It's just a shame to inconvenience you."

"Soon as we know what's going on, that there's no security issue, I can be on my way," Whicher says.

"Well, we have some good brisket and slaw and potato salad, and spiced links."

"Ma'am, thank you."

The housekeeper, Amber Lester brings out an ice bucket with chilled wine and beer and sodas.

"There's a room in the house you can have," Mackenzie

says. To the housekeeper; "Amber, is the guest room made up?"

"It's all good," she says.

Glen Carr watches, holding a longneck beer.

Whicher looks at him. "Where y'all headed in the morning?"

"Up in the hills."

"You leave out early?"

"We'll be up at four, rolling by five. You done much hunting?"

"Not so much."

"Shooting?"

Whicher nods.

"Terrain's pretty rough," Carr says. "We'll take the truck to the foothills, work a path up to high ground, try not to let the wildlife know we're there."

"He's a lawman," Eliot says, grinning, "it'll be like a stakeout..."

"I can work terrain," Whicher says.

Carr takes him in in the light-spill from the house.

"I was battalion scout commander."

"Oh?" Richardson says. "Who with?"

"Third Armored Cavalry."

The judge eyes him, silent. Takes another pull at his drink.

"You want to freshen up before we eat?" Patricia says. She smiles. "Amber, could you show the marshal to the guest room."

* * *

Black night sits above the plain to the south, now—the ragged peaks of mountains barely picked out in the glow of the moon.

Whicher stands at the compound wall, breathes the night

air. Pictures hill trails, sheltered canyons—thinks of people moving through, silent.

He thinks of night ops overseas from years back. Keyed up, tension in him.

He thinks of the man Aquino—the malign presence. The sixth sense, the first night. Heat lightning. Electricity in the air.

Stepping from the wall, he crosses the yard. Opens up his truck. He takes out the Remington shotgun, takes a box of shells.

Looking at his phone he checks for a signal. Sees a weak bar, two.

He crosses to the wall, sets down the shotgun, writes a short message to Leanne—that he's turning in, that it's been a long day. And not to worry.

He sends the message.

Stands looking out into deep, black night.

The same sense ticking in his gut.

CHAPTER ELEVEN

Sun rises above the far desert hills—dawn's light stretching over the chino grass and scrub plain to the east.

From the slope of the mountainside, Whicher picks out Glen Carr's F150 truck a thousand feet below.

Breathing from the climb, the marshal sets down a backpack. He takes a water bottle from the net pocket on its side. Settling against a flattened boulder he rests the 870, pulls at the water bottle, lowers the zipper on the camo pattern jacket, lets the chill air cool his skin. Cacti and thorn grow from every crevice among the loose scree and crumbling earth. He picks out vicious spines from a borrowed pair of gaiters covering his ankles.

Glen Carr glasses the plain below—dressed head to toe in camo hunting gear—a scoped Winchester rifle on a sling at his side, backpack still shouldered.

Richardson and Eliot sit in deep shadow on the hillside, breathing hard, wiping sweat from their faces with the sleeves of their half-zip tops. Judge Richardson cradling an Italian Sabatti rifle, Eliot sporting a Mossberg Patriot.

Carr scans the side of the mountain at the south—where a long ravine descends from the heights to a canyon floor.

Leaving the pack and the shotgun, Whicher crosses the slope low to the ground; the footing treacherous, scree loose, rolling.

Carr turns to him. Points toward the ground below. "Tigner Canyon."

The marshal studies the terrain in the early light.

"You'll get aoudad coming up the ravine there, they'll get up around this height. There's a mesa, just above us."

The ranch hand passes the binoculars to Whicher.

He glasses the slopes of the ravine before it drops into a steep cut beyond the edge of the mountainside.

"An animal headed up there won't be able to see us," Carr says. "It's real deep in there before it tops out."

"We can't see in, how we know anything's going to be in there?"

"We don't," Carr says. "But I think there'll be some aoudad up high."

"We're going up blind?" the marshal says.

"Them and us. We get up over the top of the next ridge, we're on a plateau. Another half a mile there's a ridge we can climb. Seven hundred feet or so, it's a scramble. But the ridge looks west, right over a water hole. Presa Viruelas. There's water down there, some browse. You'll get a herd, sometimes a trophy-size ram, sometimes a few of 'em."

Whicher glances at him.

"That's the best shot you'll ever see...looking down from that ridge." Carr lowers his voice. "It's rough going, though. It's a climb." He steals a look in the direction of Richardson and Eliot, both men still breathing hard on a bench of fallen rock.

"They'll make it," Whicher says.

Carr grins. "You really think somebody could be looking for that guy out here?"

Whicher hands the younger man the field glasses. "I just need to be sure, is all. Anything happens, help's a long way off."

Carr nods, takes back the binoculars. "It's wild-ass country." He hitches the rifle at his shoulder. "I guess we ought to move out."

* * *

At the crest of a mile-long ridge, the wind is strengthening.

In scrub cover Glen Carr glasses the Presa Viruelas, still in deep shadow below.

Vaughn Richardson settles against a flat hunk of limestone, aiming his rifle down into the gulch—Donald Eliot beside him.

Whicher eyes the watercourse below; dry but for a narrow green pool around a hundred yards long. Around the water hole, mesquite and whitethorn acacia and saltbush is grown dense.

Scanning the terrain he spots a dirt track crossing a high plateau broken up with hills. Beyond the plateau, a craze of mountain summits are touched with sunlight, Chinati Peak towering in the northwest.

Carr breathes; "I got eyes on something."

The marshal peers down.

A tan form slips in and out of view—a ram—browsing thin grass between the mesquite and saltbush.

Richardson looks down through the scope of his hunting rifle.

Whicher tallies the distance—around three hundred fifty yards.

Another ram steps in view beside the first.

"They'll be about twelve or thirteen years old," Carr says.

Donald Eliot looks across at him. "That okay?"

"Coming to the end of their lives," Carr says. "Trophy size. If you can get a shot, ethical shot, go for it..."

The judge comes off the scope, glances at Eliot.

"All yours," Eliot says, "it's your party. I'm good."

"Take the big ram," Carr says, "the ram to the left."

Richardson puts his eye to the scope, stays motionless, aims the rifle.

"Hit him in the shoulder," Carr breathes. "Aim low..."

"How low?" the judge says. "The scope's set for two-fifty."

"Low, but not off him..."

Richardson blows out air.

"Not off the animal..."

Whicher sees the tension in the judge.

The ram turns, moves back a yard into the brush, out of view.

"Stay tight to the rifle," Whicher tells him.

Carr nods behind the field glasses. "Wait for him, he'll come back out."

Eliot inches forward.

In the gulch the second ram moves, his head comes up.

Both rams bolt suddenly.

Carr whips away the binoculars. "Son of a gun..."

Richardson mutters behind the rifle.

"Something's down there." Carr looks through the glasses again. "Somebody's down there..."

Whicher moves up.

Carr hands him the binoculars.

From around a curve in the ridgeline below, a group of men is visible, dressed in camo gear.

The marshal counts four.

He checks for barrels—long guns at their shoulders. All four are carrying packs.

Judge Richardson gets up, moves to the edge of the ridge. "What the hell is going on down there?"

The marshal steps to him, takes a hold of his arm. "Move back, get low..."

"What?"

Whicher pulls him down, into cover.

Richardson jerks free his arm. "What the hell are you doing?"

Carr stares down. "They're gone..."

Whicher puts the glasses to his eyes.

Nobody is in sight, now.

Donald Eliot looks to Carr. "What was that about?"

The ranch hand grunts, "Border jumpers..." He turns to Whicher. "Marshal? What do you want to do?"

Whicher stares down into the gulch. "Where's their route out?"

"They go down, they can get in Tigner Canyon," Carr says. "Head for US sixty-seven."

Richardson stands stiffly, rifle between his hands. "Well, they're gone, in any case. If they've seen us they're not going to want to get any closer."

Eliot rubs his arm. "I don't know, you think?"

Whicher looks at Carr. "You have any way to call out of here?"

"Satellite phone."

"I need to call Border Patrol, let 'em know there's people out here."

Richardson steps to the ranch hand. "What about those rams?"

Carr indicates the far edge of the ridge. "There's a spring a mile or so from here. We stay on the ridge, we can look down over it. If they go there, you could get a shot. We'll be sitting right on top of them."

"There's no reason not to, surely?" Richardson says.

Carr looks to Whicher.

"Let me have your sat phone," the marshal says. "Let me speak with the Patrol."

* * *

Heat is in the air now, wind blowing warm at their backs.

Vaughn Richardson lies prone against the ground with his rifle.

At the northern end of the ridge, Glen Carr glasses downhill around the spring.

Whicher checks the watercourse running south, looking for the group of men.

On the plain below to the east he sees no sign of anyone.

Border Patrol had the position, now, near units would be alerted.

To the west, a small, sloping plateau is familiar. The peaks at its edges form an outline Whicher's seen before.

Donald Eliot looks at Carr. "See anything?"

"Not yet."

Richardson adjusts his position behind the rifle. "This looks kind of a tough shot, the range is farther."

"Close to five hundred yards," Carr says.

"Get your excuses in early," Eliot tells the judge.

The ranch hand takes away the binoculars. "Looking at four hundred feet of drop. And there's some wind starting to blow."

"Yeah," Eliot says, "you're definitely missing."

"You think they'll come down here?" Richardson says.

"They might have been through already," Carr replies. "We could get eyes on another animal. Give it some time…"

Whicher stares over at the valley to the northwest. His gaze ascending to where rough peaks block the view. "That valley," he says, "across there. Looks like the place Border Patrol found that young girl?"

The younger man looks over at it, nods.

Presa Llorona.

"There's a bunch of springs and stock tanks up here," Carr says. "People try to find them. Sometimes it's too late. They're weak already, you know? The water's no good."

The marshal thinks of the group of four men; without an organized search, the chance of locating them would be low.

"Do you think we could find a spot with better cover?" Vaughn Richardson says. "I can't lie like this too long."

From a ridge half a mile away on the opposite side of the watercourse, a figure emerges.

A second follows.

And then a third.

Whicher steps to Carr—the hand passes him the field glasses.

The marshal trains them onto three young men—dressed in camo gear—with packs on their backs.

Eliot sits up. "What's going on?"

Whicher glasses the path of the dry stream to the south. "If that other group's still back there, behind us, they're going to flank us. They've got height on us out there..."

Glen Carr regards him.

"First group is already below. I don't like two groups of men on the hill," the marshal says.

Judge Richardson sits up, squints across at the opposite ridge. "You think it's a problem?"

"They're too close. We need to get the both of you down." Whicher thinks of the route back, the distance.

Carr pulls a set of keys from a pocket in his hunting vest. "Truck's about two, maybe two and a half miles back. Stay high about a mile before you try to drop down. There's a bad ravine y'all don't want to get into." He tosses over the keys.

The marshal looks at him. "What're you going to do?"

"Rear security. I'll keep a little extra height. Watch for anyone. Anybody tries to get in behind us, I'll slow 'em down."

Richardson looks at the ranch hand. "There's no need for that, surely?"

Whicher puts the keys in a pocket, eyes the younger man. "Call your boss, have him post up at the ranch—tell him to keep watch."

"That's it, we're abandoning the hunt?" Richardson says.

The marshal addresses Carr. "Don't let them see you. Cut down once we've made some ground. Don't wait too long. We'll be at the truck."

"Got it."

Whicher nods a silent acknowledgement. "Alright." He looks to Vaughn and Eliot. "Stay tight to me. Let's go, let's move out."

* * *

Hurrying the pace across the hill, the marshal eyes the crest of the big ravine a mile south—careful not to descend too fast.

Richardson slips, falls, the rifle hits him in the side.

He winces. "What makes you think anybody out here would be a threat to us?"

Whicher moves to him. "Not us. You."

The judge struggles to his feet. "Nobody knows I'm out here."

The marshal checks back along the hillside—looks for Glen Carr. Sees him half a mile back—still high, just beneath the line of the ridge. "Prints found in Mackenzie's truck belonged to a foreign national, a South American..."

"What difference does that make?"

"South American cartels are known to target the judiciary. Shots were fired into the ranch two nights back," Whicher says. "A Honduran killer came close enough to steal that vehicle..."

"Maybe you should listen to him," Eliot says.

The marshal thinks of the first group of men—they could be down on the plain before them, they could reach the truck.

Eliot glances back up the rock-littered slope. Addresses Richardson; "If those people out there are running drugs there's no telling what they might do."

Whicher stares along the side of the hill—to the crest of the ravine. "Anybody gets too close, we don't want anything to happen..."

Richardson takes a water bottle from his pack. Unscrews the top, takes a sip.

The marshal searches the hillside and the plain below, shifts the 870 in his grip.

* * *

Dust rises from the scree on the hill. At the truck, heat rolls in waves across the scorched plain.

Oppressive silence hangs in the air, wind barely stirring.

Whicher scans the terrain as far as he can see—back toward the Mackenzie ranch—three miles along the bottom of the wide, flat canyon.

Eliot stands with Richardson by the F150—the truck's doors open, packs and gear thrown in the bed.

Glen Carr is in view now, descending—moving down fast and low, countering the weight of the big pack and the rifle.

The marshal studies the side of the ravine to the south.

He scans the scrub cover around the toe slope.

Carr reaches the bottom of the hill, swings the pack off

his back. "Everybody alright?" He wipes his brow with the arm of his shirt. "I went up to the ridgeline—two times. Saw 'em headed north, still high. Last time I looked they were dropping, starting to head down."

"Onto the plain?" Whicher says.

"From Presa Llorona. Dropping down the valley." Carr takes the binoculars from around his neck, hands them to the marshal.

Whicher checks the ground north—sees nothing.

He takes away the glasses. "Alright, let's move back to the ranch." He looks at Carr. "You call your boss?"

"I called. He'll be waiting."

"This whole thing..." Richardson says. "It's probably nothing..."

"Let's mount up," Whicher says. "Head back. See what Border Patrol have to say."

* * *

An hour later at the compound wall of the ranch, Larry Mackenzie watches the land to the south through a telescope set up on a tripod stand.

A helicopter from Air and Marine traverses the sky in the distance.

Whicher watches the A-Star out over the high ridge and the mountain plateaus. Circling, sweeping the canyons and runoffs. Hovering, descending, climbing again.

Two Border Patrol SUVs sit far off in a heat haze on the plain—agents out of their vehicles, cutting for sign.

Mackenzie takes his eye from the telescope. "There's overhangs and caves along some of those mountain faces nobody's looked in in a hundred years..."

The marshal nods.

"Indian caves," the ranch owner says, "culverts you could

get in—pull some brush over you, nobody would know you're there."

"They'll lie low," Whicher says, "with the noise from the helicopter."

Across the yard at the guest lodge, Richardson and Eliot watch the search on the hills. Grilling tomahawk rib-eye, drinking fresh-brewed coffee.

The marshal glances over at them. "Think they're fixing to stay?"

"They're paid up for another day," Mackenzie says. "I know they want to take a big ram. Glen said he's not exactly sure what all went on out there. Whether or not those folk would've crossed your path. Or tried to approach you."

Whicher cuts the man a look.

"He said they were moving fast. Like they knew what they were doing. Course, he's not law enforcement..."

"He's a good man," Whicher says. "Good man on the hill."

Over the long, high ridge, the A-Star hovers. Starts to climb into the harsh blue sky.

The marshal watches as it gains in height.

Knowing it for what it means.

No sign.

There's no sign.

They can't find them.

* * *

Standing at the Silverado in the ranch yard Whicher waits as Larry Mackenzie exits the house.

"Patrol are going to stay on the ground," the marshal tells him. "They've picked up a foot trail north of here, they'll look to track it down. They're thinking to bring in mounted officers."

"Horses?"

"Looks like."

The helicopter is gone now—a third Border Patrol unit parked down on the scrub plain, a mile and a half out.

"I'll let everybody know. That's reassuring." The ranch owner gestures at the guest lodge—Richardson and Eliot indoors, now, out of the heat.

The marshal doesn't reply. He puts away the 870 in the gun safe of the truck.

"I appreciate all you've done," Mackenzie says.

Whicher meets his eye. "I'll get an update on the threat assessment from Patrol sector headquarters at Marfa. I may be back. Right now, I have a missing person case outstanding..."

"Of course. I understand."

"Officially, you don't have any problem." Whicher swings behind the wheel of the truck. He fires up the motor, takes a business card from the glove box. "Call me, or call the sheriff's office or Border Patrol if you think something's wrong."

The ranch owner takes the card. Puts it into a shirt pocket.

Whicher nods to him, moves the shifter into drive.

He rolls by the vehicles parked in back of the ranch compound.

Steers out onto the dirt road north between chino grass hills.

He can call Fairbanks.

Richardson and Eliot were clear they intended to remain.

Border Patrol were around, everybody claimed to be happy.

He passes the turn for the barn, thinks of the stolen Dakota. Pictures the truck, in far-off Valentine. Turns his thoughts to the missing person case for the county—the young farm worker, Matias Cardenas.

He'd need to call the justice of the peace, Preston Crawford. Press for an ID on the drowning victim at the Rio Grande.

He rubs a hand across his jaw, fatigued from the hunt, from the early start.

Checking for a network on the phone he finds none.

Eight miles still, to the nearest road.

He should call Leanne, let her know where he was. At the road there might be something.

Through the truck's open window a noise slaps through the air—a shock wave, sudden, violent.

He gets off the gas.

Sits up.

Something is in his rear-view mirror.

He lifts his eyes to it—stares back in the direction of the ranch.

The mirror is filled with black smoke, with roiling orange flame.

A fireball.

As the sound of an explosion rocks the canyon, ripping through it now.

And Whicher's leg locks out—foot jammed hard onto the brake.

CHAPTER TWELVE

Flame.

Flame rolling from the wrecked chassis inside the gates.

Judge Richardson's SUV—consumed with fire.

Whicher scans the ranch, the yard.

He snaps off the retaining clip to the Glock. Jumps from the truck.

Running inside the compound wall, black smoke billows into the air.

Mackenzie steps from the porch—mouth open, face blank with shock.

Heat sears from the burning Lincoln—glass from Mackenzie's truck, from Carr's pickup is blown out, scattered across the yard.

The marshal stares into the ball of flame—makes out nothing inside the judge's car. He shouts to Mackenzie; "*Where is he?*"

The man only gapes back.

"Where's Richardson?"

The ranch owner points at the guest lodge.

Stepping back from the fierce heat, Whicher sees the

single Border Patrol unit on the plain—now racing toward the ranch, a rooster tail of dust behind it.

Glen Carr emerges onto the porch—to stare across at the burning wreckage of the SUV.

Mackenzie stands rooted.

"Where's your housekeeper?" Whicher says.

"Inside..."

"Your wife?"

"Inside...she's inside, too."

"Call 911..." The marshal starts to run toward the lodge.

Mackenzie calls back, hoarse. "What the hell happened?"

"Get law enforcement out here, get the fire department. Stay away from the vehicles..."

Glen Carr shouts, "*You need help?*"

"Car bomb," Whicher answers, "don't touch anything..."

Reaching the lodge he rips open the door.

Donald Eliot stands in a kitchen, in shorts, a T-shirt.

"Where's Richardson?"

The man stares back, mute.

Vaughn Richardson appears from a door down the hall, hair disheveled from sleep, face confused.

"Somebody put a bomb beneath your car," the marshal says.

The judge makes no response.

"Stay here. Don't come out unless I tell you—either of you." Whicher takes the Glock from the clip holster at his belt.

He turns, exits the building.

Outside, fire rages from the SUV.

He tunes out the noise, the heat, the smoke swirling. Runs across the compound yard, scans the perimeter.

The Border Patrol unit reaches the ranch at the south wall, it brakes to a stop. Both agents get out fast—armed with M4 carbines.

Whicher shows the Marshals Service badge, calls down. "*IED...*"

The driver calls back; "A bomb?"

"Vehicle IED..."

"You have people injured?"

"No injured, I don't think." Whicher makes a circling gesture at the surrounding hills. "Perpetrator could be out there—we need to check."

"We have binoculars, a spotting scope..."

"Call for backup," Whicher says, "any close unit, get 'em here."

The driver points to the Chinatis. "We've got boots on the ground there..."

"Bring 'em in."

Glen Carr appears on the porch at the house—with the scoped Winchester.

Whicher spots him. "Get inside—stay there."

"What's going on? Are we under attack?"

"Let me have the rifle..."

The marshal runs to the porch.

Carr hands him the gun.

"Go back inside," Whicher says, "get in cover."

The ranch hand nods. Steps away.

Among the sotol and mesquite and cholla on the nearby hills there's no sign of anyone. Whicher raises the Winchester, puts the scope to his eye.

He turns his body slowly, traces the line of an incline.

Eyes alive.

Breathing slow.

Searching.

* * *

Monahans, Ward County, Tx

. . .

Accelerating into the street on the west side of Monahans, Aquino sees the Red-Five Oilfield Supply.

He stamps on the brakes of the Dodge, rips the steering right, through a lot into a storage yard in back.

A Chevy Express delivery van sits parked to one side.

He stops behind it, blocking it. Reaches for the Heckler & Koch rifle on the seat.

Stepping from the SUV he runs to the front of the van. He snatches open the door.

The cab is empty.

He turns to face the store building.

Cars and trucks pass by out front on the street.

He dumps the rifle in back of the Dodge, slams the black-glassed door.

Snatching up a Sig P226 semi-automatic pistol, he shoves it into the waistband of his jeans.

He sprints to the building, runs around the side.

Two pickups are out front, a lone sedan.

He checks the street, pushes through the door to the store—steps by display shelves filled with tools and parts.

A clerk stares from behind the counter.

Aquino scans the place—looking—heat running through him, willing the man to be there.

Three customers browse near the store front window.

"Sir?" the counterman says. "I help you with something?"

"Your driver," Aquino says.

The man eyes him, wary. "We have two delivery drivers, sir. What's this about?"

"Where is he?" Aquino grunts.

"Sir?" the counterman says. "You want to calm down?"

Aquino moves closer.

"What's all this about?"

Stepping around the counter, Aquino shoves the man aside.

"Sir, you can't come back here..."

Aquino pushes open the door to a staff room.

A bearded man sits in a plastic chair, eating a chili dog and fries.

"*Sir*..." the counterman says.

The seated man stops mid-bite. "What's going on?"

Aquino looks at him. "Where is he?"

"Where's who?"

"Your driver."

"Sir, you can't come back here, you need to leave," the counterman says.

Aquino turns, stares him down.

The bearded man starts to rise.

Whipping out an arm, Aquino sends him backward, crashing over the seat. He sees no other employee in the building—steps to a fire exit, chops down on the steel bar.

The alarm sounds.

He kicks the door open.

He takes the Sig from the back of his jeans, lets the counterman see it.

Sprawled out on the floor, the bearded man only stares.

"Tell him I was here," Aquino says. "Tell him I'll be back..."

CHAPTER THIRTEEN

Austin, Tx

Downtown Austin is dark as Whicher parks the Silverado outside of the Westgate Tower on the corner of Colorado and West 12th.

Light from the Capitol building filters through trees in the surrounding parkland.

The marshal closes up the truck, stands on the sidewalk in the cool night air.

He checks his watch.

Gone ten-thirty.

Sounds of the city are on the breeze, traffic humming in the background.

He waits by the truck in the street-lit glow of night.

A gray Chevy Impala turns in from Mesquite Street.

It pulls in at the curbside. Leanne steps quickly out from behind the wheel.

She takes him in—eyes large in her handsome face, a

swathe of chestnut hair caught in the streetlamp. "Are you alright?"

He nods. Steps to her.

She looks into his face.

He puts his arms around her.

She kisses him, eases away.

"He's okay..." Whicher says. "He's in a safe house in the city. He's got armed protection. Marshals Service, plus the state police."

She lets out a long breath. "So, what happened?"

"Somebody blew up the judge's car."

Her eyes hold him.

"By the grace of God, nobody was hurt," the marshal says. "The car was destroyed. Everybody was inside, protected from the blast..."

"Was it timed to go off?"

"We don't know. FBI have people down there now. I got him out. Kept him safe till they could figure out what was happening. Drove him back here."

"What happens now?"

"They'll move him again."

"What about you, what will you do?"

"Nothing. Unless they tell me."

"Do you want us to come home?"

"To Pecos?"

"We could come back?"

"You don't need to do that."

Leanne looks into the play of shadow and light beneath the parkland trees. "Lori saw the reports. She asked me about it. She knew you went down to some ranch, she wouldn't stop asking, trying to find out if you'd been there..."

The marshal looks at her.

"I can't lie about it..."

"You don't have to lie."

"It's getting harder. Now she's older," Leanne says. "She gets really afraid."

Whicher stares out along the street. "What's been reported?"

"That a judge was targeted. That there'd been an attack, an explosion."

"They'll likely move him back to Houston," Whicher says. "USMS will protect him, a specialized team."

"The news report said it could be a cartel. A South American cartel."

"It's too early to say."

She turns to look at him. "But you won't have to deal with it?"

The marshal shakes his head. "FBI will carry out the investigation."

"I told her you were coming here, to Austin. I told her I'd just come see you were okay."

"I am," he says. "You can tell her I am."

"We can come home."

"You don't need to come home. It's good for Lori to be out here."

"Can you stay?"

"I have to see Chief Marshal Fairbanks..."

"Just tonight," Leanne says, "did you even eat?"

"It's a six-hour drive. I have a missing person case, plus a foreign national to be deported."

Leanne catches his eye. "Don't go after them..."

Beneath his breath he tells her "FBI will go after them."

"Don't try to find whoever did this."

"That's not how it is."

Her eyes are flat as she looks him over, voice hard. "Don't go after these people. Don't look for them. Whoever they are..."

CHAPTER FOURTEEN

Reeves County, Tx

A rising sun is behind him, lighting up the traffic on South Cedar.

On four hours of sleep and strong coffee Whicher drives across town, past the bank, past chain restaurants, the fire station, the sheriff's office, the jail. He pulls into the lot of the Pecos courthouse. Sees Booker Tillman exiting the building.

Tillman spots the truck, waves the marshal down.

Whicher pulls over, rolls the window.

Tillman leans in, tips back his black Stetson. "Hell of a thing with that ranch down there...what's going on, they looking to keep him back in ATX?"

"They'll move him out of Austin," Whicher says. "Is Fairbanks here?"

"She's here. We had the doc swing by this morning."

"Doc Hollis?"

"For Zambrano—he's cleared to travel. I got the job taking him to Houston, the Federal Detention Center."

"They're going to process him there?"

"According to Fairbanks," Tillman says. "DOJ and the Office of International Affairs can let the Colombian Embassy know. Court has to rule he's extraditable."

Whicher looks across the street at the brick façade of the Reeves jail facility. "You headed over?" He looks at Tillman. "Like to see him. Before you hit the road."

Tillman thumbs his salt-and-pepper mustache. "We need to get moving, but you want to see him, be my guest."

* * *

Across the street, in a holding cell, Marco Zambrano sits in an orange jumpsuit, eyes glaring.

His shifts on a steel bench as Whicher, Tillman and a jailer from the sheriff's staff enter.

The jailer, a big man in a brown uniform shirt addresses Zambrano. "On your feet. These gentlemen are taking you out of here."

Zambrano's gaze fixes on Whicher.

He stands, both hands cuffed to a Martin chain around his waist.

Tillman eyes him.

"You're going out to Houston," Whicher says. "With the marshal here. From Houston, the court will send you on back to Colombia."

Zambrano juts his chin.

Booker Tillman steps in. "There some problem?"

"*Abogado*. I want a lawyer..."

Tillman puts his head on one side. "Extradition cases, federal rules of criminal procedure don't apply." He checks the restraints on the prisoner, nods to the jailer.

The jailer fastens a black, plastic anti-pick cover over the cuffs at the man's wrists.

"You want to do yourself a favor?" Whicher says.

Tillman takes a step to one side. He cuts his eyes at the marshal.

"You want to maybe get some smokes? Something decent to eat?" Whicher says.

Zambrano's expression gives back nothing.

"Tell me something, before you go," the marshal says. "What were you doing at the border the night I picked you up?"

The man's jaw works, his mouth stays shut.

"Were you trying to get across?" Whicher feels the same strange sense around Zambrano. His agitation. Now, he wanted to speak with a lawyer—as if there was something more to say. "What were you doing? Down there?"

"I see a lawyer. *Más tarde*. After...is questions."

"I got to haul your ass halfway across the state," Tillman says, "and you know what? I'm not interested what you have to say."

Whicher eyes Zambrano. "Surrender warrant gets issued, you're on your way, mano. You don't get to appeal. But you could maybe get a cell to yourself while you're waiting. Little sweetener. That kind of a deal."

Zambrano stares past him, past the jailer. He lifts his arms against the restraining chains.

Tillman glances at Whicher, shrugs.

Zambrano turns to the jailer. "*Vamos*. Let's go."

* * *

Back across the street on the second floor of the courthouse building, Whicher enters Chief Marshal Fairbanks's room.

"You just get in?"

"I got in, I saw Marshal Tillman."

"He tell you about Zambrano?"

"Yes, ma'am. Matter of fact, I went across the street to the jail with him."

"Oh?"

"To see if I could get him to talk."

The chief marshal looks at him. "About what?"

"I want to know what he was doing down on the border. He was in the area the night the Mackenzie Ranch was attacked."

Fairbanks regards him from behind her desk through steel-framed glasses. "He was under arrest in Presidio…"

Whicher nods.

"You think there could be a connection?"

The marshal pulls out a seat. "Something about him bothers me."

"The FBI are going to need your report into the explosion," Fairbanks says. "But give me the main points." She takes a yellow legal pad from beside the computer on her desk, picks up a pen. "You stayed at the ranch overnight…"

"To accompany the hunt in the mountains."

"You weren't asked to."

Whicher nods. "Something about this whole thing bothers me. From the first night I felt it."

Fairbanks writes on the pad; "You stayed as a precaution, in view of Judge Richardson's presence…and the prior incident, the reported shooting."

"Yes, ma'am."

"Then what?"

Whicher leans back in the chair. "We went up into the Chinatis at first light, maybe three or four miles from the ranch. With a guide, the ranch hand. Plus the judge, plus another guest. We spent the morning trying to spot aoudad, Barbary sheep. We saw two groups of clandestines. I talked with the guide, told him I wasn't happy. There was no good reason for them to be there, they were most likely involved in some kind of criminal activity—I told the guide we needed to finish and head back."

"So, that's what you did?"

"The guide had a satellite phone. I alerted Border Patrol. Then we pulled back to the ranch."

"Did you see any of the group of men again?"

"No, ma'am. Border Patrol conducted a search, they couldn't find 'em. They found some tracks to follow, they were thinking to bring in mounted agents."

The chief marshal writes on the notepad. "What happened after that?"

"Judge Richardson told me he had no intention of leaving. They ate, turned in, took a siesta. Patrol kept at it. There was no immediate, present danger. I needed to resume my other duties, the rest of my work..."

"And then the device detonated?"

Whicher looks at his boss. "I was a mile or so out, I turned around, got the hell back in there. We called Border Patrol, the sheriff's department, the police department out of Presidio. And the FBI. I removed the judge from the scene, took him to safe accommodation in Austin."

Chief Marshal Fairbanks pushes back in her seat.

"Richardson says he never moved the vehicle from the time he arrived," Whicher says.

"Alright. Well, it couldn't have been a tilt fuze..."

"We don't know when the device was planted," Whicher says, "it could've been that first night."

Fairbanks lifts her glasses from her face to the top of her head.

"If it was, it was most likely triggered with a phone signal," Whicher says.

"FBI investigators will have to determine that," Fairbanks

answers. "Could somebody have accessed the vehicle while you were up on the mountain? Put an explosive charge on it, maybe a timer?"

The marshal spreads his hands.

"Could you have been observed? By the men on the hill? Could they have watched you, while someone planted the device?"

"There were folk at the ranch," Whicher says.

"Would they have seen? Were they up?"

"Maybe. Maybe not."

"So, a time-delayed device, or remotely activated?"

"A phone, maybe," Whicher says. "There's some network up around the ranch."

"A two-way radio would do it," Fairbanks says. "From up in the hills, with line of sight."

"Or a satellite phone," Whicher says.

Fairbanks stares at the desk, thinks it over.

"Sat phone's not hard to come by," the marshal says. "We need to know who'd target him."

Fairbanks puts down her pen. "Richardson has links to plenty of high-profile narcotics cases. But down here, what federal prosecutor doesn't?"

"And how did anybody know he was out here?" Whicher says.

The chief marshal looks at him from across the desk. "All questions for the FBI to answer. Marshals Service just need to keep him safe. Soon as you've completed a report, let me have it."

"Yes, ma'am."

Fairbanks takes up her pen again. "One other thing; Preston Crawford, the Presidio County JP called yesterday. Regarding the drowning victim at the river?"

"He have something on that?"

The chief marshal nods. "Crawford called the sheriff's

office, they had the dental record for your missing person sent to Fort Davis, where they're keeping the body. The Gonzales Funeral Home? Anyhow, Crawford asked the mortician to check the drowning victim's teeth."

"Oh?"

"Matias Cardenas has two teeth missing from his upper jaw—from a road accident. The funeral home checked—it turns out the drowning victim has teeth where Cardenas doesn't."

"So, it can't be him."

"Whoever it is," the chief marshal says. "Not your man."

CHAPTER FIFTEEN

Marfa, Tx

The single-wide trailer sits on a patch of hard dirt and live oak off East Texas Street, wrecked cars in a junkyard opposite, a handful of prefabricated homes either side of a crumbling asphalt lane.

Whicher steps from the Silverado, straightens his necktie. Puts on the suit jacket, sets his hat.

Out in front of the trailer home, Josefina Olvera's green Isuzu Trooper sits windows down, tires and rims covered with a fine red dust.

The marshal steps to the front door, raps hard. Scans the length of the bleak-looking street. Lets his gaze run out to low, blue hills on the near horizon.

The trailer door opens.

Josefina Olvera stands looking out. Dressed in jeans, a cut-off sweat top, her face immobile.

"Ms Olvera."

"Marshal."

"I come in?"

She steps back into a combination dinette and living area. Whicher follows.

A couch is along one wall, mismatched Lazy Boys opposite a TV.

On a thrift-store table a picture shows her with Matias, at a cookout, a family gathering.

"The sheriff's office called," Olvera says. She folds her arms. "They said you found a body in the river..."

"Three days back," Whicher says.

"But it's not Matias."

"We had to be sure."

"It took you three days to find out?"

The marshal doesn't respond. "I take a seat?"

She nods.

Whicher pulls out a chair from the table.

Olvera lowers herself into a seat, eyes hooded.

"The victim had been in the water some time, ma'am, with facial injuries. All of that can change the way a person looks."

"There's been nothing. For eight days now."

The marshal leans forward in his chair. "Ma'am, does Matias have a bank account?"

"We have joint checking..."

"Anything else?"

"A savings account."

"Have you looked at them for activity? Cash withdrawals from ATMs?"

"I look, I check. Every day, there's been nothing."

"Does he have any other account? Could he access money some other way?"

She shakes her head.

"How about cash? Could he have any?"

"He gets paid by check, mostly, sometimes in cash at the farm."

"Could he have put some aside?"

"I don't think."

"And you don't have…money problems?"

She makes a face. Looks around the room. "No more than anybody else."

"No debts? Nobody you owe?"

"We pay a loan on this." She gestures at the trailer. "We're not behind."

"You tell me anything about yourself?" he says. "You work here in Marfa?"

"I manage a bunch of guest rentals. Plus the cantina off the highway."

"And your life, together, the two of you, how is it?"

"Matias is out all day. I'm in and out in the daytime. I work a bunch of evenings."

"How about free time?"

"Same as anybody," she says. "Movies. We go visit with family. He likes his sports, basketball. Music."

"He's happy working on the farm?"

"He likes a quiet life," Olvera says. "He likes to work steady, he doesn't like…I don't know, pressure, a lot of stress."

"That why he quit working the oilfields?"

She nods. "But he works hard, his boss likes him. Oil and gas it's pretty rough. A lot goes on. People are kind of crazy. He's done with that."

"We may need to broaden this out," Whicher says, "apply for a warrant, take a look at the records for his phone. We can't get a warrant without evidence of a crime. Or something showing Matias could be in danger, at risk."

She looks at him.

"We need something to show he didn't just take off."

"I told you, he's not like that."

"He have a computer here?"

"He doesn't use one."

"Some other kind of device? If we could search his internet use, it might show evidence of something happening."

"He only has his phone. He surfs on that."

The marshal looks around the room, glances through to the dinette, feels his mood darken. Tries to keep it from showing in his face. "What can you tell me about Matias's family? Are y'all close?"

"Matias is an only. Kind of a release for him to get away. His mother wants grandchildren, you know? She says she doesn't, but she does."

"You spend time up there?"

"More around here, my family."

"How about the folk from his oilfield days, friends from back then?"

"He just kind of left all that behind. He got a job working for Zimmerman. He used to come by the cantina, where I met him. He's just a gentle guy, he's kind, he wouldn't hurt nobody..." She breaks off, swallows.

Whicher lets his eye meet hers. "We'll keep looking."

A flicker shows on her face.

"We'll look. Till we find him."

* * *

Driving East Lincoln toward the back end of Marfa, Whicher pulls in by a derelict house on the lane.

From the sheriff's department file he finds a number for Guadalupe Cardenas—Matias's mother. He presses to send a call, sets the phone to speaker.

Shifting the truck into drive, he pulls back out onto the lane.

Above the live oak, the central dome and pink stucco of the courthouse building shows a half mile ahead.

The call picks up.

"Señora Cardenas?"

"Sí."

"This is Deputy Marshal Whicher. Ma'am, I'm not calling with any news, we've had no further information at this point. But you were going to call around some of his friends? Find out if anybody heard anything?"

"Sí, yes."

The marshal yields to a farm truck at an intersection.

"I talked with a friend he has up in Monahans," the woman says. "He saw him a few weeks back. He said he thought something was wrong."

"He said that?"

"He said he seemed like something was troubling him."

Whicher gets back on the gas. "Ma'am, you have a number for this person? And a name?"

"Antonio," she says, "Antonio Nolasco."

Whicher eyes the back of the sheriff's office and the county jail. "You have the number?"

"Can you give me a minute to find it?"

"No problem," the marshal says, "I'll hold..."

* * *

In reception in the sheriff's office, the tall figure of Deputy Garcia stands in shirtsleeves drinking a cold can of soda. A female dispatcher in back talks into a phone behind twin computer screens.

Garcia sets down the can. "You made it out of that ranch in one piece, mano?"

Whicher nods.

"FBI and Homeland Security have it sealed off now—you were there when it went up?"

"I was driving away," Whicher answers, "I just left out."

The deputy gives a low whistle. "It's one hell of a mess. They know what triggered it?"

Whicher shakes his head. "We got lucky, that's for sure."

The door to the sheriff's office opens, Armando Torres steps out.

He looks at Whicher. "Marshal. Did you need to see me?"

"I'm back on the Matias Cardenas case."

Garcia cuts in; "You know we ruled out the drowning vic at the river?"

"I heard. I talked with Josefina Olvera this afternoon."

"You want to step in here a minute?" Torres says.

Whicher follows the sheriff into his office overlooking the courthouse square.

"It's been over a week," Whicher says. "Josefina says no money's been taken from their account. I talked with the guy's mother just now, she says Cardenas was with a friend up in Monahans a couple weeks back—he said it seemed like something was going on. I'm headed up there to talk to him."

"Up in Monahans?"

"Like to get a warrant to search Cardenas's phone record," Whicher says. "But I need something to put before a judge. And I think you're right, we should run a bigger search—make sure he's not out somewhere on the farm, or on the Sierra Vieja."

"I can talk to Zimmerman," Torres says.

"I'll see if I can get us some air support," Whicher says. "If he's not out there, that's another reason for a judge to grant a warrant."

"There's still the possibility he just walked."

"Right," Whicher says. "And he could've gone into hiding,

somewhere up in the oil and gas fields. Places he used to work, places he still knows people..."

"You think you could get us a helicopter?" Torres says. "Even though he could've left voluntarily, for whatever reason?"

The marshal lets his gaze rest on Sheriff Torres a moment. "Yeah," he says. "I don't think the man walked."

CHAPTER SIXTEEN

Monahans, Ward County, Tx

Two hours later, early evening sun is over the RV Park outside the town of Monahans.

Whicher sits at a picnic table on the pull-thru site.

Antonio Nolasco sits out front of a travel trailer by a Toyota pickup.

"Appreciate your seeing me," Whicher says, "at short notice."

Nolasco shrugs, rubs at a muscled arm. He slumps in a camp chair, small, lean, dressed in jeans, a work shirt, the sleeves cut off. "Most of the time, I'm not even here, I'll be somewhere working. You know?"

"Where would that be?"

Nolasco takes a drag on a cigarette. "Man camps, anywhere there's a drill site..." He takes a swig from a can of beer.

The marshal pictures the temporary lodging camps—

home to itinerant gas and oil crews—self-contained communities, miles from anywhere. "You work a long hitch?"

"Three weeks on, mano. One off."

"Doing what?"

"Trucking sand. Frack sand. Before that, driving cement trucks for the wells."

"You known Matias a long time?"

Nolasco watches through small, black eyes, smoke trailing from his mouth. "We were in high school. Like, ten years back."

"Y'all work together?"

"We worked together. We stayed some of the same camps. He was driving vans, mainly, delivering parts."

"But he quit?" Whicher says. "He didn't like the life?"

"If you can call it a life." Nolasco grins. "Pulling fourteen-hour shifts. Bunking with a bunch of animals. Bored out of your mind or working till you drop."

"But the money's good?"

"Hell, yeah."

The marshal shifts on the bench, leans forward at the table. "So, you know Matias, you know the family?"

"I know 'em. My family's in Fort Stockton. I keep a spot here, I rent the whole year. Otherwise, they'll lease to somebody else."

"You get back home?"

"Sometimes."

"You see much of Matias? The Cardenas family?"

"Not lately. Not since he's living down in Marfa. I get a week off, I'm half-dead, I got stuff to do, you know? Then I'm back on shift."

"Matias's mother call you?"

"Right." Nolasco puts the cigarette to his mouth. Draws deep. Lets the smoke curl back out.

"And she told you he's missing?"

The young man nods.

"I saw his girlfriend," the marshal says, "his partner? Josefina Olvera. This afternoon. Have you spoken with her?"

"No."

Whicher looks at him.

"I don't know her, man."

"She says it's out of character—for Matias to be gone."

"Yeah."

"How about you?"

"No, I mean, she's right."

"Mrs Cardenas said Matias came to see you. Couple weeks back."

"Three weeks," Nolasco says. "Before I started a shift."

"Here?"

"Yeah, here."

"How'd he seem?"

The young man blows his smoke out sideways. "Like something wasn't right. I could tell."

"He give you any idea what it might be?"

"I don't know, man—life stuff, you know?" Nolasco flicks his ash, stares into the middle distance. "I mean, working down there, that farm an' all?"

"Josefina said he was happy. Working regular hours, no stress."

"He made more in a couple months here than a year working down there."

"Think that was bothering him?"

"For sure it was."

Whicher lets the words sit.

Nolasco stays silent.

"He talk to you about money?"

The young man grinds out the cigarette, pushes up out his chair. "I need another beer. You want one?"

Whicher shakes his head. Writes a line onto his notepad.

Nolasco grabs a can from the trailer, sits again, shoots out his leg.

"His girlfriend said he likes a quiet life."

"Yeah?" the young man says. "Things can change, no?"

"You think something changed?"

"I mean, it gets in your blood, man. Working oil and gas. No time to think...sometimes that's a good thing."

"I guess."

"You're making money, hand over fist..."

"He talk to you about money?"

The young man lights another cigarette, bobs his head side to side. "Like, not in so many words...I mean, I think it was on his mind. He said he met someone."

"What do you mean?" the marshal says. "A woman?"

Nolasco grins. "Not a woman. Some guy, you know? Somebody that maybe had an opportunity, or whatever..."

"He tell you that?"

"You ask me, he was looking to make some changes."

"And he met somebody—he was talking to about that?"

"What he told me."

"He tell you who?"

"He just said 'this guy.'" Nolasco makes a face. "This business, people are always hiring. If he met someone, maybe they were looking for workers? For new drill sites, whatever?"

The marshal makes another note. "Could Matias be working in one of the oilfields, or gas fields?"

The young man bunches his shoulders. "I don't think he's working anyplace around here."

"Permian basin, that's a lot of fields."

"Yeah, but it's a small world, mano. People know each other. And he'd probably tell me."

"You don't think he'd be out on any of the drill sites. Or in any of the camps?"

Nolasco shakes his head. "One thing..."

"What's that?"

"He could've taken a job someplace else. You know? Like the Bakken fields?"

"Up in North Dakota?" Whicher says.

"I'm not saying that's what he's done."

The marshal thinks it over.

Nolasco takes a sip of the beer, swallows, puts the cigarette to his mouth, takes it away. "I don't know where he is marshal, that's the God's honest truth. But something was going on with him, all I'm saying. Starting to pull at him. You know? Pull him away."

CHAPTER SEVENTEEN

Forty minutes later, back in Pecos, Whicher sits in the blue leatherette booth of a Mexican diner off of East 4th.

He takes a drink from the cold bottle of Estrella Jalisco on the table. Lets his gaze run out along the dust-blown street.

Across the road the Silverado sits in the lot by the courthouse. Chief Marshal Fairbank's parking place empty, his boss long since gone.

He works a plate of steak fajitas with chile con queso, rice and beans. In his mind's eye pictures the Zimmerman farm; Cardenas's work place. And the single-wide outside of Marfa —his home with Josefina Olvera.

If Cardenas left to work the oilfields of North Dakota, it would be a long job finding him.

He'd broken no law. No crime or threat or coercion; nothing USMS could do.

A black Ford pickup rolls along the street.

The marshal thinks of the SUV Cardenas had gotten into.

Against his will, according to the farm hand that witnessed it.

Across the restaurant, two tables over, a Hispanic family eat dinner, their conversation animated, loud.

Whicher thinks of Leanne, of Lori, back in Austin. He should call them.

The phone on the booth top lights up.

He checks the number—Jeff Davis County Sheriff. Sitting back in the bench seat, he presses to answer.

"Vince Pruitt, over in Fort Davis…"

"Sheriff? What can I do for you?"

"Couple things—I couldn't get you at the office, then it slipped my mind. I hope I'm not calling too late?"

"That's alright, go ahead," Whicher says.

"Alright, well this truck, this Dakota pickup—you still want me to store it? I spoke with your boss, she told me it's now an FBI investigation. I didn't know if I was storing it for USMS, or FBI, what's the chain of custody?"

"Marshals Service can account for it up to today," Whicher says. "Maybe we'll have somebody at the Bureau take it off your hands."

"Whatever you want," the sheriff says. "Anyhow the other reason I'm calling is I had a message from El Paso PD—their crime scene officer."

"Donovan?"

"Reece Donovan, yeah. The guy sent over a message—about fingerprints he lifted."

"Oh?"

"Turns out he picked up a second hit—besides that foreign national. Another name came up, somebody on file. From the state police record. Guy name of Glen Carr?"

Whicher sits forward. "He has a record for something?"

"Agg assault. Up in Odessa, couple years back. It was no-billed, according to the PD."

"They didn't prosecute?"

"Not real sure why. Some kind of a fight. Bar room fight

that got out of hand," the sheriff says. "If it didn't go to trial, oftentimes, it would've gone as self-defense."

"Right," Whicher says.

"Anyhow, Odessa PD investigated, they printed him..."

The marshal thinks it over, thinks of Carr the morning of the hunt. Calm. No outward sign of rashness at the sight of two groups of men. Mix in a bunch of alcohol, things could get different. "If they no-billed, I guess there wasn't much to it."

"Or it could have been some mistake with process," Pruitt says. "Anyhow, I just thought you ought to know..."

"Appreciate it."

"You want me to let the FBI team know?"

"I'll do it," the marshal says.

"Did you ask the folk at the ranch for their prints?"

"I asked. There's been a bunch going on..."

"What do you think happened down there? You believe somebody tried to blow up a judge?"

"I guess we'll find out."

"Let me know if I can help?"

"You got it," Whicher says, "and thanks for the call."

* * *

Across the street at the courthouse, Whicher fishes out the keys to his truck. He stands a moment thinking. Eyes the courthouse building, the few vehicles on South Cedar. Then puts away the truck keys. Strides to a side door of the courthouse, enters a security code.

He steps inside.

An empty, white corridor and polished tile floor stretches out.

He clips along to a set of stairs, climbs to the second floor. Punches a code into a secure door. Enters.

The USMS office is deserted.

Whicher heads for his desk.

He pulls out a chair, lights up the computer terminal, enters a password, logs on. Dials up the Warrant Information System at DOJ. Slips the notebook from his jacket, flips it open, searches in it. Types a name and date of birth into the terminal—*Esequiel Aquino*.

The screen refreshes.

A listing comes up under foreign fugitives.

Warrant for Apprehension

Issued by a judge in the District of Columbia, whereabouts of the person charged unknown within the United States.

Whicher reads on.

Evidence deemed sufficient to sustain charges under treaty of extradition relating to; murder, assault, extortion, trafficking in illegal narcotics, firearms trafficking.

Warrant for Commitment into Jail...pending issue of a Surrender Warrant on behalf of the foreign government, and until such surrender be made.

Murder, assault, extortion.

Illegal narcotics, firearms.

The marshal thinks of Booker Tillman. Marshal Tillman would be in Houston, now, with Zambrano—on a similar warrant.

A hearing would take place. There'd be no bail.

When the legalities were satisfied, he'd be out of there, gone.

Two foreign fugitives on the radar in quick succession—Whicher searches for any connection. Can think of none. Foreign fugitives common enough around the border. He clicks back onto the screen displaying the warrant for apprehension—along with a photograph of Aquino. Dark-haired, his face angular, sharp, the eyes piercing. Violent. Without pity. Jaw set tight. Self-possessed.

A striking face, mask-like.

A man accustomed to instilling fear.

Aquino's fingerprints were in the Dakota taken from the Mackenzie Ranch. And then abandoned in Valentine—a highway town a hundred miles north.

Whicher thinks of the Border Patrol agent, Adriana Lozada. Her talk of new, illicit routes.

He could call her.

He checks his watch.

Better to call in the morning.

He clicks to the National Law Enforcement Telecommunication System—looks for DEA supporting files.

Several are listed against Aquino—relating to cocaine and heroin. Whicher's eyes skim the lines on screen.

He can cross-reference with DOJ archive records—look for cases involving Vaughn Richardson as prosecutor.

He clicks from the NLETS screen onto the National Crime Information Center. Reminds himself he's not investigating the case.

With a few clicks further he brings up the international warrant outstanding on Aquino.

Wanted on multiple charges in his country of birth, Honduras—listed as a person of interest in both Mexico and Colombia. Along with the US Warrant.

The marshal thinks back—thinks of the feeling out in the dark at the ranch—the first night.

Instinct had alerted him to danger.

What if Aquino never left?

What if he'd been around the whole time?

Another thought sifts forward; Glen Carr. Carr with his prints on record. A bar fight that didn't fit.

Odessa could be rough, you got in the wrong part of town. Lot of oil workers letting loose.

Oil workers.

He thinks of Matias Cardenas.

Former oilfield worker—dissatisfied, according to his buddy, up in Monahans.

The phone in his jacket starts to ring.

He takes it out. Checks, clicks to answer. "Leanne?"

"Hey, where are you? Is everything alright? You weren't home."

"I'm over at the office."

"Are you okay?"

"Sure. Just checking out a couple things, catching up."

His wife gives a dry laugh. "Are you going home soon?"

"I guess. I ate already, here in town."

"Good. Well, look, I was calling to say I think we're going to head back, maybe tomorrow. Or the day after."

"Okay."

"I think Lori had about enough. It's been fun, she's enjoyed Austin. But maybe it's time..."

"It'll be good to see you."

"Right answer," Leanne says. Her voice warm. "So, are you going to be around?"

"I'm around."

"What're you doing?"

"Right now? Looking for a missing person."

"That's why you're at work?"

"I'm looking at something else," the marshal says, "part of the case around the judge. Anyhow, when are you coming?"

"I'll talk to Lori, I'll let you know. Why are you working on that? I thought the FBI would be investigating?"

"They are."

"You know, it really worried her," Leanne says, "the thing with the judge."

Whicher sits back from the computer screen.

"She's said a couple of things. She's starting to worry more now, you know?"

"I guess."

"She just worries you'll get hurt."

"I'm fine. Tell her I'm fine."

"I told her. I tell her. But she's growing up, she thinks about things now. She's not a little girl."

Whicher turns away from his desk, stares out across the empty office—at the windows, at the night beyond them, cut with sodium light from the lot. "The guy wasn't after me. He's probably not even in the country anymore."

"Really?"

"Suspect is a fugitive from overseas—half the time he's over in Mexico. He's probably south of the border already."

"Do you know that?"

"People think so. Law enforcement think so."

Leanne pauses on the phone. A note is in her voice when she comes back on the line. "But you don't," she says. "Do you? You don't."

CHAPTER EIGHTEEN

Morning sun streams through the double-wide glass sliders in the kitchen, a half-drunk cup of coffee sits on the table, the leather shoulder holster and the Ruger on the chair beside him. Whicher keys a call to Armando Torres at Presidio County sheriff.

Looking out through the window, he checks the sky—mid-blue, clear, a few high white clouds.

The phone answers; "Sheriff Torres."

"Morning. John Whicher, up in Pecos. I'm about to put in a call to the DPS Air Station down at Alpine—for a search and locate."

"For Cardenas?" The sheriff says. "You want to do it today?"

"Weather seems good, I'm going to check availability. I need somebody to talk with the owner of the farm, get details on the extent of the property, maybe the surrounding land?"

"I'll talk to Zimmerman," the sheriff says, "if you can get us a helo."

"I don't know how extensive this can be," Whicher says. "If we can get a couple hours I say we do it. Otherwise, we might get Border Patrol in on horseback. Failing that, we could try for K-9."

"I want to be sure we didn't overlook him right here in our backyard," the sheriff says, "I owe the people in my county that."

"If there's no sign, it might tip the scale, get us a warrant," Whicher says, "we can go after the records for his phone. Right now, I don't have enough. If I can show probable cause, we might get a shot."

"I'll call Zimmerman, set up a meeting," the sheriff says, "I'll get on it."

"Alright, I'll call DPS."

"You have any kind of a feeling about this?" Sheriff Torres says. "So far? Based on what you've heard, what you've seen?"

Whicher eyes the bright sky above the yard, squinting into it. "You know you never can tell. Something happened to him. Maybe some misadventure. Or something criminal. Or he might've left of his own accord..."

"He might still come home," Torres says.

The marshal lets a beat pass. "I'll call when I know from Alpine."

* * *

Barreling down I-10 west, Whicher spots the turn for Fort Davis. He signals, takes the exit road, dropping down beneath the interstate banking toward the old Kent Mercantile, boarded out now, graffitied, the gas station closed.

He makes a left beneath the overpass, accelerates out onto Highway 118.

Reaching for the phone in the dash holder he hits the number for the Border Patrol station at Presidio.

It rings briefly, picks up.

A woman answers.

"Ma'am. Name's Whicher, I'm a US Marshal. I'd like to speak to an agent you have stationed there, Agent Lozada? Adriana Lozada?"

"I'm not sure she's in the building right now, marshal—I can check? Can you say what it's regarding?"

"I'm investigating a missing person case for the county," Whicher says, "I spoke with her about it earlier in the week."

"One moment, can you hold?"

Whicher follows the curve of the two-lane climbing through a semi-desert of sagebrush and mesquite. Denuded hills of scrub and chino grass lie ahead, the blue of the Davis Mountains rising in the middle distance.

The phone line opens up again. "Agent Lozada..."

"John Whicher," the marshal says, "we met at the Mackenzie Ranch—and down at the Rio Grande, regarding the drowning victim there? You showed me some of the local terrain?"

"Marshal, yes. What can I do for you?"

"I'm continuing my missing person investigation. We ruled out the drowning victim. Dental record confirmed it's not him. We don't yet know who it is, the county's looking to autopsy—anyhow, I'm organizing an air search..."

"Oh?"

"A sector you might know," Whicher says. "I wondered if you might be able to assist? We've got a helicopter from around noon, out of Alpine—unless they get an emergency call. We should be good for a couple hours."

"What area are you searching?"

"Farm property on the Marfa Plain, south of 90. Plus land surrounding. Extending down to the Rim Rock, maybe. Depending on how we go, how long we get."

"You think your missing person could be out there?"

"If he is, we're probably only looking for his remains—the guy's been gone ten days. But he went missing from the farm, his place of work. The sheriff ran an initial search, they found nothing—but if he's out there somewhere, we don't want to think we just missed him."

"I'll check with my boss," Lozada says.

"Property is the Zimmerman Farm," Whicher says, "west of Marfa. If you can do it, could you call me on this number?"

"I'll see what I can do," Lozada says, "I'll call you back."

* * *

The white and blue A-Star helicopter from DPS sits out on the hard pan between cultivated fields.

A sergeant tactical flight officer in khakis runs out, ducking beneath the spinning rotors.

Whicher stands with Adriana Lozada by the Border Patrol agent's truck. Emmett Zimmerman holds down his hat, passes a folded map to Sheriff Torres.

The flight officer reaches them—raises his voice over the sound of the A-Star's engine. "We're ready to roll—as soon as you want..."

The sheriff steps forward, passes the map to the TFO. "We've marked out the extent of the property..."

The man unfolds it, studies it.

The marshal steps in close. "John Whicher, USMS, I telephoned earlier. And this is Agent Lozada from Border Patrol, we'd like to come along as observers."

"Brady Keane," the TFO answers, "not a problem. We have Lieutenant Garth Newman doing the flying. We'll climb to around five hundred feet. Fly mostly between three to five hundred. Extra observers on board is all good, we get more naked-eye observation. I'll be using thermal imaging, we have forward-looking infrared, we're fueled up."

"Understood," Whicher says.

"If you can search the farm first," Sheriff Torres says, "then whatever else you can look at..."

"We'll get airborne, we'll take a view on that," the TFO says. "Standard search rate is a square mile every ten minutes or so." He opens out the map further. "We can do better than that where the land's cleared."

"We're likely looking for remains," Whicher says, "if the person is out there."

The TFO nods. "Last week, we found a guy suffering from Alzheimer's—he walked off into a desert area. Law enforcement had ground units searching for days. We got the call, we found him after about an hour, the morning of the third day. You never know."

Whicher looks at Adriana Lozada and back at Keane. "Alright. Let's get up there, let's see what we've got."

* * *

Away from the fields of cantaloupes and corn and onions, the land sprawls vast, scorched, cut with few tracks. The fallow acreage of the property is dotted with brush and broken vegetation. The A-Star runs a sweep pattern, Keane cueing the pilot through a helmet mic.

Newman flies the helicopter low and slow, the turns precise, flight lines steady.

Whicher scans the ground left—Lozada performing the same role right.

The whine of the motor is a constant, pitch rarely changing, the clatter of Starflex rotors louder in descent, smoothing out again in forward flight.

The marshal checks his watch, glances at the infrared camera display on a monitor in front of the TFO. No use if no heat signature is present. He holds down the push-to-talk switch on the audio line for the headsets. "I'm starting to think we could push out, maybe."

The TFO half turns his head. "We have just less than an hour before we need to refuel."

"Can we check the ground west," Whicher says, "toward the river? Out over the Sierra Vieja."

Agent Lozada's mic cuts in; "What makes you think he would be farther out?"

"Sheriff's deputies checked the farm the best they could," the marshal says. "If Cardenas headed west, or south, he could've gotten into that country—so far, nobody's looked."

The pilot's voice comes over the headsets. "Might be some turbulence—from the updraft at the rim. We may need to put on height."

Keane turns around in his seat. "You want to track west, or south?"

"West," Whicher says. "Shortest run to the river."

"New heading," the TFO says, "two-seven-zero."

"Copy that." Newman twists on the cyclic, the helicopter lifts, banking into a turn.

The ground rushes beyond the windows.

The helo drops, settles. Picks up speed.

Undulating folds of hills are below, now—ravines and shadowed canyons, the brush thick, grown dense around springs and watercourses.

The marshal looks at Adriana Lozada. "Recognize any of the trails from up here?"

"I'm trying to get my bearings," she says.

The TFO comes over the headsets. "You've got Candelaria to the southwest. The ninety-six gap to the north."

Lozada studies the terrain from the window.

Lieutenant Newman speaks. "We can sweep, run a grid. Or we can go along ground features."

Whicher spots a natural depression in the land at the toe slope of a long ridge. "That channel down there—that's something a person might follow—about eleven o'clock to our nose."

"Got it," Newman answers.

The A-star descends slightly.

In his mind's eye, Whicher pictures a black SUV arriving at the Zimmerman farm. Two men forcing Cardenas into it. The thought presses in again—Cardenas won't be out there.

He turns to Lozada. "Coyote routes and drugs routes out here? How do they connect to what you're seeing through Pinto Canyon? And the Chinatis?"

"There's a lowland route along the Sierra Vieja," Lozada answers. "You cross anyplace from Los Tarangos to Candelaria, you head north, climb the Rim Rock near Capote Falls. If you cross downstream, around Ruidosa—where they found the drowning victim—you can head through the mountains, or Pinto Canyon."

"There more traffic this route, the northern route?"

"Much more," Lozada says. "It's better known. Less demanding. Plus, the highway's closer once you make it up to the plain."

Lieutenant Newman's voice cuts in on the headsets. "We're coming to that area of updraft. You might feel it." He points out of the cockpit window. "There's a watercourse down there—at the foot of the ridge—I'll turn us in line we can run along it."

Whicher catches Lozada's eye again. "I've been thinking about what's happening around the Mackenzie Ranch..."

She makes a face. "Somebody blew up a judge's car, that's an FBI problem now."

"But those trails you showed me," Whicher says. "Is that the same people? The same drug runners there and here? Same people smugglers?"

"There's competition for all of the routes," Lozada says, "people fighting over them."

Whicher goes back to searching out of the window. Feels the Border Patrol agent's gaze on the side of his face.

He focuses on the harsh land beneath him. Grit scattering in the A-Star's downwash, the drone of rotor blades and the helo's engine crowding with the thoughts in his mind.

CHAPTER NINETEEN

Back on the ground in the farmyard to the side of the house, Sheriff Torres and Emmett Zimmerman stand beneath a cloud-streaked sky. The A-Star helicopter is headed back for base at Alpine—no sign or trace of Matias Cardenas apparent from the air.

Whicher eyes the farm hand's aging Buick Regal sedan—sitting abandoned in the shade of the open barn.

Emmett Zimmerman looks at Whicher and Lozada in turn. "So, what do y'all think? What will you do now?"

"The guy showed up for work here the last day he was seen." Whicher nods toward the parked sedan. "His car's still here. We can't account for how he left."

"At the time, I thought he must've gotten a ride with Santiago," Zimmerman says. "Or maybe Josefina came by, gave him a ride."

The marshal thinks of the few details from his notes. "You went into Marfa that afternoon?"

"Yes, sir, I did. I start the farm work early. If we're in need of something I'll go do it in the afternoon—I picked up groceries and some parts for one of the tractors."

"Nobody knows how he came to leave this place," Sheriff Torres says.

Lozada looks to Whicher. "You think that means he's still here?"

"Are y'all aware there's dirt roads on and off of the property?" Zimmerman says. "A person could come and go, nobody here at the house would know."

"So, somebody could've come in?" Whicher says.

"Yessir. Then left right out again."

Sheriff Torres frowns, kneads his knuckles with his thumbs.

"Santiago was here. My wife was here," the farm owner says. "Outside of temp hands, that's the only people ever are here. But neither of them saw anything the day Matias went missing."

Whicher looks to Lozada. "You think Border Patrol might be willing to run a search on horseback?"

"I could ask the station commander."

Sheriff Torres turns to Whicher. "You said Matias had a friend that reckoned he might've taken off north? To work upcountry?"

"Can't rule it out," Whicher says.

Zimmerman regards him.

"You recall what he was doing that day?"

The farm owner scratches at his arm. "He was servicing sprinkler systems. We're half irrigated, half dryland."

"That's where on the property?"

"Out back a ways."

The marshal turns to Torres, "You have anybody search around there?"

"We looked at all of it."

Whicher passes the back of his hand across his forehead, feels a light film of sweat. "Maybe we should bring in a dog."

"You mean a bloodhound?" Zimmerman says. "Try to pick up a trail?"

"El Paso PD have some K-9," Sheriff Torres says, "I could call them."

Lozada glances at the land beyond the fields. "That's assuming he's out there..."

Whicher shakes his head.

The Border Patrol agent looks at him. "You think he could be out there, alive, still?"

"I want to know he didn't die out there. I'm talking about a cadaver dog."

* * *

Ranch land stretches flat, oppressive south of Highway 90 approaching Marfa. Two horses run alongside the Chevy, their heads down, manes flying—a dun and a paint. Whicher pictures Lipan Apache riding down wild from the hills.

He sets the truck on cruise, finds the number for the FBI resident agency at Alpine, sends a call.

It picks up.

"Alec Strickland."

"John Whicher, USMS—about the investigation—into the attempt on Judge Richardson."

"Marshal?"

"I've been meaning to call. I got tied up with an air search this morning—but Sheriff Pruitt called me last night, from Jeff Davis County. They're keeping a Dodge Dakota stolen from the Mackenzie Ranch. Couple days before the bomb was set off; the night of the shooting incident."

"I'm down at the ranch now," the FBI agent says.

Whicher stares out along the arrow-straight road. "I just wanted to check the handover to FBI. Did you take a look at the truck?"

"We're focused on the site here, but we will."

"You probably need to let Vince Pruitt know what you want to do."

"I can do that," Strickland says.

"Also—the CSI working the truck picked up a hit on a second set of fingerprints—belonging to the ranch hand there; Glen Carr."

"Really?"

"Aggravated assault, Odessa police dropped the charges."

The FBI agent doesn't respond.

"It may not be relevant," Whicher says. "Anyhow, I asked for exclusion samples from everyone with access to the truck, I don't know if you got that?"

"All done, marshal."

Whicher leans back in the driver's seat. "Alright, good. Well, if y'all don't need anything I guess we're done, I just wanted to check."

"Matter of fact, we were hoping to talk to you," Strickland says. "Where are you now?"

"Outside Marfa."

"Could you come down?"

"To the ranch?"

"If you're free, we could use your help."

Whicher eyes the mountains on the long horizon south. "Give me an hour," he says, "I'll be there."

* * *

Approaching the property along the dirt road through the hills, Whicher eyes the handful of vehicles around the ranch compound—sees a dark blue Chevy Tahoe he doesn't recognize.

The burnt wreckage of Judge Richardson's Lincoln Navigator is gone now.

Driving in through the compound gates, he takes in the blown-out windows of Larry Mackenzie's Ram pickup and Glen Carr's Ford.

His gaze shifts to the deserted guest lodge.

Mackenzie appears on the porch of the main house, dressed in a striped shirt, jeans, a Western hat.

A tall man in a dark suit steps out behind him, his sandy hair neatly groomed.

Whicher parks, shuts down the truck, climbs out, fits the Resistol.

Alec Strickland emerges from the house, dressed in slacks and a white shirt. He descends the steps with the suited man.

"Marshal," Strickland says. "This is Supervisory Special Agent Boyce Kelly—from the El Paso field office."

"John Whicher," the marshal says, "USMS, out of Pecos."

The suited man extends a hand. "Appreciate your coming down."

"Agent Kelly is leading the investigation," Strickland says.

Larry Mackenzie stands out on the porch, hands stuffed deep into the pockets of his jeans. He nods. Turns around, heads on back inside the house.

"We've had to close them down," Strickland says, "while we investigate. They're not real happy."

Boyce Kelly makes a gesture toward the perimeter of the compound at the south.

Whicher follows to the low wall looking out over the stretch of desert plain. "What do we know so far?"

Agent Kelly looks at him. "We know what was used in the explosion, how it was used. Other things we're still investigating."

"You recover anything of the device?"

"Some," Strickland says. "Forensics team found a number of fragments. They've been piecing everything together—the best they can in the forty-eight hours we've had."

"Y'all know what it was?"

"There were traces of nitroamines," Kelly says, "most likely from C-4 plastic explosive. The device was probably formed up to explode vertically—directly into the vehicle—a penetrator. Collateral damage was pretty low."

Whicher eyes the vehicles in the compound, intact but for glass taken out in the shock wave.

"We found traces of the mechanism," Kelly says. "Fragments likely belonging to a cell phone. And what was probably a thyristor; a kind of switch. Plus some unburnt pieces of tape."

"Any of that going to help?"

Agent Kelly nods. "The way it was put together, we think we've seen similar."

"Like a maker's mark?" Whicher says.

"Maybe not a single bomb-maker's signature," Kelly says. "More a 'house' style. Evidence of where it was likely made."

The marshal looks at him.

"Couple years back, in Juarez—El Paso FBI gave assistance on an explosion—we shared intel with Mexican law enforcement," Kelly says. "They had a drug cartel targeting federal police, they blew up a police car, killed one officer, two civilians, wounded nine. I worked on the investigation. There's similarities between this device and the one used there."

"We talking about cartel involvement?"

"Not a hundred per cent, not yet." The FBI agent looks across the land toward the border. "Mexican law enforcement examined another device that failed to detonate, around the time of the Juarez bomb. It was similar. Made from blasting explosives, a cell phone, a thyristor wired to the speaker."

"That's not common?" Whicher says.

"Some use the phone speaker, others are on the vibrate

function. This type, it's wired to the speaker—there's extra power on the circuit, more juice."

"That's what we have here?"

"Judging from the components," Kelly says. "Plus, we found a certain composition of yellow, PVC insulating tape. The tape's manufactured in Mexico."

"They found the same tape in Juarez," Alec Strickland says.

The marshal studies the scorched ground where Judge Richardson's SUV had been parked. "You think this guy Aquino did this?"

Strickland looks defensive.

"Was he involved in the bomb in Juarez?" Whicher says.

"There's no record of him being involved."

Agent Kelly regards Strickland. "That's true. But we don't know that he wasn't."

"Aquino was here the night of the shooting," Whicher says. "What are we saying—he planted the device—then set it off remotely? Three days later, from a phone?"

"There's nothing to say it would've been him," Kelly says.

"Why wouldn't it be?"

"Anybody could call the number," Strickland says, "once the bomb has been placed."

"Anybody?" Whicher says. "From anywhere?"

Agent Strickland squints at him. "See, that's the thing…"

Whicher looks at him—then at Boyce Kelly.

"For the most part," Kelly says, "the person detonating will want to have line of sight. They want to see what they're doing, see what happens, whether the device explodes—any number of things. If they don't want that, they could use a timer. But most bombs, you want the extra level of control."

"You think somebody had eyes on here?"

"I do."

Scanning the outline of the Chinatis beyond the plain,

Whicher pictures the slopes, the high plateaus. Pack trails. The old dam, Presa Llorona. "So, they were watching as they triggered the device?"

"Most likely."

"Why trigger it when the vehicle was empty?" Whicher says.

The FBI agent's eyes cut away. "We'll get to that..."

Whicher looks to Alec Strickland.

Strickland's face gives him nothing.

"I wanted to ask about the morning you went out hunting?" Kelly says. "You and the judge. The guide, Carr, the other guest. Report says you saw two groups of men—up on the plateau."

"Right," the marshal says.

"Could they have been making their way here? Were they headed in this direction?"

"Near enough."

"Somebody among the group could have been the detonator," Strickland says.

"Border Patrol searched those hills," Whicher says, "they couldn't find anybody."

"All they'd need would be for one man to break off, and hide away," Kelly says.

The marshal thinks back to what he saw that morning.

"You don't think it's possible?"

"It's possible..."

"Somebody with a satellite phone," Strickland says. "They could wait, pick their moment."

"Nobody was in that vehicle," Whicher says. "If you were hiding out, scoping the place. You'd see nobody was in it."

"That terrain," Kelly says, "it offers up enough places to hide, don't you think?"

Whicher nods.

"And nobody knows where any of those men went to? From either group? What did they do?"

"We didn't wait to find out," Whicher says. "We saw two groups of clandestines, I dropped us down the side of the hill, got us out as fast as I could—to protect the judge."

"You didn't see them again?" Kelly says.

"No. You're saying you think it was one of them?"

"Not you?"

"Why not Aquino?" Whicher says. "If he planted the bomb in the first place."

"Because the evidence shows he stole a truck from here," Strickland answers, "and then he drove a hundred miles away."

"We think he left," Kelly says, "got out. Most likely he would've crossed back into Mexico. He did the hard part, placing the thing, anybody could've triggered it. Aquino gets out, it leaves a hard time for anybody trying to trace anything."

"An illegal crosser," Strickland says, "they just need to carry a phone. Then hide out, stake out this place. Pick the moment. And boom."

"The moment," Whicher says, voice flat, "when the vehicle is empty?"

* * *

Back at the Silverado, the marshal slips off his jacket, places it on the passenger seat of the truck.

Boyce Kelly regards him, takes in the leather shoulder holster, the large-frame Ruger revolver. "While since I've seen a rig like that."

"Faster draw in a vehicle," Whicher answers.

Kelly thinks it over.

"Habit from my days riding Bradleys."

"You an army man?"

"Cavalry. Third Armored, scout platoon."

"Did they tell you they saw a flare put up? The night of the shooting? Like a military flare."

"They told me."

Strickland crosses from the compound wall.

Kelly eyes the burnt-black earth in the ranch compound. "In Mexico and Central and South America, intimidation is an everyday tool. We think that's what happened here."

The marshal leans against his truck. "An attempt to intimidate?"

"Intimidate. Not kill," Boyce Kelly says.

Strickland cuts in; "If they'd wanted to kill Judge Richardson out here, they could've killed him."

"You're saying they deliberately made sure his vehicle was empty? Before they blew it up?"

"Why put up the flare?" Kelly says, "in the middle of a desert night? The brightest thing you could see..."

Whicher doesn't reply.

"Why shoot into the ranch compound," Strickland adds, "and not hit anything?"

"You think all of this was just a warning?"

Agent Kelly nods toward the guest lodge. "What do you think the reaction would be if someone killed a US judge?"

"We'd hunt them down," Whicher says. "We'd take 'em out."

"Exactly. Across the border, high-level intimidation is common practice, it's one step down from full scale slaughter —it creates as much mayhem. I was in Laredo when they closed the US Consulate over the border, it got so unsafe."

"There some reason a drug trafficking organization would want to shut Richardson down?"

"That's not for us to discuss here," Kelly says.

Whicher fixes him with a look. "Why not?"

"You'd have to talk to your boss. I'm not authorized to share that information."

The marshal turns to Strickland.

The man blinks back.

Over on the porch at the main house, Larry Mackenzie emerges from the house to stand mute. In the afternoon heat and a rising wind. And survey the compound, immobile vehicles, touched with shock. Glass strewn over seats, across the dirt yard. Glitter. Sharp jewels in the weight of silence.

CHAPTER TWENTY

At a food truck selling tacos at the side of the highway into Marfa, a black Toyota pickup is parked up—the Presidio County Sheriff's badge visible on its door.

Whicher slows, pulls in at the curb.

Beneath an awning at the counter, Deputy Carlos Garcia raises a hand.

The marshal shuts down the truck, steps from the Chevy. "Saw you parked there..."

Garcia gestures at the serving window. "You want something to eat?"

Whicher approaches, takes in the menu board.

"I can recommend the brisket gorditas," Garcia holds up a corn-dough pocket filled with shredded beef.

"That right?"

"Or the fish tacos, mano."

The Hispanic woman behind the counter looks at him. "We got today's special—enchiladas montados with tomatillo salsa..."

"Brisket gorditas sounds pretty good," the marshal says.

The woman nods.

"And coffee. Por favor."

Garcia takes a bite from his food. "Sheriff says you ran a search for Matias Cardenas?"

"At the Zimmerman property. And over to the Rim Rock."

"That's a lot of country."

"Nobody saw the guy leave the place," Whicher says. "But there's no sign he's still there."

"Right. So, what now?"

"He may have left the area completely. I'd like to get a look at the record for his phone."

The woman behind the counter puts up the plate of gorditas and coffee.

"Gracias." Whicher pays her. He takes the plate of food and the cup of coffee, indicates a picnic bench set back from the highway in the shade beneath a sycamore.

Garcia follows.

The two men settle at the table.

"So, what're you doing here," Garcia says, "you talk with the girlfriend again?"

The marshal shakes his head. "I was down at the Mackenzie Ranch."

"FBI have been all over it."

"They're pretty much done with the site," Whicher says. "They know about the device, how it worked, they have a bunch of ideas around it."

"They know how it got there?"

Whicher takes a bite into the shredded brisket, onion and cilantro. "The vehicle never moved from the time Richardson and Eliot arrived. They parked it, left it alone. Best guess is it was put there that first night."

"The night the place was shot up?"

The marshal shoots an eyebrow. "FBI think whoever did it was looking to intimidate—not kill."

Deputy Garcia leans back at the table. "That's their theory?"

"Some of it makes sense."

"You don't buy it, mano?"

Whicher takes a sip on the cup of coffee. "Something's not right. I don't know what."

"The bullets they shot were for real," Garcia says. "That looks like more than intimidation."

The marshal nods. "The night we were up there, it didn't feel like people screwing around."

"What's going to happen with the judge?"

"FBI will investigate. Marshals Service will keep security around him," Whicher says. "Did y'all hear anything back from any of the consulates? Anything on the drowning victim at Ruidosa?"

Garcia angles his head. "Sheriff's department has a lot of open files on deceased non-citizens..."

"There anything more about the girl they found up in the Chinatis? Out by that old dam?"

"FNU," Garcia says, "LNU."

Whicher nods, grim. Tries not to let it under his skin.

Garcia's gaze settles to the middle distance, unreadable.

The marshal eats the food, drinks the coffee. The tick of an ember starting to burn in him, despite himself.

First name unknown.

Last name unknown.

※ ※ ※

The office in the Pecos courthouse is empty save for Ramona Fonseca, working in the admin section.

Whicher scans the computer screen at his desk, finds a number for a sergeant at the Reeves Sheriff's office, Camilo Juarado.

He keys the number, cradles the phone at his neck, fills a paper cup from the water dispenser.

The call picks up.

"Sergeant Juarado? Deputy Marshal Whicher—over at the Marshals Office."

"Marshal. I do something for you?"

"I need a K-9 unit for a missing person case."

"Oh?" Juarado says.

"Down in Presidio County. A farm worker, missing ten days."

"Did you talk with the sheriff about it?"

"I just needed some advice," Whicher says. "Matter of fact, it's a not a regular K-9 assignment, I'm looking to bring in a cadaver dog. We searched already by air, the Presidio sheriff ran a search on foot. Border Patrol may be able to go in on horseback. I want to check the farm."

"You think this person's not alive?"

"I want to find out."

"We have two K-9s, plus handlers—no cadaver dog specifically."

"A dog's going to find traces," Whicher says, "the guy worked on this farm. All I want to know is could he have died there."

"I can give you the number of a specialist handler," Sergeant Juarado says. "She works with law enforcement."

Standing at the window by his desk, Whicher sees Chief Marshal Fairbanks turning in from 285. "You know where she's based?"

"Over around Odessa. She trains cadaver dogs. Her name is Suzanne Russo. Let me find you the number…"

Whicher watches his boss park, step from her car, make her way toward the courthouse building.

Juarado reads out the number, the marshal writes it down.

"She has a good reputation," the sergeant says, "I can recommend her."

"Alright, I'll give her a call—and thanks, I appreciate it."

Returning to his seat, Whicher types the woman's name into a search engine—finds a website, clicks onto it. Reads quickly. Keys the number.

The call rings, picks up.

"Ma'am. Good afternoon. My name is Deputy US Marshal Whicher, I'm calling from the USMS office in Pecos—I was given your number by a sergeant with the K-9 unit at the county sheriff's office."

"Good afternoon," Russo says, "how may I be of help?"

"I'm working a missing person case, ma'am—someone that arrived at their place of work, a farm in Presidio County—and hasn't been seen since."

"Go on..."

"In ten days no trace has been picked up, there's no sign of any activity at all. Searches have found nothing—including an air search of the property and surrounding lands today. I need to rule out that the person's not actually there—somewhere—deceased."

"Do you have reason to believe the person might be?"

"I don't have a specific reason, ma'am, I'm looking to rule it out."

"Well, you've certainly come to the right place," Russo says. "We ought to be able to help. I have an excellent dog I trust to pick up any scent of human remains."

"This is distinct from scent given off by a living person?"

"Entirely distinct from that," Russo says. "I'm referring to human remains only. Chemically speaking, that's an entirely unique proposition."

"Well, ma'am, I'd like to engage your services."

Across the room, the main door to the office opens—

Chief Marshal Fairbanks enters—dressed in a navy suit, her steel-gray hair neatly groomed.

She looks across at Whicher—gestures to her office.

The marshal nods.

"When were you thinking?" Russo says.

"Just as soon as you could do it," Whicher answers. "The family are real concerned. The individual left a vehicle at their workplace, we have no explanation for how they came to leave, or any idea where they may be now."

"And you're down in Pecos?"

"Yes, ma'am, but the area of the search is Presidio County — outside of Marfa."

"Well, we're a voluntary organization. I work full time in research on a biomedical program, here in Odessa. I can only come out with my dog on weekends."

"I understand, ma'am." The marshal chews at his lip, thinks of the potential delay.

"But I could come tomorrow, Sunday? If that's not too soon?"

"No, no," Whicher sits at the desk. "Tomorrow would be perfect..."

"I could probably make it for around eleven?"

"Any time," Whicher says, "I can be there..."

"Alright," Russo says. "I don't charge for my services, but contributions toward expenses or our ongoing work are always welcome."

"Ma'am, that won't be a problem, the Marshals Office will be happy to take care of that."

"What kind of terrain do you want to search?"

"Farmland and buildings, open country, mainly."

"No wooded areas? Wet areas?"

"It's cultivated land or desert scrub," Whicher says. "Some brush-filled drainages."

"Alright. Well, can you let me have the address?"

Whicher gives the woman the Zimmerman Farm address, along with his own number.

He finishes the call.

Pushing up out of the chair, he crosses the office, knocks on the chief marshal's open door.

Fairbanks waves him inside. "Close the door behind you," she says.

He steps in.

"How'd the search go?"

"Nothing doing. I just arranged a cadaver dog and handler. I'm meeting with them tomorrow."

"Really?"

"If there's still no sign of Matias Cardenas, I'll go after a warrant for the record from his phone."

"You think there's a chance you'd find him?"

"The guy ain't coming back," Whicher says. "I intend to find out why."

Fairbanks makes a note on the pad at her desk. Looks up. "News—on Judge Richardson—a lot of discussions have been going on…"

"I was with the FBI investigator this afternoon," Whicher says, "at the ranch. They think the bomb was deliberately set off with nobody in the car. They're talking about it as an act designed to intimidate."

"There's a developing rationale around that," the chief marshal says.

"Ma'am?"

"You want to take a seat?"

The marshal pulls out a chair.

"Judge Richardson prosecuted narcotics cases for the DA at Tarrant County—he was also a prosecutor at the Department of Homeland Security," Fairbanks says. "But now he's a criminal court judge, he's part of an initiative with the Treasury Department—looking to sanction groups and individuals profiting from the drugs trade in the US. Some of those people are based in Central America—Honduras for one."

"How's that a part of this?"

"Honduras is a key ally," Fairbanks says. "The US maintains an airbase there. If our people make it known Honduran nationals are profiting from the drug trade, authorities down there start seizing assets."

"This is based on Aquino?" Whicher says. "On Aquino stealing a truck?"

"It's a working theory," the chief marshal says. "Right now, the security of everybody involved in the asset-seizure initiative is under review."

Whicher pushes back in the chair. "You're saying our side makes waves for folk in Honduras—they send people up here to retaliate, scare them? It's that big of a deal?"

"Honduras is the first landing point for eighty percent of the cocaine coming out of South America." The chief marshal eyes him. "They move it up to Mexico from hidden airstrips. Anything getting in the way of that is a major deal."

"Big enough to send people?"

"Big enough for the US Treasury Department to get involved."

Whicher looks at his boss. "I think the guy could still be out there."

"Aquino?"

The marshal nods.

"FBI think he's long gone."

"He stole the truck, dumped it a hundred miles away, I know," Whicher says, "that's what everybody tells me..."

"They think he's back across the border," Fairbanks says.

"If he's still here, I'd like to get a hold of the son of a bitch..."

"But he's not here."

Whicher leans forward in his seat.

Fairbanks sets down her pen, checks her watch. "So, are you going home ever? It's Saturday, it's late already. You don't have family to look after?"

"Back in Austin. For Spring Break."

"Oh?"

"My wife's folks are back there. I'll probably just grab something. Catch a game. Get some rest."

She shrugs. "Well, whatever."

He stands.

Fairbanks looks at him. "Anyhow, you don't have to worry about it. Any of that, with Aquino..."

Whicher tips the brim of his hat, steps from the office.

Lets the chief marshal's words go unanswered.

* * *

In the living room of the house in Pecos, Whicher sits on the couch, feet up on the coffee table, a Spurs game playing on the TV, cold beer in his hand.

Laid out beside him on the couch is a copy of Aquino's District of Columbia Warrant for Apprehension. Plus a copy of the Warrant for Commitment into Jail.

The marshal looks at the image of the man staring back from the topmost page of the DC warrant. Mind wandering, half-watching the game. Thinking of Strickland and Boyce Kelly at the Mackenzie Ranch—their notion of intimidation.

Glancing again at the image of Aquino—the face looking out is unsettling, a mask, underpinned by a well of violence.

The game cuts to a commercial break.

He takes a sip on the beer, crunches on a handful of Doritos. In his mind's eye sees the land of the Zimmerman Farm —from the A-Star helicopter. The remote terrain, the snaking river at the border, its banks lined deep green.

His phone rings, he checks the screen, picks up.

"Leanne?"

"It's Lori."

The marshal feels a smile break on his face at the sound of his daughter's voice. He puts down the beer, sits up on the couch. "Hey, sweetheart. What's going on?"

"Mom said to call. She's getting dinner."

"Oh. Is everybody okay?"

"Uh. Yeah."

"How's Grandma? Grandpa?"

"Oh, yeah, they're fine. Mom said to see how you were."

"I'm good," the marshal says. "I'm watching the game."

"Huh."

"You know? Kicking back."

"Yeah," Lori says. "Mom said to let you know we're coming back tomorrow."

"Oh. Okay."

His daughter catches the note in his voice. "What?"

"No, that's all good. That's just fine."

She stays silent a moment.

"I might be out, is all. I might not be here..."

"Why not?"

Whicher hears a sound in the background, off the phone—Lori calling out; "He says he won't be there..."

A pause, more sounds.

His daughter again; "I don't *know*..."

And then Leanne is on the line. "Lori says you're not going to be there?"

"It's just I arranged a search."

"I told you we'd be coming back..."

"Right, I know."

"Well, how come you're working?"

"It's with a dog..."

"What do you mean? Anyhow, it's Sunday."

"Specialist dog," Whicher says, "a cadaver dog. The handler's a volunteer, she's only available weekends."

"Couldn't it wait?" The disappointment is plain in his wife's voice.

"I wasn't sure when you'd be back."

"I'd have thought you'd want to see your daughter."

"I do," he says. "You know I do. And you, too."

Leanne doesn't respond.

"The handler said she could make tomorrow, after that we'd have to wait—another week at least. It's a missing person case—looking like it could be serious."

"I thought you'd be there."

"What time will you arrive?" Whicher says.

"I don't know, we'll leave early. It's a long drive."

"I might be done...."

"Look, I have to go," Leanne says, "I have to fix dinner..."

"I'll try to be back," Whicher says. "I'm sorry. Say hi to everybody."

Leanne finishes the call.

The marshal stares at the game on screen, drains the bottle of beer. Heads into the kitchen for another.

The phone rings again from the living room.

He heads back in, picks it up. He turns down the volume on the TV, checks the caller—Deputy Marshal Booker Tillman comes on the line.

"Evenin'. Hope it's not too late for me to call."

"No problem," Whicher says.

"I just got back from Houston—taking your guy Zambrano to the FDC. There was something I needed to run by you."

"Go ahead."

"This Zambrano guy—I need to know about the arrest."

"I didn't arrest him," Whicher says. "I just picked his sorry ass up."

"You know who did?"

"Guy I saw was a police sergeant, name of Diaz. I collected him from the Border Patrol station. Down in Presidio."

"You know anything of the particulars?"

"No," Whicher says. "Why you asking?"

"I had a call from a lawyer with the Office of International Affairs—at the DOJ."

"Oh?"

"A lawyer from their extradition team. They got the job shipping the son of a bitch out of here. But they're saying there could be a problem with the surrender warrant."

Whicher walks to the living room window, eyes the darkening sky beyond the house. "Why's that?"

"The guy's refusing to eat. The lawyer says."

"He's what?"

"Refusing sustenance. And they all don't want to be forced to get a court order to get an IV into him. You know? Strap the little jerk into a restraint chair, all of that. They're saying it could put him into a mental health category. They'd have to assess for that, they could be looking at a move to a state mental institution—next thing you know somebody's saying he's not fit to stand trial. It could block the extradition. Period."

"Are they thinking it's a play?"

"Wasn't the guy acting kind of crazy the night you brought him back?" Tillman says. "Didn't you tell me that?"

"I thought he was wired on something. Maybe high."

"What if he's really a wack job?"

Whicher thinks it over.

"OIA lawyer said they could be stuck with him," Tillman says. "They have to inform the foreign extradition team, you know, their counterparts?"

"Well, how'd he seem when you transported him?"

"I didn't think he was crazy," Tillman says. "He was kind of quiet. He was asking to speak with a lawyer—matter of fact, he said he wanted to talk to you."

"Me? Specifically?"

"Yeah. Guy asked a couple times, in transit. I told him to shut the hell up."

Whicher crosses to the TV, hits mute. "Something was wrong with him the night I picked him up..."

"I guess I better call this guy, Diaz?"

"Let me call him for you," Whicher says. "I'll call him, I'll find out what went on."

CHAPTER TWENTY-ONE

A blue Honda SUV appears along the farm road—Whicher watches it behind the wheel of the Silverado in the late morning sun. He takes the USMS badge and ID from a pocket of his canvas jacket. Pushes open the door of the truck, steps out. Calls to Zimmerman over at the house, "That's her..."

The farm owner starts across the yard, dressed in a suit, not long back from church. "I sure hope all this is going to be okay..."

Whicher looks at him.

"I'm praying nothing happened to Matias, don't get me wrong," Zimmerman says. "It's just with all this going on, people get to talking. Folk were asking about it this morning, I didn't dare tell 'em I had law enforcement coming, bringing a sniffer dog."

"Just a precaution," the marshal says. "If there's nothing here, I'll start looking further afield."

Zimmerman screws up his face. "You don't think you're going to find anything?"

"He could be long gone," Whicher says.

The farm owner stares out at the approaching car.

"We let the dog do its work. We go from there," the marshal says.

The SUV drives up into the farmyard.

Whicher raises a hand to the woman behind the wheel.

She parks, shuts off the motor. Unhooks the seat belt, pops the door.

She's slim, her hair short, fair, her features petite.

She climbs out. "Suzanne Russo."

The marshal shows his ID, "John Whicher. Pleased to meet you, ma'am." He gestures across the yard. "This here's the owner of the farm, Mister Zimmerman."

"Good morning."

He nods back, "Ma'am."

"Quite the drive from Odessa." She smiles. "Beautiful country. I've never worked this close to the border." Russo steps to the rear of the Honda, she opens up the door, leans in. "Stay there..." She speaks over her shoulder; "This is Beth. She's quite excited to be here..."

The marshal moves to rear of the car—sees the black, Labrador retriever. A harness is around her chest, a short length of webbing connects to a seat-belt buckle.

Russo disconnects it. "Alright. Come on out..."

The dog jumps down, sleek, lively.

"You can say hello—let her say hello back—but don't fuss her," Russo says. "I need her calm, on task."

The marshal strokes the dog's head and neck, the soft skin around her mouth.

Emmett Zimmerman steps in closer. "Fine looking animal."

Russo smiles. "Thank you. She's probably the best I've had, the best I've worked with. In ten years of training them..."

"You do a lot of law enforcement work?" Whicher says.

"We do. Along with search and recovery. We'll work cold cases, drownings, natural disasters. Things like that. Or sometimes just people that went off walking in the woods—and never came back. We've helped convict killers," Russo says, "brought closure to folk who've lost people. Let them finally know what happened."

"What makes her good?" Zimmerman says, "her sense of smell?"

"Her drive. Her willing. She'll stay on task, she won't be thrown, she won't stop."

"That right?"

"Some dogs, they'll tire they'll get distracted."

Whicher looks at Russo. "I get you anything?"

Russo takes a bottle of water from the car. "I'll give her a drink. And if I could use the bathroom. Plus, I never refuse coffee..."

"You got it," Zimmerman says.

The dog handler takes a collapsible bowl from the car, fills it, puts it on the ground. "Alright," she says. She strokes the Labrador's ears. "Then we can get right to work..."

* * *

The twenty-year-old Buick sits low on its shocks in the shade at the side of the barn. Whicher steps to it, looks inside. "This here's the car left behind by our missing person."

Russo stands in the center of the dirt yard, the dog on a leash.

"We still don't know how he left the farm property. He showed up driving this. Nobody's seen him since."

The dog handler nods.

"You want to take a look at it? You want to know anything about it?"

"No need," Russo says. "Beth's looking for the scent of

human remains, not the scent of a person. If she finds that, she'll alert me. All I need is the areas you want me to search."

"If there was any injury to the person, would the dog pick that up?" Whicher says.

"Assuming a blood injury of any kind, yes."

"That'd register?"

"Since the blood would be in a state of decomposition."

Whicher adjusts his hat. "I want to know if we could build a picture of what went on—whether any kind of violence could've been involved."

"If anything like that happened, I'm confident we'd find it."

"How about we let her check out the car?" the marshal says.

Russo leans down to the Labrador, strokes its chest. "Alright, Beth..." She unclips the leash. "*Search...*"

The dog's head drops, she cycles in air through her nose, moving brightly around the yard. Crossing to the aging sedan, she circles it. Raises her head a moment. Lowers it, moves away, starts to walk into the barn.

"We just let her search?" Whicher says.

"Let her do what she wants to do," Russo answers.

Emmett Zimmerman emerges from the house, changed now, wearing a snap-front shirt, jeans and boots. "I can take y'all up to where Matias was working the day he went missing?"

"Good," the marshal says. "We'll let her check out the farm first—then head out onto the land."

* * *

The sun is high overhead as Whicher parks the Chevy at the edge of a field of corn miles from the house. Zimmerman sits beside him in the passenger seat, Suzanne Russo following behind in her car.

At the side of the field is a concrete water tank. Thin metal irrigation poles stand among the planted rows.

"This was where he was at, last I know," Zimmerman says.

Whicher scans the surrounding land. "He was working up here alone?"

"Yeah, alone. I asked him to come out, take a look, check everything was working."

The marshal steps from the truck.

The farm owner follows.

Suzanne Russo steps from her car, lets out the dog.

"So, he's up here, what's he doing?" Whicher says.

Zimmerman shrugs. "He was checking out the fields this sector—checking on the irrigation system. The jets will get blocked if there's dirt in the water. Sometimes, the springs get jammed up—with insects, with vegetation. You have to take the head apart, clean 'em. But do it right. I let Santiago do it, he'll just as likely fit the jets back in the wrong way around. Or let the springs fly off, lose 'em in the field. It's kind of tricky work."

"Santiago Guevara? Your other hand?"

"Right."

Whicher stares back along the track in the direction of the farm. "How'd Matias get out here?"

"Santiago gave him a ride. He had the John Deere, he needed it that day, else Matias could've had it."

"He left him out here?"

"Right. He came by later to pick him up, said there was no sign of him anywhere."

Russo brings the dog forward. "She's ready to go. Do you want me to turn her loose?"

Whicher takes in the acreage, the surrounding fields.

Turns to Zimmerman. "You know where he might've been in all this?"

"No, sir."

The marshal looks at Russo. "Alright. Well, I guess, turn her loose, we'll see what she does."

The dog handler strokes the dog's chest again, unclips the leash. "Alright girl, go on, now...*search*."

The Labrador runs along the edge of the field, toward the concrete water tank. Cuts in on a stand of corn. Weaves back out again. Trots along the side of a row. Runs in on another.

Zimmerman regards the dog handler. "Ma'am, if she picks up a scent an' all, how you know it's not just some dead animal?"

"She won't signal for that," Russo says.

"You know that?"

"It's a completely distinct scent to her—she'd never mistake something for human remains."

"I guess we just need to give her time," Whicher says.

Beyond the cultivated fields, chino grass hills rise above the scrubland, the outline of the Sierra Vieja etched into the distance.

"Let her run," Russo says. "All she's doing is following her nose. She's got no preconceived ideas..."

Zimmerman watches, hands on his hips.

The marshal eyes his truck. "I have to go make a phone call."

He steps to the Silverado, opens up, climbs in.

Lighting up the phone, he looks for a network. Checks his watch.

He dials a number for the Presidio police department.

It picks up.

"Arturo Diaz."

"Sergeant Diaz, this is Deputy Marshal Whicher, from USMS, Pecos. We met Monday night. I took custody of an arrestee from you—a fugitive on an international warrant? Name of Marco Zambrano?"

"At the Border Patrol station?"

"Right."

"What can I do for you, marshal?"

"I'm sorry to call on a Sunday. We're getting some static with the DOJ over the guy's situation—I was wondering could you give me any details on the arrest?"

"Border Patrol arrested him," the sergeant says. "We took custody, is all. The time it took for you to come get him."

"You know anything about the arrest? Where it happened? What the circumstances were?"

"Patrol picked him up," Diaz says, "they were running vehicle checks out on 67. They set up somewhere between Marfa and Shafter, I think."

"Roadblocks? Or random stops?"

"Yeah, both, I think? Looking for non-docs, narcos."

"You know anything about what happened?"

"Far as I know, he was in a pickup—with a tarp covering the bed. Kind of the thing you'll see with coyotes, people smugglers."

"That's why they stopped him?"

"I guess. They questioned him, they weren't happy. He gave a name turned out to be a known alias. When they were satisfied they knew who they had, they called the Marshals Service, impounded the truck, they called us."

"You talk to the arresting agent?"

"Just the guy who brought him over."

"He was acting up, you remember?" Whicher says. "Agitated?"

"I remember."

The marshal watches Suzanne Russo through the truck's open door.

"Is there some problem?" the sergeant says.

Russo stares at a corner of the field as the Labrador begins to circle.

"A question came up over the guy's mental health," Whicher says. "When I picked him up, I thought he seemed wired—I thought he was high or something."

"*Matón*," Diaz mutters, "a piece of work, a hood."

The dog handler starts walking toward the corner of the field—head high, her stride quick.

"I don't know what else to tell you," the sergeant says. "We had him in a holding cell a couple of hours, that's it. You came down. I handed him over."

The dog is barking, now, looking directly at its handler.

Russo calling to it.

"Alright, listen," Whicher says, "I have to go. But thanks a lot for your help."

"De nada. Anytime."

The marshal clicks out the call.

He swings down from the truck.

Stares at Russo.

Emmett Zimmerman stands looking at her.

The marshal moves fast up the side of the field; "What's going on?"

"She's got something," Russo says.

"You know what?"

"Something's here."

"Really?"

"Not a body."

"How you know that?"

"She'll give a different signal for that," Russo says.

The marshal studies the dog, agitated, no longer barking.

"Good girl," Russo says, "good girl, Beth—go on —*search*..."

Dropping her head only inches above the ground, the Labrador cycles in air.

She scampers away, toward a patch of uncultivated land.

Zimmerman comes up the field. "Where's she going now?"

Russo looks briefly at the worked earth. "I can't see anything on the ground. She's found the scent—human decomposition—it could be blood."

"She's following that now?" the marshal says.

"She is."

The dog handler starts after her.

Whicher falls in step. "So, something happened in that field?"

Russo nods.

The dog is out of sight now, gone into a stand of scrub and mesquite trees.

The marshal notices a small branch, broken at waist-height. "Somebody's been through..."

Russo stops, looks at it. "Or an animal?"

Zimmerman calls from the edge of the field. "Where's it going?"

The Labrador runs ahead, deviating only rarely—fifty yards on through the light trees—into the scrub beyond, a mix of sagebrush and mesquite and ocotillo.

Whicher follows searching for ground sign, seeing nothing.

The dog stops suddenly, circles—then moves from sight.

The sound of barking rings out, constricted, agitated.

Russo breaks into a run.

The marshal feels his heart rate climbing.

He sees the dog, now—lying flat to the ground.

Russo is at her side, breathless. "Alright, okay...good dog..." She turns, looks at Whicher. "That's down-and-stay..."

The marshal returns her stare.

"She's found a body," Russo says.

"Are you sure?"

"Oh, yes." Suzanne Russo's voice is flat, calm.

Whicher steps to where the dog is lying, heart thumping.

The dirt is disturbed, raised, moved by something.

"Good, girl," Russo says, "good girl, Beth—you *found* it..."

"Hundred per cent?" Whicher says.

"A hundred percent." The dog handler's eyes shine.

Whicher calls to Zimmerman coming up behind. "Sir—stay where you are please."

"What's that?"

"This here is a crime scene." He turns back to Russo. "You're sure?"

"Completely sure."

She gazes at the disturbed earth, then at her dog.

"Good Lord," Zimmerman says, shock in his face. "I can't believe...I mean, I can't believe you've found something?"

"I need to make a call," the marshal says. "I need a dig team out here."

CHAPTER TWENTY-TWO

El Paso County Sheriff's trucks sit line-astern at the head of the field beyond the mesquite. Alongside them, a Blazer from the Medical Examiner's office and Sheriff Torres's SUV.

Whicher stands with the Presidio sheriff as a two-man excavation team and a doctor from El Paso ME work around the exposed body.

Cardenas is lying on his back, work clothes still covered with loose earth—his body bloated, the gunshot wounds to his torso evident from the tears to the shirt and the darkened blood around the entry wounds.

Reece Donovan, the El Paso CSI shoots moving image and stills.

Despite the disfigurement, and the decomposition, there's no doubting the identity.

Whicher turns to Armando Torres. "Now that it's a murder investigation, what do you want to do?"

The sheriff looks at him.

"You asked me to find him," the marshal says, "I found him."

"I could talk to the El Paso Sheriff's Office," Torres says. "It's too much for a small department like ours…"

Whicher nods. "I'm not saying Marshals Service can't investigate. I'd have to talk to my boss."

"Murdered out here," the sheriff says, "we've got to be looking at a narco crime."

"What makes you say that?"

Torres's eyes are hooded as he gazes at the corpse on the ground. "That was brutal. They didn't take much care to hide him, either."

Whicher turns to walk back through the stand of mesquite trees. "I need to check on Ms Russo…"

Torres follows.

At the top edge of the irrigated field, the marshal sees Suzanne Russo waiting at her car, the liftgate on her vehicle open. She sits on the edge of the trunk, staring out across the farmland toward the hills.

The marshal tracks down the side of the planted rows of corn.

He steps into her field of view. "Ma'am? Is everything alright?"

"I was just thinking about that poor man. About his family." Russo looks at him. "You know? And maybe why I spend my Sundays doing this…"

The dog turns in the trunk space, tail wagging, nuzzling the woman's shoulder.

"You have a remarkable animal." Whicher strokes the Labrador. "What you do is a great service."

The dog sits, serene-looking, sun reflected in her amber eyes.

"Good girl, Beth," Russo says.

"I'd like to take your number, ma'am," Sheriff Torres says, "for our department. Your dog found the trace right here in the field?"

"Blood," Russo answers. "Almost certainly it would've been. Considering the man's wounds."

"Shot here, then dragged up into the scrub beyond the trees," the marshal says.

"But the dog could tell there was blood on the ground?" Torres says.

Russo shrugs. "If there's something there, she'll find it." She looks to Whicher. "Will you need us for anything more? I guess we should probably get going."

"I don't think there's anything else to find," Whicher says.

"I don't think so either. I took her around the field a little —and back down toward the farm, while you were up there." Russo points toward the trees.

"I think he was killed here," Whicher says. "And dragged out of sight. Quickly buried."

Sheriff Torres regards the spot at the top of the field, his eyes hard to read. "*Que Dios descanse su alma...*"

Whicher cuts a look at Torres, nods. He leans into the trunk of the car, caresses the dog's coat, the velvet skin of its ears. "Marshals Service will take care of all of your expenses, ma'am, and make a donation to your work."

Russo half-smiles.

Whicher offers his hand. "Thank you for coming here."

She takes it. "I really hope you find whoever did this."

* * *

The doctor from the ME's Office, Estrella Tirado, pulls off a pair of blue surgical gloves. She eyes the burial site—young-looking, with an angular face.

"Man's been missing eleven days," Whicher says.

The doctor steps out of a disposable zip-suit—dressed in chinos and a short-sleeve shirt. "Probably been here about that long..."

"Three gunshot wounds?" Sheriff Torres says.

Tirado nods. "Common pistol caliber, 9mm, maybe a little bigger. There are two exit wounds to the back, so one round must still be in him."

The CSI, Reece Donovan steps across. "I'll go take a look down in the field. See if I can find the slugs that passed through, or any frags."

"You know where the dog picked up the scent of blood?" Whicher asks him.

"The handler showed me."

"Did you find his phone?"

Donovan shakes his head.

Whicher looks to Doctor Tirado. "Are you going to move him?"

Tirado glances at the two zip-suited excavators, still sifting through the site. "There's no reason not to. We preserve evidence better that way. We'll go through everything here, make sure nothing is missed."

Sheriff Torres studies the corpse. "You see anything that doesn't fit?"

The doctor shakes her head. "Somebody shot him to death at close range; it's a pretty tight grouping. Most likely with a semi-automatic pistol. He was facing his assailant. We'll take him in, autopsy. Who's investigating?" She looks from Whicher to the sheriff.

"I am," the marshal says "Until further notice."

Tirado inclines her head, moves off to her vehicle.

Torres catches Whicher's eye. "This has narco hit all over it."

"We don't know he was mixed up running drugs."

"Who else is going to kill a guy like Cardenas? A farm hand?"

"We'll find out what happened," the marshal says.

"DEA say they're seeing more traffic moving through the

county."

The marshal scans the desolate-looking country beyond the worked fields.

"This morning," Torres says, "we had another report of a disturbance at a property—a woman living off-grid, out at the edge of the Rim Rock. Just twenty miles from here."

"You know what happened?"

"Garcia left out for there, I came here, I haven't spoken to him." The sheriff looks toward the body in the shallow grave. "But for sure, we're seeing activity on the rise..."

"This woman's property is where?" Whicher asks him.

"Out by the head of Pinto Canyon. Not real far."

"That's what—around ten miles from the Mackenzie Ranch?"

"Something like that. The woman reported an intrusion, overnight," Torres says. "She went inside her house, locked all the doors. She was too scared to move. In the morning she made a break for it."

Whicher takes his phone from his jacket, finds the number for Deputy Garcia.

He presses the key to send, eyes the distant line of the Sierra Vieja.

Garcia picks up the call, his voice faint.

"Yeah, this is Whicher, I'm out at the Zimmerman place. Sheriff says you went to a report of a disturbance? Out near Pinto Canyon?"

"Right," Garcia says, "I'm still here..."

"You know what happened?" the marshal says.

"I'm not real sure, mano. I'm still here looking around. But I think your truck thief might be back."

CHAPTER TWENTY-THREE

A dirt trail leads out across the high plain from Ranch Road 2810—Whicher steers the Silverado down it—taking in the rolling hills; rising and falling in waves across the land, all the way out to the big drop off at the rim.

Ahead in the scrub desert is the squat shape of an ancient ranch building—afternoon sun glaring from its weather-bleached walls of stone.

The marshal heads toward it, tires rumbling over the rutted trail—thinking of the Zimmerman Farm—and the forensic dig team, still searching. Nothing they could find would bring Cardenas back.

In his mind's eye he sees Josefina Olvera—at the trailer home outside of Marfa. And the parents at the house in Fort Stockton.

He checks the clock on the dash—coming up on three-thirty in the afternoon.

No word from Leanne or Lori.

He thinks of not being there for their return from Austin.

Ahead, by an outbuilding, Deputy Garcia's Tacoma

pickup is parked up—beyond it, a battered looking half-ton truck.

The marshal slows—takes in the surroundings. The house is one floor, made from rough stone and mud mortar, with a tin sheet roof.

Solar panels sit in a raked bank. Two small wind turbines turn in the breeze by an Airstream trailer.

Carved wooden totems and iron sculptures dot the baked-hard earth.

Whicher stops the truck as a woman steps around the side of the house—dressed in fatigue pants and a Navajo-patterned serape. Tough looking. In her forties. Her black hair streaked with gray.

Deputy Carlos Garcia appears at her side, in jeans, a pressed white shirt and Western hat.

Whicher steps from the Chevy, shows his badge and ID. "Ma'am. Name's Whicher—from the US Marshals Office, out of Pecos."

Garcia greets him with a nod. "This is Angelita Iniguez. I've taken a report, conducted a search of the area."

"You had somebody come onto your property?" Whicher says.

"I told the deputy." Iniguez's eyes are hard as she regards him. "I live out here alone. Somebody came here last night, something was going on…"

The marshal scans the house, the outbuildings, he looks out across the desert scrub. "Long ways from anywhere…"

"The way I like it," the woman says. "I can paint. Work. Live."

"That right?"

"That's why I came here."

"You're off-grid?"

She nods.

"Pretty isolated."

The woman makes a face. "I have what I need. The sun and wind. One or the other. I have batteries, I store power. There are springs on the land."

"You been out here long?"

"I've been here six years."

"With no problems?"

"Till now."

"How big is the property?" Whicher says. "It's what, an old stretch of ranch?"

"Six and a half thousand acres. But it's desert," Iniguez says, "it's dry plain, it's no good to anybody. To me, it brings peace."

"But somebody came out here last night?"

She rubs the tanned skin of her bare arm. "About two o'clock in the morning. I was asleep. I heard a noise, a motor. I looked out, I saw a shape, a black shape—a truck." She points to where a rough track continues past the house and outbuildings—out along the plain among the hills.

"Where's the track go?" Whicher says.

Garcia cuts in; "There's tracks and trails all over the land, they go to old grazing and browse."

"It runs along the bottom of the hill," the woman says, "and up onto the rim in places. But nobody goes out there—this is private property, my land. It was the middle of the night, they had no business coming in here. When the truck went by, I went out of the house to look..."

"You left the house in the dark?"

"I have a rifle," Iniguez says. "I took it, I went out—I walked out along the track to see what I could see—I saw lights."

He looks at her. "What kind of lights?"

"Just lights, white lights—in a line, I guess, set out on the ground. Out here, it's dark, real dark—you'll see anything like that."

Whicher exchanges glances with the deputy.

"I couldn't see the truck," Iniguez says, "just these lights, far off..."

"How far?"

"I don't know. A couple of miles?"

"I took a look around," Garcia says. "There's a bunch of tire tracks out there."

"I was walking back to the house," the woman says, "I saw another truck come in. A second truck." She stops, shudders. "I hid behind the trailer." She points at the Airstream. "The truck stopped. A man got out. He walked up to the house—he looked in."

"He looked inside it?"

"The lights were off. The door was closed. But he looked in at the windows. He walked all around the house. And then he walked back to his truck. I saw him in the headlamps."

"You saw him?" Whicher says. "Can you describe him?"

"He was tall. Lean. Black hair." Her eyes go flat. "His face made me afraid."

"Anglo?"

"Hispanic."

"You get a good enough look to recognize him if you saw him again?"

"I sketched what he looked like..."

"You sketched it?"

"After he was gone," she says. "I paint. I draw. I wanted to remember."

Whicher turns to Garcia.

The deputy nods. "Ms Iniguez showed me."

"I'd like to see that," Whicher says.

"He walked around like he owned the place." The woman tosses back a hank of hair.

"What did you think he was doing?"

"I don't know." Her face sets hard. "He didn't bother to

turn off his truck, he didn't care if anybody heard him, or saw him. I didn't know what he was going to do. It was...horrible. He just walked about the place, looking wherever he wanted. Then he got in his truck. He left."

"He come back?"

"No," Iniguez says, "he never came back. I ran in the house, I locked the door, I locked everything. Sat up all night with my rifle. Waiting, watching, looking out. Neither truck came back."

"Sure on that?"

"I didn't fall asleep one second. I was too afraid."

"And you couldn't call out?"

"I don't have any phone. They don't work here."

Garcia shrugs. "Mine's mainly out..."

"In the morning," Iniguez says, "I got in my truck, I drove to Marfa, reported it. They weren't even going to come—now the Marshals Service is here?"

Whicher stares along the rough track leading away across the plain. "There's been some disturbances, nighttime incidents. We're looking into everything."

"I've lived out here six years, I lived in Candelaria five years before that," Iniguez says. "We never had any trouble."

"Things can change."

Garcia tells her, "We'll look into everything."

Whicher regards the deputy. "Can you take me out, show me the tire tracks?"

Garcia nods.

The woman shifts the swathe of serape at her shoulder. "What am I supposed to do, sleep with a rifle beside my bed every night?" She turns on her heel, heads back toward the house.

Deputy Garcia looks at Whicher. "Let's take my truck."

The marshal steps to the black Toyota pickup, climbs in on the passenger side.

Garcia flips open the glove box.

He reaches over, takes out a clear plastic zip-lock bag. He hands it to the marshal.

Inside the bag is a piece of burlap sacking, folded, roughly stitched.

"You know what that is?" Garcia starts the truck.

"Strap," Whicher says, "it looks like—from a bale. A carry-strap from a mule pack."

The deputy looks at him sideways. "Hundred pounds of weed stitched inside of a burlap sack. Sometimes the straps break, pieces of the pack get ripped off."

The marshal turns the evidence bag in his hand, studying the striped, brown fabric.

He puts it back into the glove box. "You find that here?"

Garcia puts the truck into drive. "I'll show you."

***

Late afternoon wind scours the scrub plain, buffeting from the heights of the Rim Rock, raising dust along the bone-dry ground.

On a flattened stretch of the land, marks from truck tires are clearly visible in the bare earth.

Whicher stands among the traces, looking back, past Garcia's pickup, along the hard dirt trail—to the tiny ranch house—just visible above the folds of the hills. "This is where you found it?"

The deputy points to a stretch of brush beyond the tire marks. "It was lying out on the ground."

The marshal looks at him. "We spoke on the phone, you said you thought the truck thief might be back?"

Garcia scowls, stares into the scrub. "She told me he came right up to the house—most illegals won't do that. I thought of the Mackenzie Ranch." He points toward the land stretching away onto the plain. "There's more tire marks out there, headed east. I followed them a while. But there's too much ground to cover..."

Whicher nods. Twenty yards off by a clump of greasewood, a glint of sun shines from something. The marshal walks to it, picks up a thin plastic tube from the dirt.

Deputy Garcia steps over.

"Glow stick," Whicher says.

The deputy looks toward the rim of the Sierra Vieja. "I'd say we're looking at a drop by air, mano. From some sort of light aircraft."

Whicher follows the deputy's gaze to the ridgeline, a mile and a half to the south.

"They'll load up a plane or an ultralight," Garcia says, "load it from a stash house—fly over the border, then drop a bunch of bales. Somebody will be on the ground to pick them up. Law enforcement are seeing it in Arizona, we're starting to see it here."

The marshal stares back toward the house. "That's what the ground lights would've been? The first guy sets up the lights?"

Garcia nods.

"What's the second guy doing?"

The deputy shrugs. "Maybe security. To make sure nothing goes wrong. Maybe the load last night was too big for one truck. They set up a location, put out lights—make it obvious to the guy flying in. The pilot drops the load, the guys on the ground drive it out of the desert, hope nobody stops them."

Whicher thinks of the empty land all the way north and east to the highway—twenty or thirty miles. "That's why neither of them came back by the house?"

Garcia scans the ridgeline above the desert. "Here, it's new. Out in Arizona, in California they see it. We've got mountains here, it's harder. They have to fly low across the river, else our radar spots them. Then they have to get up over these mountains, they don't have the power. There's winds. Updrafts, downdrafts. Different ball game, mano. One thing they got is it's remote."

"I guess," Whicher says.

"You get over the border, you make the drop, chances are nobody will be there to see it."

"You tell her?" Whicher says. "Did you tell her all of that?"

"Folk living out here, mano..." Garcia says. "You want to live out here, I mean right out here, you got to know it's bandit country. Always was."

"You didn't tell her."

The deputy shakes his head. "It's just a theory, marshal. Not until we can be sure."

* * *

Angelita Iniguez sits on a set of wooden steps in front of the Airstream trailer.

"Whoever came by last night," Whicher says, "I don't think they'll be back."

The woman regards him, sips coffee out of an enameled mug, dark eyes glistening.

Deputy Garcia stands with his hands at his hips. "There's not much out there, ma'am. Some tire tracks, debris that might have been them—or might have been there a while."

Iniguez keeps her eyes on Whicher. "You said there have been disturbances? Incidents at night?"

"There's not much evidence of a crime taking place," Garcia says, "apart from trespass onto your property."

"That man looking into my house?"

"Clandestinos come through," the deputy says, "this close

to the border, you know that. The trucks you saw could've been picking up non-docs."

Iniguez throws the dregs of her coffee into the dirt. "Or running drugs?"

"I'll call Border Patrol," Whicher says, "see if they can put units out here."

"You have anywhere else you can stay?" Garcia says.

"Why should I leave?"

"Maybe for a night or so?" the deputy says.

Iniguez rises from the steps, starts toward the house.

"Ma'am," Whicher calls after her, "you said you made a sketch of the man you saw?"

Without answering she disappears inside.

Deputy Garcia looks at him. "I don't know what we can do exactly, mano."

The marshal eyes him.

"People crossing, if they're desperate, sometimes they'll come close," Garcia says. "If they need water, if they need help. Guys running drugs," he shakes his head, "they'll keep away..."

Whicher thinks of the man coming right up to the house. Of the Mackenzie property; barely a dozen miles south. Of the signal flare there—a light displayed.

Angelita Iniguez steps from the house. She crosses the hard dirt—in her hand a rough square of paper.

She holds out the sketch of a man's face.

Garcia leans in to look.

The marshal stares at it. "I take a photograph of that?"

Iniguez nods.

The marshal pulls out his phone, snaps a shot.

Deputy Garcia steps back, expression blank. "That mean anything to you?"

Whicher only hands Iniguez back the picture. Scans the deserted land, the hills rising toward the Rim Rock.

* * *

Back in Pecos on the driveway of the house, evening light filters through the live oak onto a parked gray Chevy Impala.

Whicher pulls in. Runs a hand across his face.

He eyes the door to the house—no one running to open it, no Lori.

Stepping from the truck, he takes his hat from the passenger seat, walks to the front door, opens up.

A scent from inside hits him—roasting chicken.

He moves through the living room.

Leanne is in the kitchen, svelte-looking, in jeans and a cotton top. Her auburn hair pulled back, her smile bright.

The marshal crosses to his wife. Kisses her, puts his arms around her.

She stays in his embrace. Then pulls away.

She takes out a skillet, places it on the countertop.

"Sorry I wasn't here..."

"I thought we'd be okay, it being Sunday..."

Whicher takes off his jacket, puts it onto the back of a chair. "Didn't mean for it to take so long." He slips off the Ruger in the shoulder holster, puts it on the top of a kitchen cupboard. "Something sure smells good..."

"Chicken with white wine and garden vegetables," Leanne says. "Mom had the recipe from a friend in Austin. It'll be about a half hour..."

"You need some help?"

"I'm good."

The marshal unclips the Glock pistol from the belt at his waist, unclips the extra magazines. "How was the trip back?"

"Yeah, okay."

"How's Lori?"

"Oh, you know." Leanne shrugs. She pours olive oil into the skillet, sets it on the heat, adds squash and blanched potatoes, garlic, thyme. "She was on her phone, messaging, listening to music mostly."

"How's your mom and dad?"

She nods. "Yeah, they're good."

Whicher looks at her.

"They're slowing down. But they're okay. They're doing things, they're keeping busy."

The marshal puts the Glock and the magazines on top of the cupboard by the Ruger. "They take you out into the city?"

Leanne gives a laugh, "Just Lori and I went, mainly."

"Where'd you go?"

"Oh, Wonderspaces...kind of an art installation, she loved that—we went out to Lake Travis, that was good. Lots of shopping, the Arboretum, 2nd Street. We ate in Chinatown, lots of things..."

"I'll go say hi to her," the marshal says. "I get you something, I get you a drink?"

"There's wine, Hill Country wine, I brought it back."

Whicher opens up the refrigerator. Takes out a bottle of white wine, plus a Lone Star for himself.

Leanne adds stock to the skillet, stirs it. "So, you were working your missing person case?"

"Murder case, now."

She looks at him.

"We found the body, this afternoon. Had to bring in the ME's office, a dig team." He takes a wine glass from a shelf, opens the bottle pours a glass, hands it to Leanne. "After we got that set up, I had to go see a woman living down on the border—somebody ran across her property the middle of the night, scared her half to death."

"Couldn't somebody else have gone?"

Whicher takes a sip on the longneck. "There's a possible connection to this thing with the judge." He thinks of the photograph on his phone—the pencil sketch.

"What kind of connection?"

"I don't know. It's too early to say. It could've been a drop, a narcotics drop, from the air. It's wild country, no one's out there."

"What happened to the woman?" Leanne's voice trails off. Her eyes cut away.

Whicher turns, looks across the room—at Lori—standing half out of sight, against the corridor wall. Dressed in a hooded sweat top and shorts—pink headphones around her neck.

He sets down the bottle.

Picks up tension in her face.

"Hey, sweetheart. How you doing?"

She gives a shrug, a fleeting smile.

"Everything okay?"

"Mom said you'd be here..."

Whicher crosses the kitchen puts his hands on her shoulders, kisses her forehead. "I know, I had a long day."

She stands awkward, slouched against the wall. "Why did you find a body? That's horrible."

Leanne speaks; "It's alright, honey..."

"Why are you always around dead people?"

The marshal looks in his daughter's eyes.

"Mom said you were finding someone. I didn't know it would be anything like that."

"Yeah," he says. "Sometimes, that's what I need to do. Find people. Whatever happened to them."

"She told me about the bomb..." Lori says.

"Okay."

"What happened to the woman?"

"Nothing, sweetheart."

"Really?"

"Sure." Whicher keeps his voice soft. "I just had to go talk to her."

"You said drug people were on her land? Like, cartels?"

"Honey," Leanne says.

"Well, that's what they *do*, cartels—they blow up people's cars…"

Whicher shakes his head. "We don't know what happened…"

"They kill people," Lori says, "they don't care who it is—they kill judges, lawyers, police…"

She looks at him, eyes shining.

Pushes off the wall, a twist in her mouth.

Then turns her back, stalks down the corridor.

Whicher watches his daughter walk away.

CHAPTER TWENTY-FOUR

Sun is climbing over the two-lane ribbon of Highway 17 as Whicher drives the route down to Marfa, the Davis Mountains blue-edged above the rolling grass hills.

Reaching for the phone on the dash mount, he scrolls the list of contacts—presses to send a call.

Chief Marshal Fairbanks picks up. "Morning—I had a message when I got in, from Ramona Fonseca, in civilian support. She says you found a body yesterday? With your K-9 team?"

"Yes, ma'am, we did. The handler came down, her dog discovered Cardenas's body—not far from his workplace on the Zimmerman Farm. He'd been shot three times at close range. Buried in a shallow grave."

Fairbanks is silent a moment. "What's happening with the body?"

"El Paso ME have it. Estrella Tirado came out. With a dig team, and Reece Donovan."

"Does Sheriff Torres know?"

"Yes, ma'am, he came out to the site. I'm on my way to see him, now. He wants to know will USMS investigate? Now that it's turned into a murder case..."

"You have any idea what happened?"

Whicher doesn't reply.

"Does he?"

"Sheriff thinks it's a narc hit." Whicher watches the road unfurl ahead. "Something went bad in the guy's life—I'd want to keep an open mind as to what."

"Wise investigator," Fairbanks says.

"I'm headed down to talk with Torres, pool the known information."

"Let me talk to El Paso County Sheriff's office," Fairbanks says, "they'll likely have to investigate, if not us. But you're already involved. You have the time?"

"I'll make the time."

"Alright, good," the chief marshal says. "I'll let you know what El Paso want to do."

"I'll tell the sheriff."

"Listen, talk to me about the circumstances on the foreign fugitive arrest—Marco Zambrano? DOJ are getting the sweats, you know he's refusing food?"

"Booker Tillman called me," Whicher says. "I looked into it. Patrol picked him up—running vehicle checks. Zambrano was driving a covered truck, they pulled him over, he gave a name that came up as an alias. They held him till they were satisfied they knew who he was. Had law enforcement in Presidio hold him till I showed up. That's it."

"Alright." Fairbanks sounds doubtful. "I'll speak to the Office of International Affairs. Let me know how it goes with Sheriff Torres?"

"One more thing," the marshal says. "Presidio County Sheriff took a report from a woman living out on an isolated ranch yesterday. Somebody came across her property overnight, two trucks—a guy in one of them cased her house, it shook her up pretty bad. One of Torres's deputies went down there, I went out there, too."

"Oh?"

"It could've been some kind of a drugs drop. The woman reported seeing lights—displayed on the ground."

"That's a DEA problem, what were you doing there?"

"There's an outside chance it could've been our guy —Aquino."

"What makes you say that?"

"It's not real common for anyone to get up close to a property. Feels kind of like the deal at the Mackenzie Ranch. Plus lights were involved; a flare was seen there."

The chief marshal makes no response.

"The woman's an artist—she got a look at the guy, she made a sketch. It kind of looks like him."

"You're still chasing that?"

"I looked him up..."

"If you're concerned about it, tell the FBI. Tell Alec Strickland or Boyce Kelly."

Whicher pushes back in the driver's seat. "Yeah. Maybe I need to think it over..."

* * *

In the sheriff's office on Highland Street, Armando Torres sits at a heavy oak desk, dressed in a suit and lariat tie, his weathered face somber.

Whicher sits opposite.

The sheriff picks at the cuff of his shirt. "I have to drive over to Fort Stockton this morning, see the parents."

"Did you talk to Josefina Olvera?"

"Last night," the sheriff says.

"I spoke to my boss on the ride down—she's going to let El Paso know USMS could carry out the investigation."

Torres meets his eye. "That mean you?"

"It would."

He nods. "Good."

"First thing I'd need is a picture of Matias's last known movements," Whicher says. "I'll speak to everybody he came in contact with. Go talk with Zimmerman again."

The sheriff sits, eyes hooded, thoughts turning.

"And the farm hand there, the other hand," Whicher says, "Guevara..."

"Santiago Guevara?"

"He witnessed a couple of guys show up; maybe he saw more than that." Whicher looks out of the window—out across the square to the stuccoed courthouse. "Somebody found Cardenas out in a back field." He looks at Torres. "How did they know he was there?"

"You suspect somebody at the farm?"

"I want to know what folk know about this. Maybe there's more to know. Plus, I'm going to need access to Cardenas's phone records."

"His number's in the file," the sheriff says. He leans forward at his desk, clasps his hands together. "You want to know what I think? You went up to Monahans, Friday? To talk with one of his friends?"

Whicher takes out his lined notebook, flips it open. "Antonio Nolasco."

"A guy working the oilfields, no? He thought something could be going on?"

"He said Cardenas met someone," Whicher says. "Somebody offering some kind of an opportunity."

The sheriff points from the desk; "He said that?"

"We don't know what it was, or who said it..."

"DEA are talking about new people operating out of Monahans," the sheriff says. "Drugs people. Starting to bring narcotics over the border, move it out from there, from Monahans."

Whicher regards him.

"The routes are always changing," Torres says. "If Cardenas went up there, he could've gotten mixed up with something. Garcia says that incident at the Iniguez property could've been a narcotics drop by air."

The marshal studies the notebook, rings Nolasco's name on the page. "I called Border Patrol, requested they have units go by there. Listen, I'll start with Guevara, and Emmett Zimmerman, find out if there's anything else to know."

Torres nods. "I guess I should head for Fort Stockton."

"Tell the parents I'll find whoever did this."

The sheriff looks at him wordless.

"Tell them." Whicher holds the man's eye.

CHAPTER TWENTY-FIVE

Over the curve of the high desert grassland, the two-story white house stands out from the barns and outbuildings of the Zimmerman farm.

Whicher steers down the dirt road toward it. Approaching nearer, he eyes the silent hulk of Cardenas's car —still parked in the lee of the open barn.

Zimmerman stands in the dirt yard squinting, slack shouldered, in jeans, a checkered shirt and Western hat.

At the house, a slight woman steps from beneath the shaded gallery. Anxious looking, her face pale, auburn hair etched with gray.

Whicher pulls in, shuts down the motor. Climbs from the truck.

The farm owner greets him. "Marshal."

The woman walks out—dressed in canvas slacks, a pale green blouse.

The marshal lifts his hat.

"We asked for somebody to come out," she says, "but they won't..."

"Ma'am?"

"This here's my wife, Kathleen," Zimmerman says.

"The deputy from the sheriff's office left last night," she says, "there's only us out here…"

Whicher looks at her.

The farm owner regards his wife. "The deputy said they don't have the manpower. It's just…we feel kind of alone."

"We're miles from anywhere," Kathleen Zimmerman says. She cups her elbows with her hands. "We've never really felt—vulnerable before. But finding poor Matias out there…"

"What if they come back?" Zimmerman says. "Whoever did this."

"You're not caught up in it," Whicher says. "Whatever he was involved with."

The farm owner only stares.

"It's just the thought that someone came here," the woman says. "And killed him, shot him to death, in cold blood."

"I'll need to talk with everybody Matias was in contact with prior to his murder," the marshal says.

Zimmerman nods.

"You, too, ma'am."

The woman blinks back, startled. "What we need is protection, not questions…"

Her face colors.

Her eyes cut away.

* * *

Dust moves in shafts of sunlight in the interior of the slat-board barn.

Whicher stands with Emmett Zimmerman staring out at Cardenas's car.

"It was a day exactly like any other," Zimmerman says.

"He was here by eight, he parked right over there. He came by the house, drank a cup of coffee with us."

"He came by the house?"

"Oftentimes, he'd do that. We'd talk about jobs of the day. I asked him to take a look at the irrigation system that morning—like I showed you."

"He head straight out there?"

"I guess he would've grabbed a couple tools."

"Anybody find them?"

"I don't know. Forensics team were here till nightfall, you'd have to ask them. They didn't tell us a thing. Except not to go on up there, or disturb anything."

"So, Matias showed up, same as usual in the morning?"

"Right."

"And you gave a statement to Sheriff Torres that you were over in Marfa in the afternoon?"

"Yessir."

"You see him again before you left?"

Zimmerman stares out of the barn. "I worked all morning, then I had to go pick up supplies, groceries, plus some parts for servicing one of the tractors. I wasn't back till gone four."

"You have the receipts?"

"Excuse me?"

"For the tractor parts? The groceries?"

Zimmerman swallows. "I guess. I got 'em somewhere."

"Tractor servicing—that'd be a business expense? There'll be a record."

The farm owner nods, a little stiff.

"What happened when you got back?"

"I don't remember, too clearly."

"Did you see him?"

"No, sir. I didn't see him again after that morning. I got back, I was running around, I just assumed he was somewhere working. We got the spring cantaloupes and squash going in, the summer onions. We're clearing land at the northern edge of the property."

"Your farm hands know what to do when you're not around?"

"They know what needs to get done. We got tomatoes and cucumbers and chilis in—there's corn for grain, sorghum, always something needing to be looked at."

"But you saw his car after work?"

"I thought maybe he got a ride with Santiago," Zimmerman says. "I didn't know if there was some problem with it, I just flat-out didn't think much about it..."

"He often leave it there?"

"Nossir. It's just not like it was that big of a deal."

"When did you start to think something wasn't right?"

"Next morning," Zimmerman says, "when he didn't show up."

"What'd you do?"

"Well, nothing..."

"You didn't call?"

"Sure, I left him a message. I called, it went straight to voicemail. I asked Santiago had he seen him. I mean, I thought it all was kind of strange. I needed help on the farm, I didn't know if I should hire somebody. And then Josefina got in touch."

"She called you?"

"She was worried sick, she didn't know where he was at, it seemed like nobody knew a thing. I guess we all started asking around—I know I did, when I went into Marfa, or anyplace else..."

"That morning at the house," Whicher says, "he seem any way different?"

"I don't know."

Whicher looks at him.

"I just don't know..."

"I'll need to talk to your wife, sir."

"We had nothing to do with this."

The marshal searches the man's face. "I'll need to ask you to wait out here."

* * *

In the farmhouse kitchen, Kathleen Zimmerman sits at an oak plank table. Between her slim fingers, she turns a bone china coffee cup.

Whicher sits upright in a straight-backed chair. "Tell me about the last time you saw Matias?"

"It was a Thursday," she says. "He showed up right around eight, at the kitchen door. I asked him did he want some coffee, he said yes. Emmett came in, they talked about work..."

"He always come by the house in the mornings?"

"If he needs to talk with Emmett or me, he'll come by."

"How about Mister Guevara?"

"Santiago will come sometimes, not all the time. It depends on the work."

"So, Matias spoke with your husband? Then what?"

"Well, nothing much. He finished his cup of coffee, he left out."

"You talk with him?"

"A little."

"What about?"

"I don't remember."

"How did he seem?"

"Well, maybe he hadn't been himself, entirely. He seemed a little—preoccupied. Or maybe I only think that now. He'd be quick to smile, mostly. But he'd seemed down about something."

"You know your farm hands well?"

She shrugs, lightly. "Not real well. Matias just a little. Santiago's more reserved, he won't say so much. I mean, the hands won't stay long, we can't pay enough to really keep them. People move on, they find something else..."

"Do you know Matias's partner," Whicher says, "Josefina?"

"Not at all."

"Were you aware somebody came here a few days before his disappearance? Two men in a black, Dodge SUV?"

"We didn't know, no. But the property here's pretty big, you could drive on and off with nobody knowing."

"Are you aware of people doing that? Folk coming through?"

She takes a sip on her cup of coffee. "You mean trespassers? Undocumented migrants?" She nods. "From time to time we'll find things. Clothing, worn-out shoes. Water bottles, bags."

"You get any trouble?"

"We don't. Or we never did. I mean, we're down on the border, we're not blind to what goes on. But we've been alright, we don't have much that people could want..."

"You're not troubled by clandestine traffic coming through?"

She shakes her head.

"You have any idea what was going on with him? With Matias?"

"I really don't."

"He talk about any plans he had? Things he was looking to do? About his family, his life away from the farm?"

"No. And I've thought about it, since then. I know he lived in Marfa, I knew he lived with a girlfriend. But our talk was mainly work talk."

"How about Guevara?"

Kathleen Zimmerman raises an eyebrow, cants her head to the side. "Santiago's a closed book. At least to me. He lives out in Valentine, I don't really know about him, or his life away from here. He's not a big talker, he'll keep himself to himself. You just never know what's going on in a person's life, do you? Especially someone like him—when they never tell you."

The marshal thinks of the stolen pickup from the Mackenzie Ranch—abandoned in Valentine. He searches for a connection, lets the thought run at the back of his mind.

"I know he's worked on farms and in construction. Day labor. I don't know what life people have had. He doesn't invite questions. But I wouldn't imagine he was mixed up in anything."

Whicher looks at her. "He was the last person to see Matias alive."

* * *

Back outside in the farmyard, the marshal sits behind the wheel of the Silverado. He stares at the twenty-year-old Buick Regal sitting low on its shocks at the side of the barn.

He thinks of his first visit—with Sheriff Torres and Josefina.

Thinks of Santiago Guevara—his story of two men showing up; making Cardenas get into a car.

He lights up his phone, searches out the number for Alec Strickland at the Alpine FBI resident office.

Sends the call.

It rings, picks up.

"Morning."

"Marshal?"

"You guys figure out what went on with Judge Richardson's car yet?"

"The IED?" Strickland says. "We're still working on it."

"Well, listen I'm calling with something you maybe ought

to know—there was an incident not real far from the Mackenzie Ranch, Saturday night. A woman living out at the Rim Rock made a report of intruders coming through her property."

"Oh?"

"It's a ranch at the head of Pinto Canyon, on the high plain. Pretty much disused, the woman's an artist—but there's a lot of land, it's remote country. She says somebody came through, they set up a bunch of lights—scared the hell out of her."

"What kind of lights?"

"I went over with a deputy from the sheriff's office, it's possible it could've been an air drop—narcotics."

"Really?"

"We found a piece of burlap sacking from a bale, plus a glow stick."

"So, that's a DEA problem," Strickland says, "how come you're calling me?"

"A flare was used at the Mackenzie Ranch the night I went out on the report of gunfire. Folk there saw it. Plus, there are other similarities. Are you seeing Special Agent Kelly?"

"Boyce Kelly? I have a meeting with him about the Richardson case in El Paso."

"Tell him the truck thief could be back…"

"Excuse me?"

"Esequiel Aquino."

The FBI agent makes no response.

"The woman at the ranch went out to see what was going on—that's how she saw lights out there."

"Where's Aquino come into this?" Strickland says.

"While she was outside, a second truck stopped at the house, the driver got out, walked around, looking in at the windows. She saw him in the headlights of his pickup."

"So?"

"So, this lady's an artist, she drew a sketch of the man she saw."

"Say again?"

"She showed me the picture—I'll send you a photograph of what she drew. Show it to Kelly."

"Seriously?"

"You familiar with what Aquino looks like?"

"I am. But how come you are?"

"I looked him up," Whicher says.

"Look, we know Aquino came through the Mackenzie property," Strickland says. "But then he stole their ranch truck, he got the heck out of there. He dumped the truck a hundred miles away, nobody's seen him since."

"Doesn't mean he's not still here."

"Listen, I appreciate it," Strickland says. "But what happened with the judge, and whatever happened with this woman, I don't think we want to confuse things. I think Aquino's a long time gone. There's no evidence he's here. Our intel says he'd have crossed the border, gone south, he would've known we'd come looking for him."

"But you're not."

The FBI agent falls silent on the line.

"Nobody's looking for him," Whicher says.

CHAPTER TWENTY-SIX

Over on the western side of the Zimmerman farm, beyond the packing shed, Whicher stands in the open doorway of an outbuilding of adobe brick—a steel frame holding up its rust-stained roof, single bulb hanging from aging electrical wire.

Santiago Guevara is at a cluttered workbench, hand resting on the jaws of a vice. His jeans and boots covered in dust, T-shirt ripped at the sleeve.

The marshal takes in the clutter of tools and gear—wrenches, saws, lengths of pipe.

Guevara's eyes are dark, still. He pulls at the bill of a sun-faded ball cap.

"Mister Guevara. We spoke regarding Matias's disappearance. Now that it's a homicide inquiry I have to talk with everybody on the farm. I talked with Mister Zimmerman, with his wife. I need to talk with you."

The farm hand shrugs.

The marshal steps fully into the workshop, takes out the notepad from his jacket, takes out a pen. "You known Matias a long time? You know him before you met him here, before you worked with him?"

"No, señor."

"So, just the time y'all worked here, the two of you. How long is that?"

"Two years, around that."

"Where you from?"

The farm hand looks at him. "Out by Van Horn."

"Y'all get along?"

"Sí."

"You get to know him?"

Guevara's eyes are hooded, face immobile.

"You see him outside of here, outside of work?"

"No."

"No?"

"I mean, maybe. A couple times. Not much."

"But you saw him here every day?"

The farm hand nods.

"Tell me about the last time? Last time you saw him."

Guevara gestures with his head at the workshop. "He came by to pick up a couple things. El jefe told him he needed to fix some of the sprinklers."

"Boss told him to come by here?"

"He came to get a wrench, screwdrivers. I had to take him to the field."

"Why was that?"

"I needed the John Deere," Guevara says. "To break up ground on the other end of the property. For planting."

"You don't have other vehicles?"

"We got a ATV. El jefe needs to get it fixed, it's not working."

"So, Matias came by here, he picked up tools, you gave him a ride out? How'd he seem?"

The farm hand's face is blank.

"He talk much? He seem different? There anything unusual?"

"No, señor."

"No? Then what?"

"I took him out. Left him there."

"How was he supposed to get back?"

"I was going to pick him up. When I got done."

"So, what happened?"

Guevara takes a long breath, exhales through his nose. "I finished up. I went back."

"How far away were you working?"

"Uh?"

"From where Matias was working?"

"I was over at the edge of the property. Five miles?"

"So, you drive on back, what then?"

"He wasn't there."

"You look for him?"

"No."

"Why not?"

"I thought he got done. Maybe got a ride with el jefe."

"With Mister Zimmerman?"

Guevara nods.

"There was no sign of anything?"

"No, señor."

"You didn't find it strange?"

The man shakes his head.

"What time was this?"

"Around noon."

The marshal writes a line in his notepad. "You see anybody come onto the farm that morning?"

"No, señor."

"Hear anything?"

Guevara squints.

"Anything unusual?"

The farm hand shrugs.

"What you do after that?"

"Comida."

"You ate lunch? Then what?"

"I went back to work."

"You didn't ask about Matias?"

"El jefe went out," Guevara says.

"You didn't ask Mrs Zimmerman?"

"No, señor."

"You didn't think it was strange?"

Guevara shifts his weight against the workbench. "I do my work, that's it. Nothing more."

"So, you went back to work? Then what?"

"I finished up. Went home."

"You didn't ask about him? Matias's car was still there. How about the next day? When he didn't show up."

"El jefe asked did I know where he was. I told him no."

"You try to find out?"

"No, señor."

"You told his girlfriend, Josefina, that you saw a couple guys come by a few days before this—in that black SUV."

Guevara nods.

"So, why did you do that?"

"I told her what I saw."

"You tell her what you thought about it?"

"I told her it looked like he didn't want to go with them."

"And that's when she called the sheriff?" Whicher eyes Guevara. Turns to look out of the open doorway. "You're living up in Valentine now, that right?"

"Sí, señor."

"I was out there last week, somebody stole a truck out of a ranch not real far from here. They dumped it there. In Valentine." The marshal turns back, looks into the man's eyes. "Know anything about that?"

"No, señor."

"You're the last person to see Matias Cardenas alive…"

Guevara gives no reaction.

"You know I found his body, right up around that field? Right where you left him?"

The man nods.

"I keep asking myself—how come anybody could find him?"

The farm hand shifts his weight against the workbench.

"Up there, you know? Where Matias was at. Who else knew that? Apart from you."

* * *

Parked at the side of the field of corn, Whicher kills the motor in the truck.

He steps out, walks the edge of the planted rows to where the dog, Beth, first picked up the trace; the scent of decomposing blood.

Eying the dirt, he thinks of tools Cardenas would have had with him. Whoever shot him could have taken them. Discarded them somewhere. He scans the surrounding land, lets his gaze run out to the chino grass hills, the lines of fences.

He can make out a dirt track—another.

Anybody could have come in—from the highway, from anywhere.

Or maybe they were already there?

Zimmerman, his wife Kathleen. Santiago Guevara.

Turning toward the patch of scrub and thin mesquite he thinks of the shallow grave, starts toward it. Thinks of Sheriff Torres. Narco people, illegal migrants.

The phone in his pocket starts to ring.

He takes it out, keys to answer.

"Marshal? Larry Mackenzie..."

"Mister Mackenzie? I do something for you?"

The ranch owner's voice is hesitant, uncertain. "Look, I wasn't real sure whether to call, but Patty insisted. Patricia..."

"That's alright, sir. What's on your mind?"

"Well, it's just that last night—we think somebody may have been out here—out on the property again. Something seemed like it was going on. We saw lights. A vehicle, maybe..."

"Lights?"

"I think a bunch of people were out here. Late; around two o'clock in the morning."

"What happened?" Whicher says.

"Kind of hard to say. I couldn't sleep, I got up, went in the bathroom, I happened to look out. I thought I saw something. Lights. Far off—over at the foot of the mountains. Patty got up, I told her, she looked out too, she could see it."

"You report this?"

"No..." Mackenzie's voice is doubtful again. "I mean, I don't know what it even was, exactly. But it shouldn't have been out there."

"Alright," Whicher says. "I'll head over, I'll come out."

"Look, I wasn't sure to call, I don't know what all happened..."

"I'm down in the county, I can be there in less than an hour."

"You think it's—necessary?"

"Sir, you just had somebody blow up a car on your ranch; a car belonging to a judge. Did you call the FBI team?"

"No, I didn't. Should I have?"

Whicher eyes his Chevy parked down the slope at the side of the field. "Just sit tight. I'll be right out."

CHAPTER TWENTY-SEVEN

The gates to the ranch compound are open, Larry Mackenzie's Ram pickup parked by Glen Carr's F150, the windshields and glass replaced in both.

The marshal steers in, sees no sign of the housekeeper's Rav 4.

Mackenzie is out on the porch at the house, watching.

Behind him, the tall figure of Patricia Mackenzie.

Whicher parks, kills the motor, climbs out.

The ranch owner descends the porch steps. "Marshal. Didn't mean to drag you all the way on out here, I guess we're all a little on edge."

"You got your trucks fixed?"

"Right. Agent Strickland said it would be okay. We went over to Presidio this morning, got it taken care of."

Patricia Mackenzie steps forward.

The marshal sees the shadow beneath her eyes.

"I told him he should have called earlier," she says.

Mackenzie shoves his hands into the pockets of his jeans. "Like I said on the phone—we were both awake half the night."

"Y'all have any idea what might've happened?"

The ranch owner shrugs.

The marshal catches Patricia Mackenzie's eye. "Ma'am?"

"I thought I saw twin beams," she says.

"Like on a vehicle?"

"It could've been people," the woman says, "it's hard to say."

"How long did this go on?"

"Around fifteen or twenty minutes," the ranch owner says.

"It was just gone two," Patricia says, "Larry was looking out of the window. We both watched the lights until they stopped. I looked at my watch, it was around two-thirty."

"Y'all see anything after that?"

"No," Mackenzie says.

"Did you go on back to bed?"

"We stayed up," Patricia says. "We were both keyed up. What with everything going on..."

"I broke out my rifle," Mackenzie says, "gave Patty my Sig. You know? Just in case."

"You armed yourselves? Then what?"

"We stayed up a couple hours," Mackenzie says. "Eventually, we went on back to bed. I don't think either of us slept."

"I told Larry he should've called the sheriff's office this morning, right off."

The marshal crosses the yard to look out over the compound wall—to the scrub plain and the rising mountains beyond. "Can you show me where you saw it?"

The ranch owner pulls out a set of keys from his jeans. "You want, I can take you right out there."

***

From three miles out on the plain, the ranch is just a dot—the line of the compound wall barely visible above the scrub-filled caliche, the roofs of the house and barns warped in a haze of heat.

Larry Mackenzie leans against the door of his pickup, the brow of his Western hat pulled low.

Whicher studies the tracks in the earth—tire marks, boot prints.

Two hundred yards to the south is the mouth of a canyon, steep sided, its north-facing flank in deep shade.

"We reckoned this to be about where it would've been," Mackenzie says. "There's no regular footfall, no vehicle use out here. I'd say this all is evidence of what we saw..."

Whicher says nothing. He eyes the canyon.

"Patty and I came out this morning. Kind of hard to tell if it's one vehicle, or more than one. But there's tire marks, you can see that. And there's prints in the dirt, footprints." The ranch owner tilts back his head. "Why do I get the feeling you don't like it?"

Whicher scans the toe slope of the hill ascending to a long, high ridge. "I was out here with Judge Richardson. With Eliot and Glen Carr—the morning of the hunt." He points at the marks in the crumbling soil. "We had the truck right around here."

Mackenzie looks at him.

"The tracks and marks we left would still be here, the earth this dry," the marshal says.

The ranch owner blows out his cheeks. "Well, I don't know what to tell you..."

The marshal nods. "No matter. Y'all saw something."

* * *

Back up at the ranch at a table on the deck outside the guest lodge, Patricia Mackenzie pours iced tea from a jug. "Larry won't tell you, but he's pretty upset about all this."

"About last night?"

"All of it," she says. "About shots getting fired in here, into the ranch—about the judge's car getting blown up." She passes him a glass. "About the FBI crawling all over the place."

"Anyone else see the lights last night?" Whicher says. "Did Glen Carr see them?"

She shakes her head. "He wasn't here. We've got nobody staying, no bookings. Nobody coming down to hunt. Nobody wants to trek out on the horse trails—or camp out on the ranch…"

Whicher takes a sip of the tea.

"Glen wasn't here, neither was Amber, our housekeeper. That's part of the reason Larry doesn't want this all getting out. We get a reputation the ranch is unsafe, that we're overrun with criminal activity, we're never going to have anybody come here again. We can't afford to run the place without them." Mackenzie sips from her glass, her eyes jittery. "I think he should've called the sheriff; I told him he should've reported it. That way, maybe we could get something done."

"It was just the two of you last night?"

"Just us."

"Is Mister Carr here now?" The marshal looks out across the yard to the Ford truck.

"Larry asked him to come up. Take a look at some of the fencing on the property."

"You have livestock?"

"We don't, no. We have a few horses. It's just to give him some sort of work, something to do. There's some water gaps that need repairing, where the creek bottoms are worn away. It's useful maintenance. We want to keep him, we don't want to have to lay him off."

"How about your housekeeper?"

"Amber's only part time," Mackenzie says. "She works for other folk, she has other things."

"This kind of thing can blow over," Whicher says.

Patricia Mackenzie shifts in her seat, adjusts the Sig in the polymer holster at her waist. She eyes the mountains in the middle distance. "It's wild country out here. Wild and beautiful. I want to stay. But sometimes I ask myself—and I don't know how we will..."

* * *

A half hour later at the compound wall, Glen Carr surveys the scrub plain dressed in paint-stained fatigues and a checkered shirt, grease thick beneath his fingernails.

"Your boss showed me a spot out there," Whicher says, pointing, "right around where we parked the morning of the hunt. Out by the foot of that canyon."

Carr shields his eyes from the glare of sun. "It's a way out of the mountains..."

"A good way?"

"You can get to the highway if you go east," the ranch hand says, "through Tigner Canyon."

"You ever see something like that before? Apart from last week?"

"Folk come through," Carr says. "Migrant folk."

Whicher looks at him.

"You won't normally see it. Don't mean it doesn't happen. They found that dead girl out there? Up at the dam?"

The marshal nods.

"I don't know what it was last night," Carr says, "did you talk with the Patrol?"

"Not yet."

"They're running after people every night," Carr shrugs,

"Larry's kind of jumpy, he says he's not sleeping. So, he saw something. Maybe things happen, time to time."

Whicher studies the harsh country—the flat plain, the peaks, the distant ridges of the mountains. "The morning of the hunt—after we saw those two groups of men on the hill? You stayed high to watch our flank?"

The ranch hand nods.

"You see anybody break off—from either group?"

Carr scratches at the stubble on his chin. "I don't think."

"FBI think somebody coming over that morning could've been the person that triggered the bomb on the judge's car. I don't know if they're right. But you didn't see that?"

"One group started down into the canyon," Carr says, "you know that. Once they went in there I couldn't see 'em. I didn't see anybody break away."

Whicher plays the memory of the morning through his mind, remembering the sense of men maneuvering—the army scout instinct kicking in.

Carr works the knuckles on his hand.

The marshal notices his blackened nails. "You know they dusted the Dakota stolen out of here for prints? They found yours. Inside of there. They matched up with a sample on record."

Carr eyes him. "That a problem?"

"You want to tell me what it was about?"

"I got into a fight. Up in Odessa. It never went to court, I was never charged. It was just a fight, a bunch of us were arrested. Cops cleaned us out of a bar, they threw us all in jail for the night. Then they wanted to make something of it. And then they dropped it. It was all a bunch of bull." Carr leans against the compound wall, folds his arms across his shirt.

"So, what happens now?" Whicher says. "You're coming into the ranch every day? You're not out here nights?"

"Work's not there. I've been home, fixing my truck. Painting my house."

"Not great for business, huh? This whole thing."

"It ain't been good."

"What happens if they can't keep you?"

"Other folk run hunting camps. This ain't the only place."

The marshal gestures toward the plain and the mountains. "You know the land? I mean, outside of here?"

"A lot of it, I know. And I'm a fast learner."

Whicher lets his gaze drift back toward the main house. "Keep an eye on them..."

Carr angles his head. "I don't think anybody will be coming back."

"Maybe stay overnight," Whicher says. "Stay out here, if you can."

* * *

Driving the dirt road away from the ranch Whicher hears the buzz of his phone.

He checks, sees a missed call from Chief Marshal Fairbanks at the Pecos office. He presses to redial the number. Steers the truck along the pitted track.

The call picks up.

"Marshal?" she says. "Where are you?"

"Down in Presidio County. The service is bad, real spotty."

"Well, listen, I spoke with El Paso Sheriff and the DA—they're happy for us to conduct the homicide inquiry on Cardenas."

"Alright, good."

"Did you interview the people at that cantaloupe farm?"

"I did. None of them saw anything, or heard anything."

"Really?"

"I'll probably bring in their hand, Santiago Guevara—try to get him talking. He was the last person to see Cardenas the day he was killed. He took him out to where he was murdered."

"Interesting..."

"Yeah, could be."

"Will you let Sheriff Torres know?"

"I'll call him," Whicher says. "I saw him this morning, he says DEA have been talking about Monahans people bringing drugs through the south of the county, new people. I'll look at that. Plus, I need access to Cardenas's phone."

"You shouldn't need a warrant," Fairbanks says.

The marshal nods, stares out through the dust-streaked windshield. "Larry Mackenzie called me this afternoon—I was just at the ranch. They had another incident overnight. Guy woke up at two in the morning—looked out of the window, he saw lights."

"What kind of lights?"

"Marker lights maybe? Or a truck? I'll let the Patrol and the sheriff's office know. And call Boyce Kelly."

"Alright," Fairbanks says. "Listen, there was something else, we had a call here this afternoon at the office—Josefina Olvera. She's asking to see you."

"She tell you why?"

"To talk about Matias, she said. She wanted you. I don't know why," Fairbanks says. "But she was pretty insistent."

Marfa, Tx

On the patch of dirt and weed off of East Texas Street, the green Isuzu Trooper sits out front of the single-wide trailer.

Whicher parks in the shade, steps from the truck, walks to the trailer door, knocks.

He takes off the Resistol.

Josefina Olvera opens up. Dressed in a T-shirt and jogging pants, her eyes reddened, her black hair wild.

Without a word, she turns, leads him inside—the air stale with the scent of cigarettes.

On the table in the living room is an overflowing ashtray, empty take-out boxes, a bottle of Big Red. She looks at him, her face slack.

"You wanted to see me?" Whicher says.

She reaches for a pack of Winstons on the table. Takes one out, lights it up, draws the smoke down deep. "You need to talk with Santiago Guevara..."

The marshal looks at her.

She holds his eye. "If you're investigating this..."

"I'm just getting started," Whicher says. "Re-examining Matias's last known movements. I'll put in a request for his phone records."

She nods.

"I take a seat?" The marshal pulls out a chair from the table.

She fills a glass from the bottle of soda. "You want some of this?"

"No thanks."

"He was lying," Josefina says.

"Ma'am?"

She sits at the table. "Santiago. He made it up."

Whicher sits. "Made up what?"

"After Matias went missing, Santiago called—he told me about those guys turning up at the farm? Getting him into that car, driving off with him..." She takes a drag on the cigarette, blows the smoke out quickly. "I've been thinking about it over and over—nobody else saw that, only him..."

"Alright. Slow down," the marshal says.

"It was lies, all of it—he wanted everybody to think Matias had gone away—far away—he made the sheriff think that, he made you think that." Her voice is animated. "He wanted everybody looking everywhere—except on the farm."

Whicher sits, watches her. "What makes you say that?"

"Nobody else saw any car; nobody saw those guys." She shakes her head. "I don't think it ever happened."

The marshal leans back, Resistol between his finger and thumb. "How well you know Mister Guevara?"

"I don't know him. We went out a couple times, Matias and me—with him and a girl I know, Sofia."

"How come he called you?"

"Sofia has my number, he must've gotten it from her."

"How long had Matias been missing," Whicher says, "when Guevara called you?"

"Like, two days." The young woman puts the cigarette to her mouth, her eyes shining. "He said he thought it might scare me—so he didn't want to call. But then he said he changed his mind, he said he wanted to let me know—in case it could help."

"And now you think he made it up?"

"Like I told you—he didn't want nobody looking on the farm."

"Ma'am, are you aware of any dispute between Matias and Mister Guevara? Any reason Guevara might have wanted to harm him?"

Josefina stares. "They used to fall out, at work, Matias told me. He said Santiago was like that; he'd start a fight, over nothing, then be like, nothing happened. He thought Matias was getting paid more than he was..."

"Guevara did?"

She nods.

"Was he?"

"No. But he'd complain Matias got the easy jobs, he was full of it. Like a kid, you know? Always complaining. And after that one time he called that was it—he never called again. I called, to see if he could think of something else—he never even called me back." She stabs out her cigarette in the ashtray. "Last night I talked with my papa, my mama, I stayed over. We talked all night. Papa knows his family, Guevara's family, he says they're trouble, always there's something with them..."

Whicher eyes the room, the clutter. The clothes draped over thrift store furniture—the photographs on the wall. "Ma'am, I was out at the Zimmerman Farm today, I spoke with Guevara. Now that this is a homicide inquiry, we'll revisit everything, dig deep. Test everybody's story. But this all could take some time."

"I'm not going anyplace."

"I'll find who did this," Whicher says.

She turns the glass of soda in her hand. Eyes brimming. "He lives up in Valentine..." She cuts a look at the marshal—for just a moment.

Time enough.

For him to lock away the image.

See the wound in her eyes.

CHAPTER TWENTY-EIGHT

In the Marshals Office at the courthouse building, morning sun lights up the window as Whicher sips at a cup of coffee, eating sausage, cheese and jalapeno kolaches at his desk.

He works the keyboard on a desktop computer, logging into a secure mail server.

A message is back from the telecoms company regarding Cardenas's phone record—*Request Referred*.

He picks up a pen, drags a yellow legal pad across the desk, makes a note. Takes another bite at the kolache, keys a number for Armando Torres.

The sheriff picks up. "Marshal. You're starting early this morning..."

"I'm calling about Santiago Guevara," Whicher says. "You know anything about him? He have a record? Ever been in any trouble?"

"Why do you ask?" the sheriff says.

"I went over to talk with Josefina Olvera yesterday—she told me she thinks Guevara made up that story—about two men coming out to Zimmerman's place, making him get into a car? She said she thinks he made it up—to get us away from there, divert us from looking at the farm."

Sheriff Torres exhales. "When she called my office, she wanted me to look into his disappearance, we did what we could…"

"Yeah, well maybe Guevara wanted her to feed that to you. She also said his family are known troublemakers?"

"The Guevaras? They make a habit of annoying folk," the sheriff says, "doing dumb things. They're a bunch of campesinos, they're not an issue to law enforcement. There'll be misdemeanors, low-level fines…"

"Nothing major?"

"Not that I know."

"Alright," the marshal says, "well, I'll keep it in mind."

"I just had Kathleen Zimmerman call me," Torres says. "Asking for a deputy to post up at the farm overnight."

"Did something else happen?"

"No. But she just spent ten minutes telling me how they can't sleep at night, they don't feel safe anymore."

"You tell her what you told me? About drugs getting moved through the county?"

"Why would I do that?"

"We need to make sure we don't put ideas out there before we know what's going on." Whicher turns the pen in his hand. "Listen, I'll call DEA, you have a contact I should speak to?"

"Delfina Ruiz."

"She know about people running drugs up into Monahans? New people?"

"It was her told me about it…"

"Where's she based?"

"Out of Odessa."

"Alright, I'll look her up. I'll check it out."

"Let me know what she says?"

"I'll be sure to do that." The marshal finishes the call.

He takes a sip of the coffee, finishes the last of the kolaches, cleans his hands with a napkin. Straightens the dark red necktie, gets up from the desk.

He crosses the office, knocks at Chief Marshal Fairbank's door.

She calls through; "Come."

Whicher opens up, enters.

Fairbanks looks at him from a pile of paperwork.

"I need to put in for a warrant for Cardenas's phone records—telecoms company want something in place."

"Maybe not a bad idea," the chief marshal says, "in case we run into any problem."

"I should be able to get it today, tomorrow at the latest."

"You have other lines of inquiry?"

"I want to set up a meeting with a DEA agent out of Odessa. Delfina Ruiz, you know her?"

"I've met her."

"Sheriff Torres says DEA are concerned with new routes opening up from across the border. I'll talk to them, see what they think about what happened at the Zimmerman Farm."

"Alright, good." Fairbanks lowers her eyeglasses, looks at him over the tops of the steel frames. "That extradition arrestee? Zambrano. Still not eating. Refusing food."

"That a problem?"

"Not to me. But according to the DOJ team, it's becoming an issue to them—if they want to get him on a flight out of the country. Another thing—the prison staff say he's asking for you."

* * *

Monahans, Ward County, Tx

. . .

In the car lot of a ranch supply south of I-20 in the town of Monahans, a gray, Ford Crown Victoria pulls in from the highway. The woman driving, a Latina in her thirties, steers the non-descript saloon into the next-but-one empty bay beside the marshal's truck.

She exits the vehicle, athletic looking, her hair cut short—wearing chinos and a pale blue shirt.

She scans the few parked cars before making eye contact.

Whicher steps from the Chevy. "Agent Ruiz?"

"Marshal?"

He offers his hand.

She takes it.

"Sheriff Torres thinks you need to talk to me?" Ruiz takes him in, the suit, the hat.

"We had a couple of incidents we're concerned with."

"You had a judge's car blown up, no?"

The marshal puts his head on one side.

"FBI have been in touch—about that." She cracks a grin. "So, what can we do for the US Marshals?"

"I'm investigating the murder of a farm worker," Whicher says, "outside of Marfa. A guy name of Matias Cardenas—he went missing nearly two weeks back. We found his body on the farm he was working at, Sunday. He'd been shot to death at close range. So far, we have no idea why anybody would want to kill him. Sheriff told me you're concerned about an increase in narcotics traffic."

"Oh?"

"There's the possibility he could've been mixed up in it."

"What makes you say that?"

Whicher gazes at a steady stream of trucks rolling along the flat highway. "Sheriff said DEA are looking into new routes opening up—coming through the south of his county, transiting to here."

Agent Ruiz regards him. "You have a specific link with this farm worker?"

"Before we found his body, he was reported missing," Whicher says, "I agreed to look for him. I got a lead for a guy out here."

"In Monahans?"

"Victim worked in oil before he was a farm worker—I talked to a friend of his who said he met someone here—somebody offering some kind of 'opportunity.'"

"He told you that?"

"He would've been making squat working on a farm—the guy here thought Cardenas could've been interested making a score."

"What's the guy's name?"

"Nolasco. Antonio Nolasco."

Ruiz shakes her head. "Never heard of him."

"We don't know what kind of opportunity it was—maybe it was legit," Whicher says. "But it could've been something else; something to put him in harm's way."

"Well, what did you want from me?"

"Put me in the picture? About what you think is going on here?"

"Here?" Ruiz says. "In Monahans?"

The marshal nods.

"I can do that. I can show you." She cuts a look at the Silverado. "I like your ride, marshal, but we're going to stand out in that, uh?" She opens up the door of the Crown Vic. "Let's keep it under the radar, take my car."

* * *

The drive to the north side of I-20 is a short one—the businesses of a Permian basin oil town everywhere—equipment rental, welders and fabricators, chemical companies, cement supply.

"We're in the middle of oil and gas country," Ruiz says. "Drilling, fracking, whatever's going on, it's going on here."

"Right," the marshal says.

"Above all, it's being serviced. Economic activity is at a high level, meaning jobs, meaning people—a transient population—movement in and out of the area at correspondingly high rates." She gestures out of the window of the car. "Take a look around, you'll see big rigs, trucks and vans everywhere—moving things in and out of here all the time."

"Headed where?"

"Drill sites," Ruiz says, "out to the rigs and back. But there's also parts and supply—a lot of materials need bringing in from outside of the area. It's a hub town, hooked into everything that goes on."

On the main drag of West Sealey, the DEA agent steers past a liquor store, a thrifty mart, a drugs testing center. Companies offering blow out prevention, hydrostatic testing.

"So, what is going on?" Whicher says.

"Some of the loads out of here are packing more than pipes or truck parts," Ruiz says. "They're hauling Mexican Green and Angel Powder, you know? Ditch Weed and Queso Blanco."

The marshal nods.

"So, marijuana and coke, illegal narcotics," Ruiz says, "brought in from over the border. You drop down to I-10 from here, drop south—a couple hours you're into Marfa, no sweat."

"So?"

"A mule crossing the border, looking to hit the road network, that's a lot of lonesome, empty country to hide out in." Ruiz cruises slow, makes a turn, crosses a set of railroad tracks onto North Main. "Most of everything coming in over the southern border is through the ports of entry—into major urban conurbations. It's still super-hard to bring in volume out here," she says. "With the level of law enforcement; plus the land is unforgiving—it's a dangerous crossing. But at low level, it goes on."

"That's what we're talking about?" Whicher says.

"Low level—in comparison to a freight train hauling a couple cars packed with coke. Out in country, it's mules looking to hike it in. Cross the river, get through the mountains—if they can do that—hike thirty miles of desert, if they can. Then try to hook up with a ride."

"That's what I think we're looking at," Whicher says.

"And the DEA would agree," Ruiz says, "and so would Border Patrol. It's a couple mules here, four or five there. They make it to a highway, somebody shows up in a pickup truck. The truck heads north."

"How come you're talking with Sheriff Torres?" Whicher says.

"Those trucks are starting to show up around here," the DEA agent says. "The loads get onto parts trucks, inside supply vans—a couple bales here or there. And sometimes, we'll find them. Sometimes not. But other times, they'll say, 'screw it', they'll load up fifty bales, see if they can get it through. You know? Get that up around Midland, on it goes. On out to Dallas or Albuquerque, wherever..."

"What do you want from Sheriff Torres?"

"We want him in the picture," Ruiz says. "We need more eyes and ears."

* * *

On the northwest side of town, Delfina Ruiz pulls the Crown Vic over at the curb a block from an elementary school on a residential street.

Whicher surveys the single-story clapboard houses and trailer homes.

"There's a guy lives in the third house down, across the block there." Ruiz lifts a finger from the steering wheel, indicating discreetly. "At night, he takes his car—you see the Camry, beneath the tree?"

The marshal picks it out.

"Couple nights a week, he drives it down to Pecos, where you're at, on down I-20, and then down around Valentine and Marfa, out on the highway there? He'll pick up a bale or two," Ruiz says, "marijuana, a couple hundred pounds maybe—then bring it back up here. He unloads it at a car wash, in the morning a guy in a truck parts van swings by, he drives it up to Midland."

"You've seen him do it?"

"We're just giving him enough rope," Ruiz says. "We'll bust him, we'll use him as a stepping stone. Low-level guys don't have money for an attorney..."

"They'll trade information for a plea," Whicher says.

"So, point one, we try to identify the source—which cartel did it come from? Is it Sinaloa, is it Juarez, is it Zeta, what is it?" Ruiz says. "Right now, we think it's probably a mix—different sources testing things out—trying new routes, small routes, seeing what happens. Somebody gets caught or killed, too bad. They lose the bundles, so what? They don't care. They try again, try another variation. Find more mules, more Camry guys, more van drivers..."

"But there's competition?" Whicher says. "Even for the smaller routes?"

"Everybody wants to control the turf," Ruiz says. "And

nobody's about to let that happen. So people step on each other's toes—sometimes they don't even mean to."

The marshal stares through the windshield at the houses on the lane.

"So, we see how much we can learn from a guy like this guy," Ruiz says, "before we bust him."

"There more like him around here?"

The DEA agent nods. "We think we know who runs it this end, who's controlling it, a guy the other side of town. New guy—we think he's organizing new routes."

Whicher eyes the Camry parked at the house.

"So, your murder victim?" Ruiz says, "What can you tell me about him?"

"He worked in oil," the marshal says. "Then he quit. Started working as a farm hand."

"You know why?"

"According to his girlfriend, he liked the quiet life. According to the buddy I saw out here, he burned out working in oil, got sick of it."

"But the money, uh?"

"Could he have been on a payroll?" Whicher says. "Helping some of those mules make it through?"

"A way in through private farmland would be something..." Ruiz says. "A farm hand could shelter mules during the day, give them food, water. Till nighttime, till they could get back moving, try to make it to the highway."

Whicher rubs a hand across his jaw.

"What if the farm owner was involved, too?"

"I don't know," Whicher says. "Doesn't feel that way."

Ruiz cracks a dry laugh. "This line of work, maybe you see the worst in people—but money as big as this can be, don't rule it out..."

The marshal shifts in his seat. "Maybe Cardenas wanted out? The victim..."

"Yeah," Ruiz says, "there's no 'out.' He takes their money for a while, then he wants to quit on them…"

"Another farm hand working there told me two men came to see Cardenas—they made him get into a car."

"Oh, hello…" Ruiz says.

"Nobody else saw it happen."

She cuts him a sideways look.

"There's nothing to say it couldn't have been the other farm hand," Whicher says, "the other hand working the angle. Victim finds out—the other hand kills him, to stop him talking."

"Or they get one of their enforcers to do it. You think your farm owner's making bank?" Ruiz says. "Growing a bunch of corn and whatever…melons?"

"I'm waiting on the victim's phone records," Whicher says. "Maybe that could help."

"You have his phone?"

"We don't."

"Then forget about it," Ruiz tells him. "If he was involved with anyone running drugs, first thing they'd do is get him a throwaway, something cheap. Any calls, he'd make them with that. And there wouldn't be any. If they came out to the farm to talk, that's why they came; no phone calls…"

"How about your guy across town," Whicher says, "the guy organizing all this?"

The DEA agent shakes her head. "That's our guy, sorry. Uh-uh. If USMS want to look at him, I'd have to ask my boss. Your farm hand getting shot is a foot soldier…"

"You're after chain of command."

"Doing my job, cowboy."

The marshal feels his mood descending. "Alright. Well, I guess I need to think about it."

"Or you can go one better," Ruiz says. "You need to do what we do. You need to catch somebody in the act."

CHAPTER TWENTY-NINE

In the car wash off the main drag through the center of Monahans, three young Hispanics wash and rinse the Silverado—ragging the wheels, cleaning the glass, stripping away the dried-on dirt and dust of the road.

In the shade thrown from the wall of a neighboring hardware store, Whicher checks his phone—sees a message from Ramona Fonseca—in admin support—about a missed call from Boyce Kelly, the FBI lead on the Richardson case. Plus a reply from the phone company; agreeing access per the terms of the warrant from a duty judge.

He leans against the wall, eyes a twisted pile of iron and metal in a reclamation yard beyond the railroad tracks. Thinks of Cardenas's phone; no drug transactions would likely be on the record. But the log could give up something, some unexpected number, a sideways lead.

He watches the young men working on his truck. Wonders which car wash the DEA were watching.

He finds the number for Boyce Kelly, calls it. Listens to it ring.

The FBI agent picks up.

"You wanted to speak to me?" Whicher says.

"Marshal, yes. Alec Strickland told me the two of you talked yesterday—about a possibility our guy Aquino is still around?"

"There was another incident," Whicher says, "at a ranch not real far from where the judge's car was blown up."

"How come you're making a link to Aquino?"

"I went out with a deputy from the sheriff's office. Spoke with a witness there. There's some similarities to what folk reported at the Mackenzie Ranch."

"We think he's long gone," Kelly says. "Our intel has him both sides of the border; more often than not we know he's south of the line. If he comes our side, he's running a risk, he knows that. Right now, he'd be a fool to be anywhere on the US side, with the FBI investigating."

"I'm letting you know what's happening on the ground," the marshal says.

"It's appreciated," Kelly says, "I want the Marshals Service to know that. But I'm not about to commit resources looking for him."

"Strickland tell you about the sketch?"

"Drawn by the witness? Yes, he did."

"Kind of looks like him."

"We don't think he's out there."

"So y'all don't want the sketch?"

"We'll look at any evidence you want to submit."

"Larry Mackenzie told me something happened down on his ranch Sunday night," Whicher says. "He saw lights—out in the dark. Something like the first night I went out there, the night they called 911. I went over to talk to him about it."

The FBI agent's voice tightens. "Why didn't you call us?"

"I'm calling you now."

"Whatever's ongoing on the terrain out there," Kelly says, "my investigation regards how and why Judge Richardson was targeted. No more, no less. I'm responsible for the focus of the investigation, I don't want to link it with everything that could be going on in the locale."

"But if he's still out there, there's a question you need to answer," Whicher says.

"And what's that?"

"If he's still out there, what does he want?"

* * *

Back at the office in Pecos, Whicher scrolls the call log from Matias Cardenas's phone. He can get it to tech support, have them run the numbers through software, see if they can generate names. Without the physical phone, ninety percent of the useful information will be unavailable—he can apply for a further warrant, try to look at iOS data.

All of that will take time.

The marshal closes the log screen, tries a different tack.

He brings up the search function on the computer—sets the filter to files for arrest and prosecution. Types in the name, *Guevara*.

A list comes up.

He scans it. Sits back.

Guevara, Tomas, in Van Horn—DUI

Guevara, Domingo, in Fort Stockton—charge of assault—jail sentence, one year.

He reads on.

Guevara, Alfonso, Marfa—public nuisance—a misdemeanor fine.

Guevara, Emiliano, El Paso—arrest and prosecution for trafficking of illegal narcotics by agents from ICE Homeland Security. He clicks onto a sub file. Reads the brief details.

Arrest made at a Border Patrol immigration checkpoint—East El Paso. Vehicle referred for secondary inspection.

Felony amounts of cocaine, heroin, meth and fentanyl found inside a spare wheel.

He writes down the details on a legal pad. Along with the name—*Emiliano Guevara*.

The door to the office opens—Marshal Booker Tillman enters.

Whicher raises a hand. "Chief marshal says our H-Town guy is still refusing sustenance. Said he's been asking for me."

Tillman nods toward the office door at the far side of the room. "You just picked him up, right?"

"Didn't even arrest him."

Tillman shrugs, sits down at his desk. Takes off his black Stetson. Lights up his computer terminal.

The phone in Whicher's pocket starts to ring.

He clicks to answer.

"Marshal? Adriana Lozada, from Border Patrol. Sheriff Torres called—about the murder of your missing farm hand—Matias Cardenas? Plus an incident at a ranch belonging to an Angelita Iniguez?"

"I'm investigating both," the marshal says. "Plus, there was another incident Sunday at the Mackenzie Ranch."

"What happened there?"

"Larry Mackenzie reported individuals on his land overnight—he saw lights."

"Alright, well listen," Lozada says, "we're running surveillance tonight, including a sweep of that sector. We have air support, we scheduled it a couple weeks back, but we're shifting the on-target zone to cover the Canyon and the Chinati Mountains. I wanted to know did you want to take part?"

"Tonight?"

"If we flush anybody out, you could get first look. Maybe it'd be useful?"

"I have to interview the family of the murder victim—let me check I can make it. What time's your op?"

"From zero-one-three-o."

"Late one."

"Yeah, well. They work late, these people."

The marshal thinks about it. "Alright, well listen, count me in."

"You want to do it?"

"I'll call, but I should be okay."

* * *

Driving down the flat highway for Fort Stockton, Whicher rolls the windows on the truck, lets air from the desert scrub blow in through the cab.

The road stretches out, power poles and lines marking out an unwavering course.

He thinks of the parents, Cardenas's parents. Questions they'll want answered. The little he can give them. Things he'll have to say.

He should call El Paso ME—Estrella Tirado. They had the body, he'd need to check for any update. The parents would want to know when they could bury their son.

Wind buffeting the cab, he stares out at the endless horizon—the tan earth, the mesquite green.

A square of bright red floats from the haze above the asphalt road—the sign for the Reeves Rifle Club.

He thinks of the big range. How long since he went out?

Nearly six months since he last requalified with the USMS firearms instructor—he'd have to book a test, set it up. Primary handgun; seventy per cent to qualify.

He passes the turnoff for the range.

He'd have to come out.

Alongside primary, he'd need to retake the tactical course

for M4 carbine. Plus the shotgun element for the 870—he makes a mental note; practice, get sharp.

He sets the truck onto cruise, scrolls the phone for a number, sends a call.

A woman's voice comes on the line. "El Paso Medical Examiner, how may I help?"

"This is Deputy Marshal Whicher, from USMS Western District—I'd like to talk with Estrella Tirado—it's in connection with a homicide case."

"One moment marshal," the woman says, "can you hold?"

The line clicks over. Goes dead a moment. Picks up.

"Doctor Tirado..."

"Doc, I'm calling about Matias Cardenas—I'm on my way to talk with the parents. We have anything?"

"There's been no autopsy yet," the doctor says. "We have preliminary findings..."

"We have an approximate time of death?"

"The state of decomposition is consistent with the length of time he's been missing," Tirado says.

"And the shots were fired from close range?"

"They were."

"Like, what, ten feet? Closer? Face-to-face?"

"Up close," Tirado says.

"There any evidence of narcotics?"

"No, marshal. And he wasn't a user, either."

"You know that?"

"We've run initial tox tests—hair and bloods show no sign of drugs use."

"Did you test his hands?"

"We did, we swabbed. We didn't find any evidence he handled narcotics either. We'll have a full report post-autopsy," Tirado says, "but it's going to be a few days."

"Was there anything else," Whicher says, "right off the bat?"

"There's some bruising around his face," Tirado says. "And partially healed contusions—consistent with being hit."

Whicher shifts in the driver's seat. "Hit how?"

"Punched or maybe slapped, no blunt force trauma."

"Somebody knocked him around?"

The doctor doesn't answer for a moment. "With the decomposition to the skin surface, we'd need to be careful about when it occurred," she says. "But it was ante-mortem, not long enough for the contusions to heal, or for the bruising to disappear."

Whicher thinks about it. "Would any of that have been visible on him?"

"Possibly. But maybe not," Tirado says. "It's not pronounced, he wasn't beaten up or anything—it looks like somebody just struck him. If you give us time, we'll do our job, we can let you know more, marshal."

"Copy that."

"We're probably looking at later this week."

"Let me know when you have more?" Whicher says. "And thanks."

The marshal clicks off the call.

* * *

Guadalupe Cardenas serves iced tea in the living room of the house on Chaparral Street, her shoulders rounded, face a numb mask, her dark eyes watery.

Whicher takes the glass she offers. "Gracias, señora."

Pablo Cardenas sits, his body coiled. "Sheriff Torres came by yesterday," he says, face bleak. "He says its better you investigate."

Whicher nods. "Marshals Service has a long reach."

"You said you'd find him...and you found him." The man's voice falters. "So, find who did this..."

The room falls silent.

Cardenas runs a hand over his face. Regains composure.

"Your son was killed at work," Whicher keeps his voice even, "the same day he went missing—most likely by somebody he knew." He looks from Pablo Cardenas to Guadalupe.

Neither speaks.

"He was shot at close range. It's rare for anybody to be killed by somebody unknown to them. So, one of the things I need to ask you to do is to try to think of anyone he knew who might have wished him harm."

Guadalupe Cardenas searches his face.

Pablo Cardenas leans forward, hands clasped together, his body braced.

"Somewhere, there could be something," Whicher says. "Could you tell me the last time you saw your son?"

Guadalupe winces at the question.

Pablo Cardenas stares at the floor between his feet. "About a week...before he went missing. He stopped by. With Josefina."

"I'm sorry to ask you this," Whicher says. He softens his voice. "Did your son seem alright when you saw him?"

"What do you mean?"

"Did he look alright?"

Confusion is in the man's face. "He looked the same as always..."

"He didn't look like he'd been in any kind of a fight?"

Cardenas stares at him. Looks at his wife, then back at Whicher. "No, señor."

"There may have been some trouble prior to this."

Cardenas blows out his cheeks.

Guadalupe shakes her head. "There was never any trouble, nothing we knew about."

"If anything occurs to you..." Whicher says.

Her eyes stay on his.

"So, Matias came by with Josefina?"

"Sí. It was a Sunday."

"They come by often?"

"No." Guadalupe clears her throat. "He was trying to live his life, make a life with her. I was...overprotective. He was my only child. They wanted to live their life, do things their own way."

"Do you know Ms Olvera well?"

"Not well. She always seems nice. She works hard, they were always busy..."

Pablo Cardenas looks at his wife, then at Whicher. "We talked—but we haven't seen her since...we couldn't bring ourselves to do it."

"We don't know what to do," Guadalupe says, "except try to blank it all out..."

"If we go there," Cardenas says, "to the place he was living..."

Guadalupe finishes her husband's sentence; "It will only make the pain worse."

The marshal stays quiet. Takes in the room, framed pictures on the walls; Christ the Redeemer, the Virgin Mary. "When we spoke before, you told me about Matias working in the oilfields, before the farm."

Cardenas nods.

"If y'all think of anything else, I want to ask that you let me know? Do you know your son's co-worker, at the farm, Santiago Guevara?"

"No," Guadalupe says.

"You know the Guevara family?"

The woman looks at her husband.

"You know of them?" the marshal says.

"Why do you ask?" Cardenas says. His eyes sharpen.

"I'm talking to everybody who was in recent contact with Matias. I've spoken with people out at the farm."

"What for?" the man says.

"Background," Whicher says, "to get things straight."

"The Guevaras," Cardenas says. "I know who they are. They're not good people."

Whicher looks at him.

"Not respected," he says.

"Your son's employer?" Whicher says. "Emmett Zimmerman? You ever met him?"

"Why would I?"

"It's just a question, Mister Cardenas."

The man only stares, his face growing hard. "You think somebody there was involved with this?"

Whicher shakes his head. "I'm not saying that. But Matias got into something with someone—and it led to some dispute or grievance. Right now, we don't know anything about that. But somewhere, there's a person or persons who had a reason to want to harm him. I need to find out why."

Guadalupe's voice trembles; "We don't know of anyone like that...I can't even imagine it..."

Cardenas sits, silent, a muscle working in the side of his face.

Guadalupe starts to sob into her hands.

Whicher looks to Cardenas. "I don't mean to upset you folks. I can leave, we can come back to this..."

The man nods.

The marshal stands.

He follows Cardenas from the room, down the narrow hallway, along to the door.

Steps out. Away from the weight, from the grief-ridden house. Feels a late afternoon sun on his back; grateful for it.

Pablo Cardenas stares, his body taut. "Why'd you ask about that man, Guevara?"

"Like I said, I have to build a picture."

Heat is in the man's face, his voice constricted in his throat. "Did one of them kill him? At the farm?"

The marshal takes a moment. Lets his gaze run out along the rural street. "Worst thing we could do is start jumping to conclusions..."

"*Monton de cabrones, los Guevara.*"

Whicher fixes the man with a look. "Sir, the Guevaras might be a bunch of lowlifes. But wherever this leads, you need to understand law enforcement will handle it."

Cardenas doesn't answer.

"I can understand if you wanted vengeance for your son's death."

"No," Cardenas says, eyes burning. "You can't understand...he was all we had."

"The law will handle this," Whicher tells him.

"You think you can make me afraid?" the man says. "About what would happen. For what do I live now? Lawman. Tell me? What could I fear?"

CHAPTER THIRTY

Five hours later, in a Mexican cantina in the border town of Presidio, Whicher half follows the ball game on a wall-mount TV, a plate of tacos de alambre with rice and beans long since finished up.

The rendezvous with Adriana Lozada from Border Patrol is still a two-hour wait. The night sweep set for one-thirty in the morning. The drive up the last paved road along the river to Ruidosa will take more than an hour.

He checks his watch. Gone ten, too late to call Leanne again. She would have picked up the earlier message, she'd know he'd be staying out, she'd be trying to get Lori into bed.

He thinks of his daughter. On the threshold of her teenage years. Growing fast, growing complicated.

He scans the groups and couples, eating, drinking, a low buzz of talk in the room.

Two men shoot pool at a table by a picture window overlooking the street.

The marshal watches passing headlamps and taillights of cars and trucks. Thinks of Pablo Cardenas, of the heat in his eyes.

If Cardenas went looking for trouble, he'd likely find it. His son dead, the brakes off—two weeks waiting for news on Matias a goad in his side.

Whicher sits back, checks his watch again. Eyes the street. Aware of his surroundings—the comfort in the cantina, the food, warmth, the companionship of people. And the night unfurling outside, beyond the lights of the town. In dark desert. Mountain passes with no light. Nameless faces in an urgent world.

A parallel reality.

Raw and wild.

* * *

On the road into Ruidosa Whicher slows the truck—he sees the Church of the Sacred Heart in his hi-beams—beyond it, in the scrub between the deserted road and the Rio Grande, sitting out in the dark, a brace of Border Patrol Chevy Tahoes.

He checks the clock on the dash—coming up on eleven-thirty. Feels the familiar tick of adrenaline—from night ops with Third Armored Cavalry, on through law enforcement. Time stretched out, then compressed.

In the rear-view mirror, a solitary set of headlights appears.

He steers the Silverado onto the hard dirt at the edge of the road.

In the Border Patrol SUVs, both drivers turn to look.

He sees their faces in the truck's headlamps—recognizes the agents from the night at the Mackenzie Ranch, the 911 call.

Matos. And Webber.

Pulling in by Matos's unit, he shuts down the motor, kills his lights.

Stepping out, he fits his hat, glances back along the road.

Agent Matos climbs from his SUV. "Marshal."

Whicher offers his hand, Matos takes it.

From the second vehicle Agent Webber steps out. He nods to Whicher. "Pulled the night shift again, huh?"

"Looks like."

"You're on this?"

"Meet here, eleven-thirty, Agent Lozada told me."

Matos looks along the road. "That should be her."

The headlights of the approaching truck grow bright.

"What time's the helo scheduled in?" Whicher says

"On station around one, one-thirty," Webber tells him.

The marshal watches the Ford Super Duty slow—then turn toward the patch of scrub.

Agent Lozada rolls her window.

"Didn't see you behind me," Whicher says. "I drove out from Presidio."

"I came down Pinto Canyon."

Matos looks at her. "Anything going up there?"

"Quiet as the grave." Lozada cuts the motor in her truck, steps out. Surveys the group. "So, everybody alright?"

Whicher nods.

Matos dips his head, hooks a thumb into his duty belt.

"All good here," Webber says.

"Alright, well we have the Marshals Service with us tonight, in connection with a homicide. Plus activity is high in this sector, we've had multiple incidents, including an IED on a judge's car..."

"It keeps on coming," Matos says.

Whicher regards Lozada. "So, how's this going to work?"

"The helicopter will fly in, they'll fly a line roughly from the foot of the Chinatis—around Shafter up, as far as Candelaria," Lozada answers. "We've asked for them to sweep away from any road. They're running forward-looking IFR, they should be able to pick up anything that's moving. We're looking for any group or individual intent on moving in stealth."

"That's how far, your search area?"

"About thirty miles," Webber says, "give or take."

"They'll be flying a line around ten miles back from the border," Lozada says, "east of the river. So, we're looking for people traversing remote terrain. If the aircrew spot anything, they'll direct units on the ground. We'll relocate as needed. Marshal, I was thinking you could take up station at the top of Pinto Canyon Road?"

Whicher nods.

"I'll be here by the river." Lozada reaches into her truck, takes out a two-way radio set, hands it to the marshal. "It's fully charged, dialed in on channel," she says. "But the radios may not work all the time, there aren't enough repeaters out here—plus, with all the mountain terrain..."

"Right," Whicher says. He studies the older model Motorola. "This thing scan alright?"

"It should scan. We'll radio check but you should be able to relay through the chopper in case of any problem. Cell coverage will be pretty much zip."

Whicher gives Lozada a look. "Top of Pinto Canyon's not far from the Iniguez property..."

"Not a million miles from the Mackenzie Ranch, either..."

Agent Matos speaks; "How about us?"

"I need one of you on the Sierra Vieja posting up east of Candelaria," Lozada says. "Anywhere you can move around, there's a network of dirt roads up there."

"I know 'em," Agent Webber says.

"You want to take it?"

The tall agent shrugs. "Alright with me."

Lozada looks at Matos. "Back around Adobes Cemetery

there's a farm road leading up on the southern approach to the Chinatis."

Matos nods. "Leading up into the canyons?"

"That's the one."

"I'm on it."

Lozada turns to Whicher. "Patrol has other units stationed on the Marfa plain, back from your position. There'll be units on the highway, too. If we need to detain or arrest, they can move in."

"You're coordinating this end?"

"Control rooms at Sector HQ and Presidio are watching thermal cameras at the river, monitoring ground sensors. Plus the aerostat radar, and mobile feeds. We're kind of out front of the line-watch," Lozada says. "The helicopter will be our eyes out here—if they see individuals, or numbers, they'll be able to tell us. Units on the plain will have our back, nobody needs to get taken by surprise."

"Assuming the helo sees them," Agent Webber says.

Whicher puts the radio set into the Silverado. "Y'all have specific intel on tonight?"

"We're responding to heightened activity out here," Lozada says. "We pick up anybody we can find. We take them in, process them, interview for intel, take it from there."

Webber and Matos look to Lozada.

"I'll radio check everybody," she says, "then we sit tight, see what happens."

Both Border Patrol agents move to their vehicles, climb in.

Matos fires up his motor, snaps on the headlamps, pulls out onto the highway, headed south.

Webber starts his unit, rolls across the hard ground—he steers out onto the highway to the north.

Lozada stands at the door to her truck, a look in her face. "I hope we don't find any kids tonight..."

"Something on your mind?" Whicher says.

"I don't know...That girl I told you about? The one found dead, at that old reservoir?"

"Presa Llorona?"

Lozada nods. "I just hope we don't find any young ones, dead or otherwise."

The marshal stares down the road after Agent Matos—the taillights on his truck twin points of red in the dark. "What's happening with that?"

"Nothing's happening with it. El Paso ME's Office have her. It's going to be way down any wait list..." Lozada avoids his eye. "There's a backlog, I don't know how to move it forward."

Whicher watches the pinpricks of red.

Wind stirs in the carrizo cane at the river.

"Look out for yourself," Lozada says. "Sometimes this can get hairy."

"I'll do that."

"If you need help, call the helo, they'll be on channel two. Otherwise, stay on three or scan—three is me, Matos and Webber. What gear do you have?" she says. "You have flexis?"

"Zip ties."

"Alright, so you can cuff people. Weapons?"

"My Glock, a Ruger revolver. Plus an 870 Remington in the truck. A ballistic vest."

"Good," she nods. "Wear the vest. Put it on."

※ ※ ※

Windows rolled, Whicher sits in the vast dark in the Silverado, surveying a desert moonscape at the head of Pinto Canyon, a wool ranch coat pulled about his shoulders, ballistic vest strapped beneath it.

Static bursts from the two-way radio.

He eyes the shotgun on the passenger seat.

The helicopter's last reported position is south of Chinati Peak—around twelve miles distant, not far from the Mackenzie Ranch. The marshal thinks of the mountain plateaus along the heights of the southern range. The old dam, the Presa Llorona. He lets his mind range, the radio turned low.

Cool wind blows in through the open window. He eyes the black sky, the few clouds—the iridescent vault of stars overhead.

Thinks of Cardenas; the homicide investigation.

He'd need to speak to Guevara, call the farm, interview him again.

He sits forward in his seat, pulls himself up against the wheel of the truck.

So far, two non-citizens have been detected—in the back of a pickup truck. Vehicle stopped by Agent Matos—on a dirt road at the southern end of the Chinatis. All occupants detained.

Whicher stares out into the dark, along a track leading somewhere toward the Iniguez Ranch.

He pictures the woman. Thinks of the sketch. Her story. Of the man looking into her house.

The same feeling in him, a feeling he can't quite shake.

He breathes the high desert air—takes in the silence.

No light shows across the land.

The radio crackles. "Air unit—reporting heat signatures..."

Whicher turns up the volume.

"Four individuals—descending a gully—to the north side of Chinati Peak. Suspects approximately one mile southeast of Pinto Canyon."

The marshal switches to channel two, holds down the key to talk. "This is Deputy Marshal Whicher—at the top end of Pinto Canyon Road—I can move down to intercept? Over."

He lets go the key.

"Air unit—copy that, marshal. Suspects are approximately —four to five miles from your position. Can you move down on the road? Over."

"Roger that..." The marshal starts the motor in the truck. "Responding..."

The radio spits static—a female voice comes over the air. "This is Agent Lozada—I'm on Pinto Canyon Road right now, around three miles south of Horse Creek—I can move up."

"Air unit, roger that. Suspects are around half a mile off-road—descending a gully—roughly to the south of Horse Creek."

"Say intel?" Whicher says. "Are they carrying anything—are they armed?"

The helicopter responds; "Heat signatures suggest suspects are carrying packages—no intel on weapons—we can't get close, we need to maintain altitude above the mountain peak. Over."

"Copy that."

Whicher whips the steering wheel around, stomps his foot on the gas.

* * *

The path down into the canyon drops steep—the truck's headlights picking out a craze of jagged peaks and ridges in the distance, wave after wave.

Tires sliding on the loose grit, Whicher follows the contours of the looping gravel road, the truck bucking, bouncing over ruts and holes.

Overhead, no sign of light from the helicopter shows.

The marshal twists the switch on the radio—selects

channel three. He holds down the key to talk. "Whicher—to Agent Lozada—do you copy?"

Only static and silence come back.

The track crosses a brush-filled drainage, turns, drops again, he keeps his speed high, chassis starting to float beneath him.

Four suspects.

All carrying something.

He grips the wheel, hits a flat section, accelerates hard.

The road descends again, he touches the brakes, scrubs speed—steers into a turn—momentum carrying him, feeling the tires break loose, the truck start to drift. Then plummet downhill, around the side of a crumbling cliff—down further into the canyon.

Ahead is a set of lights.

Twin lights, moving.

He comes off the gas. Hits the key to talk; "I've got eyes on a vehicle—Lozada is that you?"

"Roger that," the Border Patrol agent says. "I see you."

The marshal steers along the dirt road, pulls up alongside Lozada's truck.

She cuts the lights on the Ford, steps out.

Whicher kills his motor, kills the lights, pushes open the door.

"We're on foot from here," Lozada says. "Grab your radio. Bring the 870."

The marshal grabs the Motorola handset, lifts the shotgun from the seat.

In the air is a faint sound of rotor blades and the helicopter's engine.

"You have any idea where they're at?"

Lozada presses on her radio mic. "Air unit—this is Agent Lozada—we're up on Horse Creek, request direction onto target."

"Copy that. Suspects are running—moving down some kind of a drainage, they can probably hear us. They're in a gully between your position and Boulder Canyon."

"Alright, we're moving," Lozada says. "Over and out."

* * *

The pitch-black climb up the narrow-sided gully is steep—a dry wash of loose gravel and stone and scrub vegetation.

Lozada leads, weapon drawn.

The marshal follows, climbing fast, the 870 shotgun out before him.

The sound of the helo is closer now, circling in a wide arc.

Lozada's radio crackles.

"Air unit to ground."

Lozada answers. "Copy."

"You're around five to six hundred yards from the suspects."

Whicher gets on the radio. "Can you get low? If we need back up—can you get on the ground?"

"Negative on that—we're using NVG—we can't see enough to land down there. We might get down on the canyon road."

"That's a half a mile," Whicher says to Lozada.

"Pilot confirms—we can put down on the road, over."

"Copy that," Whicher says

The radio clicks out.

The marshal puts a hand on the arm of Lozada's fatigue jacket. "You know how you want to do this?"

"Get close," Lozada says, "then make sure they know we're here."

"We tell them we're law enforcement?"

"La Migra," Lozada says. "We don't want any unintended response."

She leads off, Whicher follows, keeps the shotgun clear.

Climbing the gully, he tries to pick up on anything.

The terrain starts to flatten.

The helicopter radio comes back in. "Air unit—it looks like our birds have gone to ground."

Lozada responds. "What's happening?"

"They must be hearing us overhead. We can't see heat anymore—they must've gone inside something—maybe a ground feature, a cave."

Lozada stops, looks at Whicher. Presses on her radio key. "Air unit—confirm are we still on track to intercept?"

"Copy that—confirm. At least from the last point we had eyes."

"Keep watching," Lozada says.

Whicher feels his heart rate ticking up. "You ready?"

She nods.

"Let me lead," he says. "Let me lead with the shotgun, sit off my shoulder."

Overhead, the helo is louder, circling.

The marshal pushes on—scanning the dark out front. A mass of high scrub and thin trees form shapes against the night sky.

Beyond is a low wall—and some kind of building.

He stops, signals to Lozada, squats down.

She mirrors the movement.

"That a ranch or something?" Whicher says. "You know it?"

"Never seen it. I don't think I've ever been up here."

"If they've gone inside, we need to get 'em out in the open, we don't want to go in there."

"You want to get close?" Lozada says, breathless, now.

Pressing the butt of the shotgun to his shoulder, Whicher moves through a grove of desert willow. He passes a broken-down stone wall, the remains of a rick fence, an old well.

Fifty yards on is a ranch building—an adobe house, its timber door shut.

He turns to Lozada—signals for her to push out wide.

She nods, moves. Raises her pistol, grips it in both hands.

"*US Border Patrol*," Whicher calls out, "*La Migra...*"

The sound of the helicopter overhead fills the air.

"*Come out—sal de ahí...*"

Whicher senses movement.

The door to the house opens.

A man steps out.

Through the dark, the marshal struggles to see.

A second figure emerges; a third.

"One more, somewhere..." Lozada says.

Whicher holds position, finger wrapped around the trigger of the shotgun.

A fourth man exits the building.

"*Get on the ground*," Whicher shouts.

"*Manos en la cabeza—hands on your heads*," Lozada calls out.

Whicher moves in fast. "On the ground—*en el suelo...*"

The men are dressed in jeans, hooded tops, dark jackets. They start to lie face down.

Lozada advances.

"You want to get them cuffed?" Whicher says, "I'll cover."

Lozada takes up position, speaks to the first man in Spanish.

The man lowers his hands, puts them behind his back.

Whicher watches for sudden movement.

The Border Patrol agent secures a flexi cuff at the first man's wrists.

She moves to the next man. Repeats the words in Spanish. Secures the man's hands.

Whicher stands guard as Lozada works quickly, securing the final two.

Lowering the shotgun, he keys the radio. "Air unit—we

have four suspects at a disused ranch—we've got them secured. Over."

"Air unit—we see you—copy that."

Lozada turns to Whicher. "We need to search the house—then move them down to the road."

A burst of static spits from the radio.

"Air unit—we have people moving out from the back of your building—three runners."

The marshal looks to Lozada. "You got this?"

"I got it..."

Whicher sprints past the end of the building.

Behind the house is a clearing—three figures disappearing into scrub up the side of a hill.

He dials up the volume on the radio; "Air unit, let me know what's going on..."

"Copy, marshal."

"*Policía, alto*..." Whicher calls out. He can barely make out the figures in the brush. "Stay where you are..."

The cone of a search beam spears down from the helicopter—lighting up the side of the hill—picking out two fleeing figures.

The marshal scrambles on, shotgun leveled. "*La Migra, alto...*"

The lit-up men stop.

"Get on the ground—en el suelo..."

Both men turn—raise their hands. Start to get down.

Whicher pulls zip-ties from his jacket. "Face down, on the ground. Boca abajo."

Lozada appears at the side of the building below.

"Cover me..." he calls down. He presses on the radio. "Air unit—watch the four on the ground."

"Copy that. Over."

Lozada trains her weapon uphill onto the prone figures.

Whicher steps in, places the shotgun behind him on the ground—cuffs both men fast.

Then steps away, grabs the 870, peers into the dark. "I'll go after the last one..."

Lozada moves up to the two men on the ground. "Levantarse—up, get up..."

Whicher climbs the hill, keys the helicopter. "Where is he?"

The helo comes back. "We have heat about hundred yards north of your position—moving fast—could be downhill."

"Am I on line?"

"Track left—a few degrees. Pilot's going to reposition, we'll try to get a light on him."

"Keep watching IR."

"We still have heat."

The marshal lets go the radio key.

Overhead, the searchlight cuts away as the helicopter slews—arcing out in the night in a wide circle.

Climbing fast, he weaves between clumps of brush. He feels the ground level, flatten—start to drop down into dark.

The helicopter is gone from sight, hidden by the peaks of hills at all sides.

Advancing to a rock-strewn slope, he strains to see, watches for movement—listens for any sound. The helicopter's noise now distant in the air.

He hears a fall of loose stone—tries to pinpoint its direction. Sees nothing. He keys the radio. "Air unit, do you read?"

"Copy."

"You see him?"

"Negative, marshal."

"You have heat?"

"We need line of sight. We should have IR in less than a minute—we'll get a light on him."

Whicher moves downhill into the mass of darkness—ground breaking up beneath his feet.

He stumbles, grips the shotgun, gets low, steadies. Overhead sees navigation lights on the helicopter—winking from the dark.

"Air unit—we see you."

"You see him?"

"Negative, marshal."

Whicher stares across the black slope down the canyon side. "Can you get me light?"

The cone of the helicopter's searchlight snaps back on.

"Light up the side of the canyon," Whicher says, "I can't see a thing." He pushes downhill, scanning for movement, making out nothing.

The radio crackles. "We're showing no heat signature, marshal, apart from yours."

Whicher slows, eyes the ground features.

"Suspect could be beneath rock—an overhang—or below ground. Over."

The marshal stops.

To the right of his position is a deep gash in the canyon side—the lights of the helicopter show a slashed black line in the folds of rock. "Move your light left, two hundred yards."

"Roger that."

The searchlight beam skims the ground—toward the feature in the rock.

"Some kind of overhang," the marshal says. "I'll get close, he could be in there."

Moving in the outer wash of the searchlight beam, he closes space, yard after yard.

He raises the shotgun, presses the butt to his shoulder. Stops at the edge of a rock cleft, a long, deep fissure. To peer into a dark space beneath the overhang, beyond the searchlight's beam.

He shouts out; "*La Migra—sal de ahí—come out of there...*"

The radio crackles; "Suspect is out—we see him—he's out. He's carrying something...repeat, carrying something it could be a gun, over."

Whicher strains to see along the side of the fissure in the helicopter's light.

"Suspect is back in—repeat he's gone back in..."

The marshal takes a breath, scrambles down the canyon side beneath the line of the overhang. Shouts out again; "*Policía...*"

He thrusts the barrel of the shotgun into the void. Climbs into the space, heart racing.

He senses movement. "Stop—don't move—no te muevas..."

Finger curled around the shotgun's trigger, he fights the urge to squeeze.

A face appears.

Eyes shining.

Young eyes, afraid.

The figure of a boy is before him, a boy maybe twelve years old.

"Bajar—get down."

The boy kneels, drops the stick he's holding—lies on his front.

Whicher's breath stops in his throat.

As the sound of the helicopter deafens, closer, lower, the downwash of the rotors scouring grit and dust into the cave-like space.

Cold sweat films his skin. He gathers the boy's wrists. Zip-ties them.

Sinks forward on his knees.

Stares down.

To steady himself.

Draw breath, finally.

* * *

Back down on the canyon road with Adriana Lozada, the marshal watches Border Patrol agents load all seven detainees into the back of a transport van. Last in is the young boy, slim-limbed, his hair unkempt, face closed down, his eyes round with shock.

Lozada stands by her truck. "Line watch will run about another hour without the helo," she says. "But we need to get back to the station, process everybody."

At the transport van, Border Patrol agents close up the doors. Gesture to Lozada.

She calls over. "See you back there…"

The agents climb into the front of the vehicle. Start the motor, turn on the lights.

Whicher watches it set off down the dirt road—twin headlamp beams lighting up a jagged, alien land.

Lozada looks at him. "You okay?"

He glances back at her.

"You look a little shook up."

The marshal doesn't reply.

"Let's speak in the morning," Lozada says, "we'll see how any of this relates, if any of these people give up intel. We'll need to close that old ranch building down, looks like some kind of a staging post." She looks into his face a moment. " Thanks," she says. "For tonight."

"You got it."

She turns for her truck. Climbs inside, starts it up. Pulls around, follows the receding taillights of the van.

Whicher opens up the Silverado.

Climbs in.

Sits in silence.

CHAPTER THIRTY-ONE

Sunlight streams through the kitchen window at the house in Pecos. Whicher sits, drinking coffee, eying a Colt M4 carbine from the bedroom gun safe laid out on the table.

He hears the approach of a car outside the house. Fatigued from the night before, breakfast dishes still on the countertop.

The front door opens.

Leanne bustles through the living room into the kitchen. "You're up. I didn't want to wake you. I took Lori into school, we were running late."

"You make it?"

"Just about. She needs to get to bed earlier, it's hard getting her out on time." Leanne glances at the rifle on the table. "What're you doing with that?"

"Have to stop by the range," the marshal says. "I need to requalify."

"Didn't you just do that?"

"It's six months, almost."

"Where'd that go?" Leanne steps to the kitchen table, puts a hand on his shoulder—leans down, kisses him.

"Hope I didn't wake Lori last night."

His wife looks at the coffee pot.

"It's fresh," Whicher says.

She crosses to the side, pours a cup. "So, you okay?"

"Yeah. We picked up a bunch of border jumpers. Patrol took 'em in. I'm not sure what's happening with them yet."

Leanne leans against the countertop. Takes a sip of her coffee. "What's it all have to do with your murder?"

"We're trying to figure out if something's going on down there, something different," Whicher says. "Nothing new in people coming through that sector. But a murder, an IED on a judge's car..." He runs both hands across his face. Shifts in his seat.

"You look tired," Leanne says.

"Didn't sleep too good."

"Everything okay?"

The marshal picks up his cup of coffee, takes a swig.

His wife stands looking at him.

"Last night I came pretty close to shooting a kid."

Leanne puts down her cup.

"Kid not much older than Lori." He stares unfocused across the sunlit room.

"Well, what happened?"

"We were up in the mountains—search helicopter picked up a group of people coming through." Whicher drains the last of the coffee. Sits forward, eyes the M4 carbine. "This kid ran, he got himself hidden beneath an overhang in the rocks." He turns, looks at Leanne. "It's the middle of the night, you got no idea who you're dealing with—you can't see a thing."

"Was it alright?"

The marshal nods. Rolls a shoulder. "I guess. But the helicopter said he was carrying something—a possible weapon. I was about to shoot him, you know?"

"Well, what were you supposed to do?"

Whicher shakes his head. "It's just getting too dangerous. For everybody down there. Law enforcement. Border Patrol. Anybody thinking to get through. There's no way to know who you're dealing with—a guy looking for work, or a mule, or a gangbanger. Or a girl dying of thirst or a scared kid with a stick."

Leanne frowns, looks at him. "What do you think your murder victim has to do with all this?"

"Maybe nothing." Whicher pushes back his chair, stands. "I'm pulling in a guy he worked with today, a guy out on the farm."

"Can you talk to Lori tonight; will you be home?"

"Sure." He looks at his wife.

"It's just she worries—over everything. She doesn't like it when you're out all night. I can tell her it's all fine, but it's different coming from you."

"She alright?"

"She's an adolescent girl," Leanne says. "She's alright and not alright fifty times a day."

"Alright. I'll talk to her."

"So are you getting back any time for all the extra hours you've been working?" Leanne says. "Can you stick around, eat lunch?"

"I wish I could, sweetheart. I need to hit the range, I have to run down to Presidio County, reinterview this guy. Plus, I need to speak with Border Patrol, I may need to go down there."

She gives a smile, her eyes warm. "You sure you're okay?"

Whicher picks the rifle off the table.

"Don't let it rattle you too much. You know? Nothing happened."

The marshal looks across at his wife in the sunlit kitchen. "Nothing happened this time."

* * *

On a flat stretch of desert scrub at the Reeves rifle range, Whicher sets a barricade of four-by-two lengths of lumber at twenty-five yards from a paper QT target.

The magazine of the Glock is loaded with six rounds. At the belt of his cargo pants, two spares, loaded with three rounds each.

The marshal pushes up the sleeve of his sweat top. Adjusts foam ear protectors. Eyes the grayed-out bottle silhouette, two additional bulls-eyes set at the upper left.

Glock holstered, he readies himself. Gets set.

Then draws the pistol, fires six rounds center mass, drops the magazine—reloads, kneels, fires three, reloads—drops fully prone, fires three more.

He gets up from the ground, holsters the pistol, brushes dirt from his knees.

Walks to the target.

All bar two rounds are inside the bottle, mainly in the center mass circle, a few low.

He calculates a total, based on USMS points scoring.

Satisfied, walks back, past the wooden shooting barricade to a covered area.

On a long table is a set of heavy-duty ear protectors, four thirty-round magazines of .223 ammunition—and the Colt M4 carbine on a two-point sling.

He picks up the rifle, extends the collapsible stock. Powers up a thermal imaging sight.

He locks the bolt to the rear, flips on the safety.

Fits a magazine, hits the bolt release to chamber the first round.

Fitting the ear protectors over the foam plugs to deaden out the high velocity rounds, Whicher pockets the spare magazines, walks over to the distance-shooting section of the range.

Static targets are set up—steel plate along with wood and paper, plus yardage indicators.

He shoulders the rifle, puts the scope to his eye.

A gray-scale image shows the steel-plate targets picked out in white, emitting greater heat than their surroundings.

A distance marker shows three hundred yards.

He lowers the rifle. Sets himself. Releases the safety, selects semi-automatic fire.

He thinks of the sight picture he wants to see.

Raises the M4, centers the reticle on the target, squeezes the trigger once.

The ping of the round against the steel rings out.

He lowers the rifle.

Selects another target.

Pictures it in the scope.

Raises the gun again, takes aim, fires.

Hears the round strike the target.

Selecting a steel plate at four hundred, he holds high for the distance, squeezes the trigger, the round falls short. He aims higher, squeezes again, the round hits.

He moves the selector onto full-auto. Focuses on a set of steel plates out at two hundred yards.

Holding low he fires a three-round burst on the first target. Rounds clang from the steel.

He kneels, fires short bursts switching from plate to plate.

He slows it down.

Moves the selector back to semi-auto

Shoots double tap onto each target, hits them all. Feels the bolt lock to the rear, no longer cycling—the magazine now empty.

He stands.

Sets himself to go at speed.

He eyes the plates out at three hundred. Dumps the

magazine, slaps a new one into the well, hits the bolt release with the heel of his hand, not his thumb; gross motor skill over fine, gross better under stress.

He fires single rounds, hears bullets hit, sees dirt thrown up from the misses.

He stops.

Lowers the gun.

Scowls.

Work to do.

He takes in a lungful of air through his nose.

He'll have to practice more, come back.

He clears a round from the chamber.

* * *

On I-20, approaching the intersection with I-10, Whicher reaches for the phone in the dash stand. He scrolls to the number for Adriana Lozada, sends a call. Stares across a giant swathe of desert scrub at the Davis Mountains rising in the distance.

The call picks up.

"Morning."

"Marshal?"

"I'm riding down to Presidio County, I just wanted to check in. I was wondering what intel you had out of last night?"

"Not much," Lozada says. "We've got a Guatemalan national we're looking to charge with illegal re-entry following deportation. He could be the coyote, he's a repeat offender. He was in the group of four, we think, the first group."

"What do we know about the rest?"

"No intel—it's the first time we've seen them."

"How about the three that took off?"

"Same story."

"You know what they were doing in that ranch building?"

"Looking like somebody might've left them, a couple nights back," Lozada says. "They say they were told to wait, nobody came back."

"Would that be right?"

"People move at night, they'll hide by day sometimes. I don't know why they were left there. They were hungry. Dehydrated. Scared."

"You think your Guatemalan might give up something?"

"We'll find out. We can hit him with transporting undocumented migrants for financial gain—along with illegal re-entry. He'd be low-level, but I'll talk with the investigators from Homeland Security—they're carrying out interviews. You want to talk to this guy?"

"Homeland Security has them?"

"No, we still have them, they're being processed at the station, they have their investigators here."

Whicher gazes out through the windshield at the unfolding highway. "I don't think my murder vic was killed smuggling human traffic, but you never know. Listen, I'll be in the county, let me know if you hear more, I could come down."

"Alright, marshal."

"Appreciate it." Whicher clicks out the call.

* * *

At the end of the dirt road onto the Zimmerman farm, Whicher steers into the yard, sees Kathleen Zimmerman at the house, watching his arrival.

He lowers the window as she approaches.

She stares at him. "Has something happened?"

"Ma'am?" He sees the stress in her face.

"I saw you coming in." She puts her hand to her chest. "I just thought..."

"I came to see Mister Guevara. I need to talk to him again."

"He's not here. He didn't show up..."

Whicher shuts down the motor in the truck. "You know where he's at?"

"Emmett called him this morning. He says he's sick. He says he can't come in. He's never done that before..."

The marshal steps from the truck.

Kathleen Zimmerman stares out over the fields. "When I saw you driving in—with everything going on, I just thought..."

"Was Guevara home? Up in Valentine?"

"That's what he told my husband."

"And he's never done that before?"

"Never."

"Is your husband here, ma'am?"

"He's somewhere out at the back of the property..."

The marshal reaches into the glove box, takes out a business card. "If Mister Guevara shows up here, call me."

She takes the card, looks into his face. "Why do you need to see him?"

Whicher climbs back into the Silverado. "If he comes here, let me know."

* * *

On the north side of the highway in Valentine, a battered Chevy C/K pickup sits in the shade of a lot filled with shinnery oak and mesquite. Rusted engine parts and rotted timber litter the ground in front of a one-floor cement block house.

Whicher checks the address from the folder.

Steps out, picks his way through the debris in the yard, knocks at the door.

Along the road is a brick bungalow and a clapboard house, no sign of life at either property.

A man's voice answers, rough sounding; "Qué quieres?"

"US Marshal, Mister Guevara."

Whicher steps to one side.

A lock slides back, the door opens.

Santiago Guevara looks out—his eyes screwed up, hair matted into clumps.

Whicher smells hard liquor. "Need to talk to you."

The man squints. "What for?"

"I come in?"

The marshal takes a pace forward.

Guevara turns, slouches along a hallway to a kitchen in back.

Whicher follows, surveys the take-out boxes, the food debris. Dirty dishes, empty bottles of beer and whisky.

Guevara picks a can of soda off the kitchen table.

"You didn't go into work today?"

"I got sick." Taking a cigarette from a pack on the table, he lights it up.

"I saw Mrs Zimmerman," Whicher says. "She said it's the first time. Something wrong?"

Guevara doesn't answer.

Whicher looks around the kitchen. "Live here alone?"

The man grunts.

"I need to talk with you about the murder of Matias Cardenas."

Guevara pulls down smoke, the tip of the cigarette glowing red. "I already told you everything I know."

"I'm here to give you the chance to cooperate with my investigation."

Guevara's face grows dark.

"You called Josefina Olvera? A couple days after Matias went missing?"

He shrugs, takes a pull on the can of soda.

"You never called again. Never thought to talk to her about it?"

Guevara's face grows animated. "I told her two guys showed up..."

"Nobody else saw any two guys."

His eyes widen.

"I only have your word for that."

"There was only me there..." Guevara stares at him.

"Yeah? Maybe there never was any two guys?" Whicher says. "Maybe that all was just a story you made up..."

"I didn't make nothing up."

"Sure got us scratching our heads a while, uh? Looking all over. Matias all the time there on the farm."

Fear is in the man's eyes, now.

The marshal gazes at the empty bottles on the kitchen table. "Get drunk last night?"

Guevara doesn't answer.

The marshal stares at him.

"I'm sick, is all."

"About a week back a stolen vehicle turned up out here in Valentine," Whicher says. "Right across the other side of the highway. Know anything about that? Dodge Dakota. Stolen out of a ranch not too far from y'all at the Zimmerman place."

Guevara glares at him.

"How come it ended up here?"

"How do I know?"

"Maybe you know who stole it. Maybe you were around the night it got dumped?" Whicher looks at him. "Maybe you suggested leaving it there..."

"I don't know nothing about no truck."

"Yeah, you don't know zip. That about it?" The marshal looks out of the grimed kitchen window beyond the rusted fence in the back yard. "The day Matias was killed, you took him out to that field we found him by—you were the last person to see him."

Guevara drops the cigarette into a beer can on the table. It hisses out.

"Nobody else knew where he was," Whicher says. "So, you tell me? How would somebody find him, get to him? Let alone kill him."

The man's eyes dart around the room. He grabs another cigarette from the pack, lights up. Draws the smoke down deep.

"I can't account for it, son," Whicher says.

Guevara's nostrils flare, he runs a hand through his hair. "Alright...I saw them, alright..."

Whicher looks at him.

"I saw them again..."

"Saw who?"

"That SUV...the black Durango..." Guevara nods, his eyes rounded. "I saw it on the farm."

"You saw it on the Zimmerman property?"

"I swear..."

"The day Matias was killed?"

"After I dropped him..."

"You saw that vehicle?"

"Driving down one of the tracks..."

"You see who was in it?"

"No, señor."

"You're saying it was on the farm, out beyond the house?"

Guevara nods.

"Doing what? How could it get there?"

"You turn off of Ninety—there's dirt roads out into the fields..."

"You saw the same black SUV? How come you're only telling me this now?"

Guevara slumps against the kitchen sink. Shakes his head. "These are bad people...pandilleros."

"Gang members? You know who they are?"

"*No.*" Alarm is in Guevara's face. "I don't know..."

"How you know they're members of any gang?"

The farm worker regards him. "The car they driving, the way they act, the way they are..."

"How come you didn't say any of this before?"

Guevara holds his head. "I can't say nothing about them, against them..."

"You're scared of speaking out?"

The man clamps the cigarette to his mouth.

Whicher eyes him. "Somebody pay you a visit out here?"

Guevara doesn't answer.

"That why you get drunk last night?"

"No, señor..." Guevara stares at the floor. "I'm sick..."

"I asked your boss and his wife if they saw anything that day," Whicher says, "they told me no. Nobody saw anybody that first time either—apart from you. Pretty convenient? Them showing up again?"

"I saw them," Guevara says, his eyes wild.

"The day of Matias's murder?"

"They came that day..."

The phone in Whicher's pocket starts to ring.

The marshal takes it out, checks the number on the screen—*Presidio Sheriff's Department*.

He steps away from Guevara, clicks to answer, puts the phone to his ear. "Sheriff Torres?"

"Marshal—I just took a call from a sergeant with the PD up in Monahans."

Whicher hears the note in the sheriff's voice.

He steps out of the cluttered kitchen, walks along the hallway.

"They've got a DB up there," Torres says, "they ID'd him to the county."

"Presidio County?"

"They've got Glen Carr with his throat cut—in a service alley up there."

CHAPTER THIRTY-TWO

Twin patrol cars block the street off of South Main Avenue. The marshal slows at the side of a commercial plaza as a beat officer approaches. He holds his badge and ID out of the open window.

"USMS. Out of Pecos."

"Marshal?"

"I need to talk with whoever's investigating here—it's in connection with the homicide."

Back from the road, a narrow alley of hard dirt runs between the rear of a chicken restaurant, a hardware chain, a dry clean store and a cell phone franchise.

Uniformed cops search the alley.

Behind the hardware store, Whicher sees a group of dumpsters by a fenced enclosure—a tarp screen set up around it—police and officers in zip-suits working the ground.

"Chief Morales is back there," the patrolman says. He indicates a tall officer in dress uniform by the tarp—talking to a man in a sport coat. "You want to leave your vehicle at the line?"

Whicher steers to the curb where black and yellow tape

stretches across the road. He shuts off the motor, steps out. Crosses an empty lot toward the tarp screen. Spots a female officer interviewing a man at the back of a store.

The tall, uniformed officer eyes him.

The marshal holds out his ID. "John Whicher, USMS, Western District."

"Gael Morales, Chief of Police," the man says. "And this is Sergeant Diego Cruz, CID. He's in charge of the crime scene."

He indicates the man in the sport coat, mid-thirties, thickset.

The sergeant nods at Whicher, writes onto a clipboard, checks his watch, notes down the time.

"What happened here?"

"A worker from the hardware store came out back with a bunch of cardboard packaging," Morales answers. "Found a body between the dumpsters. The manager called it in—around three hours ago."

"I take a look?"

"What's your interest, marshal?" the sergeant says.

"Victim worked at a ranch in the south of Presidio County," Whicher says. "An IED was exploded at that ranch. IED on a judge's car."

Sergeant Cruz regards him.

"Judge Richardson?" Chief Morales says. "We heard about that."

"Right," Whicher says. "Any idea how long he's been here?"

"We think since sometime last night," Cruz replies.

"We came right over," Chief Morales says, "soon as we got the call. Ector County ME are out from Odessa. They brought CSTs." Morales gestures at the zip-suited figures.

"Anybody see anything? Hear anything?"

"We're still interviewing," Sergeant Cruz says, "looking for potential witnesses—so far, there's nothing."

"Alright if I take a look?"

Cruz puts the clipboard under his arm. "If you want to see, go ahead."

Whicher steps around the tarpaulin screen.

A zip-suited doctor kneels by the body—taping bags over Glen Carr's hands.

Carr is on the ground, face-up, his eyes still open. The front of his body soaked, shirt and jeans covered with dark blood.

A livid gash runs from ear to ear beneath his jawbone. His head is canted, arms out, shoulders high.

Whicher steps away from the body. "Yeah..."

Sergeant Cruz nods. "Pretty nasty."

"I called Sheriff Torres," Chief Morales says, "asked if he could inform the next of kin."

"The sheriff called me," Whicher says. "Does Larry Mackenzie know?"

The sergeant looks at him. "Who?"

"Victim's employer."

Cruz shakes his head.

Chief Morales studies the marshal.

"FBI are investigating the bomb on the judge's car," Whicher says. "I'm conducting a homicide inquiry—with potential links here."

"Here?" the chief says.

"In Monahans," Whicher says.

"I wasn't aware of anything like that..."

"Inquiry's at an early stage." Whicher looks to Sergeant Cruz. "You find his truck yet?"

Cruz frowns.

"Red, Ford F150, about ten years old." The marshal scans the vicinity—sees no red pickup.

"You know the victim?" Sergeant Cruz says.

"Hunted with him one time. Y'all find any car keys?"

The sergeant shakes his head.

"Any idea if he'd been robbed?"

"He had his billfold," the chief says, "there was money in it. Plus his driver's license, that's how we got the ID."

"You find his phone?"

"No phone," the sergeant says.

Whicher chews on his lip. He gestures at the dumpsters. "You know where he was attacked—was it in there?"

"Back of the chicken restaurant, we think," Cruz says. "We found blood on the ground there."

"He was dragged here?"

"The ground's disturbed," the sergeant says, "we're still checking for evidence."

"Y'all find any weapon?"

"Not so far."

The marshal stares at the back of the restaurant. "You speak to anybody in there?"

"It's closed until tonight," Cruz says. "I called the manager, she said she didn't see anything out of the ordinary. We'll interview her, get a statement."

"They have cameras?"

"Two, inside. Nothing outside. We've asked for footage."

The marshal stares along the dirt alley. "Anybody find anything? Y'all taken anything in evidence?"

"We got the scene secured, marshal," Cruz says, "we're only just beginning. We don't have the officers, it's going to take time..."

"You need to find the truck," Whicher says, "guy's a long way from home, he had to get here somehow. I'll check with DMV, get a plate."

Cruz says, "I'll do it."

"We find the truck, we should get prints, DNA. Whoever took it from here probably did this."

"You're looking to investigate this man's murder?" Chief Morales says.

Sergeant Cruz starts walking to a patrol car.

"I have to make a call," the marshal says.

* * *

In the cab of the Silverado, Whicher keys the number for Chief Marshal Fairbanks.

She picks up on the second ring.

"Ma'am, I'm over to Monahans, we've got a situation here—somebody found an employee from the Mackenzie Ranch murdered..."

"Say again?"

"The PD have his body here."

"Who?" the chief marshal says.

"Glen Carr. Worked as a hand on the ranch. I don't know what's going on, but the guy had his throat cut, somebody dragged him down a back alley, left him by a bunch of dumpsters."

"You know when?"

"Last night."

Fairbanks exhales into the phone. "What's that all about?"

Whicher doesn't answer. He watches the sergeant from the criminal investigations division typing into the mobile digital terminal of the patrol car.

"Didn't Carr have a rap sheet?" Fairbanks says.

"His prints were on file with the state," the marshal answers. "He got in some kind of a bar fight up in Odessa, it was nol-prossed, or dismissed..."

"You have any idea why he might've been killed?"

"Ma'am, I'm looking for clearance to investigate."

"I'll have to check with the DA."

"We've got homicide victims at a farm and a ranch barely a dozen miles apart," Whicher says.

"Is anything happening on Cardenas?"

The marshal sits forward in his seat. "I spoke with the hand from the Zimmerman farm, Santiago Guevara. He's now claiming the Dodge SUV turned up the day of Cardenas's murder; the same vehicle he says turned up before, with a couple of gang types..."

"Really?"

"Yeah, really."

"He's only saying that, now?"

"He's either lying to protect his ass, or he was too scared to say anything before."

"What changed his mind?"

The marshal stares at the uniformed cops searching the dirt alley. "I leaned on him. Let him know he could be in the frame."

"Alright, I'll speak to the DA's office," Fairbanks says. "But the FBI team need to know about this."

"You want, I can call Boyce Kelly?"

"I'll handle it," Fairbanks says, "I'll do it. I'll call you back."

* * *

Stepping from the truck, Whicher walks past the lot of the commercial plaza—to the lights at the intersection with South Main.

He takes in the stores and businesses—a couple of banks, a Chevron station, a nail bar, oilfield supply. Nothing to bring Carr to the area. Apart from the banks—he sees ATMs at both. He thinks of the billfold, still with cash inside it—he wasn't attacked for money.

Scrolling his phone, Whicher finds the number for Agent Ruiz at the DEA.

He sends a call, watches cars and pickups on the main drag.

"Delfina Ruiz..."

"John Whicher—I'm up in Monahans. A guy connected with the case I'm investigating showed up dead here..."

"Seriously?"

"I don't know what the heck is going on. So far as I know, he doesn't have any connection to the area. I'm looking for clearance to investigate—I could use anything you have, any local knowledge."

"Well, what do you think happened?"

"All I know is somebody got mad enough to kill him—they made something of it, too, they cut his throat, they didn't shoot him—they really messed him up."

"They did what?"

"Yeah, they cut his throat."

"We had a murder outside Midland, three months back," Ruiz says, "the victim had their throat cut."

Whicher stares back down the cross street to the dirt alleyway. "Can you come down here? We're off of South Main and West Fourth."

"I'm thirty minutes away. I'll be right over."

* * *

A white panel van backs up toward the tarpaulin screen, its rear doors open as Whicher reaches the dumpsters in the lot.

Chief Morales stands to one side with the doctor in the zip-suit.

Sergeant Cruz returns from the patrol car. "We have the license plate for the victim's vehicle. We're bringing in officers from the night watch, we'll check it's not still anywhere in town."

"You let DPS know?" Whicher says.

"We've put out a statewide BOLO."

The marshal looks at the white van.

"ME's office are moving the body," Chief Morales says, "they're done here."

"I have a DEA agent headed down from Odessa," Whicher says, "wouldn't mind her seeing this." The phone in his pocket sounds, the marshal takes it out—sees the name on screen—he steps away, keys to answer.

Chief Marshal Fairbanks is on the line. "I've spoken with Boyce Kelly at FBI—and the DA's office. DA's okay with it, Kelly wants to be in the loop."

"I've got a DEA agent headed in, we need to move this fast, whatever it is," Whicher says, "it's escalating."

"Just keep everybody onside."

"Got it." The marshal finishes the call.

Stepping around the tarp screen he takes another look at the body of Glen Carr on the ground. Pictures him the morning of the hunt; working with him to get the judge down off the hill, get him back to the ranch.

The chief of police eyes him.

The zip-suited doctor stares from behind heavy-framed glasses, the hood of the zip-suit framing his face.

"DA's office think a federal investigation is warranted," Whicher says.

Morales folds his arms over his uniform shirt.

"I've got somebody from the Drugs Enforcement Agency headed here—she says they had a murder victim with their throat cut three months back, outside of Midland."

The chief addresses the doctor. "You hear about that?"

The man shakes his head. "Different county, we don't cover it."

"There's an FBI investigation at the victim's place of work," Whicher says, "and now, a potential DEA connection."

"You've got your business," Morales says, "I got no problem with any of that. My business is; I want to know who thinks they can kill somebody in this town."

CHAPTER THIRTY-THREE

At the curbside on West Fourth cars and pickups slow, looking down the street—at the PD cruisers, patrol officers, the lines of police tape shutting off the road.

Whicher surveys the traffic, trying to spot Agent Ruiz.

He searches his phone, finds a number for Larry Mackenzie—sends a call.

Groups of people have formed in the lot of the commercial plaza—to stare at the tarp around the dumpsters.

The call picks up.

"Mister Mackenzie? Deputy Marshal Whicher—sir, I need a minute of your time."

"Marshal. Is something wrong?"

"I'm calling from up in Ward County, over in Monahans."

"Oh?"

"We're dealing with an incident up here. I'm calling to ask if Glen Carr was scheduled to come in?"

"Glen's not in today." The ranch owner's voice is flat, calm. "He's only coming in part-time right now."

"Sir, when was the last time you saw him?"

"Well, here, at work," Mackenzie says. "He was here Monday, you saw him then. Has something happened?"

"He stay over Monday?"

"No, marshal. He's just been coming in odd days, going home nights..."

"The last time you saw him was Monday?"

"Monday evening. As he was leaving to go home."

"I need to know what Mister's Carr's recent movements were," Whicher says. "You know anything about what he was doing?"

The ranch owner hesitates. "He's been fixing things up around his place, working on his truck, that kind of thing..."

At the intersection, Whicher sees a gray Crown Victoria —Delfina Ruiz behind the wheel.

"Can I ask what's going on?" the ranch owner says.

"Sir, Sheriff Torres is going to be in touch, I can't really say too much about this right now."

Agent Ruiz spots him at the curbside, signals, turns in.

A patrol officer waves her down.

"I sure hope nothing's wrong," Mackenzie says, a note in his voice.

"Sheriff will have to talk to you about it, sir."

"Well, alright. If you say so."

"He'll be in touch." Whicher finishes the call.

Delfina Ruiz parks behind the Silverado.

She steps out, smooths her short-cut dark hair.

"Appreciate your coming." Whicher indicates the fence enclosure, the tarp, the dumpsters. "MEs about ready to move the body—I asked them to wait till you could get here."

"What do we know so far?" Ruiz says.

"Not that much. Looking like he was attacked in back of the chicken restaurant there." The marshal points it out. "There's blood on the ground—but the area's disturbed, people will have walked on it, driven over it. We're checking for CCTV. We'll need to talk with anybody we can find that was here last night."

"Have any witnesses come forward?"

"So far, no."

Ruiz exhales. "I better take a look, then."

Whicher walks her across the lot toward the dumpsters.

Chief Morales and Sergeant Cruz nod at their approach.

"Agent Ruiz," Morales says.

"Chief." She nods to him and to Cruz.

"Doc's about done," the chief says.

"Out of Ector County," Sergeant Cruz says, "I guess you know him."

"Doctor Jackson?" she says.

The man moves from behind the tarp screen, still dressed in the white zip-suit. He looks at her through his heavy-framed glasses. "Delfina."

"You want to go ahead and take a look?" the marshal says.

Sergeant Cruz writes the DEA agent's name onto the crime scene log, along with the time.

Ruiz takes a few steps forward, stands a minute looking down at the ground at the body of Glen Carr.

"You ever see him before?" Whicher says.

"No."

"Sure? He's not on any DEA radar?"

"If he was, it's news to me."

The marshal takes a final look at Carr laid-out flat on the ground. Blood-soaked clothes clinging to him, bags taped over his hands. "This all look anything like the other murder victim?"

The DEA agent holds her bare arm with a hand, kneads the skin. "Honestly—yeah, I'd say it does."

Doctor Jackson speaks; "We'll talk to Midland County ME, see if it looks like it could be the same killer."

"DB had that same kind of cut," Ruiz says, "up high like that, beneath the jaw."

The doctor regards her a moment. "You'd have to get up close to do that," he says, "it wouldn't be possible to do it with a slashing motion—say from arm's length."

"You'd be up in his face?" Whicher says.

The doctor nods. "Very much so."

"Brutal," Ruiz says.

"Not common, either," the doctor says.

"Alright, well I think I've seen enough." She turns around, steps away.

Whicher looks at the doctor. "You can move the body, now."

The doctor glances at the CID sergeant.

Cruz nods.

Whicher crosses the lot to the Crown Vic with Agent Ruiz. "So, what do y'all have on the murder up in Midland?"

"We're looking at it, along with the PD," Ruiz says. "There's been no arrests, no suspect has been identified."

"But you believe there was a narcotics link?"

"The Midland victim was a known courier," Ruiz says. "We knew he was driving marijuana loads, sometimes cocaine, sometimes meth or heroin. Out of Odessa, all of it from south of the border, via a network we have under observation."

"Y'all know much about the network?"

"Some, we know. The low-to-mid guys, we want the people higher up."

"Think we could be looking at the same perp, here?"

"I don't know who your DB is," Ruiz says. "I don't know what link he'd have to the victim in Midland."

The white van from the ME's office starts to back close to the dumpsters.

People on the lot of the commercial plaza turn to watch.

"Why cut somebody's throat?" Whicher says.

"I guess, no noise," the DEA agent answers. "No sound, no shot. There's the intimidation factor, also. You know? Narco killings, a lot of times we'll see that; they want to send out a message."

The ME's van pulls up at the tarp.

Whicher sees Sergeant Cruz, neck bent, talking into a radio mic.

Cruz stares across the lot. Starts walking. Gestures toward the marshal, waves his hand.

"Something going on?" Whicher says.

Cruz calls over; "Watch commander says they've found the vehicle—the victim's truck. They've got it right across town."

"Where?"

"Out past the airport, over to Thorntonville—I'll take you," the sergeant says. "They're right there, they're going to wait."

* * *

A brace of police SUVs sit across the single-lane road. Uniformed drivers out of the vehicles, weapons drawn—standing guard on a clapboard house painted red.

Overgrown cottonwoods and live oak mask the property.

A shaded gallery runs along one side.

Glen Carr's F150 pickup is parked out in front of the house in a bare dirt yard.

Whicher steps from the Silverado with Agent Ruiz.

Sergeant Cruz exits an unmarked Tahoe—runs around the hood of the vehicle, speaks with the near officer, a sergeant. Then jogs back down the street to Whicher's truck.

"Rental property," Cruz says, "tenant's name is Johnny Shillick—we don't know him."

Whicher looks to Agent Ruiz. "Ever heard of him?"

She shakes her head.

"Anybody been up to the house?"

"Not, yet," Cruz says. "They called it in, I told them to wait. What do you want to do? We can get more backup?"

"Whoever killed Carr won't be in there," Whicher says. "Nobody's going to kill him, steal his truck—then drive home and wait."

Cruz looks at him. "We don't have a warrant to go in."

"Exigent circumstances," the marshal answers. "You got a vest with you?"

Cruz nods.

"Send one of your guys around back, we can suit up and go knock. We'll still have two out front with Agent Ruiz, plus your sergeant." Whicher looks at Agent Ruiz. "You want to post up here, give us cover from the street?"

"If that's what you want."

Whicher peels off his jacket, opens up the Silverado. Pulls the Kevlar ballistic vest from under the rear seat. He takes off the Ruger in the shoulder holster, dumps it, dumps the jacket in back.

At the Tahoe, Sergeant Cruz fixes a vest in place.

Agent Ruiz pops the retaining strap on the holster of a Glock 9mm.

The marshal takes the Remington shotgun from the gun safe beneath the seat.

Cruz speaks with the patrol sergeant, then with the second officer—young, Hispanic, his eyes bright.

The young officer moves fast to a low perimeter fence at the rear of the property—he disappears around back.

Sergeant Cruz draws a Sig P226 from its holster.

Whicher signals; passes through a gap in the fence by the mailbox—gets in line with a corner of the house, away from any window.

He steps across the yard, Cruz on his shoulder—reaches the side of the house, stands a moment in the shade of the trees, listening.

Hearing nothing.

Gesturing to Cruz, he tracks along the front of the house with the shotgun.

Reaches the door to the property.

Marks are around the frame and lock—the door hangs a fraction open.

Cruz takes up station on the near side of the door.

Whicher points out the marks of forced entry. Knocks hard on the wall, steps back.

He calls out; "*Marshals Service...*"

Sergeant Cruz grips the Sig between both hands. "*Police. Open up.*"

Whicher eyes the access points, checks the walls for gunshot damage. He looks at Cruz. "Alright, I'm going in."

The sergeant nods.

Whicher kicks the door, flattens to the wall—rolls around, runs into the house—into an open living room—barely furnished, a couch, a low table. "*Clear...*"

Cruz runs past him, into a kitchen. "Clear."

The marshal moves down a tight hall, pushes open the door to a bedroom. A mattress lying on the floor, nothing more. "*Clear...*"

Cruz checks the second bedroom

Whicher looks into the bathroom.

The house is empty, practically bare.

"Somebody rents this place?"

"According to the sergeant," Cruz says.

The marshal lowers the shotgun, walks back into the living room, eyes it.

Cruz crosses to the front door, calls out into the street. "*All clear, there's no occupant...*"

The marshal stares at old drapes, a threadbare carpet. "Somebody broke in, but there's nothing here."

Delfina Ruiz appears at the front door. She scans the room.

"Why kill somebody, drive their truck here?" Whicher says. "Then break in?"

Sergeant Cruz shakes his head.

"Could be a stash house?" the DEA agent says.

The marshal looks at her.

"Maybe they were expecting it to be full."

"We'll need to process the place," Whicher says, "see what was in here."

"I'll double-check with the owner," Cruz says, "check it's still rented by this Shillick guy."

"We need to find out who he is," Ruiz says, "where he is."

The marshal lets the shotgun trail from one hand. "I want to know what the hell's going on..."

* * *

Back across town on West Fourth, Whicher stands at the edge of the plaza with Delfina Ruiz at the Ford Crown Vic—Cruz still at the rented house, an evidence tech headed in to check for narcotics, check Glen Carr's truck for prints or DNA.

"I'll head back to the office," the DEA agent says, "check for any Johnny Shillick—or Glen Carr, for that matter."

Whicher nods. "I need to see who Carr was with, find out what he was doing, who he talked to. Check out his place."

"You know where he was living?"

"I'll call the county sheriff, find out."

Chief Morales crosses the lot from the fenced enclosure around the dumpsters. "We're going to close up the site...

ME's office should find something. Maybe they'll be able to tell if the murders are connected, this one and Midland."

"You have any kind of a lead to go on?" Ruiz says.

"One," the marshal answers.

Ruiz looks at him, a question in her face.

"I'd need a warrant," Whicher says, "and a defense attorney."

CHAPTER THIRTY-FOUR

The farm road south of Coyonosa is arrow straight—through flat scrub beneath a whitening sky.

Whicher keys a call to Sheriff Torres in Presidio County. Eyes the unrelenting land, half-choked with mesquite, power line poles whumping by.

Torres answers on the third ring. "Marshal. You see Glen Carr?"

"I saw him," Whicher says. "Somebody messed him up pretty good."

"What do we know?"

"Looking like he was killed last night—in or around a service alley. There's a restaurant he could've been at, if he was meeting with somebody. So far, we got no witnesses. One thing..."

"What's that?"

"Whoever killed him took his pickup—drove it right across town and dumped it out in front of a house—like, right on the yard."

The sheriff stays quiet on the line.

"We went in the house, the place was empty. Doesn't

make a whole lot of sense. I had Delfina Ruiz come down, she said they had a throat-slash victim up in Midland with a drugs connection."

"Really?"

"We'll check it all out. What's happening with Carr's next of kin? You speak with anybody?"

"He's got family back in Big Spring," Torres says. "I called the PD there, they were going to send somebody."

"You speak with Larry Mackenzie?"

"I did."

"How was that?"

"Guy was real shocked," Torres says. "He said Carr had a girlfriend living down around Shafter—he has a trailer home there, on a piece of land. I went down, found her. She said they split up—but she was real upset."

"You go over to his place?"

"I took a look from the outside," Sheriff Torres says. "Didn't want to mess with potential evidence. Are you investigating Carr's death now?"

"I am," Whicher says. "But the FBI are going to be breathing down everybody's neck on this. Listen, how well you know Santiago Guevara?"

"I spoke with him a couple times," Torres says, "when Cardenas's disappearance was a missing person case."

"I talked to him this morning," Whicher says. "At his place in Valentine. The guy was a mess. He didn't show up for work, he was drunk from last night. He told me something, though—he said the day Matias disappeared that Dodge SUV came on the farm. He claims he saw it."

"He never said that to me..."

"Reckoned he was too afraid." Whicher stares through the windshield of the truck at a semi approaching in the distance through waves of heat. "Listen, I want to bring him in, talk to him, I'm headed down to Marfa—could you pick him up?"

"Arrest him?"

"Right now, there's not enough for that. I was thinking you might persuade him—tell him it'd be a chance to clear his name."

"And if he won't agree?"

"Last night Glen Carr was killed, I want to know where Guevara was at. If you can bring him in without violating any rights, we could lean on him."

Torres doesn't answer.

"Two dead in the county we need to get ahead of this, fast. Whatever it is..."

"Alright, I'll have him picked up," the sheriff says, "if we can find him."

"I'll be an hour and a half." Whicher finishes the call.

* * *

At a Valero station outside Alpine, Whicher pays for gas, walks back out to his truck in the late afternoon heat. He eyes the sign for chicken-fried steak at the Dairy Queen on the opposite side of the road, thinks better of it. Half an hour still to Marfa—he jumps back in the Chevy, pulls out onto ninety. Heads for Sul Ross and the center of town.

Ranger Peak and the Twin Sisters cut the skyline above box stores and chain restaurants. He thinks of the girl found up at the dam—alone in the mountains beyond the Mackenzie place.

Pulling over, he scrolls his phone. Finds the number for Estrella Tirado at El Paso ME.

In his mind's eye he sees Adriana Lozada, remembers the day the Border Patrol agent showed him the spot. Both of them silent by the stagnant water. A barren place of wind and rock and the shadows of circling birds. Looking out over the valley the girl would never come down.

He clicks to send the call.

Pulls out again. Steers on into the town.

The call answers. "Doctor Tirado."

"John Whicher, US Marshals Service. We spoke yesterday—regarding the murder of Matias Cardenas?"

"Marshal, yes."

Whicher passes the state university, eyes its landscaped surrounds.

"We're probably looking to autopsy tomorrow," Tirado says "If it goes ahead, we should have results by early next week."

"I appreciate it..."

The doctor waits for him to continue.

Whicher pulls himself up behind the wheel. "Matter of fact, I'm calling about something else..."

"Oh?"

"A related matter. Your office has the body of a young girl, I believe. Recovered from the Chinati Mountain range around twelve days back. I'm calling to check if there's been any attempt to identify her? I'm working two homicide cases connected to the immediate surrounding area where she was found."

"This is a girl listed how?" the doctor says. "Non-documented, non-citizen?"

"I believe she would be. But I'm calling to ask if the ME's office could expedite an identification."

Tirado sounds doubtful on the line. "You think this relates to...a homicide case?"

The marshal weighs his words; knowing them for the lies they are. "Two homicides, the latest last night, I think there could be a connection..."

"Well, I'm not sure," Tirado says, "I'd have to look into it…"

Whicher hits the one-way split through town. "If there was a way of finding out who she was, where she came from, I'd like to know it…"

He steers the curving highway behind a slow-moving pickup and horse trailer.

No way to take the words back.

Not wanting to.

"Well, look…"

Whicher hears the note in her voice.

"I could amend it onto the file, if you wanted, marshal… the file for the Cardenas case…"

"I'd appreciate it, doc. I'd be obliged."

Silence.

"Alright. Well, alright," Tirado says. "I'll make the amendment. I'll upload it onto the system, I'll see what we can do."

"Understood."

"Was that all?"

"That was all, doc."

Whicher moves out to pass the pickup truck and trailer.

"And thank you."

He shuts off the call.

Thoughts working on the inside.

Turning over in his mind.

* * *

Marfa, Tx

Santiago Guevara sits with Armando Torres in a small interview room at the sheriff's department off the courthouse square.

The marshal settles into a steel-frame chair, puts a slim leather tote onto the desk.

Sheriff Torres sits forward in his seat. Clasps his hands together. Glances from Guevara to the marshal and back again. "For the record, you're not under arrest, you're here of your own free will..."

Guevara nods.

"You're not accused of anything. You're free to leave at any time. You've agreed to try to answer some questions that could help an ongoing inquiry, is all."

The sheriff looks to Whicher.

The marshal clears his throat. "Last time you saw Matias Cardenas, you told me you took him out to his place of work? Fifteen days ago. To a field where he was fixing the irrigation system?"

"That's all I did," Guevara says.

"And then you left him, you were working elsewhere on the property. Far from there."

"Right."

"How far?"

"Like, eight miles."

"How you think somebody found him? To kill him?"

Guevara spreads his hands. His face stressed. "I don't know..."

"You think it would've been hard?" the marshal says. "For somebody looking for him?"

"There's farm tracks—like I told you. You can drive around the place. I saw that SUV out there..."

Whicher opens up the tote, slides out a notepad.

Guevara shifts in his seat.

"You told me you saw a black, Dodge Durango SUV. Same

vehicle you think, as one you previously reported to Sheriff Torres. When two guys showed up and took Matias someplace—under some sort of duress."

The farm hand nods.

"You didn't tell anybody it came back the day Matias was killed—because you were afraid. That right? You thought the people in the car were pandilleros, gang members?"

Guevara doesn't answer.

Whicher sniffs. "How come you seen this vehicle—eight miles away an' all?"

Color steals into the farm hand's face.

"Eight miles is a ways," Sheriff Torres says.

"I was near there," Guevara says, "later that morning, I saw them."

Whicher angles his head.

Guevara stares at the floor.

"You think they just found him?" the marshal says.

"Right."

"They just drove around, till they found him? Or could somebody have told them where Matias was at?"

Guevara doesn't respond.

Sheriff Torres eyes him.

"I talked with Mister Zimmerman, your boss. And his wife. Asked 'em did they see any vehicle that day—they said not."

The farm hand still says nothing.

The marshal keeps his tone light. "I don't know... First, you're eight miles away from there, then you're around—you didn't see nothing, then you *did* see something..." He looks down at his notepad, decides to change it up. "You know a feller name of Glen Carr?"

Guevara's eyes flick away.

"Do you?"

"No, señor."

"No?" The marshal leans back a fraction in his chair. "See I'm working another case, alongside Matias's murder. I told you about a truck getting stolen—ending up in Valentine?"

The man doesn't answer.

"That truck's part of this other case I'm working. Thing like that happens, you ask yourself; how come it was dumped there, you know? Little place like that—nothing much there. Maybe it's just random? Or can you find some kind of connection?" The marshal stares at Guevara. "Some little connection. Like Valentine. You know? Where Santiago Guevara is at."

"It don't have nothing to do with me."

"Less than half a mile from your place."

"So?"

"Yeah, I don't know. So, Glen Carr? Sure you don't know him? Ranch hand. Works the Mackenzie Ranch—other side of the canyon, not real far."

"I don't know him."

The marshal picks up his notepad, reads a few lines to himself. "Monday I went to see Josefina Olvera. She thinks you lied to her—about that SUV. About those men."

Panic is in Guevara's face, now, he turns to Sheriff Torres. "He's accusing me of being a liar?"

Whicher cuts in; "I'm not saying I think you're a liar. I want to know why Josefina Olvera does." He reads on in his notes. "She says you never offered to help but one time. She reckons all you wanted was an alibi, or whatever—like that was why you really called. Her words."

No response.

"She also said you and Matias used to fight?"

"No..."

"You thought he was getting paid more money—getting the easier jobs on the farm."

Guevara shakes his head.

Whicher looks at him. "That's what she told me."

"That's not how it was."

"Where were you last night, Mister Guevara?"

"What?"

Sheriff Torres looks at the farm hand. "Where were you last night? It's a simple question."

"Home."

"Anybody with you?" Whicher says.

"No."

"You see anybody?"

"No."

"Anybody see you, talk to you?"

"No..."

"I came by this morning, you looked like you had yourself a late one..."

"I got sick."

Whicher searches in the tote, takes out the sketch drawn by Angelita Iniguez.

He lays it flat on the desk.

"Either of the two men you saw with Matias look like that?"

Guevara glances at the picture. The edges of his mouth downturned.

From the tote, the marshal takes out the print-off from the DOJ Warrant for Apprehension. The photograph of Esequiel Aquino on the top sheet. "How about this?"

Guevara sits rigid, his face a mask. Eyes returning to the photograph, widened slightly.

"You know this man?"

No response.

"Name of Esequiel Aquino?"

Sheriff Torres speaks. "That's something you need to answer."

"This one of the men you saw? On the farm, with that SUV?"

"No," Guevara says. "I don't know…"

The marshal changes tack again. "You ever visit up to Monahans?"

The farm hand squints at him. "What?"

"You have friends there? Family?"

No answer.

"How come you got drunk last night?"

"I wasn't drunk…"

"There some way you could prove you were home?" Whicher says.

The farm hand stands.

"Glen Carr was killed last night…"

"You alright?" Sheriff Torres asks Guevara.

The man's face is drained. "I don't need to listen to this. I'm free to leave?"

"Yes, you are."

Guevara nods, swallows. "Then I'm leaving."

CHAPTER THIRTY-FIVE

Inside the sheriff's office, Whicher stands at the window, eyeing the cars and trucks on Highland Street, shadows slanting from the trees in front of the domed courthouse.

"I guess that's the last time he talks without a lawyer," the sheriff says.

"Guess you're right."

Torres sits on a corner of his desk.

"His whole thing with the SUV coming onto the property?" Whicher says. "He make that up? Or did it really happen?"

Torres regards him.

"You get a look at his face when I showed him the photograph? He either knows the guy, or he's seen him."

The sheriff inclines his head.

"Aquino's a killer, we know that. We know he's been here," Whicher says. "He left his prints in that truck he stole. Maybe Guevara told him where Cardenas would be that day..."

"Why would he?"

"Because he was afraid?"

"If Guevara was the last person to see him alive," the sheriff says, "he could've killed Matias himself..."

"I know it."

"But we don't have evidence..."

"Maybe I could find some," the marshal says. "Search his house, his vehicle, maybe there'd be something."

"You can't get a warrant without probable cause."

"Something went on with him last night," Whicher says. "He was drunk this morning, he never showed up for work..."

Torres frowns.

"I know...it's all circumstantial."

"You think he has something to do with a guy blowing up a judge's car?" the sheriff says. "Or killing a ranch hand?"

"If he saw this guy—Aquino—recognized him for what he was," Whicher says. "A gangbanger, a killer, that'd make more sense. I think he's scared we'll ask him to testify against a guy like that."

The sheriff nods.

"They'd probably take him out before he could even make the stand," Whicher says, "maybe that's what happened last night? Maybe they took him out there, to Monahans, made him watch."

"So, how's a guy like Glen Carr get a death sentence?" Torres says. "How is he connected to someone like this Aquino?"

"Maybe it wasn't him?"

"Then who the hell was it?"

The phone in Whicher's jacket starts to ring. He takes it out, checks the screen. "I need to get this."

The sheriff rises from his desk.

Whicher clicks to answer, steps out of the office into reception.

Chief Marshal Fairbanks is on the line. "I just took a call

from the DOJ in Houston—one of the lawyers from their international extraditions team."

"Ma'am?"

"This Marco Zambrano character...he's still refusing sustenance, it's getting to be a major problem," Fairbanks says. "They have issues with his mental state, his health, his general competence to undergo due legal process."

"They're worried they're getting stuck with him..."

"He's asking to speak with you again," Fairbanks says.

Whicher pushes open the door from reception to the street. "With me, really? Specifically?"

"He claims he has information—says he knows the whereabouts of a murder victim."

"Come again?"

"A murder victim. In Presidio County. Buried out on a farm."

The marshal stands on the sidewalk, staring out over the courthouse square.

"A farm," Fairbanks says, "right?"

"He say where?"

"He won't—he wants to sit down with you."

"Matias Cardenas?" Whicher says. "That's who he's talking about?"

"I don't know. I do know you're dealing with a body found on a farm..."

"He know who killed this victim?"

"He won't say. According to the lawyers. Only that it's close to the place you took him, the ranch."

"The Mackenzie Ranch?"

"That's the implication," Fairbanks says.

"I took him out there responding to a 911 call."

"Listen, the DOJ team called me, I thought you ought to know all this."

"What's going on?" Whicher says. "He looking to trade information? Cut some kind of a plea?"

"That's how it sounds," Fairbanks says. "Extraditees can ask to serve out sentence here, rather than the home country..."

"He could trade?"

"It happens."

The marshal moves down the sidewalk, eyes his truck.

"Where are you?"

"Down in Marfa. I just reinterviewed the hand from the Zimmerman Farm."

"You have two homicide cases," Fairbanks says, "one of them at a farm, the other, a victim from a ranch undergoing an FBI investigation. I think you should do it. I think you should go..."

The marshal leans up against the Silverado.

"We can get you on a flight to Houston in the morning, it's an hour and a half. He won't talk to the DOJ lawyers," Fairbanks says. "He only wants to talk to you."

* * *

The gray Impala is parked on the driveway in front of the house in Pecos as Whicher pulls in off the street.

He checks the clock in the dash—7.25 in the evening.

Grabbing the leather tote from the passenger seat, he slides out of the truck, steps to the front door, opens up.

Inside, in the living room, Lori is sprawled on the couch—phone in both hands, TV on low, the smell of cooking coming from the kitchen.

She looks up from her phone screen. "Hey, dad."

"Hey, sweetheart." Whicher dumps the tote on a chair "How you doing?"

"I'm okay."

"Something smells good." He nods toward the kitchen.

"Uh-huh."

"Mom back there?"

She smiles. A little blank.

The marshal walks through into the kitchen.

"You finally made it?" Leanne steps away from the stove.

He kisses her.

"I made chili."

"You need me to do something?" Whicher says.

"No. Go talk to your daughter."

He steps back, looks at Leanne.

She smiles. "You want a drink? There's beer in the fridge."

"Do you?"

"I'm good."

Whicher takes off his jacket, walks from the kitchen down the hall into the bedroom.

He hangs up the jacket, sets his Resistol hat on the bed. Takes off the Ruger, the Glock at his waist. Puts the guns up into an armoire. Heads back to the kitchen, takes out a Shiner. Pops the top.

"So, you alright?" Leanne says. "You know? After last night?"

He nods. Takes a sip from the bottle of beer.

"You have a good day?"

"Busy one." He lowers his voice. "Had another homicide last night. A worker from the ranch where that bomb exploded."

Leanne looks at him.

"I have to go to Houston in the morning."

"What for?"

"I brought a guy in—the night this all started? DOJ reckons he has information to trade."

"You're going out to talk to him?"

"Looking that way."

"About what?"

"A homicide."

"Well, you're here now," Leanne says. "We can sit down and eat, be a family."

The marshal looks at her.

"Go talk to your daughter."

He takes another sip of beer.

She smiles.

"Alright. If you need help, let me know?"

"Go ahead."

Stepping through to the living room, Whicher eyes the TV—a dance troupe and singer he doesn't recognize—a talent show.

He eases down onto the couch.

Lori glances at him over her phone.

"What's going on?"

She shrugs. "Nothing much."

"So, you okay? I wake you up last night?" He takes a sip of beer.

She shifts on the couch, lowers the phone a little. "Sorta..."

"I was trying to be quiet."

"I was half awake. Mom said you went down on the border...or something."

"Right."

"Doing what?"

The marshal slides down into the couch. "It's the case I'm working..."

"The one with the judge?"

"Connected with it."

Lori watches him over the top of her phone.

She glances at the TV. Looks back at him again.

"We're trying to figure out what's going on," Whicher says. "It's kind of complicated."

"So why were you out all night?"

"We were running a search. This certain sector, down there. With a helicopter. And Border Patrol."

Her face is still now. "And what happened?"

"We picked up some people coming through." He takes a pull at the Shiner. "We're looking for information, trying to figure out what's going on. If you're a beat cop, you shake-down the streets you work to find things out. Out here, this is kind of our version."

"Why's it complicated?"

The marshal stares at the TV screen, eyes unfocused. "Well, I guess things are happening that we don't understand."

"People are always crossing over," Lori says.

"They are. Mostly, the last thing they want is trouble—they make trouble, we're all over 'em. What they want is to be on their way, nobody noticing..."

"So?"

"So, now, we've got trouble."

"Like with the judge?"

"Kind of..."

"So did you find out who blew up his car?"

"Got an idea."

"You know why?"

The marshal shakes his head. "There's things we have to find out, a bunch of things."

"But why do *you* always have to do it?"

He looks at her.

Lori's face is sullen, her eyes downcast, studying her phone.

"It's not always me. A lot of people are handling it—you know? Border Patrol. Local law enforcement." Whicher grins at his daughter.

She avoids his eye.

"It's my job."

"Well, is it dangerous?" Her voice is tighter now. "Down there?"

"It can be."

She looks up, eyes wide. "Yeah... well, that's what I mean..."

The marshal studies the TV a moment. Takes another sip of beer. "I've been doing this a long time..."

"So?"

"I'm always careful."

"I don't like it...when you're out all night."

Whicher nods. Leaves his daughter's words unchallenged.

"Mom doesn't either."

"Your mom's used to it..."

"She doesn't like it."

Whicher looks at her.

"You don't know that," Lori says. "You don't know it—but I do."

CHAPTER THIRTY-SIX

Houston, Tx

Across the airport arrival hall at George Bush Intercontinental, a woman in a navy suit holds up a hand in greeting. The marshal takes in the Department of Justice lawyer—toned-looking—in her mid-forties, with subtle make up, lob-cut sandy hair.

He makes his way across the hall toward her.

She steps forward to greet him. "Joanne Krueger."

He raises his hat, offers his hand.

She takes it.

"John Whicher."

She gestures past a line of bright-lit concessions. "I have a car outside. It's a thirty-minute ride downtown to the Federal Detention Center."

"That where you're holding him?"

"Unless we have to move him into medical care," Krueger says, "or a psych ward."

She starts to walk toward the signs for the exit and the terminal road.

"He's still refusing sustenance?"

Krueger inclines her head. "Yes, he is."

Waiting passengers in the hall part for the sharp-dressed woman, the big man in the suit and hat.

"How was the flight?"

"Just fine, thanks. How is he?"

"I haven't seen him in a couple of days," Krueger says. "In general, he's pretty weak. Subdued. Uncommunicative. I hope your visit will be worth it, marshal. We've tried talking with him to find out what he has in mind." The lawyer glances at Whicher, not breaking stride. "You're the only person he seems to want to talk to. Why do you think that would be?"

At the exit of the terminal building Whicher follows the DOJ lawyer outside into late morning sunshine on the wide sidewalk.

"Border Patrol picked him up in a vehicle stop," the marshal says. "A foreign fugitive warrant was live on him. I went down to Presidio to get him. That's about it."

"Really?"

"My boss told me there's an outside chance a foreign extraditee can cut a plea. Serve sentence here, rather than in the country of extradition. Negotiate for a lighter sentence?"

"They'd have to have something we really want," the lawyer says.

She pulls out a set of keys, presses on the fob—the lights flash on an E-Class Mercedes.

The marshal walks with her toward it. "Who makes the decision on that?"

"We do."

"How about if it's useful to me?"

Krueger reaches for the driver door of the Mercedes, brushes her hair behind her ear.

She smiles with her mouth but not her eyes. "I mean, the decision will be taken at senior level, in consultation with others, including legal representatives from the extraditing country."

"But?"

He looks at her.

She says, "Still DOJ."

* * *

On the top floor of the eleven-story Federal Detention Center on Texas Avenue, a two-hundred-and-fifty-pound CO leads the way along a restricted access corridor.

The corrections officer reaches a door, enters a code on a keypad.

The door opens into a secure interviewing room—a space divided in two by a floor-to-ceiling glazed-block wall—a steel-mesh grille set within it.

Marco Zambrano sits behind the mesh screen, dressed in prison whites—slumped forward on a metal stool.

Two chairs face the security screen.

Krueger takes the left-hand seat, the marshal sits to her right.

The CO stares briefly through at Zambrano—checks the steel-bar door at the back of the room is firmly closed.

Whicher takes in the surveillance cameras—two, at ceiling height.

The corrections officer catches Joanne Krueger's eye.

She nods.

"Ma'am. Sir. You're all set."

The CO leaves the room, closes the door behind him.

Krueger addresses Zambrano. "I work for the Department of Justice, you know who I am. And you know who this is..."

Zambrano eyes the marshal.

"You've asked for an informal hearing to evaluate information you have."

"Sí. Yes."

"You claim to have information related to criminal activity?"

Zambrano sways on the stool, his face emaciated, skin sallow. He hunches his shoulders in his scrubs.

The marshal takes in the cannula in his arm.

"Let's hear it," the lawyer says.

"I know where is a body. A murder victim," Zambrano says. "I can show you."

"You know where a body is?" Whicher says. "How do you know?"

"I was there."

"You witnessed a murder?"

"Sí."

"You know the name of the victim?"

"No."

"But you know where the body is?"

"I know where," Zambrano says. "Una granja."

Whicher sits forward. "A farm?"

"Sí."

"What kind of a farm?"

"I don't know, is just a farm."

"Where?"

"La frontera. Near to...the border."

Whicher eyes the prisoner behind the mesh screen. "Who killed this person?"

"A man I was with—I didn't know it. I thought it was...to talk. We drive to this farm, to see this man."

"Describe it," the marshal says. "Describe the place."

Zambrano stares at the steel countertop. "Maíz. Campo de maíz."

"A field of corn?"

"Sí."

"Victim's buried in a field of corn?"

The man shakes his head. "Close."

"This field have irrigation?" the marshal says. "Irrigación?"

Zambrano's eyes widen.

"Fifty yards from there, behind a stand of mesquite—you buried the victim, we already know about it."

Zambrano sinks on the stool.

"That's your trade?" Whicher says. "You got nothing."

Joanne Krueger looks at Zambrano. "Did you kill him?"

"No. No."

"The victim's name is Matias Cardenas." Whicher turns to Krueger. "He was a hand on a cantaloupe farm in Presidio County."

The lawyer says nothing.

"You know the name of the man who killed him?" Whicher says.

Zambrano broods on the question.

"It's not enough to know," Krueger says, "or say you know. You'd have to testify. Your testimony would have to convict."

Whicher sees apprehension in the man's face.

Zambrano stares down at the ground, shifts his cuffed hands against his knees. "Is a man...named Aquino..."

Whicher sits back, folds his arms, stares.

Zambrano nods his head.

"Esequiel Aquino?"

Confusion is in the man's eyes now.

"Esequiel Aquino killed Matias Cardenas?" the marshal says. "And you were with him?"

"I didn't know he would kill..."

Whicher leans forward. "Why were you there?"

"El chofer..."

"You're his driver?"

"This man," Zambrano says, "he took money."

"Cardenas?"

"Sí."

"From Aquino?"

"Sí, sí."

"For what?"

"Seguridad. Mulas," Zambrano says.

"For drug mules? Money to protect drug mules?"

"To hide them…"

Whicher thinks of the oilfield worker up in Monahans, Nolasco, Cardenas's friend—his story; of Cardenas meeting someone.

"Mulas cross at night," Zambrano says. "They hide by day…"

Krueger speaks; "Why was this person killed?"

"He wanted to stop." Zambrano picks at the sleeve of his scrubs, sits mute. Mutters, barely audible; "No puedes…"

The lawyer says, "Right. You can't."

Whicher watches through the steel-mesh security screen. "Not enough."

The man's eyes flick to him.

The marshal shakes his head. "We don't have him. We don't know where he is. We don't have any prospect of apprehending him."

Joanne Krueger sits silent.

"You wanted to see me," the marshal says. "Why?"

Zambrano runs his tongue over thin lips.

"Why me?"

"Because…"

"Because what?"

"Because I know…" Zambrano nods, eyes glazing, as if deciding something to himself.

"What do you know?"

"The night you take me? I know about this, too." Zambrano's face is suddenly animated.

"You know about what happened that night?"

"Si, si."

The lawyer looks at Whicher. "Hold on, what?"

"I had to drive," Zambrano says. "Drive him."

"Drive Aquino?" Whicher says.

The man nods his head up and down.

"You were supposed to be there?"

"La Migra," Zambrano says, "La Migra...stopped me..."

Krueger mouths a silent question; *What?*

The marshal thinks of Zambrano on the night—wired, hyped. "I picked him up, there was a 911 call—reports of shooting, at a ranch. Aquino stole a truck from there."

Krueger eyes him. "The ranch the explosion took place at? You're talking about the attack on the judge?"

The marshal nods.

Zambrano squints through the security screen, eyes like slits, his face screwed up.

"What were you going to do that night?" Whicher says.

"Intimidación."

"You were trying to intimidate the judge?"

"Qué?"

Whicher stares at the man.

"No entiendo."

"You don't understand?"

Zambrano shakes his head.

"Who were you trying to intimidate?"

"Competidor..."

"A rival?"

"Yes. Rival."

"What do you mean?"

"Organización rival. New. Una pandilla."

"A rival gang, a new gang?"

"Burreros, bringing niños over the border…"

"Kids?" the marshal says.

"Not…kids," Zambrano says. "Drogas. Drugs. A new route."

"A new route through the ranch?"

"Sí. The land of the ranch."

Whicher stares at the man. "Who were you going to intimidate?"

"Seguridad," Zambrano says, "like the other…"

"What do you mean, like Cardenas?"

"The man of the ranch."

Whicher eyes Zambrano behind the steel-mesh screen. "Somebody helping drug mules come through the Mackenzie Ranch?"

"Mano de rancho, sí."

"The ranch hand? You're talking about Glen Carr?"

CHAPTER THIRTY-SEVEN

Whicher stands with Joanne Krueger in the secure corridor eleven floors up in the Federal Detention Center.

"He's giving me the perp on two homicide cases."

The lawyer stands arms folded over the front of her navy suit. "He's giving up one, Cardenas, the farm hand..."

"Glen Carr was found dead in Monahans yesterday—if they were trying to intimidate him at the ranch the night I went up there, I say Aquino went ahead and killed him."

Krueger stares along the length of the corridor at the waiting corrections officer. "Why would they blow up the judge's car?"

"I don't know," Whicher says, "I need to know—I need to know we can talk to him about a deal..."

The lawyer's face is clouded. "If there's no connection to the attempt on Judge Richardson, FBI won't be interested—neither will DOJ."

"DEA will be," Whicher says, "if I can get him to testify. I think the guy's still out there, Aquino..."

"FBI are investigating," Krueger says, "what do they think?"

"They think he's gone—across the border. Back south."

"They don't believe he's in the country?" She looks at him.

"I believe he still is." The marshal thinks of the gut feeling, stretching all the way back to the first night. "I think he's out there, somewhere. And I want to nail the son of a bitch." He turns to the CO, catches the man's eye. "You get us back in there?"

The corrections officer steps forward, unlocks the door.

Whicher re-enters the interview room, pulls his chair closer to the mesh security screen.

Joanne Krueger follows, she sits.

"The day Border Patrol arrested you," Whicher says to Zambrano, "I want to know about it?"

The man's eyes are rounded, stress etched into his face. "I have names," he says, "people in Odessa—jefes, distribuidores, many people..."

"Not enough to tell, you'll have to testify, go all the way. First, I need to know everything—otherwise, no deal."

"Why'd you blow up the judge's car?" Krueger says.

Zambrano doesn't answer. He swallows, stares at Whicher.

"Start with what you were doing—when Border Patrol picked you up."

"I drive him," Zambrano says. "From Odessa. Leave him. Not far from the ranch."

"Where?"

"The highway. To walk in the desert—to the ranch."

"To walk?"

"Sí."

"How far?"

The man shrugs. "Is so nobody sees..."

"To enter...unseen?"

"He walks. Waits for night." Zambrano licks his lips, swallows. "To put the bomb."

"He went there to place the bomb?"

"Sí."

"Why?"

"We tell already, for him to stop."

"Who? Glen Carr?"

"He didn't stop. So we show him."

"How'd you get the device?"

"Contacto. In Juarez."

Whicher notes the detail. "Why that car?"

"Más caro."

Whicher looks at him. "The most expensive?"

Zambrano nods.

"That's all, that's it?"

"After, I drive to him, from the north—from the canyon."

"Pinto Canyon? What was he going to do?"

"Fire many shots, bengalas..."

"Bengalas? Flares?"

"So everybody sees—comes out of the house. Then explode the car."

"But you never made it?"

"La Migra..."

"Because Border Patrol picked you up..." The marshal thinks of Zambrano on the night at the ranch; sweating, amped up. Knowing Aquino would be there; knowing he was waiting for him.

Joanne Krueger speaks; "So, this Aquino targets a vehicle at random? The most expensive looking car? Nothing to do with it belonging to Judge Richardson?"

Zambrano's eyes are blank.

The lawyer looks at Whicher. Shakes her head. "Not interested..."

The marshal thinks through Aquino's actions—firing flares, firing shots out in the desert, getting people's attention at the ranch. But nobody had come out, instead, they'd called 911. Whicher had come up, law enforcement had come up.

Zambrano, his driver, hadn't showed.

And so he couldn't blow up the car—not with law enforcement everywhere—and no way out. He'd changed his mind, trekked out on foot, found the barn, stolen the Dakota.

"You know a man named Guevara?" Whicher says, "Santiago Guevara?"

Behind the mesh screen, Zambrano's eyes show no sign of recognition.

"No?"

Zambrano shakes his head. "I know many people—many names—narcotraficantes, personas importantes."

"What about this rival gang?" Whicher says.

"Es una guerra."

"A war?"

"We defend our land. They cross la frontera—nuestro camino."

"They use your route? Through the mountains, the Chinatis?"

"Sí."

"Then through the ranch land?"

"Sí, sí."

"Then where?"

"Monahans. Midland."

The marshal eyes him. Feels his heart rate tick up. "Monahans? Then up to Midland?"

Zambrano nods.

Whicher turns to Joanne Krueger. "I have to call DEA."

***

At the far end of the corridor, Whicher eyes the busy street below through a slit window. Two calls to Delfina Ruiz at DEA have gone unanswered; he keys the number for the lead FBI investigator on the Judge Richardson case.

Boyce Kelly answers on the third ring.

"I'm in downtown Houston," the marshal says, "I know who acquired the bomb on the judge's car."

"Say again?"

"I'm at the Federal Detention Center, I've just been talking to him."

"Marshal. You want to tell me what the hell's going on?"

"I picked up a guy on a foreign fugitive warrant—last week—he just told me about it."

"Is this legit?"

"It's straight-up legit. He told me he got the IED from a guy in Juarez..."

The FBI agent clears his throat. "Current evidence suggests it came from Juarez..."

"Right. So, we have him in custody, we're holding him. And the guy's talking. He wants to deal."

Kelly doesn't respond.

"They weren't targeting the judge," Whicher says, "they weren't after him. They were looking to intimidate the hand —Glen Carr. This guy says Carr was helping drug mules cross Larry Mackenzie's land. They warned him to stop, they were escalating it, South American style."

"Is this credible?" the FBI agent says.

"Aquino went out there, picked the most expensive-looking car to light up—it happened to belong to the judge." Whicher glances back up the corridor—sees Krueger—talking fast into her phone. "This guy can point you to the bomb-maker. He can give me the perp on two homicides. Plus, he has information useful to DEA."

"Look, if there's no link with Judge Richardson," Kelly

says, "no de facto case around it, I don't think the FBI would want to get involved. This guy acquired the IED?"

"He says so."

"Did he place it on the vehicle?"

"Aquino placed it," Whicher says, "the guy told me how they did it. Aquino tracked in on foot—my guy was supposed to pick him up—but he got himself arrested by Border Patrol."

Kelly thinks it over a moment. "So, he's an accessory—but we don't have Aquino. If you could get him, we could deal..."

"This guy's on a warrant for extradition—he's out of here unless we deal."

At the end of the corridor, the DOJ lawyer finishes her call.

"So, do you want a piece of this?"

"Right now," Kelly says. "As of right now—I don't."

* * *

Joanne Krueger steers the Mercedes along the terminal road toward the airport. The car dips beneath a concrete overpass, she switches lanes for the domestic flights.

"Think he'll keep on with the hunger strike?" Whicher says.

The DOJ lawyer shrugs.

"You're stuck with him if he's not fit to undergo due process."

Krueger maneuvers the big sedan toward the departures building, saying nothing.

Whicher eyes the flights coming in beyond the air traffic control tower—still no word back from Delfina Ruiz at Odessa DEA.

The lawyer looks at him from behind the wheel. "It's not my decision to make. I came to hear what he had to say, and report back. There's an entire legal extradition team involved in this—not to mention the foreign extradition lawyers in Colombia."

"Think they want him back?"

Krueger slows beneath the roof pillars in the covered drop-off area—brings the car to a halt. "Maybe they want to bring him to justice—and be seen to do so. Maybe he has information they want?"

"Keep him alive," the marshal says, "don't let him starve to death."

"Not my job to do that."

"If I can get a deal, I'm coming back."

"FBI don't want him," Krueger says.

"Maybe DEA will."

"You really think anybody will care at DEA?"

The marshal pushes open the door of the Mercedes. Steps out. Tips the brim of his hat to her. "I guess we'll find out."

* * *

At a window seat at the front of the airplane, Whicher gazes out at airport buildings and the city of Houston stretched out beyond perimeter fencing and the freeway as the Boeing 737 taxies at the side of the runway.

He thinks of Zambrano, emaciated in his prison whites—of the desperation in his face behind the interview room security screen.

The phone in his suit pocket starts to ring.

He takes it out, checks it—Delfina Ruiz.

He picks up.

"You've been trying to call me?"

"I'm on a plane about to take off out of Houston…"

"Your message said you were talking to somebody in the FDC?"

"Arrestee on an international fugitive warrant."

"What's going on?" Ruiz says.

"I'm flying into Midland. Can you meet me?"

The 737 starts to pick up speed, moving along the taxiway to the far end of the runway.

"I'll be landing in an hour-thirty. I've got something I think you ought to hear…"

CHAPTER THIRTY-EIGHT

In a Mexican kitchen off the service road at Midland International, Whicher sits in a booth watching as the unmarked Ford Crown Victoria pulls into a parking bay outside in the lot.

The young Latina woman stepping from behind the wheel is dressed in shorts and running shoes, a gray marl T-shirt. Wraparound sunglasses on top of her short brown hair.

The marshal drains his cup of coffee, traps a twenty under the mat.

Walks out of the restaurant.

DEA agent Delfina Ruiz leans against her car. "We can't do this here." She gestures to the Silverado. "Follow me in your truck."

The marshal takes out his keys. "Where are we going?"

She opens up the Crown Vic. "Just sit right in behind me."

* * *

Fifteen minutes later, the exit road from I-20 into Odessa runs past the back of a subdivision at the southern edge of the town. Condominiums mix with single properties, new-built churches, low-rent motels.

A wide expanse of short, burnt grass is up ahead—sports lights and batting cages—a roadside sign reads, *McKinney Park*.

Delfina Ruiz signals, pulls into a near-deserted parking lot. She stops beneath shade trees.

Whicher pulls in alongside her.

Stepping out, the DEA agent lowers her sunglasses. She scans the lot, the surrounding park.

The marshal climbs from his truck. "So, we good here?"

"We're good." She pushes the dark glasses up into her hair.

Across the empty sports fields, past deserted batting cages, a playground stands empty but for a handful of mothers and young kids.

Ruiz indicates a running trail through a patch of wood-land—live oak and cottonwoods.

Whicher walks beside her.

"Tell me about Houston?"

"I spent the afternoon talking with a Colombian," Whicher says, "on an extradition warrant. Guy with information. Looking to trade it for a plea."

The sound of traffic on Interstate Twenty drifts on the breeze, a green canopy of leaves throws deep shade inside the woods.

"What kind of information?"

"Narco trafficking," the marshal says. "Names of people. Distributors. In West Texas. Here in Odessa."

The DEA agent angles her head.

"He told me who killed my missing farm hand. And cut Glen Carr's throat in Monahans, most likely."

Ruiz stops. Looks at him directly. "How'd you get this?"

"A guy I picked up. Ten days back, the night of the ranch

attack—the ranch where Judge Richardson was staying? This guy was supposed to be driving for the guy who did it—another foreign national—named Aquino, Esequiel Aquino. You know him?"

The DEA agent doesn't reply.

She turns, walks on, the marshal falls in step beside her.

"Listen," she says. "Today I was working undercover. Meeting with a confidential source."

"An informant?"

"A source," Ruiz says, staring straight ahead. "This source told me the guy that killed Glen Carr is receiving a narcs drop—tonight."

"Aquino?"

She shakes her head. "No names. They'll hardly ever use names. Everything's a code or a number. But he told me the guy that cut up the *vato* in Monahans is taking a load tonight—from across the border."

"He tell you where?"

"He didn't know." She throws a look at the marshal. "But this is a trusted source, a former cholo, a gang member. And something else—that house where Glen Carr's truck was abandoned? The house in Monahans? Rented out to a Johnny Shillick? There's evidence of narcotics all over it."

Light filters through the trees as the woods begin to thin.

The path emerges into another, smaller park—soccer pitches surrounding an empty picnic pavilion—beyond the park, an upscale Catholic church.

"The arrestee in Houston told me they were looking to push out a rival gang—intimidate them," Whicher says.

"So, this guy Shillick's one of the new people bringing drugs over the border?" Ruiz says. "Up into Monahans?"

Whicher walks with the DEA agent toward the pavilion. "Maybe. And maybe Aquino cut Glen Carr's throat for helping his mules come in over the Mackenzie land."

"Nobody's seen him," Ruiz says. "It looks like this Shillick hightailed it."

"Carr's truck was dumped outside his house," Whicher says, "maybe to send a message—maybe even to try to put him in the frame."

From the open doors of the church the sound of music and singing drifts in the evening air.

Ruiz lowers herself onto a bench at a picnic table.

The marshal sits down opposite.

"These Monahans people," Ruiz says. "They're going up against a much larger organization—here, in Odessa."

The marshal watches traffic on a four-lane highway—delivery vans and big rigs prominent among the trucks and cars. "So, two rival drugs gangs," he says, "trying to run two routes, too close to one another. My homicide victim, Cardenas—working with Aquino, for the Odessa people. Cardenas wanted to quit—Aquino killed him."

Ruiz nods.

"And Glen Carr working for these Monahans guys."

"Is what it looks like," the DEA agent says.

The marshal leans his weight into the table. Stares into the lengthening shadows of the trees, their branches moving in a soft wind. "I want to go after this guy..."

Ruiz doesn't answer.

"If he's down on the border tonight, you think DEA would make up a combined op?"

Her face is doubtful.

"If you believe your source?" the marshal says. "It sounds like he could be out there."

Ruiz shakes her head.

"No?"

"No."

"Are you interested in my Houston guy's testimony?"

"We would be," Ruiz says, "yes. But we don't have time or

agents available to set up for tonight. Plus, I have to protect my source. DEA make a move we'd hang him out in the open. You could put the word out to Border Patrol…"

"That's not going to blow his cover?"

"Not if it's the Patrol. You tell them intel points to mules coming over tonight—have them target your suspect area…"

Whicher nods.

Delfina Ruiz eyes him, leaning in against the table. "But you want more than that?"

The music from the church floats to silence on the wind.

Whicher answers; "I want to take him off the board."

* * *

Van Horn, Tx

The living room of the cement-block house in Van Horn is empty. From behind rusted-steel security bars on the windows, Aquino watches the barely occupied lane on the eastern edge of town.

At his feet on the concrete floor is a long, canvas carry bag, unzipped.

Inside, the Heckler & Koch 416 rifle.

He looks out past the parked Dodge Durango—out along the street. No vehicles are moving, scarcely a sign of life showing at the handful of run-down houses and prefabricated homes.

At the far end of the lane, a Toyota pickup turns in. Aquino's hand brushes the Glock 17 pistol at his waist.

One man is inside the pickup.

It drives up to the house, stops directly outside, behind the Dodge SUV.

The door opens.

Aquino recognizes the mustachioed man stepping from the truck.

Carlos Mendoza—a replacement for the hick Colombian.

Mendoza looks up and down the street. Crosses the dirt yard. Knocks at the door.

Aquino unfastens the locks, slides back the security bar. Opens up.

Mendoza stands wordless.

"Inside," Aquino says.

The man steps into the room.

Aquino locks the door, checks the street from the window.

"¿Qué pasa?" Mendoza says.

Turning from the window, Aquino looks Mendoza up and down. "Here is where you come. After..."

The man nods.

"You wait here. Somebody will arrive."

"¿Cuándo?"

"When they come," Aquino says.

Mendoza stands mute, leans his stocky frame against the dry wall.

"You don't do nothing. You stay here. Watch over. Don't open any package. Don't touch a thing."

"I wouldn't touch nothing."

"If you take something..." Aquino lets his stare sink into the man's eyes.

Mendoza doesn't blink.

"The truck? Outside?"

"Is okay," Mendoza says.

"The plates?"

"Robadas."

Aquino nods. Stolen.

Mendoza pulls a pack of Marlboros from inside his jacket.

"You don't smoke in here," Aquino says.

The man nods. "Outside..."

Aquino shakes his head. "You don't go outside."

He reaches into the canvas bag, lifts out a pistol-grip Mossberg 500 shotgun.

He gives it to Mendoza, eyes him.

The man's face is stone.

"This doesn't leave your hand," Aquino says.

CHAPTER THIRTY-NINE

At the house in Pecos, Whicher changes into a sweatshirt and jeans. He hangs up his suit in the walk-in wardrobe in the bedroom, stares at the gun safe mounted on the wall. Thinks of the message left for Fairbanks, updating her. He runs a hand over his face. Eyes the safe a moment longer.

Stepping from the bedroom, he tracks down the hall into the kitchen.

Leanne looks up from picking off the meat from a rotisserie chicken, shredding it between her fingers into a bowl. "How was Houston?"

He leans against the countertop. "Downtown looked pretty good from the window of a detention center."

"You get the best jobs..." She eyes a pan of tomatillos and chiles serranos heating on the hob. "You want to stir that for me?"

"What's cooking?"

"Green chicken enchiladas..."

Whicher picks up a spoon, stands at the stove.

"So, was it worth the trip?"

The marshal nods. "Worth it to me."

Taking a fry pan from a kitchen drawer, Leanne puts it onto the stove, puts the shredded chicken into it. "You find out why he wanted to talk?"

"Guy was involved the night I got called out to the ranch. Hooked up with what went on. He knows who killed my farm hand."

Leanne makes a question with her face.

Whicher stirs the saucepan. "Only good if I can get him into court," the marshal says. "Where's Lori?"

"In her bedroom, I think."

"She doing okay?"

"She's finishing up her homework." Leanne adds oil into the pan, sets the heat, takes a plate of chopped onion, adds it in with the shredded chicken. "So, what will happen?"

"Looking like he could still be deported."

"Even though he could help clear a homicide?"

"Two homicides. The ranch hand killed up in Monahans could be the same guy."

Leanne stirs the onion and chicken in the pan. "Well, then?"

Whicher takes a pinch of crumbled queso fresco from a bowl by the stove. "Foreign fugitives, there's already a prior call. And no automatic right to enter into any kind of plea. Extraditing country has first rights, I'd have to build a case…"

Turning down the heat, Leanne strips more meat from the chicken, shreds it.

The marshal stirs the saucepan. "Matter of fact, I need to make a call."

"I got that," Leanne says, "go ahead."

Whicher puts down the spoon, takes another pinch of the queso, grabs his phone from the table.

He heads back to the bedroom, steps to the walk-in wardrobe. Enters the combination for the gun safe. Opens it.

Takes out the scoped M4 carbine and a brace of loaded, thirty-round magazines.

He puts everything onto the bed. Checks the magazines over. Powers up the thermal imager on the M4, checks the level on the battery.

He sits a moment. Lays the rifle down. Finds the number for Adriana Lozada at Presidio Border Patrol.

He keys the call, stands.

Lozada answers.

"Marshal."

"Evenin'."

"I do something for you?"

"Maybe. I was calling to let you know about a DEA tip on a possible narcotics run tonight. In your sector."

"Really?" Lozada says. "That's news. We hadn't heard?"

"Might be just a couple of mules crossing the river," Whicher says. "There's a possibility it could involve a guy I'm looking for..."

"Oh?"

The marshal clears his throat. "Did you know that Glen Carr was found up in Monahans yesterday morning?"

"Sheriff Torres called," she says. "He told the station commander..."

Whicher surveys the bedroom—checks the hallway is empty.

He sits on the bed, lowers his voice. "DEA aren't acting on this, it's low level, they're not ready to make a move. But their intel is, the person involved is likely responsible for Carr's death. I think it's a guy named Esequiel Aquino. I'm pretty sure he killed my farm hand, Matias Cardenas."

"You think he could be down here? Tonight?"

"That's the word."

"What do you want to do, you want to come down?"

Whicher eyes the M4 carbine. "Thinking about it."

"But DEA don't want to act?"

The marshal picks a magazine off the bed, presses down on the top round against the spring. "I'm not alright letting these sons of bitches have free rein—to kill, and get away with it..."

"Nobody is," Lozada says. "Listen, we're running line watch tonight between here and Ruidosa—up the San Antonio valley. Extra unit on the ground wouldn't hurt."

"Right."

"Weather's not looking great, though. We're expecting high winds, and maybe some rain."

"Oh?"

"That means the aerostat's probably going to be down. I don't know what radar we'll have. Drones might be grounded. Anyhow, we'll head out from the station around ten—unless we're called out sooner."

"I'll come down," Whicher says. "I guess it might all be a long shot..."

"If you change your mind," Lozada says, "let me know."

Whicher finishes the call.

Lori appears in the hallway, holding a jar of crema Mexicana. Lips pursed.

"Hey, sweetheart."

His daughter's eyes are bright, indignant. "Did you just arrange to go out again...tonight?"

"What?"

"Down to the border?"

The marshal doesn't answer.

Lori stares at the rifle and the magazines on the bed. "What's all that?"

He looks at her.

She grips the jar in her hands, color rising in her face. "You're going after that drug cartel again?"

"No..."

"Yes, you are…"

"I'm looking for an individual. Alright? One man—not a cartel."

"*Why?*" Lori's voice is shrill.

Whicher keeps his voice soft, even. "It's my job sweetheart…"

"You were just down there…"

The marshal puts away the phone, gets up from the bed. "We think a suspect could be there tonight. Somebody involved in a murder."

"Exactly—that's what I *mean*."

"I'm running a homicide investigation, sweetheart…"

"Somebody else can do it. You were just talking to someone—they can do it."

"Border Patrol," the marshal says. "They can't be everywhere."

"Why can't you just let someone else do it?" She stares at him, voice rising; "Why does it always have to be you?"

Leanne appears in the doorway behind her daughter. "Sweetheart, it's alright…"

"It's not al*right*. Cartels kill people—they don't care who it is."

"Lori," Leanne says, "don't speak to your father that way."

Whicher eyes his daughter—careful to measure out his words. "I can't back off from folk because they're dangerous."

"You could."

"It doesn't work like that."

She stares at him, mouth clamped shut. Her eyes brimming. "If you don't care about how we feel…then don't expect us to care about you…"

She pushes past her mother, runs from the room.

* * *

US 90 is slick with rain. Aquino eyes the land south, black cloud etched into a darkening twilight sky.

The road ahead is empty.

In his rear-view mirror, only the headlamps of Mendoza's truck.

Set back from the highway is the Border Patrol tethered aerostat—the blimp radar. He stares at it—grounded. Smiles to himself, behind the wheel. He looks up into the rear-view —wonders if Mendoza will take it on board, notice.

A shower of rain hits the windshield suddenly. A gust of wind rocks the truck.

The weather is set to worsen. No matter.

He hits the wipers. Turns them off again as the rain just as suddenly stops.

Steering along the tar-ribboned road, window down in the Durango, he smells the wet earth, recalls his native Honduras. Thinks of dirt-poor villages, long behind him now.

On the back seat of the SUV is the canvas carryall— inside it, the Heckler & Koch. Everything else in the Toyota pickup, Mendoza's truck; Mendoza running all of the risk.

Recognizing the terrain beyond the fence line, Aquino slows—he looks for the bump gate onto the dirt road. Considers for a moment whether to use it. Whether to cross the land there.

But who would stop him?

Nobody.

Even if anybody saw.

He checks the highway is empty—no oncoming headlights. Sees the gate, now, along the fence line, slows, brakes, turns in from the road. Steers the front end of the Dodge onto the opener—nudges at it, the gate swings open.

He drives the SUV through.

Before him is a sea of chino grass and dark red earth— disappearing into failing light.

The buildings of the farm and the house miles off—beyond undulating folds of hills.

The Zimmerman place.

Wide open to him, the whole property. Despite the loss of the lookout. One less fool to pay.

Behind him, he sees Mendoza slow, make the turn, steer the pickup through the gate.

Nothing ahead of them now, till the river, the border. Save for mountain and ravine and high desert.

No road, no settlement.

Nobody out across the land.

No eyes. No ears.

CHAPTER FORTY

At the Border Patrol station in Presidio, Whicher listens to the rain on the window. He studies a large-scale topo map at the back of the room. Adriana Lozada fastens on a ballistic vest over olive fatigues.

Agents Webber and Matos position radios on their vests, adjust their holsters, check ammunition pouches, cuffs.

The marshal takes in the network of farm and ranch roads and trails along a thirty-mile stretch of border on the US side —from Presidio, northwest along the river to Ruidosa.

Lozada steps across the room.

"Lot of ways in," Whicher says.

She nods. "A lot of the main trails have ground sensors on them. Military grade. They'll send signals here and up to control in Marfa."

"No way to know what triggered 'em, though," Agent Matos puts in, "till we can get out and take a look. Whatever it was will be gone—could be animals, could be non-docs. Could be drug mules. Only one way to find out."

"How about if people are moving away from the trails?" the marshal says.

Lozada shakes her head. "Most won't. They'll pick remote routes—there's plenty of them. But they won't try to cross open desert. They don't have the skills, or the strength, they know it. They're not going to survive."

"How about narco traffic?"

"You're talking about young men," Lozada says, "ready to risk more. Even then, for the most part, they'll stay close to some sort of known route."

Agent Webber speaks; "We've got thermal imaging cameras at the river—but we can't detect everything..."

"So, what's the setup for tonight?" Whicher says.

"Post up twenty minutes apart," Lozada answers, "a little like the sweep, Tuesday." She turns to the map. "Agent Matos to the south—away from the road. The Chinatis behind him."

Matos gives a thumbs-up.

"Webb's going to head north, post up east of Candelaria. I'll be somewhere in between, around Ruidosa. I'll move up and down the river road. Like the last time, but without air support," she says. "And with the weather how it is, downward-looking radar will be minimal."

"The guy I'm looking for was trying to shut out people coming through the Mackenzie Ranch," Whicher says. "I think that's what a lot of this has been about. If he thinks he's closed down a route so a rival faction can't use it, maybe he'll go ahead and use it himself."

"Through the mountains?" Lozada says. "That's real tough terrain."

"Maybe he won't," Whicher says. "I'm just saying...it's a possibility. There's also an outside chance someone could come up near to Pinto Canyon."

Lozada shoots an eyebrow. "How so?"

Whicher fastens a two-way radio to a loop on the Marshals Service Kevlar vest. "Somebody was on the Iniguez

Ranch five nights back—that's right off of there." He tightens the vest straps against a navy sweat top.

"Stay close to the foot of the canyon," Webber says. "Near to the river, so you can get to the road."

"Faster if we need to move," Lozada says. "You don't want to get stuck in the canyon—lot of dead zones in there." She taps her radio.

Agent Matos grins. "Best chance is always nail them on the flats—before the ground rises. They get in the hills..." He shakes his head.

"If a sensor gets triggered," Lozada says, "we'll need to check it out, find out what it was. Did DEA give specific intel?"

"Nothing they shared with me," Whicher says. "Their source reckoned a shipment would be arriving. Most likely, I'd guess mules packing bales of dope on foot. Nothing major. Else DEA would want in."

"Yeah, nail them at the river," Matos says.

"They get across, they'll look to get up a trail," Agent Webber says. "Have somebody pick 'em up."

Lozada looks again at the map. "You think they could try at the Mackenzie Ranch?"

"They might," Whicher says.

Lozada looks to Agent Matos. "If they do," she says, "you'll be the closest to that."

* * *

In the scrub mesquite at the foot of Pinto Canyon Road, Whicher sits in the Silverado, lights out.

The Sierra Vieja is to his back, the Rio Grande five miles to his front.

Gusts of wind hit the truck side-on, rocking it.

Squalls of rain blow in the air, disappear in the night.

He huddles in a wool ranch coat, scanning the dark. Picking out only shapes. Mesquite and creosote bush and cactus. The slopes of hills, outlines of rocks.

He thinks of Zambrano in the prison room back in Houston.

His mind flits to another image—formed half from a file photograph, half from the sketch by the artist, the woman ranch owner, Iniguez.

In the desert silence he thinks of two murders—Cardenas and Glen Carr. The throat-slash victim up in Midland. Who knew how many more.

A single point of light is out in front of him—somewhere down on the river road at Ruidosa.

He shifts his gaze from the pinprick of light—sweeps the dark land, the empty desert.

A burst of static spits from the radio.

Adriana Lozada's voice comes on speaker. "Marshal?"

Whicher holds down the key to talk. "Yeah, this is Whicher, receiving, go ahead."

"We have a sensor triggered down near the old Adobes Cemetery. A dirt road—not real far from Agent Matos. It could be foot traffic—heading up into the Chinatis. Over."

The marshal keys to speak. "He need backup? I could go down there."

"I'll go," Lozada says. "I'm already down on the road. He's headed out, he'll see if he can find what triggered it. I'll go help him. It may be nothing. Hold the middle ground here, you've got Webber to your north. We don't want to leave too big a gap."

"Copy that," Whicher says. "Let me know if you need help."

* * *

Fifteen minutes later, Lozada is back on the radio. "I've got Matos cutting for sign in a canyon south of Cinco de Mayo —a mile or so from where the sensor was tripped—it looks like a group passed through, maybe five or six, headed north."

The marshal feels his heart rate tick up. "That could be mules, no?"

"Could be. Current course puts them into Cinco de Mayo."

Whicher thinks of the place—Lozada showing it to him the day they met—the day she took him to the Presa Llorona. "If they go up, over the high plateau, they're on Mackenzie land. Over."

"Copy that," Lozada says. "We're going to head north, see if we can catch up to them. If they see our lights, they're going to run and hide. We've got infrared binoculars, we should be able to find them. Unless they get in the hills. Over."

"Let me know what happens?" the marshal says. "Keep in mind the guy waiting on those mules is a killer."

"Copy that, marshal."

"I can get there fast if you need me."

"Understood. Over and out."

The radio falls silent.

Whicher sits back. Looks out through spots of rain on the windshield of the truck. Eyes the M4 carbine on the seat beside him.

Stares out into the black.

* * *

Flicking on the dome light of the cab's interior, Whicher takes the Border Patrol map from the seat in back.

Unfolding it, he traces the mountains, the main canyons

with a finger. The paved road at the river, the networks of trails—dirt roads crossing ranches and farms.

Cañón Cinco de Mayo is just a few miles from the border.

Anyone headed north through the mountains would emerge the way the group had appeared the morning of the hunt. Stalking out of the dark like a four-man patrol; looking for trouble.

He could drive up Pinto Canyon—pick up the dirt road to the Mackenzie Ranch.

Head in, set up from the rear.

Have Lozada and Agent Matos drive them to him.

He thinks of radioing Lozada—stops himself.

Better to wait.

Sit it out.

Hold the flank for Webber.

Hold ready.

* * *

The clock on the dash shows 12.30am. Shapes shift as moonlight streaks across the land between strips of low, ragged cloud.

The radio at his Kevlar vest beeps into life.

"Marshal?"

"Receiving."

"This is Agent Lozada—we have contact with a group of six—repeat, six individuals."

The marshal sits up. "Mules?"

"Negative. They're non-citizens, two adult males, two women, plus a boy and a girl. We're detaining them now. We're going to run them down to Presidio, have them processed. I'll head back up to Ruidosa just as soon as we've dropped them at the station—it's probably going to take me forty minutes."

"Copy that."

"Everything alright up there?"

"Yeah," the marshal says.

"Still quiet?"

"It's quiet. Wind's picking up. Getting wild out here."

"Always wild," Lozada says. "I'll call when I'm leaving the station—over and out."

* * *

The lone light at the river road is gone now. Anyone slipping by the thermal cameras, getting past the sensors—if they made it into desert or into the hills, they could lose themselves under cover of night. Unless the Patrol spotted them, Whicher tells himself. Or unless a rancher saw something, noticed something.

They'd be next to untraceable.

Like the group discovered off-trail by the helo—coming in along the remote ravine close to Horse Creek.

He stares out over the empty land in the darkness.

Pushes down a nagging thought.

* * *

1.15 in the morning—Lozada's voice is back on the radio.

"I'm coming up the river road," she says, "about ten minutes from Ruidosa. I'll post up when I get there."

"You take those folks in?"

"They're at the station now."

"I'm thinking to take a look up into Pinto Canyon," Whicher says, "if you're covering the river. Unless you want me to wait?"

"No problem," Lozada tells him. "Matos is in position around Adobes. Go ahead..."

CHAPTER FORTY-ONE

Five miles up the twisting road the marshal starts to recognize stretches of the pass. The truck's twin headlamps pick out silvered rain, crumbling dirt cliffs, gravel washes, boulders. A sudden steepness is in the sides of the canyon—a length of flat-lying gradient before him, distinctive faces of rock.

The stone ruins of the old schoolhouse at Horse Creek loom out of the dark.

He brings the truck to a halt.

Stares out of the window up the side canyon, impenetrable in the black.

Thinks of the helo calling down directions.

Heading up—to another ruin, full of non-docs.

In his mind's eye he pictures running in the darkness, chasing the fleeing figure, the young boy.

He comes off the brake, gets back onto the gas. Steers along the trail of dirt and gravel. Thinks to signal-check the radio. Presses down on the key to call.

"Whicher—to Lozada. You read? Over?"

Lozada's voice comes back faint. "Receiving. Over."

"I'm about halfway up the canyon—nothing doing here."

"Roger that."

"Anything with you? Over."

"No alerts from dispatch," Lozada says. "No sensor triggers. It's all quiet at the river. Mobile radar picked up signal on a low-flying aircraft over on the Mexican side. Dropping in and out. Slow moving, the only reason they'd look at it. In case it's crossing over. Could just be a truck, sometimes it happens. Are you staying in the canyon?"

"For now," Whicher says.

"Keep your eyes open."

"I'll do that," the marshal answers. "Over and out."

* * *

The dirt road climbs sharp now, crossing creek beds and gulches—he visualizes the route ahead, along the contours of the steepening canyon.

He moves the shifter to a low gear.

Climbs on into night—over loose gravel, patches of volcanic rock. Pushing on for the top of the pass where the Sierra Vieja flattens to the wide expanse of grassland, the Marfa plain.

He thinks of the turn—past the head of the canyon.

Out onto remote ranch country.

The Iniguez Property.

* * *

The southern edge of the Rim Rock sweeps down out of night, folds of hills descending into desert scrub.

At the far reach of the truck's headlamp beams, beyond creosote bush and guayacan and lechuguilla he sees the walls of a one-floor ranch house, half a mile up ahead.

No light showing from it.

A feeling starts to tick in the pit of his stomach.

He drives along the dirt trail. The clock on the dash coming up on one-forty-five.

Thinking of the woman.

Iniguez.

Her fear describing the man looking into her house.

He stares out through the windshield. Something in the visual wrong, presenting wrong; disturbing the picture.

He comes off the gas, squints, tries to make it out.

Then stops.

Sits entirely still behind the wheel.

Faint marks are in the dirt road stretching toward the house and the buildings. He sees it between beats of the windshield wipers. Clear. Then blurred out again.

He unhooks the seat belt, opens up the door.

Steps out. Walks forward of the truck.

Kneeling, he stares at the ground, at tire marks pressed into wet soil.

A vehicle has driven through, over the damp earth—recent, since the rain started to fall.

Rain that'd come since nightfall.

Alarm grows in his gut.

He steps to the truck, climbs in. Drives on.

Approaching the ranch, he slows, draws level with the first of the outbuildings. Spots the battered-looking half-ton truck—her truck.

In the sidewash of the headlamp beams the wind turbines beyond the house are picked out—the carved totems, the iron sculptures—the Airstream trailer.

He stares down the dirt track leading farther out onto the property—the track Garcia took him on; the barely used trail onto former grazing land. In the hi-beams, he makes out marks in the wettened earth.

He stops the truck. Grabs the M4, takes a flashlight from the glove box, gets out. Crosses the dirt yard, checks the wheels and tires of Iniguez's vehicle—they're dry, no earth on the sidewalls nothing in the treads, it hasn't moved.

Something else has driven through.

He plays the flashlight beam along the ground toward the house, sees the door hanging open.

He starts toward it, a feeling building inside.

Stepping to the door, he pushes it wide—into darkness. He takes a pace inside the blackened space; "*US Marshal…*"

No response comes back.

Moving further inside he calls out again, "*US Marshal—anybody in here?*"

He fits the light to a holder on the M4 carbine. Checks each of four rooms in the small, stone house.

No one inside.

Stepping out, he runs to the Airstream trailer. He tries the door. It's unlocked.

He opens up. "*Ma'am? Anybody there…*"

He sweeps the interior with the light on the M4. The trailer is empty.

Moving fast, he checks an outbuilding, another. Feels his pulse climb, his breath come short. The image of Glen Carr in his mind's eye suddenly, Glen Carr with his throat slashed, dragged away, dumped like garbage in a service alley.

He stares at the house, the trailer, the few built structures. Afraid now; for how he might find her.

Out at the edge of the Silverado's headlamp beams is a small corral, a stone shelter beyond it. He runs to it. Stares at a door of rough wood planks. Yanks it open.

Shining the light inside, he sees her—at the back of the shelter on the dirt floor.

Her eyes are wild, she holds out a rifle.

"*Marshals Service, ma'am—it's alright, it's alright…*"

She stares, holds the gun rigid.

"I'm a US Marshal, I was here with Garcia..."

"They came back..."

"Somebody came through?"

She nods, grips an AR-15.

"They're on your land?" he says.

"I heard something go by—I got out..."

Whicher offers his hand.

"I just wanted to get out, to hide..."

She takes a pace forward.

He leads her from the stone shelter. "Ma'am, go back inside your house..."

"What if they come back?"

"Go on inside, lock up, you'll be safe. I'll get law enforcement out here."

She stands clutching her rifle.

A rip of sound is in the air, on the wind—somewhere overhead. Something motorized, some kind of engine.

"I have to go after them," he tells her. "Go, go on inside..."

He runs for his truck, jumps in.

Sees her race for the house.

He drives out, past the Airstream, past the last of the outbuildings—into darkness, blasts of wind howling out of the night. Intermittent bursts of rain lash the windshield. He follows the twin wheel marks in the ground.

On into the abandoned grazing land

In the wet smear on the windshield, lights appear.

Far off in front of him.

Lights.

In a line.

* * *

Snapping out the headlamps, Whicher grabs the M4 carbine from the passenger seat. He cuts the motor, whips open the door, keeps low to the ground.

Pushing away from the truck, he scrambles up the rising grade of a hill.

An outcrop of solid rock looms in the dark.

Flattening behind it, he pulls the M4 to him, flips on power to the thermal imaging sight.

Searching out a flat spot on the rock, he places the rifle.

They must have seen him—seen the truck lights.

Hunting for dots of white on the plain he spots something. He pivots the rifle against its resting point on the rock.

Puts his eye to the scope.

* * *

Aquino stands with his back to the big SUV—he stares out across the scrub plain.

A black nothing is all that's out there.

Carlos Mendoza waits by his Toyota pickup at the edge of the marker lights on the desert floor. He stares up into the night sky.

An ultralight aircraft circles in the air above.

Aquino watches it, for only a moment. The tiny craft slews in the gusting winds.

Breaking off, he reaches inside the SUV for the HK 416 rifle. He shouts to Mendoza to watch for the bales of drugs suspended from the harness on the ultralight's frame. "*¡Cuidado!*"

Mendoza turns, gapes at him.

Aquino points at the sky.

Switching on the night vision scope of the rifle, he raises the weapon, rests it on the roof of the SUV.

Looking out across the desert plain a green image forms—

the lens capturing available light and infrared. He searches for the source of the light he saw.

Finds it—a truck—stationary—on the track from the ranch, headlamps out.

He tries to make out a driver—any occupant, sees none.

Zooming the lens, he focuses the image.

He dials in the range finder, tries to estimate distance— it's out at 500 yards.

The slope of a rounded hill is to one side of the track— another rises from its other side, up in the direction of the mountain rim.

Beyond it, the track is invisible.

Zooming out, he waits for the image intensifier to readjust.

Sweeping right to left, he searches.

The noise of the ultralight loud overhead.

Aquino looks from the scope into the night air.

The pilot of the craft struggles with a lever on the frame —releases a clutch of bales. They fall, deadweight to the ground.

Mendoza starts to run toward them.

More bales will fall; Aquino shouts at him to wait; *"¡Espere!"*

The man swivels his head.

Returning to the rifle scope, Aquino scans the land—the images jerky, his hands unsteady, anger building now as he searches for the occupant of the truck.

* * *

Whicher keeps his eye to the thermal imager on the rail of the M4 carbine. He sees the man at the SUV—sweeping back and forth, a rifle held before him, head canted to a scope.

A second man stands within a square of marker lights—

hacking at the netting around objects on the ground. At the top of the picture an ultralight dances—it's motor bright, a white spot, hottest of the heat signatures in the gray-scale image.

Nobody else is down there—no other heat sources within the field of view.

Two men. A third in the aircraft.

Jackrabbits and javelinas watch set back in the scrub desert.

Two vehicles. The SUV and a pickup truck, glowing from their hoods, their wheels, their brakes.

The SUV is big—a Durango, maybe; Whicher stares at it.

Stares at the man with the rifle.

Aquino.

Maybe Aquino?

He feels his heart rate climb, looking at him in the reticle of the scope.

The man hacking with the knife frees something from the netting on the ground. He fills both hands, carries objects to the pickup, throws them into the bed.

The ultralight circles in the air above the glow sticks.

Then turns away to the south, toward the Sierra Vieja.

The man searching with the rifle breaks off—runs toward the man with the knife.

* * *

Dragging everything from the net across the dirt, Mendoza hoists the bales one by one into the pickup bed.

"Go," Aquino tells him.

"*¿Qué?*"

"Take the drogas, go east—*este.*"

"Back?" Mendoza says. He points. "Past the ranch?"

"No, no—a truck is back there."

Mendoza's eyes widen.

"Head east," Aquino says, "I'll go north. Over the desert."

"What truck?" Mendoza says.

"Go to the house—in Van Horn. Stay off the road."

Mendoza stands rooted at the side of the Toyota.

Aquino shifts the rifle between his hands.

Steps to his own vehicle. "Go. *Vamos...*"

* * *

Zooming onto the tailgate of the fleeing pickup truck, Whicher makes out a series of letters—among them a Y and an O.

He pulls back from the scope, presses down on the radio key. "Whicher—anybody read?"

Only silence comes back.

Through the scope, he sees the man with the rifle, now inside the SUV.

The vehicle starts to move.

A burst of static crackles on the radio, followed by a faint female voice. "Lozada."

"This is Whicher."

"Receiving," the Border Patrol agent says.

"I'm up at the Iniguez property—I just witnessed a narcotics drop from an ultralight. I have a suspect vehicle—probable Toyota pickup—traversing ranch land, headed northeast. Over."

"Roger that."

"Vehicle is likely headed for Farm Road 2810 out of the canyon—or Highway 90."

"Copy," Lozada says.

"It's carrying narcotics in the bed. You need units up the Pinto Canyon Road—and on the highway out of Marfa."

"I'll get out an alert," Lozada says.

"I've got a second vehicle here."

"You need assistance? Over."

"Going to be gone before you can make it," Whicher says. "But send units to the Iniguez Ranch." He checks the scope again. "Vehicle is headed northwest. Will pursue. Over and out."

He clicks off the radio, sprints downhill to the truck. Fires it up, sticks the rifle in the footwell, hits the lights.

The SUV is out ahead of him, half a mile or more, taillights glowing.

He shifts into drive, mashes down on the gas, the truck lurches forward.

Away from the trail the land rises at either side, twisted outcrops of rock, alien, grotesque in the play of the truck's beams.

The SUV out front disappears, reappears as the track twists and turns through the hills at the Rim Rock's edge.

Whicher thinks of the man in the SUV—a drug runner and a killer.

He thinks of his daughter's words.

His answer to her.

The taillights on the SUV vanish.

The marshal waits for them to reappear.

Pushes the truck on faster.

* * *

Out of the car, Aquino steadies his rifle against the roof. He zooms the night vision scope to the blind bend; the spot where the track re-emerges from around the side of the hill.

Adjusting for the range he guesses the approximate height of a windshield.

Leans his body weight into the SUV, steadying the rifle's barrel, finger curled against the trigger.

The scope fills with phosphorescent green light—lens saturating as the truck's headlamps appear.

Squinting, Aquino fires—venting pent-up rage since the truck's arrival, projecting the violence inside him, loosing round after round.

He pauses, lets the scope adjust to the light source—only the headlamps show clear.

He works to zoom back, expand the picture.

Now frantic to see.

* * *

Scrambling from the truck Whicher dives into the scrub mesquite. He pushes down shock, crouches, raises the M4— sights on the muzzle flare out in front in the dark.

He brings the flashes to the center of the thermal image scope.

Incoming fire is directly in line with the stationary SUV.

He steadies the rifle.

Single-fires three rounds. Hits the back of the vehicle with the second, the third. Shoots for the glowing tires.

Then holds on a faint outline—a man's head visible behind the car.

* * *

Aquino feels the rounds hit the taillight cluster, the D-post— he flinches, he can't find the shooter. He flips the H&K to full-auto—sprays both sides of the track—empties the magazine.

Running around to the driver side, he gets in, stamps on the gas, ducks low at the wheel.

A bullet cracks the rear glass, passes straight out through

the windshield—a second explodes the headrest on the passenger seat.

Aquino weaves left and right.

Rounds hit the bodywork, low down.

The track passes the side of another hill.

He makes the turn around it—out of sight.

CHAPTER FORTY-TWO

Whicher runs from the brush keying the transceiver on the Kevlar vest.

He stares after the disappearing lights of the SUV, blood running.

"Whicher. Anybody copy?"

No response comes back.

He keys again. "Anybody read this? Over."

He rolls the volume, a flat hiss is all he hears.

Dead zone.

Standing, breathing in the dark, adrenaline surges.

He can wait for backup.

None may come.

The desert stretches out, hundreds of square miles to run in.

He jumps into the truck. On anger and instinct and the rush of blood inside him. Drives on, steering around another bend in the track.

The taillights are gone.

No pinpricks of red.

No wash of headlamps.

Nothing.

Accelerating, he tries to make out features in the surrounding land.

To his left, the ground rises into black, toward the drop off at the cliff edge of the Rim Rock. A thousand feet of fall.

To his right a maze, undulating hills.

He swings the truck up the steep grade toward the rim. Higher and higher, straining to spot the first sign of the cliff edge. Looking for the highest safe point.

Braking to a stop, he grabs the rifle, jumps out, climbs in the bed of the truck.

He puts the scope to his eye—high-spotting, scanning, breath held, fighting to steady in the wind.

Nothing.

He sweeps back and forth.

Spots it.

Twin dots of white—moving fast—the SUV.

3,000 yards in the scope. Mile and a half, maybe more.

Headed east.

* * *

Aquino grips the wheel as headlights blink in and out behind him once again. He can't lose him.

Whoever it is, he can't shake him, can't get him off of his tail.

Up ahead is cover; buildings and barns he knows. He can dump the Dodge, hide it. Strike out into desert, he's done it before. He can walk out, have Mendoza pick him up—find him somewhere, a stretch of highway, up in Valentine, anywhere.

He glances in the rear-view mirror, sees nothing.

Focuses ahead—sees a fence line, a gate.

Outrun him.

Evade or kill.

He thinks of killing whoever is behind him—willing it, one thought running into the next. Filled with hate, with vicious force burning through him.

The specks of white reappear in his rear-view mirror—lighting up the blood in his veins.

He stares ahead at a zinc gate—chained and padlocked.

Steers the Durango straight for it, teeth bared, flooring out the gas.

* * *

Whicher grabs the radio unit, puts the channel selector into scan.

Static and noise spit from the transceiver—a burst of radio chatter—silence.

And then dispatch.

Border Patrol in Marfa.

He keys to speak. "This is Deputy Marshal Whicher—I have a suspect vehicle south of Highway 90—in open country. I'm in pursuit. Over."

A female voice comes back. "Dispatch, copy that, marshal."

"Vehicle is a Dodge Durango—request assistance, urgent."

"Roger that. What is your position?"

Whicher steers the truck along the side of a stand of greasewood and scrub mesquite. "I'm in desert south of 90, coming onto farmland...I think...the Zimmerman property."

"We'll roll units, marshal. Over."

"All officers, be aware—suspect is armed and dangerous."

"Copy that."

Ahead is an open bar-gate—its frame bent up, twisted.

Whicher keys the radio; "Entering the property now."

"We'll get back up rolling, marshal, if you can wait..."

"Understood," Whicher answers. "Over and out."

* * *

Descending the dirt trail between worked fields, he can no longer see it—no sign of the SUV, no Aquino out in front—no pinpricks of taillights, no red, no wash of white.

Outlines of barns and buildings form out of the darkness.

Up ahead a pole light glows dim, a yard lamp—he thinks of the buildings about the Zimmerman property. Brakes the truck to a sudden stop.

Ambush country.

The farm, the outbuildings.

Staring through the windshield, he tries to pick out the fleeing vehicle—it can't be gone, it can't be that far ahead.

He shuts down the motor, kills the lights, snatches up the M4 carbine. Stuffs extra magazines into pockets on the Kevlar vest.

Slipping down from the truck, he presses the M4 to his shoulder—stares into the thermal imaging scope—sees the house, barns, farm equipment—stationary vehicles, Zimmerman's truck.

Nothing shows hot, nothing warm. He keeps low, moves in, advancing behind the rifle. Sweeping, looking for heat spots, for the SUV—for Aquino. A feeling inside like leading a zone op, dismounted from the Bradleys, every sense on high alert.

An AC unit glows at an upstairs window of the house.

Whicher pushes wide, flanking out beyond the packing shed.

At the edge of the scope's field of view, a patch of white registers, a blur.

The marshal levels the rifle, moves into cover behind an old stone wall.

He searches out the heat again—finds it; a bright glow bisected with a hard edge—he zooms the scope.

The hard edge is a barn doorway—a barn set away from the rest of the buildings; he pictures the farm workshop—thinks of interviewing the hand there, Guevara.

Adjusting the lens on the scope, Whicher sees the source of the heat—rear wheels and tires on a vehicle, part hidden inside the workshop space.

The SUV.

Aquino—waiting on him to pass the farm—to lose him.

An outline appears—the figure of a man—moving out from the house.

Whicher shifts onto it.

Places the reticle—out at two hundred yards.

A second outline appears—a second figure—at the far side of the workshop building. The marshal stares, momentarily confused.

The figure by the house carries a long gun—a rifle.

Zimmerman.

Emmett Zimmerman.

The marshal hears him call out into the dark.

Whicher stares, mind turning.

Holds the farm owner in thermal image sight—thoughts working inside; was Zimmerman in this?

The sound of shots cuts through the air—he sees the farm owner hit.

He sights on the shooter, shouts out; "*US Marshal, drop your weapon...*"

The figure runs from view.

Zimmerman is on the ground—not moving.

The marshal cuts left and right, sprinting—closing down distance.

He reaches the farm owner. Kneels, scopes the ground back to the workshop.

Zimmerman stares, doubled up, gasping. "I heard vehicles...I came out..."

Whicher sees the man's bloodied hand over a wound.

"I'm shot...in my side."

"Press it, press down..."

Another figure rushes from the dark—the marshal levels the rifle.

Kathleen Zimmerman runs into view—face taut, her eyes shining. "What happened, what's going on? I heard shots..."

She sees her husband, drops to her knees.

"He's hit," Whicher says, "put your hands on the wound, press down on it, you need to stop the bleeding..." He keys the radio. "This is Marshal Whicher—at the Zimmerman property—I have a gunshot injury, adult male—request medical assistance, urgent."

Dispatch comes back. "Marshal, we have units coming out —medics among them."

"Roger that. Injury victim is the farm owner—I'm in pursuit of a shooter."

"Marshal, units will be with you in minutes..."

"Copy that. Out."

Zimmerman stares up from the ground. "What's going on? What's happening?"

Kathleen Zimmerman's eyes are round with fear. "What do we do?"

"Stay here. Keep pressing on the wound," Whicher says, "I have to find him."

The farm owner croaks; "Don't go out there..."

The woman's eyes are wild; "What about us?"

"Law enforcement are headed in," Whicher says.

Zimmerman winces.

The marshal sweeps with the scope, stands. Runs to the workshop.

Anger is in him now—at the man murdering his way

across the county, gunning Zimmerman down, slipping into the vast night, breaking free. Gone into the scrub desert between the farm and the highway—miles and miles of it.

They could search for hours, never find him.

Running into the workshop, he grabs a ladder, drags it outside, throws it up against the wall. He climbs, gets up on the roof. Squats. Puts the thermal imager to his eye.

Scanning the darkness around the farm, he picks up white dots of animals out in the brush.

Sees a heat source—moving.

Focuses the lens—struggles to make it out.

But the blur of moving image is a man.

Scrambling down from the roof, the marshal jumps from the ladder, runs into the scrub, tracking the line of a drainage gulley—following the fleeing man's course.

He could be making for anywhere—to buy time, have somebody come out. Air units will all be grounded.

Adrenaline mixes in with anger, the marshal feels his heart pound, running on into the blackened night. Mesquite and creosote bush start to thin; the ground descends, rises.

He stops.

Raises the scope of the M4 to his eye.

Breath coming hard, he steadies his arms, his body—searches the ground forward.

Sees him—a lit-up figure in the thermal scope—rifle trailing from his hand.

The marshal fires—three times.

Aquino runs on—stops—drops down to the ground, brings up his rifle.

The marshal squats, checks the range—out at three hundred yards.

He aims high, fires at the prone figure.

Then scrabbles to a hummock of dirt, throws himself down in the chino grass. Hears a high crack, another—

followed by the thump of the report—five-five-six rounds, supersonic, overhead.

Sliding to the side of the dirt slope, he aims the M4. Steadies the reticle on Aquino, fires six more rounds. Rolls back in cover.

He pulls a fresh magazine from the Kevlar vest, loads it.

More rounds cut the air, followed by the whump of the reports. No knowing how close the bullets are. But close.

He sets the M4 to full-auto—slides to the far side of the grass hummock, kneels.

Takes aim, starts to unload—gets to his feet, runs behind the suppressing fire—emptying the magazine.

Then drops to the dirt, pulls a fresh mag, reloads.

Squinting through the sights from the ground, he sees the man back up; running.

At a fence line on a farm road, he jumps out of sight into a ditch.

Whicher sprints, moving wide in an arc.

Aquino appears at the ditch. He fires out.

The marshal fires a single round, hits him. Fires another.

Aquino ducks from sight.

Lights are somewhere out in the dark—the flash of emergency lights—the whoop and scream and wail of sirens.

He can stay back; hold short.

Muzzle flash bursts from the top of the ditch.

Whicher runs, blood up, sprinting.

Tight to the dirt slope, Aquino sees him. His left arm is hit, he holds out an automatic rifle in one hand, like a pistol.

"*No se mueva,*" Whicher shouts, "*don't move. You're under arrest...*"

For a split second, nothing.

"*Estás bajo arresto...*"

Aquino's face contorts, eyes blazing—he squeezes off wild shots with the rifle.

The marshal drops, shoots him in the chest.

Knocks him backward.

Aquino sprawls in the dirt, tries to whip up the rifle.

Whicher pumps three rounds center mass. Moves up, deafened, numbed. Half-blinded.

Over the lifeless body.

Until the keening sirens rouse him—break the overload.

He turns.

Leaves the man on the ground, leaves his dead eyes staring.

Shoulders arms.

Backs off, finally.

EPILOGUE

Three weeks later.

In the courthouse building on South Cedar, Whicher eyes an on-screen preliminary report from the DEA at his desk.

He skim-reads lines on his computer screen, half listening to Ramona Fonseca in admin support, typing notes onto a keyboard, speaking with a caller on the phone.

He stands, refills a cup of coffee from the drip filter machine. Settles again at his desk.

Takes in the updates, reads the notes from Delfina Ruiz—a senior Special Agent now negotiating with Marco Zambrano at the Houston FDC on Odessa's behalf.

Sworn statements from Zambrano covered the murder of Matias Cardenas. They gave up information significant on the attempt to intimidate Glen Carr—Carr's subsequent murder. And the murder of the prior throat-slash victim, up in Midland, by Aquino.

Beyond that, his information related to the whole narco-trafficking network in Midland and Odessa, plus the emerging rival network in Monahans—now largely dismantled. Arrests were already made on the stash house owner, Johnny Shillick, delivery drivers, the car wash guys—Whicher thinks of sitting with Ruiz in her unmarked car in Monahans, the DEA agent laying out what they already knew.

Aquino's accomplice, Carlos Mendoza, was now in custody. Along with street-level people, they had mid to upper-level in the distribution chain—from Zambrano's testimony.

The marshal thinks of Cardenas and Glen Carr—foot soldiers pulled into a war they couldn't hope to understand. For easy cash; nothing more than looking the other way. Cardenas tired of farm hand money. Carr maybe thinking of a life beyond the ranch.

Cardenas's family had a hard time believing in their son's involvement. So too Josefina Olvera.

Larry and Patricia Mackenzie—the people around Carr said they couldn't understand.

Whicher thinks of Delfina Ruiz; of her easy cynicism, the dark edge to her laugh. Well versed in the power of narco money.

Cardenas had wanted to stop. They wouldn't let him.

Glen Carr had had a warning. And wouldn't listen.

Zambrano's testimony would likely yield more—Joanne Krueger and the DOJ lawyers would drive a hard bargain—the DEA in Houston would squeeze him dry.

The marshal checks his watch, clicks off the report on the screen. Pushes back from the desk.

He crosses to Chief Marshal Fairbanks's door, knocks.

Hears her voice.

"Come..."

He enters.

Fairbanks looks up from her desk.

"I have to head out," he tells her. "I have a meeting with the JP for Presidio County, south sector...."

"Preston Crawford?"

"Plus Sheriff Torres. And Agent Lozada. Developments on the DBs," the marshal says.

"Identifications?"

"I guess I'll find out," Whicher says. "I just got done looking over the DEA report from Delfina Ruiz—I'll let Torres know we're not looking for anybody else."

"You can let him know the FBI are standing down from further investigation into the Mackenzie Ranch IED," Fairbanks says. "It's all DEA turf now."

Whicher nods. "They're welcome to it. What's happening with the judge, anyway?"

"The security reviews are clear, Judge Richardson will be taking up post in Austin," Fairbanks says. "I'll probably be seeing him."

"Yeah." Whicher shoots an eyebrow, squares his hat. "Tell him I said hi."

* * *

The dirt road onto the Crawford property passes a sheet-metal barn, thin pasture, a handful of cattle scattered beneath mesquite trees. Ahead is an old ranch house—the marshal spots Sheriff Torres's SUV, Adriana Lozada's truck —plus the Nissan pickup belonging to the justice of the peace.

A rusted windmill turns beyond a rick fence, pumping water to a livestock trough.

Whicher pulls in, parks the Silverado. Walks around to a shaded porch along the front of the house.

Preston Crawford rises from a table, descends a set of wooden steps, Robusto cigar trailing from his hand.

Seated on the porch, Sheriff Torres nods a greeting, along with the Border Patrol agent, Lozada.

"Marshal," Crawford says, "thank you for coming out."

"Mister Crawford." Whicher follows the JP up the set of wooden steps.

"I get you something to drink?" Crawford raises a glass jug of iced tea.

The marshal nods.

Sheriff Torres pulls out a chair from the porch table.

Whicher takes it from him, sits.

The JP fills a glass from the jug.

"I saw Kathleen Zimmerman this morning," Torres says, "she reckoned Emmett's getting out of the hospital next week."

"In El Paso?"

"They're moving him to the clinic, back in Alpine."

Preston Crawford hands the glass to the marshal.

Whicher takes it. "Thanks."

The JP sits.

"She told me they're thinking of selling up," Torres says.

"Selling the farm?"

"Looking that way."

The marshal takes a sip on the iced tea, thinks it over.

Adriana Lozada regards him, a question in her face.

He glances at her.

She says; "So how's everything? Are you doing okay?"

He puts down the glass, shifts his weight in the seat. "Two weeks administrative leave is all done," he answers. "The post-shooting investigation is pretty much complete."

Preston Crawford takes a puff on his cigar. Streams out his smoke. Lets a moment pass.

"Good to see you back," Lozada says.

The JP tips his ash. Sits forward, leans his elbows on the table. "Ordinarily, I wouldn't ask everybody over," he says.

"But since this thing is multi-agency, I thought for once to do it this way..."

Sheriff Torres clears his throat. "So, what's on your mind?"

"I had a call from the forensic pathology lab in Lubbock. On the drowning victim at the river," Crawford says. "The bill's going to run to several thousand—to get him up there and get an autopsy—the county finances won't run to it."

The sheriff nods.

"I can't ask the funeral home in Fort Davis to keep the body much longer. They don't have the space." The JP looks around the table.

"So, what're you fixing to do?" Torres says.

"I've spoken with the cemetery in Marfa. They've agreed to donate a small plot..."

Adriana Lozada regards him.

"I'll inform the consulates. We'll keep a hair sample, something for DNA. But somebody from the man's family would have to come forward looking for him. They'd have to provide a sample of DNA for us to have a chance of matching an ID."

"First they'd have to report him missing," the sheriff says.

The Border Patrol agent speaks; "And if the family are non-docs living here..."

"There's no chance of that happening," Sheriff Torres says.

Preston Crawford inclines his head, his shoulders slump an inch.

"So you'll bury him?" Whicher says.

"What else can I do?"

"Recorded how?"

"The river body will be ruled as a drowning on the death certificate. So far as the Texas Code of Criminal Procedure goes, we're in compliance. There's no evidence of foul play,"

Crawford looks to the sheriff, "so your office won't be required to investigate."

"I get it," Torres says.

"But marshal, you've been running two homicide investigations in the county," Crawford says, "I want to know you're okay with that?"

Whicher looks at him.

"The ME's office in El Paso said they had a request from USMS to autopsy—in connection with this..."

"The girl from the mountains?" Whicher says.

"That young girl, right."

Adriana Lozada searches the marshal's face.

"They're ruling cause of death in her case as exposure," the JP says. "They can't keep her remains, they're not offering to bury her. I've asked the county for funds to bring her back here. Bury her in the cemetery."

"And that's it?" Whicher says.

"They can't identify her. There's just no way," Crawford says. "I'll inform the consulates. ME say they'll send DNA to the state's identification program." The JP spreads his palms. "One day somebody might come forward. We might repatriate her..."

"One day," Lozada says.

"I wanted to know is everybody alright with it?" Crawford says. "Do Border Patrol want to take it further?"

"That's not our role," Lozada says.

"Or the Marshals Service?" the JP says. "In relation to your homicides?"

"We've closed the homicides." Whicher looks at Torres. "We're not looking for anybody else."

Torres nods.

"FBI are pulling their investigation. Everybody's out of here..." The marshal takes a sip at his drink.

"Which brings it on back to me," Crawford says, "and the

county. And the burdensome nature of it all on finances—which y'all know are basically zip..."

Nobody at the table speaks.

Whicher swirls ice around the inside of his glass. He stares out at the mesquites choking the fields beyond the house, at a rooster and hens pecking the threadbare earth.

"I wish I could tell you different. Every justice of the peace I speak to, every border county it's the same. We're struggling. Or overwhelmed. I keep body bags and tags in my truck, now," Crawford says, "I never take 'em out..."

Wind turns the sails of the old windmill, creaking, grinding against the rusted gears and bearings.

"I do the best I can. I'll bury them, stand over them," Crawford says. "Treat them decent."

Lozada nods.

"I'll plant a cross in the earth. Pray for them."

The marshal meets the man's eye.

"There's nothing else I can do." The JP sits back from the table. Smokes the cigar. Regards his empty glass in silence.

"Let me know," the marshal tells him.

"What's that?"

"When you do it. Let me know," Whicher says. "I'll be there..."

* * *

High cloud scuds across a bright blue sky on Easter Sunday. The view from the mountain plateau takes in Chinati Peak, Tigner Canyon, the plains south of the Mackenzie Ranch.

The land is empty, under a harsh sun, a world of stone and thorn and rock and spine.

Whicher descends a slope at the eastern side of the plateau with Leanne, the ground falling steep into a dry watercourse choked with scrub.

Below, sunlight glints on a body of water.

The marshal takes the lead over the crumbling ground.

The wall of the old dam curves above the reservoir, anchored into the sides of the hills.

Approaching it, Whicher slows, turns to check on his wife.

She picks her way down over treacherous footing.

Whicher reaches a flat hunk of fallen rock by the water. Waits.

"Is this it?" Leanne says.

He nods.

She climbs down to the side of the Presa Llorona. Stares at the dark water, shades her eyes in the glare of light. Scans about the barren earth and rock, the dry scrub.

Whicher moves to stand beside her. He points down to the small plain below—to buildings just visible in the heat haze in the distance. "Down there is the ranch..."

"The Mackenzie place?"

"She was most likely with a group. Looking to get by there. And then she got too sick. She couldn't go on."

Leanne hugs her sides, lightly. "I don't know how you could leave somebody out here."

The marshal doesn't reply.

He stares at forty feet of stagnant water. Weathered concrete. "You know the old legend—La Llorona?"

Leanne looks at him. "About the weeping woman?"

"What they call this place." The marshal takes a pack from his back, puts it onto the ground. Takes out water bottles, gives one to his wife.

Leanne reaches inside the pack, takes out cut lilies, tied, wrapped in paper. "Somewhere somebody will be waiting for her..."

She stands, with her husband, takes his hand. Closes her eyes.

Whicher takes off his hat, stares out over the hard land. Says a silent prayer for an unknown child. Tells her Godspeed. To a better place.

He thinks of a boy he almost shot, in the downdraft of a helicopter, in blinding light.

Feels the wind in his hair.

Listens to the deep silence.

Leanne lets go his hand, places the flowers in a nook in the old dam wall.

Arranges them. Steps back.

Neither one of them speaks.

Whicher crosses to the piece of fallen rock.

Sits.

Leanne sits.

To bide a while.

In the unbroken peace.

Printed in Great Britain
by Amazon